IN THE
NAME OF
MERCY

IN THE NAME OF MERCY

NICHOLAS DELBANCO

WARNER BOOKS

A Time Warner Company

Warner Books, Inc., 1271 Avenue of the Americas, New York, NY 10020

 A Time Warner Company

Printed in the United States of America
First Printing: September 1995

10 9 8 7 6 5 4 3 2 1

Library of Congress Cataloging-in-Publication Data

Delbanco, Nicholas.
    In the name of mercy / Nicholas Delbanco.
       p. cm.
       ISBN 0-446-51711-9
       I. Title.
PS3554.E44215 1995
813'.54—dc20   95-4046
                                                                  CIP

Book design by Giorgetta Bell McRee

For
Bernard and Aurora Greenhouse
To Whom I Owe More Than Words

Acknowledgments

It is no doubt unnecessary to state this, but what follows is a work of fiction. Any resemblance to persons living or dead is coincidental, and anyone with a map of Michigan will find neither Lakeview nor Bellehaven in the state. Trueman-Andrews Hospital does not exist, nor does the hospice next door. I did have help, however, while trying to make this imitation of reality more plausible than would otherwise have been the case. Those who read this book, in various stages, and kept me alive to its possibilities are, in alphabetical order, Charles Baxter, Andrea Beauchamp, Andrew Delbanco, Dawn Delbanco, Elena Delbanco, Jill Delbanco, Richard Elman, Russell Fraser, James Landis, Rob McQuilkin, Anton Shammas, Bruce Wallace, B. Joseph White, Jon Manchip White, and Mary White. To these colleagues, friends, and family I want to repeat in public what I've said in private: thanks, thanks.

Once again I am grateful to the Corporation of YADDO, for its provided privacy while I completed a draft. My agent, Gail Hochman of Brandt & Brandt, and my editor at Warner Books,

Jamie Raab, as well as its president, Laurence J. Kirshbaum, have been exemplary in their several roles; no author could dream of or receive more gracious and intelligent support. Dr. Alexander Gotz, Dr. W. Joseph McCune, and Dr. Amnon Rosenthal have each furnished help; my brother Dr. Thomas Delbanco served as teacher and close critic from first to final page. This manuscript would not exist without him; its errata, however, are mine.

Primum Non Nocere

"First, Do No Harm." No one's condition should be made worse because of having visited a physician. This is an idealistic but virtually unattainable goal, because there is no medical procedure, operation, or drug that does not have the potential for harm.

Taber's Cyclopedic Medical Dictionary, 17th ed.

Prologue

WHEN THEY entered the apartment it was Thursday night. The hall door was locked and bolted, but the master key did function and the sheriff had a warrant. The foyer and living room reeked. The windows had been locked. As it had done since the start of the story, the *Lakeview Clarion* would report on what they found; it would also print a floor plan, with black arrows pointing to "the death room," and photos of the rear facade of Hospitality House. The lights were off.

The two of them were sitting upright in matched chairs, dressed, facing each other, and in the man's case—Harry would swear to it—smiling. The chairs were high-backed, upholstered in black leather, and the table between them was walnut. On the table was a copy of the poems of John Donne, with a bookmark at the sonnet that begins "Death be not proud." The power for the CD player was still on, though the music had played itself out. It was Mendelssohn's *Songs Without Words*. There was an empty ashtray and the "Handbook for Dying" pamphlet and a deck of cards.

His eyes were open, hers shut. Her left ear and the hair above it and three-quarters of the cranium remained intact; the rest of her face had exploded. There were no suicide notes. There was a bottle of Rémy Martin VSOP, with one snifter on the table and one overturned on the dark floral rug. The rug could take a stain. Her breasts—Harry registered this without thinking— were good; her ankles had swollen, however, and her legs were blue. Her shoes were off. It took some time to see the rope, because the nylon filament was the same color as her clothes, and it would take some time to slip the knots. Her partner had tied them expertly; his own restraint was Velcro and could be self-attached.

"Jesus," said Bill Cutler.

"Jesus Christ," the sheriff muttered.

"Jesus H. Christ," said Harry, not to be outdone.

And then they set to work.

Book I

I

"How do you feel?"

"Fine."

"Tell me the truth," Peter said.

"I wouldn't lie."

"No."

"I've not ever lied to you, ever. Why should I start now?"

"All right. How do you feel?"

The moon outside their window was a sickle moon: bright white. She shut her eyes.

"It's the reason why they say you shouldn't treat your family."

"Who says that?"

"Everyone," said Peter. "It's the first thing they tell you in medical school."

"The first thing?"

"Well, maybe the second. The seventh. I can't remember exactly what they told us when."

He cleared his throat. He watched the moon. It pointed north-northeast.

"You and your bedside manner," said Julie. "They don't know anything about it."

"No."

"You've been perfect. Wonderful."

"Except?"

"Except for just one little thing. You keep on asking where it hurts."

"I'll stop," he said.

"Don't stop."

"I will. I promise."

"The answer is, oh, everywhere. It's killing me everywhere, Doctor."

He took her hand. He had known that already. She squeezed with her no-force remaining.

"What time is it?"

Her bedside clock read 9:21. "Nine-twenty-one," he said.

"What time was it last time I asked?"

"A while ago. I don't remember," he lied. "Let me get you some water. Or apple juice."

"To keep my strength up," Julie said.

"Of course."

And then, as he had known she would but never when exactly, and never what would trigger it, she turned on him. "To keep my strength up, right? To make it last longer, correct?"

"No."

"So what's the point?" she asked. "Why don't you tell me that, my Mr. Bedside Manner? What time is it?"

"Nine-twenty-three."

"I *know* that," Julie said. "What day is it?"

"It's Thursday."

"Christ," she said. "What month is it?"

"November. And you know that too."

"I'm making conversation, Doctor. Isn't that what we're doing, what we agreed? We're discussing things, we're talking. I'm whispering sweet nothings in your ear."

"Not nothing," Peter said.

"If you had the slightest notion, if you had any idea . . ."

There were two pillows. He plumped them. When her breathing quieted, she asked again: "What time is it?"

"Nine-twenty-four. I love you very much."

And it was true. She was his wife, and he was a doctor, and she was going to die. There was nothing he could do. There was something else he could have done, perhaps, but now it was too late, and no amount of pretending or cheery bedside chatter would make any difference; she yawned. There was supposed to be a second chance, an alternative procedure. They had been married three years.

Peter thought of what he could have done instead. "I'm Peter Julius," he'd said. "And you are?"

"Julie Watson."

Later they would joke about it; later she would tell him, "I can't marry you. No way. Who'd want a name like Julie Julius?" And he'd say, "I can't change *my* name, I can't be Dr. Watson." But at the party that first night there'd been no talk of changed last names or jokes about "Julie Julius" or the stalwart companion to Holmes; they talked about a movie they both had happened to see.

"It's fake," she said, "it candy-coats reality," and he had noticed the phrase. "All those accidents waiting to happen," she said. "Coincidence. It's Hollywood's notion of fate."

Peter thought the story line was good. She had been right, he admitted, but did not admit he was wrong. They agreed to disagree. They were standing by a picture window, next to a poster of the Leaning Tower of Pisa and a reproduction of a woman by Degas. They discussed Edgar Degas: his failing eyesight in old age, his use of bright pastel. He asked how well she knew their hosts, and she said, "Not at all." He asked what brought her to the party, and she said something he couldn't quite hear, and in the living room, between the couch and pushed-back chairs, they danced. There were other couples dancing, and therefore not much room. They stood on the shag rug and held each other and, in a dazed preliminary version of what would follow, embraced.

"You could just leave, you know," she said.

He shook his head.

"We wouldn't want to compromise your precious"—she paused for breath, panting—"integrity. The Hippocratic oath, correct?"

"Correct."

"Don't be so brave about it, Doctor. I'm much better. Really, better. Don't feel you have to stay with me."

"Are you thirsty?" Peter asked.

She shook her head.

"Do you want fruit? A slice of apple, maybe?"

Julie made no answer.

"A cracker?"

"No."

He tried their old joke. "Some bedside manner I've acquired. Now you don't *want* anything."

"I want to die," she said.

The music had been loud. The room was hot. They could have separated and not traded telephone numbers; she might have failed to answer when he called. He might have left that week for Knoxville, attending the conference there by himself, and not been lonely or hoping for her company or able to arrange the extra airplane ticket and the rental car. When he asked her if she'd like to go, if she would care to travel south, she could have told him, "No."

But Julie answered, "Yes. I happen to be free this weekend; you checked my dance card, didn't you? Coincidence as fate, remember?"

The doctor shook his head. Except it *was* coincidence, an accident waiting to happen. It might have been winter, not spring. They could have spent Saturday night at a honky-tonk near Knoxville, being tourists, being bored. They need not have driven eighty miles away from everyone high up into the mountains; it could have been raining, not clear. They might have found no pine-protected hideaway, no stream that burbled by the porch; the Dew Drop Inn Kamp Kabins could have been closed, or full.

And even though that weekend worked, something else might have gone wrong. She could have been leaving, not back from the Peace Corps; she might have been married already or in the vengeful throes of a divorce. She could have said yes to that job with the refugee service in Thailand; the paperwork might have gone through. She had not been looking, Julie told him later, had very definitely *not* been looking—and that was why they found each other; it never works when you look.

They might have been living in Greenland or Iceland or Labrador or Lapland or Newfoundland instead. He could have suggested a honeymoon in a rain forest or somewhere overcast like Scotland, not the Round Hill Hotel in the sun. She might not have been a redhead; she could have been a brunette. He could have insisted they stay off the beach, or that she wear a hat.

There need not have been a problem with the ozone layer lately; there might have been no doubling incidence of the disease. He could have been less stupid and they might have caught it earlier; he could have been less busy establishing a practice or impressed by her suntan or blind. She could have responded to treatment; there might have been a treatment that would work.

In the hospital bed he'd installed in their house, the patient shifted, shuddering. "I know it's made me awful."

"It hasn't. Not at all."

"I can't control it, Peter. When the pain comes, I get vicious."

"No."

"I'm sorry. I'm so sorry." Julie made a sound high in her throat.

"It's not your fault, or anyone's. If you want to blame someone, blame me. Or the man who invented the aerosol can. Or all those hydrocarbons and what they do to sunlight. It's the planet's fault."

"I must look hideous."

"You look beautiful."

Weighing eighty-seven pounds, wearing a wig, she attempted to rise. "You mean it?"

"Yes."

"You'll miss me?"

"Yes."

"You won't ever blame yourself? You won't get all morbid about it?"

He spread his hands.

"There's only one problem."

"What's that?"

"I can tell when you're lying," she said.

So this was what they'd come to in three years. The courtship had been brief. They flew back from Knoxville together but saw no point in separating and could not stay apart. After two months, he proposed. They were naked; they'd been making love; he came back from the bathroom and looked at her between the sheets and felt so purely grateful for the long lithe shape of her, the sunlight slanting by the bed, dust motes suspended there—the sense of grace conferred, of luck within his reach—that he settled to his knees. He wanted to be on the floor. Peter felt a little foolish and more than a little clumsy, but he observed the ancient way and asked her to marry him, though naked, on his knees.

Then they were engaged and very much in love and, they told everyone, happy. Over the telephone, both sets of parents approved. His mother wept, his father said, "*Mazel tov*, Pete." Her own family would be relieved, said Julie, that he was a doctor. They would have preferred it, of course, if she'd done the proper thing; they had intended her to marry someone southern, someone not Jewish, somebody rich. It was why she'd joined the Peace Corps: to escape. They worried the whole time she'd been away; they were certain that she'd bring back someone unacceptable, someone foreign or—Julie dropped her voice and drawled it—*dark-complected, strange.*

Then she smiled at him, so welcoming, so vivid, that he also smiled. "You're everything I ever wanted," Julie said. "And they have to recognize that."

Her parents lived in Savannah; the party took place at their home. Bright flower beds profusely bloomed within a wide expanse of lawn; the wedding tent was yellow, with pink climbing roses as trim. There were close-barbered men and well-tailored women and many wedding gifts. A Dixieland band with old black musicians played beside the pool. "As the father of the bride," said Julie's father, in his toast, "I want to tell you, everyone, that this is the best girl there is." Then he blinked back tears.

They honeymooned in Jamaica, at the Round Hill Hotel. One of Julie's father's partners owned a cottage on the hotel grounds, and he loaned it to the couple for a week. There was a basket of fruit in the kitchen, a bottle of Taittinger waiting on ice, and they felt as if they truly had been welcomed into Eden. They were the single couple in the exuberant world. There was a lock on the cottage, of course, and padlocks at the entrance gates—but they were fair-skinned honored visitors who had been given the key.

It did look like paradise. They swam and played tennis together and lay beside the water in the annealing light. No other two people ever, they assured each other, had ever been so much in love or so completely happy. They drank rum punches at the bar and struck up a friendship with the bartender, whose name was Jack. One afternoon Jack confided to Peter that the lady looked more like a mistress than wife, and everybody was jealous, and he was a fortunate man.

"That redhead you got there, she's *something*," said Jack, and the proud husband agreed.

He told Julie he believed himself the luckiest man alive, and she said, most deserving. He said, "I hope I do deserve you," and she said, don't even think that way, it will spoil our luck.

"I'm lucky now," he said.

"Don't talk about it, really."

"I've been crossing my fingers all day."

Then Julie reached behind her back, her high breasts rising, her arms taut, and undid the hooks of her bikini and released and let it fall. "Come here and deserve me," she said.

"Do you remember that dance? What was it called? The limbo?"

"Yes."

"In Jamaica. The one where you lie on your back?"

"Not lie," he said, "you balance. The point is to keep balanced, to not let it touch the ground."

"And they keep lowering the bar?"

"That's right."

"And everybody claps? And they stuff dollars in their G-strings? And am I inventing this or didn't they have fire?"

"Yes. The bar was burning."

"What time is it?"

"Nine-fifty-two."

"I must have been sleeping."

"A little," he said. "Do you want something to drink?"

"But why's it called the limbo?"

"What?"

"That dance. Do they mean 'limber,' maybe? Why did they call it that? Do you have to be limber to stay off your back?"

The moon was gone. Clouds covered it, or it moved past the window, or he shifted in his seat; the moon was not a constant, Peter knew. Or, rather, it *was* constant, but seemed to be a changing thing. He sat in the one chair. He did not know the reason that they called that dance the limbo, and it did not matter to him, and he fought to stay awake. He had kept watch for three days.

"Because the dancers are in Limbo," Julie said. "That must be why."

He shifted in his seat.

"They were such extravagant athletes," she said. "Those dancers. All of them."

He watched the wall.

"Those brilliant acrobats. Remember how we envied them?"

He shook his head.

"How long will it take me to die?"

II

ON THE night of his thirty-first birthday Dr. Julius was offered—
and one week later accepted—a job in private practice. He and
Julie discussed this at length; it was, they knew, a turning point
and choice of a career. He had thought about research instead.
He had been trained in internal medicine and specialized in
gerontology; the cell structure of old rats held, he was certain, a
clue to the degenerative syndromes he intended to explore. She
asked him what he wanted, what he *really* wanted, and Peter
said he had become a doctor to diagnose and then alleviate the
suffering of others. It embarrassed him to say so, but that was
the whole point.

Julie's father had a friend who owned a summer home in
Lakeview, on the east shore of Lake Michigan. His name was
Harley Andrews and he was, said Julie, mega-rich. He went fishing with her father when the Watson family had summered in
the area; she remembered "Uncle Harley" vaguely: his bald
head, his walrus mustache. He smoked cigars and laughed a lot
and told what her mother called off-color stories and was ex-

travagant and fat. She herself had been—she squeezed Peter's hand—just a baby then.

J. Harley Andrews played the oil-shale commodity market in the years when oil shale had a future; then he invested in robotics; then he bought a bank. He owned ten thousand acres of a ski resort in Colorado, with the buildings and boutiques and lifts. He owned a bottling plant and shopping centers and an assortment of mines. Therefore, in gratitude, and since he had not married and had no children of his own, he donated the J. Harley Andrews Clinic to the inhabitants of Lakeview. The structure faced Lake Michigan; its equipment and facilities were fine.

Now they needed additional doctors. Julie called her father, and her father called his good fishing buddy; an interview was scheduled and a job as internist proposed. It seemed just as simple as that. It would be, said Andrews, his belated wedding gift. He hoped to meet the happy couple soon; he sent congratulations to the bride and was amazed that she'd grown up so fast and was delighted to help. He couldn't be in town that week—he had to be in Switzerland—but he had every confidence in Julie's choice of husband and was sure they'd like the place and surely hoped they'd stay.

The interview went well. Dr. and Mrs. Julius spent the night in a lakeside hotel. Her parents had presented them with a bright red Saab convertible; they traveled with the top down, listening to B.B. King and Billie Holiday, getting lost on purpose on the back roads and the narrow lanes that bisected orchards and farms. There were vineyards and billboards with pictures of grapes; there were signs inviting tourists to stop and taste and buy the local wine.

"Do you want me to accept?" he asked, and she told him yes.

Julie was excited at the prospect; she remembered Lakeview as a Main Street lined with elms. She remembered candy stores and carousels and a band shell at the beach. She pointed out to Peter where she'd hidden by the boardwalk, and where she had been bitten by a dog. She showed him the old ice cream stand and the fire station and the bowling alley where, their final summer in the town, she went on her first double date.

This vision of prosperity had altered with the changing times; the elms had been cut down. The church required paint. But willows had been planted by the Andrews Clinic, and they tumbled greenly where the honeymooners strolled. They liked the town, its rural feel, and dreamed of their own house someday nestled in the dunes. They discussed the transition from research to practice, and whether he would miss the hours in the lab.

"You're sure you won't miss it?" she asked him, and Peter told her no. He hoped to make a difference in the health of a community. He wanted to meet patients, face-to-face.

"Have you noticed, darling, how I do all the talking here? I'm doing all the talking."

"Yes."

"I'm making conversation, and I hope you notice. I just hope you remember. It's your turn now," she said.

"We don't have to do this."

"We do."

"You have a choice still. You can wait."

"I can't," she said. Her breathing was rapid and shallow. "Let's not discuss it anymore."

"All right."

"Let's talk about anything else. Let's talk about the weather. What time is it?"

"Ten-seventeen."

"What were we doing last year, do you think, on this day in November at ten-seventeen? Two years ago?"

"I can't remember," Peter said.

"That's all I ever think about. It's what I ask myself. What was I doing just this minute when I still could do it? Ten years ago, maybe, or two, or five. In my old life, I mean."

He shook his head.

"What was on the bureau, for example, or the bedside table? Where did I keep the flashlight? Did we have this color pillow? Kleenex?"

Her speech had slurred. She licked her lips. "What time is it?" she asked.

Peter waited every day for what the night would bring. It was always worth the waiting for; it was perfect and exciting to sit together on the porch or walk by the shoreline in moonlight. It was fine to dream together of the future—the way they would spend it, and where. They rented a converted boathouse two miles from where the Watson family once owned a summer place. They met lawyers and bankers and real estate brokers— but mostly they kept to themselves.

He played the piano; she sang. Julie was an artist, he hastened to tell strangers; she had a way of looking at the world and a special sort of knowledge that took him by surprise. She knew about gardens and fabric and stenciling and quilting and egg tempera paint and General Sherman's march through Georgia and needlepoint and the difference between a strawberry cobbler and buckle, a grunt, a growl, a fool. She decorated rooms with cloth from Indonesia and rush mats from New Guinea and twig chairs and tables fashioned in northern Michigan. She was in no rush, she told him, to become a proper citizen; she wanted to play house. She had seen enough privation and misery and sickness in her two years in the Peace Corps, and she needed not to think about it for a while. She needed, instead, to have fun.

He was Jewish and she was Episcopalian, but it did not seem to matter; he was one year older and they were the same height. Shoeless, they saw eye-to-eye. They agreed to be true to each other until death did them part; they intended to honor each other in sickness and in health. For better or for worse, they said, forever and ever, amen. He told her of the families he dealt with at the clinic: his patients and their problems and the way they could be solved. The work was hard, the schedule long, but he respected his associates and liked the office staff. They planned on children, but not yet; they wanted to enjoy and share their freedom first.

Julie spent hours on the Sunfish, drifting in lazy circles and tacking in the cove. It reminded her of happy summers; it made her feel, each evening, like a kid. Lake Michigan was clear and calm, and the sun was brilliant, often, and the nighttime stars were brilliant, and they told each other secrets in the hammock slung between two cedars in the dark. When she told him she was pregnant he was shocked.

"How did it happen?" he asked her, and she said, "Ask the doctor, darling," and they laughed. It had been pure accident, a coincidence waiting to happen, but they agreed it was good news. Though they'd been careless as to birth control, they'd be careful hereafter, he vowed.

"It's my turn now. I'll talk. I used to think," said Peter, "that there were things that mattered, distinctions that counted. Divisions. Like the ones between the rich and poor, the young and old. Or the educated and the ignorant, the stupid and the smart. Or the male and female, the beautiful and ugly, the brave person and the coward—all those things that used to matter once. But it turns out all that matters, the only important distinction, is between the well and ill."

He continued with his speech. He told her how the first time he had seen her at that party she gathered up what seemed to him the light of the room entirely. He repeated that he loved her and would love her forever and ever and would never ever forget. Peter rubbed his eyes. He saw her now as what she was reduced to by the cancer: a terminal patient, a suffering heap. She should tell him what she needed, and he'd do it if he could.

"You'll stay with me?"

"Of course I will."

"You'll be here the whole time, you promise?"

"I promised that already."

"You'll marry someone else. Not next week, but soon enough. I give you my permission. My blessing. But if you have children soon, and if it's a daughter . . ." Julie said.

"Don't talk about it. Save your strength."

For an instant, febrile, she flared up again. "Don't name it after me."

"All right," he said. "I'm sorry. I keep thinking that it's better if we don't make you talk."

Through her lips he saw her teeth.

It should be emphasized that lentigo maligna melanoma and superficial spreading melanoma may exist for several years in the preinvasive stage. Females have greatest aggregation on the lower legs and back. Torso lesions have a worse prognosis than lower extremity lesions. The management of metastatic disease presents real problems, since chemo- and immunotherapeutic techniques are ineffective in the majority of patients. There was nothing more he could have done and nothing left to do.

So he counted out the pills. She had been taking them for months, to dull the pain. She was losing her ability to swallow, and it was important to her that she could still swallow and that she take the morphine by herself. She had made him promise early on that—before it grew too difficult and the pills stopped working altogether—she could decide; she hated not having a choice. She wanted, she told Peter, to decide about it on her own; she hated the regalia of the hospital, the solemn faces at her side, the apparatus of relief and delusion of improvement and monitored recovery. She hated the IV.

When he promised that he would not let her suffer, that he wouldn't let it go too long, she asked how could he ever know that long enough wasn't too long? It's been too long already, it feels like forever, she said. There's spontaneous remission, Peter told her, and she said yes but you've said that before; spontaneous remission is not an option now. Why, he asked, what makes you so certain, and she made the sound high in her throat that once had been the keening wail of pleasure and now meant, merely, pain. You know it too, she told him, there's nothing left to—what did you call it?—remit.

He could give her a shot later; he could wait till she was

sleeping and do it while she slept. "Not on your life," said Julie, then arranged her face to smile.

She couldn't bear, she told him, the hopeless prolongation; she hated what was happening and what it did to her and how she had to suffer and was being brave. She hated their decision to perform the operation, to terminate the pregnancy, to try radiation, to try medication, to wait. He told her that she needn't talk, and that he understood. She shook her head. They had watched the hard things grow impossible and simple things grow hard.

Arthur Pomerantz discovered it when she was three months pregnant. It was March 18. It rained. Arthur was Julie's ob-gyn; the visit had been routine. When he called Peter into the office and, pointing to the left axilla, said "You'd better feel this. Here," then cleared his throat and, shuffling papers, said, what do you think, what's your sense of things, I think we'd better go for it, I think you might want a second opinion but mine is get her out of town and find the best surgeon you know and tell him to biopsy tomorrow or, better yet, last week—when Dr. Peter Julius drove his pale pregnant silent bride in the car they'd planned to take vacations in back east across the wide flat state to his old teaching hospital, and his teachers shuffled schedules and the surgeon laid it out for him, when he palpated the left axilla and felt his stomach fall, when he noticed at last and too late the spreading mole above the clavicle, when he held her and explained it and put on his cheerful face, all through the operation, through the post-op and the second set of biopsies and radiation and the course of medication, all through the nearly twenty months of arrested and then steep then slow decline—Peter tried to be responsible. He tried to be of use.

His family had visited, but his father too was dying; they blessed her and withdrew. Her family had visited, but they did not stay. Julie's mother wrung her hands; she could not keep from crying, and she would not speak. Her father said, "I gave you a daughter so perfect, so healthy, and you married her and now she's ruined and you're a son of a bitch."

Dr. Julius did not disagree; he did not justify himself. There would have been no point. He maintained his wife in the hospital until discharge was appropriate; he consulted on the treatment plan with specialists in Boston and Chicago and New York. He kept in touch with the surgeon; he spoke with his collagues; he rehearsed the course of malignant melanoma and read the latest articles and wrote to their authors for clarification. He went through the motions scrupulously; he drove home every day for lunch and took over for the day nurse nightly and, for the final weeks, he took a leave of absence from his work.

In the clinic and in public, he tried to be polite. But in silence, once she fell asleep—or driving to work, or brushing his teeth, or examining a baby, or doing the grocery shopping, or explaining carpal tunnel syndrome, or bronchitis, or sinusitis—he raged. He had fits of white wild room-leveling fury; he swept their set of soup bowls and the lacquered Chinese teapot and the wedding photographs and old glass bottles from the shelf. He did not replace what he broke.

The moon was down. The room was dark. The lamp beside the bed had a pink sixty-watt bulb and ocher shade. He placed the tablets and a glass of water and a pitcher on the table; he arranged them in a triangle, with the white pills at the apex and at her right hand. "We don't have to do this," he said.

"We do," she said. "We'll do it now. I don't think I can wait."

"I love you very much," he said.

"What time is it?"

"Ten-fifty-six."

"Do you wish we'd kept the baby?"

"We couldn't have," he said. "Not once we started treatment."

"Don't you wish we hadn't tried? Don't you wish there'd been a baby?"

"No," he said, and this was true. "I'd do it exactly the same way again. I wanted you to live."

"Except I can't," said Julie, and she turned from him—not out of fear or reticence or lack of resolution or any sort of shame or wish for privacy, because they'd long since given up on shame and privacy, because if you provide the sponge bath and arrange the wig and change the dressing for the bedsores and empty the bedpan and, when the constipation starts, you give your wife an enema, there's not much point in downcast eyes or the forms of modesty—to drink.

Her face was averted; he watched. She swallowed two pills at once. He stopped counting at fourteen. When she shook her head or gagged, he handed her the pills. He filled the water glass. It grew harder for her, slower, but she did not say a word and raised her right hand to her mouth repeatedly and drank.

This procedure took some time. It would take time, he knew, for her to fall asleep. These were his last minutes with her, and he tried to make them count. They had neglected to warn him in medical school; they didn't say "Don't marry, or if you must marry, don't let your wife burn in the sun." "Dr. Brownie's Blues" was in his head, and the lines about bad blood:

> You've got bad blood, baby, I believe you need a shot.
> You've got bad blood, baby, I believe you need a shot.
> On your back now, baby,
> Let the doctor see what else you got . . .

Arthur was a jogger, bald and beak-nosed and efficient; he had trained at P&S. Betsy Pomerantz raised golden retrievers, and their younger daughter was deaf. Peter tried to remember these things. He studied the wallpaper seams. He distinguished two separate patterns in the wallpaper behind the bed—a cluster of eleven grapes and a vine that curled around a trellis then back to the cluster of grapes. There were redheads everywhere, and most of them had freckles; he wondered why the God that neither of them believed in had chosen Julie to wreck.

His mind became a riot of avoidance. He recited the Lakeview pharmacist's telephone number at home. He tried again to focus not on the course of treatment but on that brief period before she had been diagnosed and the procedures began. He tried to remember the name of the maid at the Round Hill Hotel. He remembered their first night together in the Great Smoky Mountains. They had rented a Thunderbird: white. He remembered the name of their cabin: Peony. It stood adjacent to Oleander on the left and Quince on the right. The name was carved in wood above the cabin door. There were curtains; there was a wicker rocking chair; there had been a rag rug on the wide plank floor. The doctor reached to dim the light, but she said, "No, I want to look at you," and shook down her hair.

More slowly still she drank; her eyes were shut. Now Julie stretched her mouth and, making no noise, as if underwater, through aqueous resistance, raised the glass.

He tried to see her once again in all her tensile strength, her beautiful agility; he watched the wallpaper, its filigree, and tried to reconstruct once more, in its intricate arrangement, the shape of their embrace. They had promised to be true to each other forever and ever, until death did them part. Well, now death would them part. It would do so just as surely if she did not choose to kill herself, if he did not kill her, but would take a year or month or week.

This is called, he told himself, the management of pain. This is how the doctor deals with grief. He counts the pattern of the grapes and ties his shoe a second time and coughs and, in his head, noiselessly, repeatedly, idiotically, he mouths the blues. He watches the patient relinquish the glass and how her hand goes slack. He watches how she dribbles and her eyelids flutter and her head falls back. He tries to think of what to say, what comfort to provide. But there is nothing left to say to the young lady in the bed and no kind of comfort to offer but shared silence and—as her breathing grows stertorous, her respiration irregular, the nictation of her closed left lid and blue vein in her yellow wrist still palpable, spasmodic—not even that. This is called, he told himself, my own precious life's fucking work.

So he knew it to the minute when she died.

III

PETER STAYED in Lakeview, working. His first intention was to leave, but there was nowhere else to go and nothing else to do. Everything reminded him of Julie, and he had no desire to forget. Friends urged him to forget. They did this not unkindly but after a suitable interval and out of what they assured him was concern. They said he should mourn her, of course. They all mourned her also, of course. But everything must have its season, and their marriage had its season, though it had proved bitterly brief.

For the first months they repeated this: he still had his life left to live. He turned thirty-three years old. There is—or ought to be, they said—a limit to the period of mourning and of grief. They suggested he should think about the early time with Julie, the happy time when she was well; they urged him to take a vacation, to move into an apartment, to focus on and deal appropriately with loss. The word they did not use was "morbid," but they suggested nonetheless that he need not be morbid; the word they avoided was "eligible," but Peter had become a bachelor again. He ate their casseroles and drank their wine and listened to their consolations and tried to pay attention while they offered him advice.

The men were supportive; the women were kind. They took him to movies and basketball games; they brought him to picnics and bars. Julie's death had been a problem, and they wanted to solve it, he knew. They had great faith in fixing things, as if death were a problem to fix. What it came down to, always, was "Physician, heal thyself."

Arthur Pomerantz urged him to jog. "There's nothing like ten miles a day to work your way out of depression," he said. "I know, believe me, Pete. Or handball, maybe, squash . . ." Peter thanked him and promised to jog.

The wife of his accountant led him back into her pantry, where she mixed a second highball and looked at him beguilingly. "If there's anything you need me for," she said, "if there's ever anything . . ." and then she dropped her eyes and raised the glass. She licked its brimming rim.

He was grateful, he told her; he'd call.

"I'd really like that," she said.

He did not call, however, or invite her to the house. He stayed in what now seemed to him the elaborate structure alone. He trimmed the boxwood hedge and mowed the lawn. He met no one in Lakeview who distracted him from Julie or who justified the species to which she once belonged.

The clinic closed at six. "I can't be late," said Penny Lampson, leaving. "It's my busy social schedule. It's Friday night bingo, remember?" She was rueful, self-absorbed, no longer even flirtatious. "Have a good weekend," she said.

Then J. Harley Andrews arrived. He announced himself over the intercom system and he filled the door. "Condolences."

Dr. Julius stood.

"You free for a minute?"

"Of course. I'm glad to meet you, sir."

"Harley. Uncle Harley. You should call me Uncle Harley, just the way your poor wife used to . . ."

They shook hands. Andrews wore blue linen pants, a red belt, and a shirt with pineapples. His grip was strong. He looked the way that Julie had described him: plump, prosperous. What hair he had was white. "You're Pete, correct?"

He nodded. "Peter."

Andrews settled to the couch, behind the coffee table. He put his feet on *Wellness* and *American Heritage Magazine*; luxuriantly, he stretched. "I been away, you understand, been out of touch too long. I haven't passed through Lakeview since we cut the ribbon for this place."

"We were grateful to you, sir."

"Three years it's been. Too long, too long. Julie died, what, last November?"

"Yes. She didn't much want visitors, so in the end we . . ."

"That was one terrific kid." Andrews waved a wrapped cigar. "I never got to see what kind of grown-up she turned into, never had the pleasure. But that was one great kid."

He had flown in for the fishing, he explained. He wanted to see old-time friends and check out Mickey Muskellunge and track down Billy Bass and Tommy Trout. He had heard about Julie, the crying shame of it, he was sorry that what happened happened, and he wanted Pete to know. She died too goddamn young. "Condolences," he said again, then sighed.

Dr. Julius studied, as if for the first time, the diplomas and the illustrations on his office walls. Julie had selected them: a matched set of prints by the couch.

"She *went* too soon. She *passed* too young. Notice all the ways we have of not just saying 'died.' Dead—what's the expression?—untimely." Andrews shook his head. He had rings on several fingers and a necklace of bright beads. "The hell of it, if you want my opinion, is how many people got nothing to live for. How many are enduring things in pure plain misery, and want to get it over with."

There were caricatures of the profession. Old-time surgeons

plied their trade with saws and bloody tablecloths and whiskey bottles to anesthetize their patients; they waved hammers and forceps and sheets.

"Nice place you got here, Doctor." He considered his cigar. "*We* got here, come to think of it . . ."

The moral of the framed series was: *See how much more we know now. This is the twentieth century, there's been medical advance. You can trust us, you can rest assured; admire what we know . . .*

"Not to change the subject, Pete, but are you still happy?"

"Happy?"

"What I mean is, is it working?" Andrews waved his hand, inclusive. "You know, the town, the clinic, the whole damn operation. When you got these people everywhere who only want to die. And who *deserve* to, dammit. Whose 'every third thought shall be'—what's the expression?—'my grave.' Who want to quit and aren't allowed to." Andrews placed the cigar in a case of red leather, with his initials embossed. "Who need your help to die with dignity and, not to change the subject, can't find any goddamn dignity or any way to do it since 'the Almighty fixed his canon 'gainst self-slaughter,' am I right?"

He seemed to need no answer. Improbably, he yawned.

"The whole entire system is, if you want my opinion, screwed up. It costs twelve dollars nowadays just to send a bill. You pay more in malpractice insurance than most people make in a year. The rich are paying thousands—hundreds of thousands, maybe—to keep their miserable selves alive, the poor can't make it past the emergency room, can't get the hell out of the hallway, and if they do, God help them if they don't speak English. We should be feeding crack to everyone past eighty, giving heroin to ease the pain and passing out the needle. So *that* should be the population most at risk for AIDS . . ."

In the silence that followed they stared at each other. "Why are you here?" Peter asked.

Andrews laughed. "Just checking on the paint job. Passing through. It's been, hell, *years* since I dropped in and you know

what the Romans say—what's the expression?—Tempus *fug it*."
His laugh was more convincing than his previous solemnity.
"And if a person comes along and says, 'I can't take it any
longer, can't *bear* to just keep keeping on,' then do yourself a
favor and pay him some attention." Now Andrews stood. "Condolences. I'll tell Daddy Watson we met."

"Good luck with Tommy Trout," said Peter. "On your fishing
trip, I mean."

A hundred years from now, he knew, and in whatever func-
tioned as the hospital of the future, there would no doubt be illustrations also: the operating theater, the CT scan, the X-ray
machine. And the moral would be similar: *See what fools those
doctors were, see how much we've learned since then.*

"You'll be hearing from me, Doc. I may just need your help
sometime."

And Andrews left abruptly as he came.

The Watsons had no use for him; he had known this all
along. When he called on holidays the maid claimed they were
out of town; when he sent a smoked turkey to Savannah they
sent no message of thanks. He remembered how her father—not
saying it, never quite coming out with it as an accusation—
blamed him for her death.

The Watsons had had it all planned. They had looked forward to croquet and badminton and paddle tennis back behind
the patio, with weekends of sailing and golf. They had arranged
to play four-handed bridge and drink mint juleps in retirement;
they assumed that their beautiful daughter would give them
grandchildren to spoil.

Then the dream became a nightmare; she married Peter instead. The last time he had called, Mr. Watson did take the receiver. He said, "I'm warning you, I'm warning you . . ." then
spluttered into silence and hung up.

So he returned the wedding silver and the linen with her
monogram; he kept the wedding album but returned the CD
player and the microwave and crystal and the blanket chest. He

donated the wheelchair and walker and Porta Potti and arm-chair and adjustable trays to Shady Acres Retirement Home. He dismantled her hospital bed and painted the wallpaper white. The Kiwanis Club collected clothes; he gave her clothes away.

Arthur and Betsy Pomerantz sent a postcard from Barbados. "Having a terrific time. Wish you were here," they wrote. The divorcée across the street invited him one Sunday for coffee and croissants; she told him she was lonely and had been unable to sleep. The son of a bitch she'd married had been pathological; he lied so much he wouldn't recognize the truth if it walked right up and slapped him in the face. He'd lied about the weather and if he fed the cat, not to mention little things like money and his boyfriend out in Cedar Rapids and if he'd been promoted or why he was fired at work. He'd taken back the necklace that he gave her last September, he took the car, he'd cleaned out their savings account. She sighed. The world is full of trouble, of starvation and war and disease; she didn't mean to make it sound as if her own particular trouble was all that inter-esting, all that remarkable, really, but she cried into her pillow every night. "Do you *hear* me?" she inquired.

He said yes.

There were foghorns off Lake Michigan and, when the wind blew southerly, the smell of pickles in brine. Boxcars from the pickle plant rolled past. The houses were shuttered, the boat-yard defunct, the drive-in bank for rent. He drove through Lakeview's empty streets, in winter snow and summer rain, and often in a predawn dark so thick with mist that—had he not known with certainty each intersection and the curves—he would have had to stop.

Peter crossed three sets of tracks. The road banked back above the hardware store, and there he braked with caution; by the statue of a Potawatomi brave, brandishing a tomahawk, wearing a headdress, he parked. Fleetingly, glancingly, he did notice strangers: the way a man walked, left foot splayed, or the goiter on a waitress in the truck stop off I-94. He saw the way boys hitched their pants before they swung and missed the ball;

he observed the furtive way that balding men tousled their hair. He assessed the inflamed earlobe of the clinic's blond receptionist, and the imprint of her overbite on the sandwich she devoured during lunch break at her desk. He watched parents with their children, and children with each other—the hissed hint in the waiting room, the veiled threat or the open hand, the jostling for position in the backseat of a car. It was a peculiar world, and Peter took no joy in it; he studied the behavior of survivors: those who lived.

IV

ONE FRIDAY morning in October, Alan Eliot walked in. The man was tall, gray-haired, disheveled; he took small, cautious steps. He shuffled his right foot; his right hand shook. He seemed at ease, however, and happy to enter the office; he stank. He did not sit. When Penny Lampson closed the door, she rolled her eyes the way she did when there was trouble coming.

"Good morning," Peter said.

"Good morning. Yes."

"What seems to be the problem?"

"Problem?"

"You wanted to see me?"

"Why not?"

"You spoke to Miss Lampson outside?"

"Who?"

"The nurse who had you fill this out?" Peter gestured to the clipboard and the signature—ALAN ELIOT in large block let-

ters, and then in a child's cursive, with the last word underlined.
"Your name is Alan Eliot?"

"Why not?"

"Our records indicate that this is your first visit here."

"I think it is." His speech was slow. "I think it must be, yes."

Carefully, lowering himself by stages, attentive to the chair
and having positioned the cushions, he sat. He had been born—
Peter looked at the medical history—in Madison, Wisconsin,
on 10/11/29. In the space for occupation, Eliot marked "Retired"; in the space for next of kin he listed "None." The rest of
the page held a pattern of checkmarks; the "Reason for Visit"
was blank.

He was wearing a tweed jacket, and he kept his right hand on
the left lapel, scratching and then smoothing it. He wore no
socks. His shirt was torn. His tie was tied on top of and not underneath his collar; his cheeks were smoothly shaven but his
chin bristled with hair. His nose was red.

"To my knowledge, Mr. Eliot, we haven't met before. I'm
Peter Julius."

"I don't remember." He coughed. "You."

"But you *did* make an appointment."

"I'm sorry. I just don't remember."

"So what brings you here this morning—what can I help you
with?"

"Doc, my elbow's killing me." He threw back his head; then
he laughed. "One, two, four, six, eighteen, five hundred twenty-
eight"—he could remember number series the way other people
knew names. The pleasures of arithmetic, said Eliot, were few.
Once the pleasures of arithmetic were many, did not fade, and
he could keep balance sheets suspended in his head, whole
columns of figures—and telephone numbers and license
plates—like rhyme.

The sun through the window was strong.

"My Sarah's gone, you understand. I lost my dear wife also."

"Also?"

"Just the way that you did, Doctor," said Alan Eliot. "I wanted you to know."

And then his speech grew rapid. Inequity made sense. But the comfortable balance of an equation solved—exactness—mattered less. He had calculated, always, that his own wife would outlast him. On an actuarial basis, he had been correct. The women of his family outlived their men, had always done, as women everywhere lived longer. Sarah died at sixty-three. He did not know how to proceed. He had done so for two years. He assumed she would survive him, and had planned for her survival like the certainty of taxes, like the cost-of-living increase with inflation factored in. But there had been no increase, only loss.

The square root of minus one is i. The square of the hypotenuse of a right triangle is equal to the sum of the squares of the two adjacent sides. While he waited at a register he would do the total and the tax before they punched it in. The girl behind the counter totaled up. Then he himself would inform her, sixteen dollars and forty-two cents, or twenty-eight thirty, or two hundred seventeen fifty before she had the answer, and she would look at him, startled.

"Nothing to it, miss," said Eliot. "I pay attention, that's all." And then he would give her the money and tell her how much to give back.

He had been, he told Peter, depressed. He coughed. He knew with total accuracy what had happened on the second Tuesday of the second month of 1957, at two o'clock that afternoon—but he could not remember last Tuesday. Last Tuesday he fouled his own sheets. He knew what was going to happen, and therefore he made this appointment. He knew what was happening now. His wife was dead; they had no children; there was no one to take care of him or keep him from the hospital. The square root of forty-nine is seven; the square of forty-nine is two thousand four hundred one.

"You've guessed it, haven't you?"

"Excuse me?" Peter said.

"Pretend you haven't guessed." He coughed.

The factory noon whistle blew.

"It's senile dementia of the Alzheimer type, Doctor. It's what I have. Incurable Alzheimer's, yes."

Outside, there was laughter. A screen door slammed.

"Just like Rita Hayworth, in fact." He coughed. "Just like that man you read about in Portland, was it, or Spokane? They found this man, this *gentleman*, at the dog track without any papers, with his clothes in a suitcase. Sitting in a wheelchair." His fluency deflated. "Yes."

"Who made this diagnosis?"

"They left him there, that's all."

"Who told you this?"

"The disease was first identified by Alois Alzheimer in 1907."

"Mr. Eliot, please answer me. Has anyone examined you?"

"I don't remember. Everyone."

"Why did you come to see me, then?"

"I don't remember. What I have is Alzheimer's disease."

"There could be other possibilities. It isn't always that."

"I knew your wife," said Eliot. "Believe me when I tell you I've made inquiries. I believe I knew your wife."

"There may be something we can do."

"I want to die," he said.

So this is what it comes to, Peter told himself, and what I have become. He checked his watch. The man had had a stroke or was a drunk or was clinically depressed or suffering from Pick's disease or Huntington's chorea or Creutzfeldt-Jakob disease with Alzheimer's thrown in, the smell of whiskey in the room, the tang of urine also, and Penny Lampson wondering how soon he would buzz her for help.

The patient blinked. It was lunchtime, with a scheduled break, so Peter ran preliminary tests. He drew a triangle; Alan Eliot tried to copy it and failed. He drew a set of circles; Alan Eliot could not. He recited a series of numbers, and these presented no problem; he asked about the story of Little Red Riding-Hood and which side won the Civil War and how many blackbirds were baked in a pie and who ran up the clock. The answers were precise.

He held up a ballpoint pen and asked its name; Alan Eliot sat mute. He showed an outline map of the United States; it proved unrecognizable. He asked what day it was, and Alan Eliot said, "Friday. Don't take me for a fool." He inquired what had happened on the second Tuesday of the second month at two o'clock in 1957, and Eliot regaled him with the list of those who attended their high school reunion, and how he had planned it with Sarah, since she was their class secretary and that year they decided not to hold the dance in June but February instead. Billy Williams was the principal investor in a hotel in the Poconos and had offered them the place for free, because Billy always went after a buck and knew which side and slice of bread to spread the butter on. He filled the place in June but had no paying guests in February, and it was warm enough, and so they took the Packard—he was still driving Packards then, though later it was Oldsmobiles—and Sarah brought along a hamper, the straw one with the wooden handles she found in the market in Williamsport, with hard-boiled eggs and oranges and her fried chicken with the pecan crust she'd learned to make in South Carolina the summer she worked on her Aunt Elsie's farm and—his favorite—her special sticky buns. Then they picked up the Andersons, who lived at 2231 Lookout Circle, the yellow Tudor, the one with brown trim and white shutters with the hearts cut out, and lilacs by the driveway and that ivy on the chimney on the north side of the house; he had had his flask along for when they planned to stop. So the whole way through Ohio they sang four-part harmony—his own voice was a baritone and Jim's was bass, and sounded just like Vaughn Monroe's, and Sarah had the sweetest alto you could ever hope to hear, and even Betty Anderson push come to shove could hold a tune—so it was music music music, it was I got rhythm, it was fascinating rhythm, although of course he had to drive and therefore concentrate. The Packard was reliable but you couldn't trust the trucks, the way those sixteen-wheelers nowadays will take a curve, where was I, *music, music,* and Jim and Betty Anderson, who was wearing her white sweater, the one with the basketball above—you should excuse the expression, Doctor—her right tit that proved she'd been a cheerleader. The sweet acrid whiff of leaf smoke nowadays is something kids don't get to know, and if you ask me it's their loss, their cross to carry, *that old rugged cross.* But Phil and Ethel Chamberlain—the other set of sweethearts from their class, so that made six of forty-two, fourteen and two-sevenths had married each other—had been to the Pocono Mountains the season before, or maybe two, and they were telling everybody about Billy Williams's hotel: the wide verandah, the view of the valley, the rocking chairs in every single room of—what was it called?—the Hi-Daway, the Bide-a-While, and what was the question again?

"What am I holding here?"

"A pen. It makes no difference."

"What *is* this, Mr. Eliot?"

"An outline of America. Don't take me for a fool."

"Do you drink whiskey? Bourbon?"

"Yes."

"How did you get here?"

"Driving."

"By yourself?"

"There's no one else. I told you that already."

"You live alone?"

He nodded.

"And your address is . . . ?"

"I know what's wrong. I know it won't get better if you ask me twenty questions."

"We'll try to help."

"I want to die."

And then Penny Lampson did knock.

*   *   *

His father's heart attack had happened in the final month of Julie's life; there had been no occasion to mourn. Peter flew east for the funeral, then back to Lakeview that night. "When everything is finished," his mother told him, weeping, "that's when we start again."

Peter patted her back. He agreed. But he had had no notion what she meant, or wanted; his father's passing had been—so she assured him—peaceful. This was something to be grateful for; this at least was a blessing, she said.

Frederick Julius went without pain. He had been reading Isaac Babel and marked the page with his usual precision and closed the book and folded his hands and closed his eyes and did not wake up in the morning. When she herself awakened, he had been rigid: cold.

"I'm sorry that I wasn't there."

"Your father was," said Esther Julius, "remarkable, a remarkable man."

There had been a series of small strokes, and then a massive occlusion; his health had been failing for years. The company he worked for closed and inflation was a problem and the neighborhood grew dangerous and their rabbi had lymphoma and a six-foot yellow swastika had been spray-painted gaudily on the Temple door. Then, once they replaced the door, black swastikas sprouted on walls. She herself had been tempted to curse.

"When we had half a glass," said Esther Julius, "he always thought it halfway full. Myself, I thought 'half-empty.' "

"He was an optimist."

"May your own end come so peacefully. May we both have such a death."

He called his mother once a week and wished he were a better son and offered her a room in Lakeview since he knew she would refuse. "What would I do in Michigan?" she asked. "I know nobody there."

He did not contradict her, or insist. Peter sent a subscription to Quality Paperback Book Club, so she would have something to read. He enrolled her in Fruit-of-the-Month and had grape-fruits and oranges and apples and melons delivered, but he could not bring himself to visit or endure her mute reproachful-ness. He sold the Saab; he bought a secondhand Dodge Dart. He sent the profit to her so that she could take a cruise; she lived alone in Yonkers and might enjoy the change.

His mother called. "That trip you were talking about," she said. "Maybe we should take it together."

"I can't."

"Unspoiled St. John's and exciting St. Thomas, it says in the pamphlet. Those beautiful islands. The sun . . ."

"Take Lotte Bornstein with you. Remember, I have patients . . ."

"What I remember," said Esther Julius, "is that you're a busy man and when your mother asks for company her son the doc-tor can't afford it. Because he's not married anymore he's not now rich enough, and every old person in America can make an appointment. Every sick and lonely person can turn to him for comfort. Except, *natürlich*, me."

The blood tests, the neurological exam, and the CT scan confirmed the diagnosis: Alan Eliot was suffering from Alzheimer's disease. There was benign senescent memory loss, but also the ability to retain and manipulate numbers; there was early nominal aphasia when he spoke about his marriage. He re-peated Sarah's name. He was circumlocutory, often, with a ten-dency to pun. Peter ruled out Parkinson's and multiple system atrophy and Sydenham's chorea and viral encephalitis and mul-tiple strokes and meningitis and Hallervorden-Spatz disease.

Alan Eliot could not be sure if he had seen a doctor or had taken medicine or ever been incontinent before. He had forgot-ten his age. When, six weeks after their first meeting, Peter showed him his medical record and the indicated birth date—10/11/29—he smiled and shook his head. There was optic atro-phy, and Eliot seemed to alternate between the rigid steps of frontal lobe gait apraxia and the wide-based cerebellar gait of

the alcoholic. He did drink. The complicating factor was dia-
betes mellitus, with the attendant difficulties of maintenance;
the patient could not be relied upon to monitor his diet or self-
administer the insulin. There were two episodes of hypo-
glycemic collapse. Retinopathy was evident, and ulceration of
the feet; in December, and against the doctor's recommenda-
tion, he insisted on and was fitted with an open-loop insulin
pump.

Alan Eliot paid cash. He sported a thick roll of bills. He
handed out ten- and twenty- and fifty-dollar bills to women and
construction workers and avid wide-eyed children in the waiting room. He arrived for his appointments at the scheduled
hour, smiling, nodding, affable, in a white stretch limousine that
idled by the door. A chauffeur wearing livery stayed inside the
car.

On the first full day of winter, there was snow. They plowed
and salted and spread sand, and then the sun came out again
and turned the streets to slush. The wind blew thick flakes off
the lake, and then it rained and then it froze and everything was
covered in a carapace of ice. Alan Eliot grew worse. As winter
turned to spring once more, he showed an agitated intermittent
clarity: he knew that he'd know nothing soon. He had, he said,
disconnected the stove and reduced the temperature in the
water heater so he would not burn himself and unplugged the
toaster oven and put pillows on the steps. He could surely use a
drink.

Peter went to visit, to assess the patient's need. It proved severe. The apartment was a shambles, with clothes and books
and newspapers and food and candy wrappers and Aspergum
and empty bottles and rags and sugar and an artificial Christmas
tree and cans heaped in corners, a rank fecal smell on the
couch. Above the couch a sizable stuffed tarpon hung, and there
was a photograph of three men standing on a dock.

To his surprise, he recognized them all: J. Harley Andrews
and Julie's father linked arms around Eliot's shoulders and
pointed to the tarpon at their feet. They wore white pants and

sneakers; Eliot sported a cap. A net, a gaffe, a life preserver occupied the upper left quadrant; water glittered at the right. The picture was yellowing, grainy, and the silver plate had worn to black in sections of the ornate frame.

"I didn't know you knew them."

"Who?"

"Harley Andrews." He pointed. "Daddy Watson."

"I knew your wife," said Eliot. "I told you so, remember?"

"Yes."

"A first-rate girl. A charming girl. A pearl."

There was a photograph also of someone who might have been Julie at ten, poised waiting for a backhand. "Do you like tennis?" Peter asked.

"What?"

"Tennis," he repeated.

"Yes. I used to like so many things."

Alan Eliot brought out a handkerchief; he blew his nose. He studied the handkerchief closely, then folded it and put it away. What he most missed, he said—and it would come upon him without warning, while stacking the dishes or tying his shoe, during the six o'clock news, bending for the morning paper, joking with the girl behind the register who called him "Professor" and had that fashion of dipping her head, biting her tongue while she punched out the numbers—was companionable presence, Sarah by his side. What he most wanted, Eliot explained, was his wife's soft bulk beside him in their blankets in the double bed, the pattering trill of her gossip, the telephone extension cord she coiled around her wrist. There was twice the room without her, but he nonetheless felt halved.

A bottle of Jack Daniel's lay empty by the sink. A pocket comb protruded from a glass of orange juice. There were *The Three Musketeers* and books by Agatha Christie and a third photograph (tilted, out of focus, in a black frame, eight by ten) of a white-haired woman the doctor assumed to be Sarah. She was wearing a polka-dot dress. She was standing by a door; she held but did not lean on a thin furled umbrella. She smiled toward the camera: lips pressed together, teeth hidden.

Alan Eliot opened his shirt. He fumbled with the second button, scratching at the cannula and the rash above the belt. "Hold still," said Dr. Julius, "don't move," and stretched the wattled skin. He swabbed it carefully.

"Some weather," the old man announced. "Some weather for fishing. Correct?"

The patient's prognosis was clear. The days would be mere integers in a long dull series, and they would end at zero, the sum of everything. Alan Eliot would lose his sight to retinopathy; then he would lose what remained of his memory, then mind. He would turn sixty-six. The adults taught to handle him as if he were a baby would be younger and not older than their charge. They would strip him of autonomy, the right to live alone. He would lose his way while walking, then prove unable to walk.

They would take him to the county home or the V.A. Hospital; they would let him rock, mild evenings, on the balcony. The patient would require feeding; he would need his clothes and bedding changed. They would wheel him down for dinner until he forgot how to eat. He would forget, in quarantine, the reason he resisted it, and tap his way through corridors on the way to watch—for he would call it watching, although he could not see the screen—TV. When certain advertising jingles played, he would hum along.

Peter shut his eyes an instant, breathing out. And all of this would come to pass except that they had met. For did not J. Harley Andrews, come north to check out Tommy Trout, find his old friend wandering and urge him to make an appointment, saying or not even needing to say, *trust me, let me arrange it, the kid has got no father the way you've got no son.* And if this were in fact the case then Andrews also had monitored things, with an absolute chill foreknowledge dropping by that afternoon as though on the spur of the moment and stopping in on feigned planned impulse had satisfied himself: *this* one has also lost his wife, *this* one will understand because they share each dawn the endless gray day's prospect of survival, and what goes on between you two goes no further, *I give you my promise, I give you my word.* Then, later, Harley would have sent the white stretch limousine with the tinted windows, and the silent chauffeur and the rolls of cash—since nothing in the man's apartment otherwise suggested wealth, the venetian blinds skewed, sprung, the linoleum cracked in the kitchen, the bathroom faucet dripping and the tub awash . . .

"Some weather," the patient repeated, and Peter said, "Hold still." He bowed his head. He doubled the insulin dosage, and then he injected a third. Alan Eliot smiled up at him confidingly and yawned and closed his shirt. Outside, it rained.

Now the patient remembered or claimed to remember the child that Julie used to be, the married woman also when she returned to Lakeview. They had been standing in the checkout line, discussing the wet weather, the boardwalk and the blighted elms, the girl at the register saying, "Morning, Professor," and "Have a good one," and "Take care." It had been March 18, it was, yes, March 18. Julie told him she was married and he asked about her family and she told him she was pregnant and going to the doctor that very afternoon. Then she asked about *his* family and he told her about Sarah and said they shouldn't discuss it, it will ruin your good luck. They walked together to the car and she promised to meet him tomorrow for lunch, except tomorrow had been March 19 and late, too late, irrevocable . . .

Peter knew what he must do: he left the insulin in numbered vials beside the outstretched hand. The fellowship of death does lodge a claim.

"You're leaving, Doc, you're going?" asked Eliot, incurious, and Peter nodded: yes.

"You'll come back tomorrow?"

He nodded again.

"The day after tomorrow?"

"Don't worry," Peter said. He shut the door.

V

PENNY LAMPSON bought a mountain bike and pedaled through Lakeview to work. She did this all year long. She had an athlete's rangy frame, and a snub nose with freckles and an air of perpetual astonishment that made her seem much younger than her actual twenty-eight. Her hair was blond. She was living with her parents but remained an optimist; she told Peter that she hoped to travel soon, and anything worth doing was worth waiting for.

Penny had attended Notre Dame. There, she played lacrosse. She liked to pack a picnic lunch—in a yellow lunch box with pictures of Snoopy wearing goggles and an aviator's scarf—and eat beneath the willows by the lake. She told Peter it was funny—not funny strange but ha-ha—the way the men of Lakeview treated her because she hadn't married yet. Half of them believed she must be disappointed; the other half were certain she was gay. That their brilliant and seductive selves had failed to impress her, she said, never entered what passed for their minds.

She invited him to dinner the first Saturday in May. He did not want to go. He suggested they could eat together after work, in town, but Penny insisted she had it all planned. She waited till her parents left to visit her kid sister in Milwaukee, because otherwise her mother would supervise the cooking and her dad would want to show his entire cache of baseball cards, with the Ralph Kiner and the Mickey Mantle from 1955. His Roger Maris from that year was frayed in the upper right corner, so that meant maybe two hundred dollars off the price for mint condition, but the 1951 Sal Maglie and Whitey Ford and Eddie Lopat and Vic Raschi and Allie Reynolds were factory-new. Her father had collected cards since 1948. He was always announcing their value, always reminding her that this was her inheritance. She hoped that Dr. Julius liked whitefish and wouldn't hate her cooking and could use a home-cooked meal.

Spring had come to Lakeview; dogwood trees flared in the Lampson front yard. There were rocks along the driveway, painted white. Plastic geese traversed the lawn. The sun was setting as Peter arrived, and its red reflected glow turned the clapboard roseate. Two doors down from the number she gave him, balloons had been tied to a mailbox, and they bounced jauntily.

She greeted him wearing an apron, with a smudge of flour on her cheek. She had been baking bread, she said, and the domestic ease of it, the picture-perfect scene at the door, made Peter pause, uncertain; he proffered his bottle of wine.

"Don't tell me," Penny said. "Blue Nun."

"It's not that bad." He smiled at her. "A little better, maybe."

"I'm not," she said. "A nun, I mean. I mean, I *used* to be, but not since parochial school. I mean I used to *want* to be . . ."

"It's nice out here."

"It's not. It's where I live now—nowheresville." She pouted at him prettily. "*Soyez le bienvenu*, Doctor. That means you're welcome, in French."

A pair of foot-high ceramic springer spaniels sat at attention by the fireplace. There was a gun case by the Pianola, with hunting rifles on racks. There were sofas and matching arm-chairs covered in a brown and yellow plaid; the mantel had a photograph of Notre Dame's women's J.V. lacrosse team, with Penny in the center, bottom row. A mahogany file cabinet, with crossed baseball bats on top, held her father's collection of cards.

For the next hour, while she cooked, he sat in the kitchen and drank. She was nervous, she confessed, and she always talked when nervous; before each game at Notre Dame Penny ran right through the rosary and as much as she could remember of that poem by the guy who wrote *Alice in Wonderland*—what was his name?—Lewis Carroll. Did Peter know—what was it called, "Jabberwocky"?—'Twas brillig and the slithy toves, and all the rest of it, the gyre and gimble in the wabe, it wasn't him that was making her nervous, it was the carrot soufflé.

She had been working at the clinic since three weeks out of nursing school; she did aerobics, evenings, and for the last year—just in case the right man came along and invited her to travel—had been studying French. Now she could get around the corner and find the bathroom and locate the American embassy in Paris on the map and say, *garçon*, there's too much salt in this soup and I need a *jeton* for the phone and thank you very much. She wanted to be ready, just in case. Don't laugh, she said to Peter; stranger things have happened and they happen every day. This meal, for example—the bread she baked, the carrots and the lemon sauce—well, not the whitefish, maybe, but the recipe, was French. She had a tape full of phrases and listened to her Walkman and repeated them while biking: *on sait jamais*, she said, one never knows.

She asked him, had he been abroad, and he told her yes. I *knew* it, Penny sighed. Then she asked about Paris, *la ville des lu-mières*, the City of Light, and he said he was no expert: what do you want to know? Everything, said Penny, tell me every little thing. The French are terrible drivers; there's too much traffic, he said. Her disappointment was palpable, so he spoke about the Tuileries and Montparnasse and cafés in the park and chairs for rent from old ladies who wiped them with rags; he described the

Seine River, its populous banks, the narrow cobbled streets. She sucked her lip; she listened intently, intensely. He described the Eiffel Tower, Notre Dame, the Arc de Triomphe and—running out of monuments—the Hôtel des Invalides. He told her that the Louvre was the name of that section of Paris where wolves rampaged in time of famine: *louvre* means "wolf" in Old French.

After the salad and the cheese, after the brandy, things changed. They were standing at the sink. He was helping with the dishes, scrubbing out the pots and pans, and Penny said how strange it felt to be here playing grown-up, with her parents out of town and entertaining the boss.

"I'm not your boss," he said. "I don't think of myself that way."

"Oh yes you are," she said. "Oh yes you do."

"I don't," said Peter. "I promise."

And then it all whelmed over him: the loss, the loneliness, the slack exhaustion at week's end and horror of returning home, the rigor of his isolation undermined by wine. He touched her cheek, her neck. But then he turned his face away and once more withdrew from her and said, "I can't, you're kind, I don't know what . . ." and would have left in darkness except she would not let him.

She pressed herself into his hip. She shrugged herself out of her skirt. She put her wet hand on his mouth to silence his stuttering caution. Then he told her of his abstinence, his celibacy since Julie died, his chill grief-trammeled aloofness, and she said, "That's over now, that has *nothing* to *do* with us, baby," and led him to her bedroom—chintz curtains and a teddy bear still nestled in the pillows, a floral pattern on the rug, a framed poster of Mick Jagger and one of Jimi Hendrix by the window, her blue eyes wide, her white back broad, her body pliant in his arms—"I thought you'd never," Penny said, "thought you'd never notice . . ." and fell back on the bed.

A MichCon Full Service Maintenance Plan man found the corpse of Alan Eliot on Tuesday afternoon. He had gone to the apartment twice to adjust the water heater; the second time he notified the super, since the service order required that the customer be home. They used the master key. The smell was overpowering, and though they did not touch it they covered the body with sheets. The windows had been locked; they opened these also, for air. There was no sign of forcible entry or suggestion of foul play. He had been dead, the medical examiner reported, forty-eight hours at least.

Alan Eliot lay facedown on a couch beneath a large stuffed tarpon; he died from insulin shock. Underneath a raincoat were a bottle of Jack Daniel's and empty quart bottle of gin. Given the patient's history, the malfunction of the pump and the improper dosage were readily explicable. A tennis racket and chess set and a much-thumbed *Child's Primer of Arithmetic* lay at Eliot's right hand.

His testamentary instructions were precise. The deceased left no survivors; he was to be interred next to his wife of forty-one years, Sarah, of beloved memory, and what remained of their estate would endow a scholarship in both their names at their alma mater, Woodrow Wilson Technical High. On the day of the funeral service, it poured. Dr. Julius woke with a headache; his dreams had been fierce. The last one had to do with Hitler; his parents had been gnawed by rats, and there was a treadmill turning, and there were storm troopers marching, goose-stepping, conducting a house-to-house search. The downspout by his bedroom window had worked free, and it banged against the shutters and the gutter overflowed.

At Muehlig's Funeral Parlor he recognized none of the mourners; the minister reminded them that the meek shall inherit the earth. Ashes to ashes—Peter joined in the chorus—dust, dust. He heard nothing from J. Harley Andrews or from Daddy Watson, but a large floral wreath had arrived at the clinic. There was a wreath at Muehlig's also, and lilies on the bier.

"Do you know what we call you?"
"No. What?"

"At the office." With her fingernails she traced his calf, then knee. "You have a nickname. Guess."

"I can't imagine," he said.

"That look of injured innocence. That 'butter-won't-melt-in-my-mouth.' It kills me," Penny said.

He kissed her hand.

"Do me a favor, baby. Don't look so serious. Don't be so god-damn *scared* of me."

"All right."

"I won't blow your cover, I promise."

"What cover?" Peter asked. He tried to make a joke of it. They were naked, on top of the sheets.

"We call you Dr. J."

"Who calls me that?"

"Oh, everyone."

He cupped her breast.

"Julius Erving," Penny said. "You know, that basketball player. The amazing Dr. J."

He played with her nipple. It stiffened.

"There's been an office pool," she said. "I win."

"Win what?"

"Just keep on doing that. The office pool. Don't stop. The prize."

"Win *what?*"

"It's twenty questions, Doctor. Except the first nineteen don't count." She took his cock and slipped it back inside her and rocked above him wetly. "It's my turn now. I win."

In the moonlight through the curtains, her face looked drawn, drained, flayed. Penny beat at him; she moaned. The cross between her breasts grew slick with sweat. She moved above him urgently, with shuddering abandon, crying "God, my God, *God*, God." And then her whole body convulsed.

His dead wife's ghost was in the room, and he required air. The taste in his mouth was of ash. Yet Penny held her teddy bear; she kissed the little woven nose and said, this is the best,

the *bestest*, the only friend I have. All mimsy were the boro-
goves; did he remember how she'd warned him that she talked
too much when nervous?—well, now she wasn't nervous but it
did feel good to talk.

She told Peter of her love affair with the neurologist from
Stanford and the day she lost her faith. The prick had made her
see that "happily ever after" is a fairy tale, and nobody goes to
the seashore and no one lives that way. She told him of her passionate conviction, at age seven, that Christ's wounds could be
fixed with iodine and Band-Aids; she told him how she used to
own a pet rabbit, an iguana, a pair of canaries, a dog, a horse, a
Muscovy duck. All of them had died.

First do no harm, said Penny, that's the doctor's motto, isn't
it: make sure to do no harm. When loverboy the neurologist
prick from Stanford headed south for points unknown she
thought she might be pregnant, and that had been no fun.
She'd been wandering the wilderness; he, Peter, must have noticed; she'd spent forty days and nights in what passed for the
wilderness here. He had been going home alone—so noble, so
decent, so goddamn *aloof*—while she went to Friday night bingo
and then to the Quality Bar. And though her faith had not been
lost it had been sorely tested; those forty nights out by herself—
at the Watering Hole or Nineteenth T—were not a *good idea*.

She continued with her speech. Since Jesus suffered on the
cross, the name of the game is repentance: they fill you so full of
it all. But a Catholic has to *believe* in redemption, in stigmata as
a sign of hope and the visible proof of concern. If God took
mercy on the world why didn't He take mercy on His servant,
Penny Lampson; he, Peter, wasn't Catholic and couldn't understand. They make you feel so guilty for every little pleasure; they
make you think an ice cream sundae or a bounced check or a di-
aphragm inserted, say, before a dinner date will send you
straight to hell.

At two in the morning she told him to go. She had had
enough. Her cunt, she said, was sore. He should call again tomorrow, her parents would be in Milwaukee till dark; she'd be

waiting for his call. She was sick of playing Goody Two-Shoes, and handing him his lab report or the printout on an EKG, when what she really wanted was his finger up her ass. She'd had it up to here, she said, with "holier than thou," this *noli me tangere* shit. Did he believe what she believed: that everything was perfect now, and all their problems had been solved and they could go to France? She'd wanted this since way back when, since the day he arrived at the clinic, and she'd grown tired of waiting; do you always taste so sweet, she asked, or is it the carrot soufflé?

VI

WHEN HARLEY Andrews called next morning, it was with an offer. He wanted Pete to work for him and not in Lakeview anymore; it was time to move along. He was starting a hospice, he said. Pete was ambitious, wasn't he, and that meant changing things around; he ought to be director of some high-class world-class hospice attached to a real hospital and not some rinky-dink clinic in the middle of nowhere like Lakeview, with no chance to get ahead. He apologized for saying so, but after all, he *built* the place and had his name up there in lights and he knew just exactly what the clinic could accomplish; it wasn't rinky-dink exactly but too far out of the way.

"Here's the deal." His voice was static-riddled, distant. "You remember when I came last fall. Remember what we talked about?"

"I do," said Peter. "Yes."

"The thing is I'd been fishing. I did in fact go fishing. But that afternoon I went to see—I guess you knew this, didn't you, I guess you must have figured it out—Chip Eliot. It's what we used to call him, old Chip-off-the-Block Eliot, he could sit so quiet in the rain. I miss him," Andrews said.

"He died peacefully."

"Correct. You got the flowers?"

"Yes."

The connection was faulty. The telephone squealed.

"They're calling people *murderers* who work for Planned Parenthood. Christ. We don't mind dropping bombs all over downtown Baghdad and blowing up the desert to test the damn equipment; we don't care how many goddamn Kurds and Croats and Haitians and Cambodians and Tutsis and Muslims and Hutus and God-knows-what-all foreigners get slaughtered every week. But just try to call it quits as a citizen of America or decide *not* to have a baby or pull the plug on some suffering loved one and it's 'Hold it, fella, you're under arrest.' They want to lock that doctor up for helping people kill themselves who come in and ask for his help. It's the right-to-lifers and the ones who want to legislate that there's no right to death: the Constitution Keystone Cops, the Vatican Police . . ."

"There's a difference," Peter said.

"Not from where I'm sitting, pal. Not in my humble opinion . . ."

"Dr. Jack Kevorkian. That's who you're thinking of?"

"Correct. The guy out there in Royal Oak. The one with the van and machine."

"He has no patients of his own. He's a pathologist, understand; he has no prior knowledge of the people that he works with. They come to him prepared to die; they're strangers who've made up their minds."

"Hold on," said Harley Andrews. "Can you hear me?"

"Yes."

"Well, that's exactly why I'm calling. It's what I want to discuss."

"There's all this static on the line."

"I'm up here in the plane, that's why. I maybe shouldn't call on Sunday—what's the time there, nine o'clock? You awake?"

He nodded. "Yes."

The phone was white. It blared again. "Know what I heard lately?"

"What?"

"When you look back down at planet earth from where the spaceships get to, all you can see—the only evidence of human habitation—is, you'll never guess it, Pete, the wall. The Great Wall of China, I mean. There isn't any New York City, no Rome or Buenos Aires or railroad tracks or airport or graveyard or garbage dump or anything to let us know there's intelligent life on the planet. Except for the Great Wall. And what I think is, sometimes, intelligent life—or what passes for it nowadays—leaves a whole lot of room for improvement . . ."

"Why a hospice?" Peter asked. "And why should I want to direct it?"

"Because I asked you to, is why. Because I'm doing you a favor and you're doing one for me."

There were whitecaps on the lake. The wind was high, the first day-sailors in the cove, and gulls preened along the roofline and the boathouse chimney. Dr. Julius spat; the wind turned his spittle to spray. Like that catboat beating northward, he had been blown off course.

J. Harley Andrews had astonished him; he'd talked for twenty minutes from the plane. His own health had never been better, a little trouble with the ticker, maybe, but there was nothing personal at stake. That taste in your mouth in the morning, he said, why it's the smell of death—it's everything inside you breaking down. Still, he was in the fortunate position to help his fellow citizens, since all of us start dying, don't we, from the first minute we're born. But we refuse to see it and just don't want to deal with it, no matter what the politicians say we're the only major nation with no workable health-care delivery system, unless you count South Africa which he, Andrews, wasn't counting; as a citizen of the republic it devolved upon him, didn't it, to provide the tired and the hungry and the huddled masses with a respectful venue where death has no dominion or grave its victory. I used to sing it with old Chip: thy *sting-a-ling-a-ling*.

He told Peter he was serious and had never been more serious: those guys at the Hemlock Society have got the right idea. He was thirty thousand feet above the Rocky Mountains, and it did wonders for perspective: *Memento mori*, pal. Get off that front-porch rocker, and into the kitchen and turn up the heat. So why he called was simple: Trueman Hospital back in Bellehaven had agreed to his funding proposal. He was starting up the Trueman-Andrews Regional Medical Center and wasn't it exactly the sort of place where a hospice with an outreach program could maybe make a difference, where we could do some *good*! Old Trueman and his son-in-law, the guys that used to run that shop, they're two control freaks, understand, and they don't want their cus-tomers—that's what they call their patients, Pete, can you believe it? *customers*—to have any kind of input in the treatment plan . . .

So on behalf of human choice—the right to die, to choose to sign off—he, Harley, had taken control. I'm offering a chance, he said, a change for the better, correct? And there's your title on the door, your brand-new Bigelow on the floor, and all you have to do is think about it, buddy, then agree.

In a final burst of static, Andrews had hung up. The wind in-creased. Peter found a captain's cap, then a sand-buried bottle of wine. When he returned to the boathouse at noon, there were three messages on the machine.

The first said, "Morning, baby. It's your wake-up invitation. It was wonderful last night." The second said, "Paging Dr. Julius. I'm waiting for you; come for lunch?" The third said, "Where *are* you, you bastard? Call. Call."

Yet Nurse Lampson seemed to understand that nothing would change at the clinic between them; she greeted him on Monday with her standard "Morning, Doctor," and bent back to the desk. A salesman was leaving; technicians arrived. A man in a wheelchair ascended the ramp.

"Good morning." Peter paused beside her, looking down.

"Your eight-thirty's waiting." She gave him the clipboard. "Room C."

There were two earaches, one acute sinusitis, his seventeen-year-old with lupus, a dental hygienist with herpes zoster who had filed for disability. There was his epileptic, a phlebitis, and his patient with M.S. There were two compensation cases from the pickle plant. On his appointment schedule she had attached a memo sheet; it showed a man and woman, naked, embracing. Underneath, the legend read: *Things to do today.*

At lunch he joined her by the lake, where she sat beneath the willows. The perfume was familiar. "How are you?" Peter asked.

"My parents send their best. My sister sends her very best."

"And how was their time in Milwaukee?"

"I waited all day yesterday. You didn't call."

"I tried," he lied.

"When did you call? On Sunday afternoon?"

"No."

"On Sunday night? On Sunday morning, maybe?" She looked at him in pure opposition. "When? *When?*"

"All right." He sat. "I didn't call."

"There isn't any office pool. I'm not about to *brag* on you."

He peeled his apple, quartered it.

"You son of a bitch," Penny said.

The man in the wheelchair threw bread at the water; gulls wheeled.

"Don't make me ask this, Doctor, don't make me regret what I'm going to say."

High clouds scudded past them, and the wind was cold. "Just say it," Peter said.

"Was Saturday the only time? Was that our wham-bang, thank-you-ma'am?"

He resisted the impulse to touch her white arm.

"Can I come by this evening? And disturb your precious— what would you call it—privacy?"

He offered her an apple quarter. She refused.

"Because maybe you don't understand, I've got no other sister.

In Omaha or New Orleans, or any other place my parents would go for the weekend." Her voice was high. "Just tell me. I just want to know."

A helicopter traversed the beach. Then it banked back above them, and the willows shrilled.

"All right," she said. "Okay."

He shook his head.

"Oh," Penny said, "I almost forgot to tell you."

"What?"

"You had a call from Mr. Moneybags. Our savior, our great founding father—Mr. J. Harley Andrews himself. He wanted to give you a message. I forgot." She smiled at him, teeth glinting. "Well, I didn't exactly forget. When I'm nervous, remember, I talk. But there's no time like the present, is there, nothing like our *tête-à-tête*. That's French, if you've forgotten, and it means head-to-head. The way we were, in case you've forgotten, on Saturday night. Well, not exactly head-to-head, if you need reminding. When you promised to take me to Paris."

A flock of geese wheeled, honking. "What did he want?"

"He called about old Eliot. Your Alzheimer's patient—he called him Old Chip. He said 'Congratulations, pal,' he said you were terrific, and did just what he wanted. I told him I'd give you the message."

Dr. Julius stood. "What message?"

"That I know what you did."

At six o'clock his last scheduled patient arrived. Sam Green let himself in and sat down. Sam wore khaki coveralls, with his name in red stitched on his chest. He had gray curly hair and the lined face and features of an Ibo warrior. He had, he told Peter, no reason to live; the pills made no damn difference and the pain was getting worse. The nerve blocks and the acupuncture and the weeks at the pain clinic failed; he'd been unable to sleep. Truth is he didn't want to sleep, and wasn't getting used to it, since every time he shut his eyes he saw the gush of blood again, his dead sons and their murderer. It wouldn't go away.

His arms, still thickly muscled, had been crosshatched with a knife. It looked as if Billy Morris had tried to carve initials there, or to play tic-tac-toe. Green rolled up his sleeves to display this, and then the medallion of scars at his neck. "Forty-four times he cut me." For so big a man, his voice was small and soft. "I took two thousand stitches. Maybe more."

Billy Morris had been let out on parole. He had been convicted of rape. Eight years earlier he let himself into the basement of the apartment complex—Huron Acres, Building C—pulling the fuse and waiting for Sheela Johnson to come down to fix what was wrong. What was wrong was Billy Morris and his gun. He had asked her for a date, and she refused. So he used the barrel on her, raping her repeatedly while holding the gun to her head. Two days later he decided he would try again, and this time there was no one home so he shat on the coverlet of Sheela's bed; he wiped himself with the pillows and pissed on the blankets and took the TV. They caught him three days after that.

Billy's mother said that Sheela Johnson had driven her boy crazy, leading him on like she did. The defense had been insanity, but it did not work. The accused had known enough to stake out the building's basement, after all, and to return two days later. The conviction had been rapid, and the judge, Michael Sikorsky—persuaded by the evidence of premeditated rape, "since premeditation may well be compatible with sudden violent assault"—gave Morris thirty years. Parole should be considered only after ten, and then only after evidence of satisfactory psychiatric testing and under close supervision: "So manifest a threat to society cannot be ignored."

Time passed. Billy Morris stayed quiet in jail. The prison at Jackson filled up and the parole board changed and, eight years after sentencing, Morris was let out. Parole was granted not so much in defiance as in ignorance of the psychiatric profile and the mandated instruction; Sikorsky had retired in 1989.

Then, three days after leaving Jackson, Billy went lethal again. He did so in the same housing complex, in the same basement space. He climbed through the same window and found the fuse box and, as before, pulled the fuse. After eight years, however, the tenants had changed; Sheela Johnson had long since gone west.

Now Sam Green and his family lived rent-free in the building, in the first-floor apartment by the elevator shaft. In exchange for rent Sam swept the sidewalk and front steps and lobby and fixed the lightbulbs and locks. He had rigged a bunk bed in the boiler room, since his two boys liked to sleep down there and pretend they were out camping; they were six and eight years old.

Billy Morris slit their throats. Their father was returning from his Wednesday night shift at Big Joe's Warehouse, and thought he maybe heard something—a cat on the loose or a valve in the boiler room, maybe—and took his flashlight and his Allen wrench and replacement fuses and went downstairs in the dark. Morris jumped him with a knife. Green fought off his attacker, but he received forty-four stab wounds and nearly bled to death.

The case had been sensational enough to gain wide coverage. It was headlined for a week. It raised issues of the penal system, capital punishment, the criminally insane, court-ordered supervisory procedures, inequity in housing for the disenfranchised black. Billy Morris was apprehended next morning, behind a Dumpster in the Huron Acres parking lot, sleeping off what he insisted was only one bottle of beer. He appeared to have no memory of what he had been doing, or why; he said he didn't mean to kill no baby boys.

Peter knew the language; he had read the feature articles in the *Lakeview Clarion*. Sheela Johnson was discovered in a shelter in Sonoma, and she said her life was not worth living ever since that rape. The only thing that kept her going was the thought of her attacker still in jail. Judge Michael Sikorsky, reached in Lookout Mountain, said he remembered the case. There had been a "blank, methodical malevolence to Morris," declared the judge; in thirty-four years on the bench he had seldom seen the like. He felt entitled, now, to speak his mind. There were two dead children whose only mistake, whose fatal miscalculation, was to have slept in their beds.

The janitor's face was impassive, a mask of stately grief. His wife had quit, he said. She couldn't handle it out there at Huron

Acres, it was just too much blood in the basement; you don't wash a nightmare away. She'd gone off to Kentucky which when they first come north she swore she'd never see again, but even that old hell beat Lakeview anymore. She'd left him, she wouldn't be back. Green said again, "It hurts too bad," and Peter said perhaps you should go back into the hospital, and Green said there's no way to pay. What can you do for me, Doctor, the Demerol ain't working, the Percodan ain't working, I feel like what would fix me and the onliest thing to do it is a gun. You don't mean that, said Peter, and the patient looked at him: I asked you a question, Doctor, I asked what you're planning to *do*.

Peter changed the dressing at his shoulder and right arm. We can monitor your medical progress, he said, we can maybe up the ante on the pills. It's not the pain, said Sam, it's Billy Morris getting fed and dressed at Jackson while I try to find someplace to live that don't smell like a butcher shop, while I try to get me some rest at night without seeing my poor boys, my boys, and that miserable cocksucking shitbrained motherfucker don't even goddamn *remember* what he did. If I'd only been home sooner, if I'd only not stopped on the road. You mustn't think that way, said Peter, it's this violent country we live in, it's not your fault at all.

Okay, I read you loud and clear, said the custodial superintendent of the Huron Acres Apartment Complex, and it don't appear you'll *assist* me so I won't be back tomorrow. Because time is the best healer, like you say.

Sam Green departed with a stately gait—bent over, hunched, deliberate—and entered his pickup and sat. He pulled his cap low on his head. He rested his head in his hands.

Dr. Julius watched through the window, in the gathering blue dark. Green lit a cigarette. He let the engine idle, then eased the truck into reverse. The side panels had been painted red, and the right front fender was missing; the cab was rusting out.

Then Green rolled down the window. He flipped out his cigarette ash. He rolled the window up. He left the parking lot with such considered caution, waiting so long to make the turn, his blinker on, that Peter turned away again, and therefore did not see him go but only learned later from those who were witnesses how the Chevrolet nosed slowly out, how its driver worked the gears and ran a light and picked up speed and made a U-turn at the post office and, careening wildly, bearing down upon the horn, accelerating, tires squealing, came back again at fifty miles an hour and slammed into the clinic's rear cinder-block retaining wall and exploded there.

Peter heard it; it sounded like bombs. He ran to the suicide's site. The truck was framed in flame, and by the time he reached it he could get nowhere near. Inside, Sam Green was burning, and the smoke was thickly billowing and fire so high and heat so intense the clinic roof ignited also. The pine tree by the north wall flared and fell.

Then there were sirens wailing and many other vehicles and foam and spray and men with high-pressure hoses and axes and he was ordered back. The police arrived, and the ambulance crew. They removed the body and a melted jerry can of gasoline and impounded the wreck of the truck. They took his deposition and took photographs. They measured the arc of the tracks.

Then members of the clinic staff appeared and, at eight o'clock, a TV truck and live report from *Channel 7 Eyewitness News*. The reporter wore high heels and a purple blouse; she reminded viewers about the Billy Morris case and announced— facing forward, raising her voice and slowing down her speech for emphasis, staring at the camera—that the tragedy continued for Sam Green. But it was over now.

For Dr. Julius, however, it was not over now. A man in great pain asked for help, and he had withheld it. The Lakeview fire department hosed the roof, then hauled the shriveled pine away and picked through wet charred rubble; they cordoned off the parking lot and raked the area down. Peter drove home through familiar streets that had grown alien; there was no comfort in the boathouse or, when he walked it, the shore.

Book II

I

THE PATIENT was lying upright. This was imperative. The patient lay propped in her hospital bed, at Trueman-Andrews Medical Center, in a private single room, breathing lightly, shallowly; the digital clock read 11:56. The hall clock read three minutes faster: 11:59. Which one of these two readings was accurate—or, perhaps, less inexact—it seemed unimportant to know.

The door closed noiselessly. The patient slept. She did not stir. According to the chart that hung above her bed the place of Alice Tucker's birth was Toledo, Ohio, and date of birth 2/17/59. She was divorced and lived—though here the entry had been smudged—at 1147 Lenawee Ave., #2, in Bellehaven, Michigan. The nearest living relative was a father, John J. Burckert, of Fresno, California; the mother was deceased. Alice Tucker had been transferred to room 516 from the I.C. unit on Friday afternoon. She had been admitted to and released from the hospital often; this most recent visit had lasted for three weeks.

Her history was brief. Two years earlier, in the postcoital shower, her lover had discovered a lump in her left breast. Even in warm water and the pungent foam of VitaBath, even when she dropped the sponge and reached for him he failed to respond to her fond ministrations.

"Is something wrong?" she asked him, and he told her, "Yes." Then he told her to get herself dressed.

"What's wrong?" she asked. "Got another appointment?"

"I want to help," he answered. "I'm trying to be helpful here."

"It's not your problem," Alice said, "and none of your damn business."

"I thought it was."

"Well, think again," she said. "You're not my doctor, are you?"

"Of course not. No."

"So leave me alone," Alice said. She couldn't bear, she told him, to have his hands all over her and wonder every time just what he was feeling or felt. She handed him his shirt.

The metastases proved rapid and the love affair collapsed. Ms. Tucker had been thirty-four and pregnant and in otherwise excellent health. Her most recent physical had been three months before. At the beginning of treatment, pregnancy was terminated; two separate courses of chemotherapy were sustained without result.

Then, after some discussion, the hospital's bone-marrow transplantation unit had been deployed. By agreement with her surgeon, Ms. Tucker was to provide a test case of the hospital's new resource. There was a flurry of excitement and publicity attendant on the operation; when she left Trueman-Andrews the first time, looking well (rendered photogenic once again by the wig and makeup from the expert cancer-care cosmetics unit) the procedure had seemed a success.

Nonetheless it failed. The metastases advanced once more, and the bone-marrow transplant proved irrelevant; there was nothing left to do. The patient was admitted to the hospice program in order to display the continuity of care that Trueman-

Andrews provided. As its new benefactor liked to say, "A full-service hospital is what we're after here. What we offer is cradle to grave."

In the photographs the patient's face remained attractive, and she gamely raised two fingers of her right hand at the camera in a V-for-victory sign. When interviewed she claimed that she had no regrets; the administration and the doctors and the nurses all were swell. The Good Lord would watch out for her, said Alice Tucker to the press, like in that oratorio they sang in church where He watched over Israel and slumbered not nor slept. She pursed her lips while saying this, and a shadow of her old flirtatiousness hovered in her smile.

The chart was on its clipboard and the clipboard hung suspended from the foot rail of the bed. There were two IVs attached. R.T. had signed off on the eight o'clock medication, and C.B. had signed off on the eleven o'clock medication. The blinds were drawn. Something (coffee? a thumbprint?) had obliterated the patient's home telephone number. The office number listing was left blank. There were the names of attending physicians; at the appropriate intervals blood pressure had been listed, as well as the patient's temperature and pulse and respiration rate.

There was, however, no hope. Alice Tucker had been terminal for weeks. A member of the Internal Review Committee of the hospital suggested that the bone-marrow transplantation may well have been a mistake. It was costly and misguided; it was technology-driven; it alleviated nothing and the patient's suffering had thereby been prolonged.

Now Ms. Tucker, her doctors agreed, was to be made as comfortable as possible, but without heroic measures; a *Do Not Resuscitate* order hung at the foot of the bed. There was a written order also that, under no circumstances, should the head of the bed be let down. Pulmonary edema posed the immediate risk. The patient had been well controlled with morphine for pain, but the tumor in her pericardium could not be contained. She was positioned bolt upright in order to keep the heart pumping; at anything less than the vertical, the heart had no capacity to clear the lungs.

The controls of the bed had therefore been masked; the patient was too weak and drugged to move the tape. She had begun to hallucinate, insisting she was pregnant and that her lover should be called; she needed, she said, to confess. She made a friend in the next room, Scott Raposo, who had AIDS, and when he came to visit he sat by her side and they talked. Alice whispered wheezingly; she paused often in order to breathe. "Suffocation is awful," she said. "It's like having a pillow inside you. Don't let them do it, Scott."

There was a sign, *Do Not Lower,* hand-lettered in red ink and tacked above her head. If in her confusion she requested that the angle change or that the bed be lowered or that her pillow be taken away she was to be refused.

The clock read 11:58. It was a simple matter to unstrap the tape. The controls were simple also, and the bed responded. Its machinery hummed gently, briefly; it sounded in the darkened room like a refrigerator switching on, an elevator shifting floors. At full horizontal, it stopped.

Ms. Tucker's eyelids fluttered, but she did not seem to see. Her breast—so round once, its nipple so pink, so ready to stiffen—stayed slack. Her breathing altered slightly: already more liquid, perhaps. Spittle glistened at her mouth. The walls were white. It would be difficult but not impossible to ascertain the moment of the patient's death. To wipe the down button clean of prints then reattach the masking tape was simple; to make certain that the hall was empty and slip across it and enter the stairwell was but a moment's work. The night was cold and clear. The clock read 12:03.

March 21

To the Editor:

Don't ask me who I am. You don't want to know. You may want to know anyway but you don't need to and anyway you won't find out I'm no fool. This letter tells the truth and sometimes the truth is too scary to tell like in the Branch Davidians or with O.J. that football player and people who're crazy like that. Have you noaticed how when people go into the hospital here they come out usually dead? Have you noaticed what they call the Harley Andrews Hospice is just another form of Killing, Mercy maybe, but mostly it's organized murder like the abortionists or Hitler did, and anyway I ask you how many is too many how fast is too damn fast? Do you think I spelled noatice that way on purpose in order to see if you're paying attention alias notice a.k.a. or because I didn't know any bitter guess again.

You ought to check it out. They pretend that they're angels of deliverance but what they do is kill. And pretty Alice Tucker was the first. And I promise you, won't be the last. The last shall be first, as it says in the Bible and also there are Revelations writ in FIREY LETTERS to come. The way I see it is that Who Shall Live and Who Shall Die is the business only of our Creator-Creature and not some pewny mortal: Him Who Holds us in the Palm of His great Hand and you'd better watch it Buster or that Glove becomes a Fist. Because their's a whisper campaign.

Because all we want is the peace we had, the system that used to purtain. The way it used 2B. Did you notice how I speled *purtain* did you notice how I roat To Be and isn't it funny and isn't it strange how different things can be and mean exactly the same thing? Because what I'm remembering and want you to remember is how nobody but God decides Who Lives and Who Shall DIE. But today a doctor does it and that's wrong. So listen Mr. Editor there are honest citizens in Sodom and it's not as simple as you think to bury an entire town in well let's call it salt. We like it here. We *elect* because it's our United States of American priviledge to stay. Some of us go to the palace and some of us go to the outskirts of town, but everybody's pleased to know the story's over now.

In the privacy of your own home I ask you and I ask you think it over check it out. For vengeance is mine, Saith the Lord.

II

IN BELLEHAVEN, Dr. Julius focused on his work. Where before he had attempted to restore his clientele to health, he now confined his practice to the terminally ill. The first day at the hospice, he visited with patients. There were ten.

The Harley Andrews Hospice was attached to Trueman Hospital, and the hospital itself was now called Trueman-Andrews. The poor benighted multitudes, the downtrodden and don't-tread-on-me's: the hungry and the tired would be welcome, Harley said. Dr. Julius had pharmacological consultants and family outreach counselors and a unit administrator and a volunteer as well as paid staff.

Two white-haired women greeted him. They introduced themselves as "old-timers" and told him to make himself comfortable and take off his coat. They asked him if he wanted tea—Lapsang souchong or Earl Grey or Lipton's. The doctor said no thank you, no, he had already had breakfast but he wondered how they felt about the hospice and if they had suggestions.

"We get to bring our furniture," said Polly Winternitz. "Anything we want."

"The comforts of home," Hilda Gulickson said.

"But there's a limit, Doctor, there's only so far we can go. I couldn't bring my sideboard, if you follow. Or my candlesticks. No use for those dining room chairs, no need for family things."

"May I sit?" asked Dr. Julius.

"Yes. They're very good to us here. And we put anything we want to on our bedside table."

They smiled at him and drank their tea contentedly. He understood, he said, that theirs was a special arrangement; the majority of hospice patients remain in their own beds. In England, where the movement started, the idea of the hospice had been firmly rooted in "home." But there were those who had no such surroundings or family to turn to, and it was this constituency that Harley Andrews served.

"We get popovers each Saturday." Polly held a magnifying glass. It was tied to her neck with a ribbon. "Each Saturday morning they give us a treat."

"It's like a rest home," Hilda said. "You'll appreciate it soon enough. Rest in Peace." The woman cackled. "You follow? *Rest in Peace.*"

"Fudge," said Polly Winternitz. "Would you like fudge?"

"No thank you."

"Don't be shy. Her granddaughter sends it, it's fudge for a *horse*. We couldn't possibly eat all this sweet stuff." Hilda raised her cup and drank. "No matter how hard we try."

"She married a doctor," said Polly. "My granddaughter, I mean. A neurosurgeon, if you please, and he's very famous."

"Congratulations, Polly."

"One day he saved the life of someone who was grateful. Well, everyone's grateful of course. Or so they like to say. They shake your hand and send you checks and bread-and-butter letters and say how grateful everybody is, the ones who want to go on living, who say they have something to live for. But this person *did* something about it, he actually *did* something."

"What did he do?" Peter asked.

"Well, his life was saved, you understand. And he owned racehorses. And he had so much money he named his personal favorite after my granddaughter's husband. Dr. Billy Peck, it's called."

Across the hall, a telephone was ringing.

"Don't listen to her," Hilda said. "She isn't making sense. She's talking about a person who happened to own horses. That horse is a disgrace."

Again, the fudge was offered. Again, Dr. Julius refused it.

"That horse is glue by now."

"Don't *say* that," Polly said. She glared at Hilda through the magnifying glass.

"The horse is glue. It's holding up somebody's wallpaper. Your famous Billy Peck."

"Ladies, please . . ."

"It's true. He never won a single race. Not one race in his lifetime." Hilda spat the words, envenomed. "Billy Peck."

"Don't listen to her, Doctor. Don't pay her any attention. She doesn't deserve it."

"I don't?"

"No."

"She knows nothing about it," said Hilda. "Nothing about it at all. Would you bet the fifth chute at Saratoga, for example, would you bet anything above the fifth with that wide-angled turn?"

"Glue. Elmer's glue. Her Billy Peck. Her Billy *Pecker*, that's what she means."

"You're just jealous," Polly said.

"Ridiculous," said Hilda Gulickson.

"Ridiculous," repeated Polly. She mimicked her companion's intonation—shrill and high-voiced, rising. They stared at each other as if they might spit, or pull each other's hair. Yet when Peter said, "Don't argue, *please*," they turned on him together.

"Why not?" asked Hilda.

"Give me one good reason . . ."

"For example," Hilda said, "if you don't mind my asking, compared to the doctor we've been discussing, just who's the neurosurgeon? Which one of you's the specialist, okay?"

"Okay," said Polly. "You're new here, aren't you, anyhow. You don't know the first thing about it." She addressed the wall, complicitous. "He doesn't even know about my nephew Billy Peck."

"I understood he was your granddaughter's husband."

"That shows how much *you* know."

"Get lost," said Polly Winternitz. "Maybe you understand *that* much, Mr. Doctor Know-It-All. Just get lost."

All this was a form of instruction. Dr. Julius visited daily and stayed on call at night. He worked long hours, hard. As medical director of the Harley Andrews Hospice, he admitted and supervised patients and prescribed their medication and monitored their progress and attempted to reduce or at least control their pain.

They died, most often, painlessly. He signed the paperwork. Polly Winternitz and Hilda Gulickson expired without incident, having each ingested a quantity of morphine with their fudge.

"Do you smoke?" asked Joseph Cleary.

"No. I'm sorry."

"Got a smoke?"

"I don't," said Dr. Julius.

"Too bad," he said. "I smoke."

"How old are you?"

The old man made no answer. He gazed at Peter unblinkingly. "Smoke?"

"I'm sorry. No."

"Got a drink?"

"No, not that either. Not right here."

"Too bad," he said. "I drink."

"Well, at your age," said the doctor, "I don't suppose it hurts you."

"That's right," he said. "No pain. No pain no gain. It's an expression."

"Did you sleep well? How do you feel this morning?"

Joseph Cleary wore clean green clothes and black workboots. His belt buckle read: U.S. Navy. His workboots were unlaced. "A smoke," he said. "I know you smoke."

"How are you *feeling* this morning?"

"Fine morning," Joseph said. A chewed pipe stem protruded from his pocket.

"Yes. Well, in that case I'll be moving on."

"You do that, Doctor. Go ahead."

"I'll come by again tomorrow."

Joseph smiled. His upper plate was missing.

"If there's something I can do for you . . ."

"Smoke. You got a smoke?"

He had been in Bellehaven six months. It was an improvement. The town lay east of Lakeview, in a region of what once were farms, with a river running through. There were municipal buildings faced with Indiana limestone; there was a junior college and a newspaper and outlet stores and an Amtrak station and an industrial park.

Home was a furnished apartment, the west-facing side of a two-family house. A tall blue spruce outside his window blocked the view. His new neighbors were reclusive, and he rarely saw or spoke to them or heard them through the walls. He brought his clothes and chess set and music from Lakeview, and nearly nothing else; he wanted no reminders of the vanished past. For whole nights he slept without dreaming of Julie, for days at a time he saw patients and drove home without regret.

Dr. Julius did find a job, however, for Nurse-Practitioner Lampson. He praised her experience to Personnel, assuring them that she would make a competent addition to the staff; she was efficient and reliable, he said. But that was as far as it went. Though once or twice she told him she was grateful and would like a chance to prove it, Peter kept his distance. What he wanted was a colleague; what he needed was a friend.

The hospital president, Trip Conley, invited him to dinner.

They met at the Hermitage—Bellehaven's best. This assessment had been printed on the menu and above the anteroom where guests removed their coats.

Trip was tall and thin and elegant; his shirt was white on white. He wore his hair slicked back. "The wife couldn't make it," he said. "Not this evening, anyhow. Apologies . . ."

There were few other customers, sitting in upholstered chairs or in the pink plush booths. The background music was baroque: a harpsichord, two flutes.

Conley ordered a bottle of wine. "Have something else, if you prefer." He waved his hand, proprietary. "Have anything you want: my treat. The big boss told me, 'Treat him well.' "

"The big boss?"

"Uncle Harley—that's what you call him, right? He sings your praises, Doctor. He says if Trueman-Andrews is going to be noticed you're the one who'll do it. But let me ask you something, if you don't mind me asking . . ."

"What?"

"What brought you to this town?"

Trip was known in the restaurant, clearly; their waiter brought bread and olive oil and a crock of seafood pâté. He made a great show of producing the bottle, then pulled and proffered the cork.

Dr. Julius arranged his napkin. "Change."

"Change?"

"I was, oh, restless in Lakeview. I needed a challenge. Someplace a little bit larger."

Conley smiled. He understood, he said, the need for change; a person could go stale. He explained to Dr. Julius that he himself had shifted jobs; his own particular training was in business administration, and two years ago he'd been looking around for some new kind of opportunity when Dick—my father-in-law, Richard Trueman—said why not come on board? So Trip had done exactly that; he'd been a point man for the hospital and had liked the job.

But now things were changing again. It was Harley Andrews,

wasn't it, who had bought them out and bailed them out and was suggesting, not gently, that Richard Trueman consider retirement and maybe Trip would stay awhile and maybe he wouldn't, he'd see. With all the trouble nowadays about capitation and billing, with the beds they looked to lose to all this competition, with HMOs and "covered lives" coming out of every goddamn closet it hadn't been much fun. This new wrinkle of the hospice was an extra added attraction like, if Peter didn't mind his saying so, that nurse-practitioner he'd brought with him from—where was it?

"Lakeview," Peter said.

"You don't have to answer this," Trip said, "you can plead the Fifth Amendment but I do have a question . . ."

The waiter brought shrimp bisque. He ladled and withdrew.

"Ask ahead," said Dr. Julius.

So after they had tasted it, after Conley had a second glass and remarked upon the weather and the pleasures of Bellehaven, he cut, as he said, to the chase.

"Why do we need your patients, Pete?"

"Need?"

"Well, what if they're not welcome?"

"Then we write a contract with another service facility. We find another hospital."

"*Mi casa su casa,* correct?"

"Excuse me?"

Your house is my house, Trip said. It was nothing personal, not for him at any rate, but his father-in-law, Richard Trueman, did take the hospice personally and was dead set against it—no pun intended—and had been from the start. Between the two of us, he confided, we two don't always get along; old Tricky Dick and I don't see exactly eye-to-eye. He's what you'd call a fundamentalist, a real tub-thumper Trueman is, and he and Harley Andrews are what you'd call water and oil. Old man Trueman thinks a hospital is where you have the right to life and not what Daddy Warbucks thinks, a right to death instead. So there's some opposition here to what you and the big boss are doing; forewarned is forearmed, Conley said.

Then he reminded Dr. Julius that this Friday they would hold grand rounds and get a chance to make the case, to lay out the *philosophy* of what was going down: on grand rounds, if he had it right, they'd be focusing on AIDS.

And speaking as we were just now of, what would you call it, *associates*, we might as well agree to keep the lines of access open and maintain accountability if you follow what I'm saying. I mean you wouldn't want to furnish transport for your old people to Chicago or, heaven help us, South Bend; ours is the only health game in town so we'd better play it together; any friend of Harley Andrews's will be a friend of mine. And while I'm on the subject there's someone else Pete ought to meet, a lady who's arrived just now and will be in the audience for grand rounds on Friday morning: our visitor from England, our expert on dignity-death. You've heard of Cicely Saunders, correct, the patron saint of hospices?—well, Rebecca Forsythe is a whole lot better looking, and have you met her yet?

Dr. Julius said no.

And then Trip told a joke. "There's this old geezer, see, this widower. And the bell rings and he answers the apartment door and there's this terrific number, this *pulchritudinous* person." He pronounced the word with relish, raising and wriggling his hand. "Great tits, if you follow, with a lot to show and wearing just about nothing to hide it, and she leans against the doorway and says, 'Sir, your children and your friends have been concerned for your well-being. And so they've purchased my services and I'm here to provide you with a night of super sex.' "

The hospital president emptied his glass. "And so the old guy answers, 'Thanks very much, it's kind of you, I believe I'll take the soup.' "

Trip laughed. "Get it, Julius? 'I'll take the *soup!*' " He wiped his lips. "Myself, I recommend the salmon. Or the rack of lamb."

*　　*　　*

They discovered Joseph Cleary the next morning, in his bed. The patient was methodical; he had known just the way to proceed. He hoarded painkillers for weeks. He placed a plastic bag securely over his head, tying it under his chin. There was a slice of toast half-eaten on his night table, and two empty bottles of Ativan and one of Halcion. There had been twenty tablets in each. Joseph mashed them into and then swallowed them in raspberry yogurt, washing the meal down with whiskey. On the floor beside him lay a quart bottle of Southern Comfort, empty and uncapped.

Using a typewriter he had written, according to the formula suggested in his Hemlock Society Book:

I have decided for the following reason to take my own life. This is a decision taken in a normal state of mind and it is fully considered. They say my cancer's in the liver now, there's so much cancer in my bones I just about can't move. I break things when I move. These painkillers make no difference and that's why I've saved them out. And they won't let me smoke, the doctor tells me not to. If you put them all together and make a Hospice Cocktail why then maybe it will work. I sure could use a helping hand but nobody is offering so what I do instead is mix it up myself.

I have the right not to be handled or treated against my will, and I absolutely forbid anyone to interfere with me while I continue to live. Anyone who disregards this notice will be committing a civil and criminal offense against me.

Joseph Cleary. Bellehaven, Michigan. April 6.

Penny Lampson found him; he was lying on his side. The plastic was translucent and his face appeared swollen inside it. She released the plastic mask, untying the black ribbon and peeling the bag back. He had probably not needed it; the pills and alcohol would have been sufficient.

"How did he know how to do this?" Peter asked.

"To kill himself?"

"To use a plastic bag."

"It's common knowledge, isn't it?"

"But all those pills. The tea and toast. The whiskey to increase the action of the drugs. It's textbook procedure . . ."

"He wasn't taking prisoners." Nurse Lampson wore white. "He wanted to be certain."

"It's overkill," he said.

"Will you sign the death certificate?"

Dr. Julius nodded.

"Will he be autopsied?"

"Yes."

There were three more deaths that week, but all of them took place outside the hospice, in the patients' homes. The coincidence was notable and methodology precise. The suicides had been effective and preplanned. Dr. Julius returned from each of his site visits with a similar report: sedatives in conjunction with alcohol had been engorged in quantity, then a plastic bag placed on the head. In each of the three cases also a formal note lay by the pillow, disclaiming coercion and insisting on the right to self-determined suicide. One called Dr. Jack Kevorkian a saint. She hoped she would meet him in heaven, which was where—if there was any justice, if God's mercy meant a thing at all—he deserved to go.

Two of the sufferers were male, one female; all of the cases were terminal, though Etta Heisinger had been in remission. The obituary notices that Saturday were brief, but the *Bellehaven Daily*, in its Community section, ran a two-column story on depression and its risks. According to the article, teenage suicide is more widely reported on but no more prevalent than suicide among the elderly. A workshop would be held on the subject, sponsored by the outreach program of St. Paul's Lutheran Church.

III

"GOOD MORNING, friends, and thank you all for coming here today. My name's Trip Conley and I'm the president of True-man-Andrews Hospital—so it's my official duty to welcome you this morning. My pleasure also, of course. I'm pleased to see so many colleagues and associates assembled for what promises to be a most unusual grand rounds. As many of you know, I've no expertise in medicine as such; I'm the least learned person in this room when it comes to the clinical aspect of AIDS. I'm not a doctor and, before accepting the presidency of this great insti-tution, I had no direct experience of the challenge and the pos-sibilities involved in such a job. I'm Joe Six-Pack, John Q. Public, and that's the role I play.

"But I happen to believe that it's a useful role. I like to think the gulf between the caregiver profession and those it serves is not unbridgeable. And it's been my purpose all along to try and represent the layman's point of view—to bring Joe Six-Pack and John Q. Public's concerns to the boardroom and consulting room and, yes, even to grand rounds. Which is why I'm glad to

stand up here and play the fool and demonstrate my ignorance"—Trip paused, allowing the appreciative titter to subside—"in order to try and remind you how little we really *do*
know."

This was a speech he could give in his sleep; this was the president's patter song, and he had it cold. In every venue in the hospital, and for every talk-show host and camera and journalist in
town, across the state, across the country and three weeks ago in
London he'd been asking the same question: what's going on
here, folks, what do you think you're up to and how can we assist?

"It's a little like the story of the Emperor's new clothes." Trip
smiled. "The one about what happens when a rich and powerful
character—in this case, the Emperor—gets fooled by a fast-
talking tailor into failing to acknowledge his own ignorance.
He's told, as you remember, that only the *most* intelligent people
can judge the value of these clothes, their beauty and expense."

Involuntarily, he glanced at his own sleeve: the weave was
excellent, the buttonholes hand-sewn. "And because he doesn't
dare seem stupid, the Emperor says, oh my, yes, this costume is
surpassing fair. And he puts nothing on. Then everyone else in
the kingdom falls for the same ploy; they tell him that he's looking well, in the *pink* of health, in fact, and remark on his splendid new clothes."

His tie was watered silk. His socks and his handkerchief
matched. His cuff links were silver: T/C.

"It continues this way for a while," Trip declared. "They say
he sets an example for all; they refuse to believe what they see.
Then there's a party to celebrate this gorgeous suit he's wearing,
and he struts his stuff all over town. But a wide-eyed child
points out what no adult could dare admit: the Emperor goes
naked. And everyone agrees. So the head honcho finds a dressing gown or nice fur coat or whatever they wear in wherever
he's Emperor, and everything gets fixed again and everyone lives
happily ever after. Except, of course, the tailor. Who gets
killed."

Trip waited for the laugh. This time it was uncertain.

"All right. So I'm *not* Hans Christian Andersen and there's a limit to the value of analogy. We're not discussing fables but the practical matter of patient supervision and its cost-effectiveness, the way to bring our hospital to speed. Yet here—and by *here* I mean not merely Trueman-Andrews and Bellehaven but all across the country—we have a kind of similar confusion, a *collective* inability to look the problem in the face and say wait a minute, something's wrong. And it's got to be said and it's got to be shouted or we're all in deep, deep trouble, and that's why I don't hesitate to tell you fairy tales this morning. Because I *want* to be the kid who shouts, hey, the Emperor's wearing no clothes. I *do* want to stop the parade."

And this was true enough. His big-time speech this season was a sermon on input, collective decision-making and the value of feedback and participatory management and all the rest of it. He liked to talk consensus, but anyone with half a brain would see how the process itself could be processed: the buck stops here, Trip reminded himself, the fuck-offs stop fucking with me . . .

He had been an only child, his dad an army officer, and home was brick split-levels and six different schools by the time he was ten. He'd been what they call an army brat, but always in America, since when his dad went overseas Trip and his mother stayed home. Except that home had been a suitcase and a bag of books and her red rusted station wagon and a basketball, no hoop, and the one thing he learned was mobility, how to keep on keeping on. When he was twelve years old and they were stationed at Fort Benning, his mother had enough and ended up in bed with Harry Stringfellow, who sold and fixed TVs and showed up on a service call because of the antenna; it was supposed to rotate and pick up directional signals, except it wouldn't turn. His father was out on maneuvers but Trip came home early from school (or what he said was school that day but really was walking the red clay ditches and counting the beer cans and reading the Hardy Boys, watching the crows), so when he slammed in through the kitchen screen door, blowing his nose, saying, "Mommy, my throat hurts," what he found was a fat stranger with no pants on in the living room and his mother in only a towel.

"Aw, shit," said Harry Stringfellow. "You didn't told me, Doris, you had kids."

"Just one of them," his mother said.

"Aw, shit," said Stringfellow again, and walked into the bedroom and came out holding his pants. "You never did," he said.

"Meet Harry Stringfellow," his mother said. "He was just stopping by."

So then the two of them packed up the car and went to Potsdam in upstate New York, where his grandparents worked a dairy farm—twenty holsteins and a goat—and they could watch the snow all winter till it drifted past the windows and he couldn't see. By the potbelly stove in the kitchen Trip read *Treasure Island*, and books about the Civil War, where one brother fought for the North and one brother fought for the South. In the graveyard there were monuments to the citizens of Potsdam who gave up their lives for the sake of the Union, and for the sake of the country. His father called, but Doris wouldn't answer, and she told her parents to say they hadn't had a visit, not in weeks.

His grandparents had a freezer full of chicken parts and a sprung-roof chicken coop, and a thermometer outside the bathroom that one March morning at seven o'clock fell to –42. His mother was a pretty woman, everybody said so, and soon enough she met an assistant professor of chemistry at Clarkson who had an apartment on Main Street just past the Roxy Theater, above the travel agency, and she gave Trip the money for movies and popcorn and visited with her professor while he went to the show. Later they had pizza, or maybe they went bowling, and it was pleasant when the ice broke up along the Raquette River and he could ride his bike.

This happened each Friday till May. There had been a test that day, last period, on algebra, and Jenny at the next desk let him copy down her answers, so it wasn't difficult, and he had scored the winning run from second base when lard-ass Freddy Merkin dropped a pop. It was after Stanley Kubrick's *2001*, Trip remembered, when he had been supposed to meet his mother in the lobby, but who was waiting for him was his father, not in uniform. There was an ambulance and fire truck outside the professor's apartment, and there were people watching, but his father took him by the arm and pulled him to the parking lot across the street and made him get into the car and locked the door.

"We're getting out of here," Joe Conley said. "We don't need this two-bit town."

"Is everything okay?" said Trip.

"Fasten your seat belt," his father said. "It's A-OK. You bet."

There had been blood on his shirtsleeve, and his right cuff was torn, but when Trip tried to ask about it, all his father did was talk about *2001* instead, and if that freaking HAL had freaked him good or not. "Not me," said Trip, "not ever," and his father said that's A-OK, space travel's the wave of the future, computers is the coming thing and you got a ticket to ride.

"Ride where?" he asked.

His father lit a cigarette. He cracked the window, inhaling.

"Ride *where*?" Trip asked again.

His father would not say.

When he retired from the army Joe Conley had been forty-five. He bought a used thirty-foot Slip-Stream and racked his guns and fishing rods above the second bunk, and when Trip couldn't sleep at night he said, just go to sleep, shut up and shut your face. They drove to New Mexico, then north to Nevada, and then Trip went to school in Florida and Kansas and, for two whole years, in Spokane. This was where he washed dishes and worked mowing lawns and then as a busboy and learned about manners and wine. This was where he watched his father get hired by the packing plant then fired for slicing the time clock with the fire ax.

They got along together, reading the Bible out loud, playing rummy and hearts and canasta, and Trip learned how to bluff at poker and win at solitaire. His father had health benefits and an

army pension, and sometimes he brought women to the Slip-
Stream or their rented rooms, but mostly he brought rye. They
never did speak about Potsdam or what happened near the Roxy
to who Joe called "your mother, my ex"; when Trip dared to ask,
much later, when he was seventeen, his father said, why nothing special, except she's not so pretty anymore. And neither's
her professor, since you ask. Don't fuck with me, he said. That's
the lesson, ain't it, don't *ever* fuck with me. He bent back to the
shoe he was trying to tie, his foot up on the chair.

By then he was a half-deaf drunk—all that artillery had done
in his right ear, he said, and refused to wear a hearing aid—and
never heard it coming. Trip gave him thirty pounds but was two
inches taller, and he had the reach. So when he hit his father it
was like kicking over a tree, not needing an ax or a chain saw
because the trunk was rotten, hollow, just waiting to go down.
When Joe Conley fell he hit his head, making a soft light unimportant sound, and the folding chair fell next to him and he lay
there with his eyes closed, breathing, spittle on his cheek, while
Trip took their money from the canister above the stove and the
backpack he would need.

In years to come it puzzled him, how he'd walked out on his
parents—first his mother, then his father—when they required
help. There'd been no ambulance or fire truck where Joe lay on
the linoleum, out for the count, and his own sleeve wasn't
bloody though his knuckles had been skinned. Trip wasn't
angry, really, at the old man by the kitchen sink, but what it all
came down to was an eye for eye and tooth for tooth, not so
much *revenge* as *reciprocity*, an evened score, a way of doing unto
his father what his father did before.

He hit the road. He went straight south, thumb up, head high,
and there were truckers who helped him and one who called him
"baby face" and skinny guys in Oldsmobiles who wanted to tell
their life stories, not because he cared to listen but because they
had to talk to stay awake. Once, a girl in a Mustang convertible
offered him a joint then pulled behind an overpass and gave him

a blow job and then, when he got out to take a piss, she drove away, backpack and all, in the middle of nowhere with night coming on. Trip lay behind the overpass—not cold because it was July, but shivering, staring up at the amazing stars, and hearing trains and trucks and planes in the distance—till dawn. He recited to himself the story of Jesus in the desert, being tempted for forty days by Satan, and he swore he would resist temptation and, if he ever saw that bitch again, not do unto her the thing his father would have done. In the morning he did find his backpack where she'd tossed it, a red nylon heap by the side of the road, so he fixed himself up and moved on.

It took three weeks to make Mexico City, and then he went to San Miguel de Allende and found work as a jewelry salesman and hung around in the zócalo with other artist types. On his nineteenth birthday he took stock. The man who owned the jewelry store had a heart condition, and he had quit the rat race and come down from Chicago, but he said to Trip you're young, you're healthy, you should *do* something with your life not only just piss it away. It happens anyhow, he said, the pissing it away, I mean, you don't need to help it along. So Trip accompanied the shipment north and with his share of the profit—all fair and square, aboveboard, signed over as commission—he enrolled at Western Michigan because the guy in San Miguel he worked for had a cousin in Kalamazoo.

This was when he first looked in the mirror and saw a handsome stranger smiling back. Clean-cut Trip Conley of Michigan bore no resemblance he could notice to that kid with the milk pail in Potsdam or the waiter he'd been in Spokane. In exchange for help around the house—mowing, raking, painting trim—his landlord halved the rent. They sat together on the porch on summer evenings, rocking, nodding at the neighbors, for all the world like family except that Trip was fucking his landlord's sister when she got off early from work. He was polite and literate and when they asked him where he came from he perfected a self-deprecatory shrug, as if anyone not born or raised in Kalamazoo would be too embarrassed to say so, and the only thing he wanted was to be buried there.

But the only thing he wanted by the time he was a senior was a ticket to anyplace else in the world, and Trip made it through college and business school and by the time he was finished was nobody's baby or fool. That was when he got ambitious and began to hit the big time and get hired for what players call the show. He liked to give orders, not take them, and he liked control. That was when he understood how most people want to be told what to do but not to know you're telling them, how what they want are orders they imagine they've made up. And that was when he met Christine and fell in love with her, of course, of course, and struck it rich.

Chief Resident Kelly and Dr. Julius, the next two scheduled speakers, sat level with his feet. In the second row, not opening her notebook, Rebecca Forsythe watched. As if he needed time to think, as if he would in fact consider their opinions, Conley scanned the hall.

"So to repeat my moral: it's as if all over America people understood at the same instant that the Emperor's wearing no clothes. The medical establishment looks naked. And it makes some of us furious, and it makes some of us scared. No wonder the tailor's in trouble, no wonder we've come to a crisis of confidence: something just *has to be done*."

He was at his best, he knew, when he appeared to improvise; he lifted the glass, paused, drank.

"My own approach derives from a set of management principles. The basic assumption here is that people desire to express themselves in *all* of their life situations, including where they work. So why not in a hospital? I'll take your silence to mean you agree—since I don't want to think you're afraid to express disagreement. In which case our theory's wrong."

Again he waited for the laugh; again it did not come.

"These positive attributes of workers are most evident when, in the first place, all members of the organization are enabled to participate as fully as they can in its activities and, in the second place, they feel that they have been recognized personally and will be equitably rewarded for participation. I'm a layman, I use layman's terms. It means you own your shop.

"Some of you may remember the radical dictum so current in the sixties—'If you're not part of the solution then you're a part of the problem.' Well, in my opinion, to be part of the solution is to *reduce* and *isolate* the problem, whether you solve it or not. And what this means in practical terms is *all* of us are in this boat together, and we can steer it or sink.

"We've already had some real success, as many of you know, in two separate situations within Trueman-Andrews. The staff in the admitting office recognized more quickly than did top management, for example, that with the advent of same-day admissions in ambulatory surgery, the admissions process—which was an efficient one for the conventional admissions of yesterday—had become no longer viable. Because they themselves identified the problem and could propose solutions, they did not become discouraged or—as so often elsewhere—alienated from the system.

"And delays in patient arrival at the endoscopy unit had been seen as 'somebody else's problem' by the radiology technicians, unit coordinators, transporters and floor nurses involved; each group was blaming the other. When we challenged them to solve the issue of delayed arrivals by themselves, they formed a project team. Now ninety-five percent of endoscopy patients arrive within five minutes of schedule—and there's not only patient and employee satisfaction involved but also the matter of money. Time is money, friends, as Harley Andrews keeps reminding me and it's my business to keep reminding you. In this case we're discussing something on the order of a million dollars per annum in operating costs. And, since time is money, I'll use only two minutes more . . ."

He tapped the mike for emphasis, then glanced at the photographer. The photographer offered thumbs-up.

He smiled. "Okay. If there's a rule I want us to hold golden, friends, it's *pay attention to procedure*. Empower the entire constituency, with each of its competing claims, and you'll end up—flawed, no doubt, imperfect, no doubt—with a result you can defend. And out of that defense, that process *shared* and *justified*, you go one little step further. That's the true march of medicine, the one-step one-step one-step; it's not a broad jump or high jump or sprint but a kind of marathon, it's one little step at a time. Slow but steady wins the race."

Horseshit, Trip told himself. *Crap*.

"So I believe grand rounds this morning can serve an important purpose. It's a chance for us to air our thoughts, to engage in constructive debate. In this particular area we're confused about priorities, and I've therefore invited two speakers—Dr. Kelly, Dr. Julius—to air opposing views.

"Nowhere does the issue seem more pertinent than in the case of AIDS—for those afflicted with the disease, of course, but also those affected by it in their near and dear. I've visited this morning's patient more than once in the last days, and—on this subject of competing claims—he has a good deal to say. Believe me, he's an interesting fellow; when they write the case management textbook he'll be a textbook case . . ."

Here, Trip consulted his notes. "Before I close, however, I'd like to say one last thing. We have the visit of a specialist from England—an expert, that is, in the only specialty that counts: the experience of suffering, and the layperson's point of view. Ms. Rebecca Forsythe is a name that will be known to you as the much-praised and best-selling author of two books on the topic of assisted suicide. She has confronted this gravest of issues in unsparing personal terms, recounting her personal loss. She's asked me *not* to turn this into a promotional tour and very particularly *not* to treat her as a celebrity during her visit to Bellehaven. So I'll limit myself, right now, to giving public thanks that she's agreed to a site visit—to see what we are up to, here at Trueman-Andrews, and to offer us the benefit of her experienced advice. There you are, Rebecca. Please stand up."

She stood. He himself led the applause. Then Trip stepped aside and took his chair and let the show go on.

IV

SHE ADORED these American boy-men, with their fervor and their insecurities, their membrane-thick thin skin. They all had such childish assurance, so desperate a need—a performance anxiety, really—to please. They behaved in bed or on the tennis court or, just now, on the podium as if their lives depended on applause; they needed you to tell them they were perfect, wonderful, the best there'd ever been. Americans could never have enough of your approval, and they worked hard for it too.

Trip Conley had persuaded her the journey was worth making and she could be of use. His success had been no accident; he was good at what he did. Since service was her weak point—the last corruption, really, of the charitable impulse, her old habitual confusion of the giver with the gift—Trip pressed her into service yet again. He had known just what to say. He fixed her with those big brown eyes and batted them and, positively pleading, said, "Rebecca, you *have* to, you must."

She had had her fill of him already—his iced negroni cocktails and two dozen long-stemmed roses delivered to the flat, his triceps and his pectorals absurdly flexed each time he caught himself reflected in the mirror, his orgasm out of a textbook and the way he clenched his fists. She intended to refuse. Her last book tour exhausted her; she heard herself mouthing inanities all over Sussex and East Anglia and knew she needed a rest.

Death's Kingdom was a huge success; it was doing better than her *Undiscovered Country;* it was in the fifth printing already and they couldn't print it fast enough to keep it on the shelf. Everywhere they wanted her to talk about her husband's suicide and then listen to their histories, their own remarkable sorrows, and to give advice. They wanted her to help. If she, Rebecca Forsythe—they seemed to be saying, though never quite out loud—could reach so large an audience with a book about Arthur and how he had died, why surely they could do as well, and no doubt better, splendidly, with the unwritten stories of their lives.

So what they really wanted was for her to step aside. What they hoped for from Rebecca was a kind of reciprocity, *you've touched me, I touch you.* She could almost hear them saying it: I've lived your life and bought your book and watched your husband choose to die, and now it's my turn, lady, step aside. It would have been all right with her; she had nothing left to give.

But that was Conley's talent: his instinctive salesmanship. Rebecca Forsythe was an inspiration, he maintained, a source of strength for thousands, and she could draw strength from that. He urged her to visit Bellehaven and examine the new hospice at the Trueman-Andrews Hospital; he suggested that the trip would do her good. He had recognized exhaustion, her bone-deep inertia, and refused to take no for an answer; he had been persuasive, and so was the size of the check. And he had been so ardent, so very much committed to the notion of her visit to America, so certain she would make a difference that she caught herself thinking, Well, why not, well anyhow it's possible and what's the risk and why not just say yes?

So flattery had got him somewhere after all. It had got her to this godforsaken city in the middle of nowhere, the middle Midwest. She landed in Chicago and he met the flight—with two bottles of champagne and a box of chocolate truffles and the roses once again. They had had a lovely evening at the Drake. He could be sweet when he wanted, and he told her that he wanted her—just whose phrase *was* it anyhow, Rudyard Kipling's, Noël Coward's—"to bring the wretched heathen to the light." So Rebecca told him yes, all right, and then Trip entered her and worked those narrow hips of his and then she fell asleep.

Next morning they made their way east. He drove into the rising sun along a road that made the M-25 out of London look like a country lane: so full of commuters and lorries and diesel fumes she had her migraine by the time they reached Bellehaven. There were lakes the size of inland seas, and steel plants and quarries and rubbish and factories everywhere along the verge. She rolled down the window; it stank. The town itself was gray.

In this place Trip had to be careful; his wife was, he told her, possessive and would be jealous of her fame and had this notion of fidelity and would—he laughed, making a joke of it—cut off his balls if she guessed. He maundered on about suspicion, how his enemies were waiting for his first miscalculation and how everybody hoped—expected—that he would make a mistake.

"You understand, don't you?" he asked.

"Of course."

"There's the question of professional"—he touched her knee—"behavior. They've been watching. They'll be watching all the time."

"I understand," she said.

What Rebecca did not tell him was that she preferred it this way. She had grown used to solitude in the three years since her husband died; she took pleasure in her privacy, and thank you very much. She refused to be Trip's conscript, his famous recruit to the cause.

"I can't tell you what this means to me," he said. "Or to the hospital staff. When you agreed to come to town . . ."

"Don't bother, Trip. You mustn't . . ."

"I'll see you this evening," he said.

Then he dropped her at the hospital apartment for distinguished guests. Hospitality House, its president explained, was built for those whose child or spouse or parent had been flown in for emergencies and who needed a roof for the night. They might as well have placed a sign above the portal: "Abandon Hope, All Ye Who Enter Here." She despised it at first sight.

Trip signed her in and drove away and as soon as he rounded the corner her self-possession vanished, her brave good humor fled. The migraine had remained with her, or flickered at the yellow edges of her vision, an old familiar come to call. She should have stayed at home. There were No Smoking signs and fire extinguishers and bowls of plastic flowers in the hall. There were photographs of the Grand Canyon and a geyser called Old Faithful in Yellowstone National Park.

Rebecca knew herself; she canceled that night's dinner and the next day's schedule and kept Trip Conley at bay. She would visit the hospice and leave. She did not want him pawing her between appointments, with his wife around the corner. Here it was nothing like the Drake: all lime-green carpeting and ice machines and inspirational pamphlets on the bureau and the Gideon Bible coyly stuffed into the dresser by her bed.

Therefore she lay in an airless dark room, drinking ice water, a wet washcloth over her face. She should have gone to Greece. And she kept seeing Gytheion—the bright green sea, the spitted lamb—each time she closed her eyes.

This aimlessness—though she preferred, of course, to call it spontaneity—was new. It came with widow's weeds and a bank balance, and the one depended on the other. If Arthur hadn't killed himself and if she hadn't witnessed it, she would not have written *Undiscovered Country* or have struck it rich. Their marriage had been good. It had not, of course, been perfect, but perfection in such matters is a matter of degree. They had had their share of trouble, what Arthur used to call domestic squabbles; they had hoped for children and a cottage in the Cotswolds but had not had the chance.

Sometimes Rebecca felt restless and sometimes he too would appear self-absorbed, too busy with his work at Lloyds to look up from his morning paper or his desk at night. He was making a career. They went to a concert on Thursdays and the theater on Saturday night. They had sex after the theater on Saturday if he was not too tired, and if he was too tired they had sex on Sunday instead. It seemed a life like many others, satisfactory, but then he came home not from the office as she thought but from his consultation with the doctors at Kings' Cross.

It had been raining, she remembered; it was March 18. Arthur urged her to sit in the orange plush chair, his favorite one by the hearth; he was formal, ceremonious, and poured them both a drink. She could remember thinking that he planned some sort of announcement: *I've been promoted, fired, I've fallen in love with the cook.*

But it had been nothing like that. It proved unexpected, utterly. One minute she was sitting near the fireplace, holding a martini and considering what she would say if he were sleeping with the cook, and the next minute everything changed. He was going to die, Arthur said. He had been judged: weighed in the balance and, alas, found wanting. The verdict, he informed her, was pancreatic cancer. It explained his recent loss of weight and his digestive troubles; it was a death sentence as absolute as hanging, but with less hope of commutation or reprieve.

"I didn't want to worry you," he finished. "Not till it was absolutely necessary. Now it is."

"Of course," Rebecca said. "Naturally, now it is."

She could remember thinking that the pillow on the footstool should be cleaned. The fringe of the curtain was stained. She supposed she must have been in shock—which would explain the feel of clinical displacement, the sense of acting merely as a witness to the drama of their lives. This was, she recognized, the climactic moment of their marriage; this was her chance to weep or tear her hair or make a scene or speech. But she remained mute, motionless; she had noticed his button was loose. She had just the right color of thread. She would mend it, later, when he removed his coat.

It was Arthur's final wish that they should have a holiday in Greece. She had never been there, and he had not been there in years, and he wanted to show her the Acropolis and see the Bay of Corinth and the Hermes by Praxiteles again. They flew to Athens and drove to the Mani peninsula and lazed through the Peloponnese. It would be, he told Rebecca, a last chance to control the pain; he would need to learn to do so on the trip.

He had been thirty-eight. Three years before, because it was the middle of his life (and not, he had assured her, because he'd had an inkling or any sort of premonition of this news), Arthur subscribed to the Hemlock Society. He told her that he had made plans. It would become imperative, he said, to move beyond the pleasure principle and then beyond discomfort through the outer edge of suffering to bliss.

They had been married for eight years but this was the true consummation of their marriage. They exchanged what he called deep-sworn vows. Arthur shed his old decorum like worn-out clothing; all propriety and inattention fell away. They ordered ouzo and retsina wine and she ate grilled lamb and mullet while he took small bites and tried to swallow; they made love, when he could manage it, with a bodily abandon engendered by despair.

Gytheion, Rebecca learned, was where Paris and Helen had spent their first night; the town had been called Kranae then. Now Gytheion was a tourist town, a ramshackle port with ferries bound for Italy or, perhaps, Patras. By the waters of the blue Aegean she saw only a shabby modernity, and nothing of the glory that was Greece. There was a clutch of dispiriting restaurants and second-rate cafés. There was a lighthouse with graffiti, thorns and brambles underneath. Where Helen and her darling

Paris lay together, blissful, there were fishermen on motorbikes and the occasional caïque.

Everything, she could remember reading, begins as mystery and ends up as politics: *tout commence en mystique et finit en politique.* But in their case it proved the reverse. What had started out as politics became, instead, mysterious; she adored him as never before. When she glanced at herself in the mirror, she saw a wide-eyed creature thunderstruck by grief. For somehow Arthur Forsythe, beside her in their old hotel, became a creature out of fable: both her red-haired implacable husband and doomed illicit prince. Nothing in her life alone or in their life together had been similar, remotely; she prayed for every day to last a month.

And then it was as if her prayer had been granted, and the dream came true. Each hour was a day, each day did last a month. Only she should not have wished it; she should have known what lies in store when such a wish is granted: an eternity of pain. He said, "I think it's time, don't you?" and Rebecca said, "Yes, I suppose so," and booked the tickets back.

He slept the whole flight home. When they returned from Athens he could barely swallow, barely speak; the brilliant light upon his face faded and went dark. And when Arthur killed himself it was as though the turning motion of the earth, the very laws of gravity had altered in her case. She could not leave the room. They had had no children, and her family was in Dorset, and her husband's family were prim, formal, stiff-lipped strangers with whom she had nothing in common but him, and now not even that. She had wanted to die *for* him, then *with* him, and then survive for only one reason: to tell his story right.

He asked her to do it, of course. He whispered one morning, effortfully, you could write this down. So Rebecca felt compelled to work, to stay in touch with their struggle by preserving it on paper—on what they used to call, only half-jokingly, her winding sheet. Of his tapes and their conversations and his journal entries and her daily log she compiled a testimonial. Once back in London with him dead she wrote the whole book in a month, and did so in a trance. She could not remember eating, nor if and what she drank.

And then her neighbor Noel said just show me what you're writing, darling, let's just have a look. Noel was a publisher, and he knew the trade. He'd been sweet about Arthur, considerate, and she in turn had rather liked his oriental houseboys and his collection of jazz records and—as if anyone still dressed that way—his silk striped foulards. So when he asked to see her work she said she couldn't possibly, it wasn't for public consumption. I know this business, he assured her, nothing ventured nothing gained.

Then he took her heap of pages (so rapid they hadn't been numbered, so much an effusion she'd not kept a copy) away. He removed them on Friday and came back that Sunday and all his temporizing—Rebecca used to tease him for his finicky indulgences: the apricot poodle called Mopsy with her own embroidered pillow, the sherry on the silver tray, the hedge he had been training into topiary—disappeared.

He was excited, she could tell; his guess had been confirmed. We'll use your photograph, he said; we'll publish it, and well.

She'd felt forlorn all weekend, as if not merely a widow but the victim also of some wrenching accident that left her completely alone. Those sheets had been her company, the last lingering trace and residue of Arthur left behind. When Noel brought them back to her he said he'd made a copy, and suddenly there were thousands and then hundreds of thousands of copies and, as he predicted, her photograph was everywhere and she was a cult figure, Xanthippe in the British press, the beautiful and grieving wife of Hemlock's famous Socrates—as if, from all that barrenness, she'd grown fertile: birthing death.

Now the next speaker stood up. She fought to stay awake. Since she, Rebecca Forsythe, must not fall asleep in public she would have to pay attention; she rubbed her ankle, hard. Chief Resident Jim Kelly began his presentation; he cleared his throat and squinted out against the light. She adored these American boy-men, except all of them were fools.

V

WHAT JIM Kelly hated was the zodiac above him, with its silver glitter-stars embedded in the ceiling, and its rainbow coyly arced above the stage. He was looking at, he told himself, the single brightest orange row of seats they could possibly have ordered, the single most electric green they might have painted the walls; the carpeting was crazy: multicolored, plush and—according to the press release—fashioned for their millionaire by Tibetan refugees.

He tapped the mike. It worked. "Okay. Let's get started," he said. As chief resident he was supposed to introduce the problem; then Julius would have his say and then they'd disagree. Conley liked to watch them fight it out and to play judge not jury; it was his new management mantra: *process, consensus, progress*—those buzzwords for this joke of a debate.

"Good morning. Glad you're here." It was 8:05. He cut the lights and lit the screen behind him; he launched into the details and started his routine. "All right. The patient is a thirty-eight-year-old, single, white male, a stockbroker; he was admitted this week to the Trueman-Andrews Hospital for the fifth time in the past year. His complaints on this admission were cough, chills, fever and sweats, of five days' duration. Mr. R. is known to have AIDS.

"S.R. led an active, promiscuous sex life, beginning in his early twenties. He's a native of the area with no history of drug abuse or recorded blood transfusion; it is presumed he has been infected for ten or twelve years with HIV. He felt well, however, until about two years ago—when he began to notice weight loss and saw lesions on his torso which proved to be Kaposi's. Shortly thereafter, generalized lymphadenopathy appeared, accompanied by splenomegaly. Biopsy was consistent with well-differentiated small-cell lymphoma, and he received standard chemotherapy six months later when he became symptomatic with pruritus, sweats, loss of appetite, and continued weight loss."

Kelly paused. There was no one in the auditorium to whom this came as news. It was, so far, the standard story and it happened every day; he hurried through the history in order to get to the point.

"Mr. R. has had other symptoms and signs characteristic of AIDS—increasing weakness and strong suggestion that the lymphoma is now in his lungs. His recent admissions have been triggered primarily by severe, persistent syncope, which has often accompanied dehydration from his diarrhea—and two episodes of pulmonary Pneumocystis infection, the last of which appeared despite his fairly careful attention to chemoprophylaxis.

"On physical exam at admission, the patient was an emaciated, intelligent man, breathing rapidly with a deep nonproductive cough. His vital signs were unremarkable, except for a respiratory rate of thirty-four, and temperature of thirty-nine degrees. There were diffuse crackles throughout his lungs, generalized lymphadenopathy, and remarkable hepatosplenomegaly. There were physical findings of peripheral neuropathy, and several small skin lesions compatible with Kaposi's on the right upper hemithorax."

He enjoyed these sessions usually: the chance to strut his stuff. His first slide was a photograph of the patient's face, dark glasses perched in place.

"Laboratory tests included moderate anemia, with cell indices consistent with the anemia of chronic disease. Liver function tests were compatible with mild biliary obstruction. The creatinine was 5.2, and BUN 78. Chest films showed diffuse reticular-nodular infiltrates, perhaps more marked at the bases. EKG was normal.

"Suffice it to say for today's rounds that we treated him for Pneumocystis again, with IV pentamidine, and as I speak he is breathing more easily and looks a little stronger. Renal failure is the present major risk."

On the platform where he stood they should have invited a stand-up comedian, or cast a crooner as chief resident instead. The audience arranged itself—unconsciously, it seemed—by rank: the interns huddled in the rear, the residents ahead of them, then the nursing staff and the attending doctors and up front, in the first two rows, the seats reserved for consequential guests. Sitting where he'd asked her to, so he could watch her while he talked, Penny Lampson waved.

"Of particular note for our discussion this morning, the patient's mental status has remained intact—a feature somewhat different from many of our sufferers with AIDS. While Mr. R. is perhaps not making as much money as he would like on the market, he has kept up with his work." Kelly paused. "The reason he has been able to do so is that his devoted companion and lover, J.B., has been with him for four years. J.B. does all the housework, has virtually stopped his own employment—he worked for a real estate agency—and has devoted night and day to efforts to keep S.R. comfortable. He has shown himself to be absolutely indispensable for the last twenty-four months.

"However—and here we have the complicating factor of the

case—J.B. is reaching the end of his rope. A chronically ill patient, with an inevitably fatal prognosis, says he wants to continue living. And the person who takes care of him says it's time
to stop. S.R. is full of fighting spirit but his lover and principal
caregiver—the reason, in effect, that S.R. feels *able* to survive—
is ready to throw in the towel. J.B. has requested us to help the
patient die, whereas the patient himself insists he wants to live.

"Psychiatrists have evaluated both S.R. and his roommate—
who, by the way, is HIV negative. They find them both of
sound mind, so we cannot easily invoke a third party to make
judgments as to management; there's no legal basis for us to in-
tervene. And, to complicate things further, the patient absolutely refuses to leave his own home except on an emergency
basis; if we suggest a chronic-care venue such as an AIDS hospice, he rejects the idea out of hand. There have been, at times,
violent disagreements between him and his roommate about
their shared quality of life; they've reached a critical juncture
and cannot continue this way."

Jim swallowed; his head hurt. The Percodan was wearing off;
he'd halved the dose this morning in order not to lose his edge
but it was blurring anyhow and feathering back into pain. He
could feel it spreading softly through the nerve ends and the
ganglia, the old familiar messenger and powdered solution: *help,
help.* He pulled at his left shoulder and squinted in the light. He
had made the move from pharmaceuticals to medicine too late;
he was thirty-four years old.

And Marjorie, his wife, had been practicing her own kind of
avoidance; she worried about unmonitored blood and HIV and
if he could contract it. She kissed their new miniature schnauzer
with more evident pleasure than him; she watched TV talk
shows each afternoon about spiraling medical costs. She told
him horror stories every evening over cold cuts, about so-and-
so's nephew who fell off a ladder and how it cost them half a
million and they had to sell the house. Next day there would be
someone's uncle with an aneurysm that popped while he was

driving so he plowed into a school bus and killed eleven sixth graders on their way up the hill . . .

When he suggested maybe they might use a cleaning lady once a week she said housecleaning's not my thing and it would be terrific, wouldn't it, if you were home sometime to help. He understood, of course, that what she really needed was for him to pay attention, that she was telling him, hey, Jimbo, wake up and smell the coffee, hey, *here's* where we live.

But it was hard to focus in the house. There was the radio blaring, and the rotator cuff he tore while lifting something that he hadn't even noticed at the time, and the multiple injections and the arthroscopic invasion that made no difference, none. There was television always on, and dog shit on the floor; there was the leak in the toilet and the wasp nest by the porch and the article he'd promised on open-label sedatives that was six months overdue . . .

Jim wiped his glasses carefully, then returned them to their case; it was time to finish up. "S.R. is a realist and expects no miracles in the near or distant future. Yet he also insists he has every intention of trying to continue with his present mode. His roommate, on the other hand—whom we have come to know pretty well—has had it. He has sacrificed his own income, has lost friends—several others in their circle have died within the year. J.B. is becoming severely depressed and is drinking quite a bit. The best solution, clearly, would be to hospitalize him also and supervise his diet and alcohol dependency. With his own medical problems—ulcerative colitis, principally—we've been a bit uncertain as to how to treat J.B.; I've prescribed an MAO inhibitor and we'll keep our fingers crossed.

"There is, of course, no way to compel J.B. to continue as caregiver, and in a certain sense it's not even our concern. He's a free white male past twenty-one, and able to make up his mind. We're doctors, after all, and—contrary to what others in this room might think—not marital or romance counselors. But it's pretty clear to those of us who have gotten to know both of them that if the roommate gives up on his program of assistance, the patient will die quickly."

Kelly waited to let this sink in. The medical logic was simple: you do what's possible to do and then you send them home. But why should it matter to him?—the overworked and underpaid and insufficiently photogenic chief resident of the Trueman-Andrews Hospital—who had a daughter with scoliosis and a son in private school with what they were beginning to suspect was attention deficit hyperactivity syndrome.

That Englishwoman, Forsythe, was watching him like royalty; she had her notepad on her lap and might condescend to write. He hated how things slipped away—how what he thought he could control turned out to be someone's agenda. And he had lost his love of disputation, the querulous need to get things *right*, the urgent passion for exactness that alone keeps the profession and its members honest . . .

"There's one more aspect of this case that may be relevant to the unusual grand rounds we are conducting today. I've added up the hospital bills for just the last year—exclusive of doctor's charges—and to my astonishment they total in excess of $130,000. S.R., as it happens, can handle the costs, but he's an exception to what has become the rule of AIDS . . .

"Our problem therefore is not medical—we know how to keep him going—but managerial. On this aspect of the issue I yield to Dr. Peter Julius, the new director of the Harley Andrews Hospice. Pete?"

VI

PENNY COULDN'T get over it, really: this bullshit they were laying down in the name of progress, this holier-than-thou discussion right after the one in the staff lounge, just when things were percolating and Jim Kelly poured her her coffee and snapped his plastic spoon. It snapped right in two while he stirred. Watching his knuckles, she'd wanted to laugh; he'd been so cute this morning—so anxious and puppy-dog needy and proud. He said, just watch me, please just come along. She said I don't need to listen to Dr. Saint Peter Julius or President Night-Tripper Conley, I've heard them too often before, I'm sick of them both, tell the truth. But Jim had made that face of his, that I'm-no-good-at-small-talk what's-wrong-with-me-anyhow face, and Penny had felt sorry and walked in at his side.

What he meant to say was *comfort me, I want you to lie down.* We've got ten minutes anyway before the room gets busy; open your mouth and open your legs and let's get it on. I'm the chief resident here, and you're a nurse-practitioner; let's fuck. That's what he really meant.

But he was far too shy, of course, and offered her a Lorna
Doone instead. He smoothed what remained of his hair. Then
he said he thought he had a right, a duty even, to speak his
mind at such events, and he asked her what she thought of
management procedures in this particular case. She agreed with
his opinion, Penny said. She smiled and said, not meaning it,
that the whole house staff agreed.

Then she asked if he had noticed how their pretty-boy president kept his hands in his pockets that time by Scott Raposo's
bed; no bodily fluids for *him*, you could bet, no messing around
with a needle and blood, no way, no thanks, no chance. Jim
said, I hadn't noticed, no, and she said—reaching her hand out
to flick a crumb from his lapel and resting it there, just an instant, lightly, not pressing—that's because *you* were doing the
work.

So Penny got this aisle seat and an hour to chew gum. She
yawned. She needed no lecture on uremia in conjunction with
AIDS, and which symptom you try to treat when. What it
meant was renal failure, and one of the symptoms was itching,
and she'd been hired, hadn't she, to scratch just where it itched.
Trip Conley gave his TV talk, then Jim gave his let's-look-at-
the-facts talk, and now Peter Julius was climbing to the podium,
accepting the respectful scatter of applause.

She yawned again. This discussion was missing the point. She
knew more than she wanted to about the management of pruritus and the proper dispensation of potassium; she was their local
expert on weakness, irritability, nausea, twitching and shortness
of breath. The man they called S.R. was a funny man and true
believer who hoped to stay alive. He was undeluded as to the
prognosis; he wasn't crazy for Mexican quack remedies or chick-
pea mustard plasters or even AZT. And so he asked her every
day, what's new, what's the news on the rialto, how'm I doing
now? Penny told him fine, just fine, and then he said tell me the
truth.

They spent time together. It turned out he knew Lakeview

well, he himself had been born in Michigan City and had gotten out as quickly as he could. He'd done so for different reasons, of course, but they both had made it here to Trueman-Andrews and even in his pain and fear and worst cold midnight trembling he told her he'd do it again. He told her, no regrets. So they discussed what happened to him and how he had made his escape; they talked about growing up Catholic, quitting, and wanting to go somewhere where there wasn't always someone peering over your shoulder or in at the window, outraged by what they saw.

What they would see of Scott Raposo now was nothing to write home about, not even to Michigan City. He couldn't walk; he weighed a hundred pounds. And his lover, Johnny, was a case; Johnny minced past the nurses' station with more perfume and mascara on than any of the nurses wore and seemed to think they'd care. The only one who cared was Scott; they fought about the newspaper and what would happen to the parakeet and if the BMW needed a paint job and where they would go for vacation. These two were always at it, always squabbling about rights of proxy and surrogate powers and the level of potassium and what Scott wanted done at home and who pulls which plug. When she listened to them argue Penny felt jealous, nearly; it was like a conversation, a habit of discussion and the way they could agree.

S.R. gave her tips on the market. *Plastics*, he advised her, except that you're not old enough, and when she asked him old enough for what he said *the joke*. There was a movie, *The Graduate*, and it's what some old fool tells Dustin Hoffman: plastics. But as long as we're discussing it I'll give you some advice, my dear, in my capacity as broker: avoid commodities and make sure your partners use protection and don't ever *ever* borrow someone else's needle. Not likely, Penny said, and then he rolled his eyes and pursed his lips and did what he said was his Fats Waller imitation: one never knows, *do* one, he said. I can talk to you, darling, he said.

At seven she had checked on him, since the doctors would be

by. He rolled over carefully, trying to make a joke of it, saying there's no salt on my tail this morning, is there, homegirl, not enough salt in my food. If you'd just let me have a little more potassium my night sweats might amount to something, right? No salt, she'd said, no sweat; you didn't wet your bed. When I get out of here, he whispered, I'm buying you some dancing shoes and we'll go out dancing. If we decide on Mexico, we're taking you along. Then she told him what she'd heard and what she hoped would please him; he was to be the subject of grand rounds.

Visibly, Scott brightened; he said maybe that means someone has built a better mousetrap, maybe they've got a new drug. Penny told him maybe, and she plumped the pillows and checked and replaced the IV. He asked her for a mirror and said—*shrieked* was more like it, really—sweet Jesus just look at this face.

It's not so bad, she told him, you look fine. Then he did what he could to disguise it, combing his hair and brushing his teeth and wearing his alpaca sweater since company was scheduled to appear. He chattered with her happily, he said surely it's a sign. God help you you poor fool, she thought, because no one else is likely to; the intervention he was hoping for would have to be a miracle or it just plain wouldn't work.

Now, moving up the aisle beside her, Jim Kelly brushed her knee; lightly, she pressed back. She'd been in Bellehaven six months. The town wasn't Paris, not even Chicago, but anything was better than that jailhouse by the water where her father nodded off each evening in the Barcalounger and her mother scrubbed the dishes twice and sluiced down the counter afterwards with her special mixture of vinegar and Comet and ammonia in order to kill off the germs. She had moved to Trueman-Andrews at the same time more or less as Peter, and with his professional help. She'd been offered the position on the strength of her résumé and blow job, though she stressed the former to her parents and reminded Dr. Julius of the latter; she could blow the whistle on him just as well, she said.

He said it didn't matter, he had nothing to hide or explain. Penny said that may be true but not when I'm done telling it, and anyway all that I'm asking is a chance to improve my prospects, I promise I'll leave you alone. He'd asked, starting when? starting now? She said the truth is, Doctor, I just wanted to be friends with you, that's all I ever wanted in the first place mostly.

It had worked out, after that. She'd been certain all along that he was still in mourning, that he was sleeping with a ghost, and she wasn't part of the program. And he said, you'd be a distraction and she said so get me a job in the hospital but not in the hospice itself. I won't bother you, I promise, as soon as we're both in Bellehaven. And he had done what she asked him, with his Jewish rectitude, and she also did what she promised with the exception of once in March when she had had three margaritas in the Rooster's Pen and called him from the pay phone to come get her, please, *please*, there was this guy in the corner who wouldn't let her walk out by herself and it was midnight and she was scared and, she admitted it, tipsy and needed him, Peter, to help.

He showed up in his raincoat and did drive her home. The roads were slick. She said, I've missed you, Dr. J., have you been missing me? She ran her hand through his hair. Then she whispered, come on in, why don't you come on in and come, but he said not now, Penny, and she said then never again.

So she flirted with Jim Kelly and let him touch her knee. He'd been telling her his troubles, lately, his problems with the mortgage and the kids. Pretty soon—not right away, because he was married and nervous and slow—he'd make his move. She was in no rush, she told herself, and signed up for aerobics class and took bike rides by the river and Bellehaven's excuse for a lake and did second shifts and overtime at work. The work was hard enough, Lord knows, and after she got home at night she felt too tired for even TV; she'd grab a yogurt and a Miller Lite and take a few swallows and sleep.

When loverboy the neurologist prick found a job in points unknown he'd left her with a parting gift, a burgeoning surprise. She'd not been using birth control; she was a good Catholic girl. But there was no way she could carry it, not in Lakeview, not at home, and therefore Penny suffered little children to come unto Him: the gift of life became the gift of death . . .

Her father would be putting Mickey Mantle next to Roger Maris and his personal hero, Ralph Kiner. He had acquired his Ralph Kiner for twenty bucks and a dog-eared Jimmy Foxx. He liked to say it was the best thing he had done in years, the only acquisition—that, and the Motorola—of which he could be proud. He stared at her, eyes narrowed, and said I hope you take my meaning, girl, and I'm including *you*. So I'm not a goddamn nun, she said, and without changing his expression, open-handed, he hit her. She fell back against the counter, hard, and her mother looked up from the dishes and said Penny, watch your tongue.

So that was when she knew she'd have to leave. She'd burn his baseball cards and smash his precious springer spaniels if she didn't get out of there soon. She'd take the Barcalounger and douse it with paint thinner or his gallon of antifreeze from the garage, and she'd bring him his slippers and pipe and kneeling down before him, begging his pardon, smiling up at him like any proper daughter performing her act of contrition, inquire if he'd like a light and then she'd strike a match.

She would have done it, too, except they went off to Milwaukee. And then she got Peter to visit and then he killed, what was his name?—the guy with Alzheimer's, the old one?—and when Harley Andrews called she knew she'd got her passport and her ticket out of town.

"You're my ticket, Doctor," she could remember saying. "And you're the horse I'm betting. Giddyap."

He had that solemn way about him, and it made her laugh. "This isn't a race," Peter said.

"I've told you before. You *owe* me."

He stared at her, unsmiling. "What?"

"A ticket," she repeated. "Take me with you, I can't stay."

"Listen, *you* were the attending nurse on Alan Eliot. If you claim I got the dosage wrong, I'll say it was your fault. And who are they likely to listen to?"

"Me."

"Get out of here," he said.

"That's exactly what I want. Just what I was hoping to hear. So tell me, when do we leave?"

Now her Saint Peter Julius was talking. His delivery was good. When he tapped the podium for emphasis you could *feel* the way the audience warmed up to him, the older ones respectful and the younger ones holding their breath. They loved his compassion, his grace under pressure, his brown unruly hair. He was putting the best face on things and thanking the chief resident, although he knew they disagreed, for this chance to air his views. I'd rather argue with Jim Kelly, Peter told the audience, than agree with most anyone else. I'd rather all of you, she told herself, quit acting like kids in a sandbox or playground or classroom debate; I'd like to get back to the question of endotracheal intubation and mechanical ventilation and how to get some sleep at night and stop seeing my dead baby every time I lay me down.

VII

"LET ME remind the audience," said Peter Julius, "of the history of grand rounds. Traditionally, and this is a tradition some of us can still remember, the name meant just what it implies. A distinguished doctor went about his business, making rounds. One of our teachers would walk through the wards, and we medical students would follow, and he'd explain what we were looking at or ask us to explain it by ourselves. It was, as many of you will agree, instructive and a little scary; it was—I'm speaking for myself, of course—an exciting way to learn what our profession used to consist of, and watch it at its best.

"Like any other tradition, however, it had its share of problems. We jostled for position by the great man's elbow, we couldn't always follow or even hear or see. We got lost in the hallways or bored by the ego trip; all too often grand rounds turned into a performance by an actor with a stethoscope as prop. The *medical* component lost its focus and looked vague. So this—as one of my professors called it—'perambulation' came to seem besides the point. The pretense of improvisation was dropped; we focused on a few predetermined cases and were treated to a lecture or display.

"Then, in turn, it began to seem silly to walk through the hospital at all. The patient was introduced to some sort of room such as this one, while the teacher and the students gathered round. That was a matter of efficiency; why should twenty people walk to two or three beds when the 'beds' could be brought here instead?" He smiled. "Lately, we've come to a further refinement: we dispense with the patient altogether and discuss our hypotheses or findings with lab reports and slides. It's been turned into a research discussion, a report on work in progress. So grand rounds can be conducted without the annoying need to consult reality so often, or to deal with suffering as such.

"I've told this tongue in cheek, but it is nonetheless true. Nowadays, the business of medicine seems further and further removed from patient contact, patient awareness of discussion and involvement in the treatment plan. We've come a long way in a little time from that 'hallowed' old tradition, where we were encouraged to *listen* to what the sufferer says.

"Now, S.R. is a perfect example of a man who can make his own case. He's knowledgeable, articulate; he knows just what he wants and why he wants it and is, it's fair to say, vociferous on his own behalf. When I went to see him yesterday evening, he questioned our procedures and the remedy for renal failure and the proper monitoring of his potassium level; as Dr. Kelly informed you, he's been admitted five times within a year and has every expectation of coming back five—indeed, *fifteen*—times more. He's very conscious of his rights and could prove, I'd guess, litigious. That our resources are strained and his prognosis hopeless does not deter him in the slightest; that he and his roommate, J.B., run the house staff ragged fails to interest him at all."

As always in such sessions, Peter worked to remember the patient—who was labeled by initials and who therefore seemed abstract. Scott Raposo would be in his armchair, staring out the window, holding his copy of the *Wall Street Journal* and maybe the business section of the *New York Times*. He was busy trading, selling, or pretending to—stockpiling assets for his nonexistent future, as if he could or would be there to reap next season's profit or absorb the loss.

Scott folded the paper meticulously, since one of the things he couldn't abide was the slipshod way that Johnny read, the crumpled paper coming to him if his lover assaulted it first. Scott said it's not so hard to be careful, do you have to make it seem as if a hurricane blows through this room every morning along with the breakfast cart; can't we have some order here, just once?

But Johnny said nothing; he smiled. He had that single dimple and the gap between his teeth. Starting last Saturday, therefore—it was little enough to do, Lord knows, and cheap enough, he was conserving energy for the more serious disagreements— Raposo ordered two newspapers so they both read undisturbed. He would be wearing glasses, bundled in his crimson robe and trying to make it through breakfast; he would have a cup of tea with honey cooling at his side . . .

At the hall's rear, someone sneezed.

"Now, Trueman-Andrews is," said Peter, "one of those special places where a man *can* have valuable input in the treatment plan. But even here, and even though you've heard President Conley urge our collective participation, we've moved too far too fast from the ideal of the attentive, the *attending* physician. That was a system, I needn't remind you, where the doctor's trained to listen, and the patient speaks his or her mind.

"Well, S.R.'s mind is clear, my friends, and has been made up. He believes that time, far from his enemy, is on his side; he hopes that medical advance in treating if not curing AIDS will be sufficiently rapid so that he can profit thereby, and he wants—as he expresses it—'to stay the course.' He thinks, in short, that there's a gambler's chance he can survive. And he's willing, in considerable pain and at considerable cost, to take that gambler's chance.

"As it happens, however, he's wrong. His time is limited: extremely so. His kidneys are close to collapse. Although we must stay well aware how often physician judgments as to futility should be uncertain, there's no uncertainty here. In particular cases our medical knowledge may be incomplete, there may be a reversible condition, the clinical information may be missing, and so forth; none of that in this instance pertains.

"And therefore it's no kindness—I'm speaking now in ethical or, if you prefer, *moral* terms—to permit S.R. this option or privilege his choice. We can only help a little bit and it costs us all too much. More precisely, what we should not do is deploy what are limited resources that might be better put to use within the Bellehaven community on an a priori hopeless attempt to assist one of our citizens in his delusional conviction that we as his doctors can help."

Here Peter rocked back on his heels. He could hear the proverbial pin. If they wanted detail, he would use the question session; he'd tell them more than they needed to know about who broke which glass, and why, about the argument last night that brought them to the corridor, Johnny with his suitcase packed, Scott wrapped around the IV tree in only his undershirt, screaming . . .

Johnny had been drinking; you could smell it clear across the hall; he lurched and dropped a plate. But Scott thought it was funny. "I'm laughing," he declared, "two big strong men like you two are and only little me to deal with—can't handle it? Buck up!"

"That's not to say," Dr. Julius continued, "that we should offer no assistance or fail to alleviate pain. We should and must do what we can. But the hospice not the hospital is the appropriate venue for such a course of treatment; it's cheaper, less invasive and in that sense more humane. You have heard from Dr. Kelly that S.R. dislikes the hospice, and would prefer to go home. This last option has been rendered moot by the refusal of J.B.— who is, again as we've been told, not easy to persuade. The patient, moreover, considers entry in a hospice tantamount to declaring defeat; it means he knows he has to die, and soon. As I've said, S.R. is a lucid man and he had judged—correctly, in my estimation—that his chances of survival are slightly increased by a stay in the hospital. Or, shall we say, his survival may well be prolonged. We cannot *increase* his chances, but we can extend them here.

"With the best will in the world," he said, "and good old American know-how, and the belief in progress that has always marked this nation, we've backed ourselves into a corner and—I'm speaking now of health-care delivery in general terms—must learn to start again. The President knows it, Congress knows it; so does the man on the street. We're the envy of the whole wide world in terms of our resources, our medical technology, our 'can-do' approach to a problem.

"But our hospitals go bankrupt while our level of health care declines. We employ seven caregivers per patient and another four for maintenance, we have empty beds that cost too much to sleep in, while—according to whose figures you read—some thirty-two to thirty-seven million Americans go uninsured. You know all this—the statistics on our infant mortality rate, our drug-dependent population, skyrocketing equipment and insurance costs—and it's not my plan this morning to remind you of the facts. It's easy enough to recite what's gone wrong and then attempt to fix it: mine is not a lone voice crying in the wilderness, everybody and his brother's out there wailing too.

"Dr. Kelly has provided you with the facts of the present case. He represents the very best we can do in a situation where, as I assume he would also agree, our best's not good enough. We do what we can, and that's all. I myself speak for the hospice alternative and to the issue of AIDS management in an age when our resources are no longer limitless. They never were, of course, but for many years we in this profession behaved as if they were virtually infinite, and as if all problems could be solved. Today most of us fear the reverse. We're cutting corners right and left and charging premiums that even a few years ago would have seemed unthinkable; the system's in Chapter 11—so say the nay-sayers and prophets of doom—or it will be soon."

He poured himself water. He drank. He had schooled himself to wait.

"The truth, as usual, lies somewhere in between. It's neither black nor white, but a gray area we're looking at; we're not in medical heaven, though it certainly isn't a hell. *Primum non nocere*, let me remind everyone here assembled that it's our first and primary duty as healers to do no harm. But everything beyond that primary duty is, I think, now subject to legitimate debate. First, what's the point or purpose of heroic measures? The hospice accepts only terminal patients, of course, but with this particular syndrome it's a matter of degree; it isn't a problem of whether but when. The verdict has been handed down, and the verdict is absolute: death.

"So I'd like you to consider the argument for patient transfer and—in particular cases, with full prior familial agreement and contractual sanction—the viability of some such alternative as the Hemlock Society. The issue is difficult, dangerous even, but we as a society can no longer afford to be judgmental. You all know the panic occasioned in Michigan by the recent spate of doctor-assisted suicides, and the national debate and uproar over an unlicensed pathologist's work.

"I therefore oppose Jim Kelly's position, for reasons that now should be clear. I urge upon you all the sufferer's imperative privilege, which must include the family. S.R.'s parents have written him off; he is, as you know, unmarried and childless—and J.B., his actual 'family,' is not recognized by law. We should treat and release S.R. rapidly, as rapidly as possible; we should not permit ourselves, as caregivers, to provide this kind of care. That he's a subject for grand rounds is in itself instructive and, I believe, a mistake.

"Because, *and this is the crux of it*, his self-proclaimed lucidity is nonetheless half-baked. He thinks that J.B. is willing to help him; he's wrong. He thinks that he can manage by himself or with paid assistance; again, he's quite likely mistaken. S.R., in my opinion, is not too very different from those deluded folks who have themselves deep-frozen on the chance of immortality; it's—in terms of sheer medical management—unrealistic at best. DNR is the prescription here: Do Not Resuscitate. The patient has his reasons and desires and is entitled to them, but not—I repeat, *not*—at our collective expense and in the face of verifiable reality: S.R. is going to die."

VIII

KIDNEY FAILURE, just kidding, kiddo, steak and kidney pie. Kid gloves, Kid Gavilan but not Kit Carson, New Kid on the Block. And what was that Durante sang: Inkadinkadoo? Kidney trouble, kidney stone, I own or used to swim in once and share and share alike a kidney-shaped and bright blue swimming pool, kick the kid's knee, kid the can. No, what he meant was *kick* the can, that must be what he meant to say, he mustn't get it wrong. I kid you not. Here's looking at *you*, kid. There was what they told him was a fix and it was called potassium and then there'd be dialysis and nothing in the stiff improbable bed he now called salvation would ever need fixing again. Oh Johnny, darling Johnny, why can't we march on home?

He used to love to sing. He used to be able to play. He was thick-fingered always, a little, but had a guitar and voice and used to like to wail away when nobody joined in the chorus, when Johnny comes marching home again let's see how does it go?

And therefore Scott Raposo hefted his guitar. It was badly out of tune. It was, sadly, a balloon. It was fashioned out of rubber and cotton and plastic and elastic and it had a metal sounding board strapped to his right arm. I am, he told himself, drifting, I must strive to be precise—for what is grammar but the comforting and codified arrangement of intention, and we do wish to be clear: subject is subject to kidney failure and predicated to be here in room 517 of the Trueman-Andrews Hospital in beautiful downtown Bellehaven. There was a word for it: renal. There was a bird for it: venal. Nonetheless he played and sang and the multitude of nurses and the army of orderlies danced.

Well you haven't an arm and you haven't a leg, *haroo, haroo,* well you haven't an arm and you haven't a leg, *haroo, haroo.* And so there was a problem, and in plain truth in absolute honesty if you'll forgive me saying so the problem isn't Johnny. Johnny, it would seem, was doing well. Swell. Johnny, from all available evidence, was in the fucking prime of life and feeling, thank you, no pain. Johnny had his legs and arms, Johnny had his liberty, Johnny had the key to the apartment and could eat the guacamole in the fridge and be raising a storm window or screwing in a lightbulb with that hard right hand of his or reading—no, *tormenting,* tearing through—the paper or swallowing his Nardil or soaping himself in the shower; Johnny might be sleeping by the time I get to Phoenix, with that fleck of saliva gathered on his lower lip that always escaped in the morning, the saliva I mean but not the lower lip or morning, *oh my darling dear, you've changed, I fear,* you're goddamn right I have and wouldn't you?

Nonetheless Scott sang; he entertained the troops. In room 517 of the beautiful hospital in downtown Trueman-Andrews he marched the gimp-legged legion home and shut his eyes and, within the echoing arch of his skull, screamed tonic and dominant both. *Well you haven't an arm and you haven't a leg, you're an eyeless boneless chickenless egg. And you'll have to be put with a bowl to beg,* oh Johnny we hardly knew you. Therefore and accordingly and because the occasion seems suitable and since the commodity markets are closed this morning let's get acquainted, why not? I, Scott Raposo, thirty-eight, Caucasian, male, being of sound mind and body *which came first* or, as we used to say in tenth grade, *who*, so baby it's lean over, *whom*, Johnny, *the chicken or the* being of sound mind and rapidly deteriorating although still to some degree or at least until recently acceptable body, wherein where*on* the ravages of HIV and AIDS—all those initials, have you noticed? the fucking acronymic first letters— have done their mighty work and wreaked their awful will, do give and bequeath, do herewith convey Kaposi's sarcoma, the *egg*.

He had been a Catholic. He had, as they like to say, lapsed. Except you don't ever leave the Church, you just take a vacation. Except you don't ever grieve the Church, you just fake a vocation. And he had wondered, idly and from time to time and with some fervor latterly, what it might mean in his own particular and specific and individual instance to return. He wondered for example who would offer final comfort, and what it would entail. He wondered with increasing urgency what renal failure signified and when it would succeed. Because he used to love to sing, because he could be locked inside a tree trunk and through the hollow cleft of it see nothing but the sailing sky and *still* discover, as he liked to tell Nurse Lampson—who *listened*, dammit, who knew why he wanted to leave—an occasion for praise, for dialysis and our agreement, girl, because it was important once to have a hedge fund in reserve and he'd be damned in any case so why not for a sheep as lamb, but particularly in this instance if he failed to take advantage of the opportunity afforded, availing himself as so often before of the miracles of modern medicine, its excellent administration and beneficent effect.

With your drums and guns and drums. He coughed. There was someone in the room. White shapes went flitting past him like talkative floor-bound birds. He coughed. They brought clipboards and glasses of juice. Their faces were frequently black. *With your guns and drums and drums and guns*. They bore trays and cups with pills. They produced rubberized gray ribbons—

somewhat, he wanted to suggest, irrelevantly—to wrap around his arm. While they were taking his blood pressure, always, they studied the wall; always they told him the numbers and said, Scott, you're doing fine. Then they frowned and wrote things down.

"Are you all right?" Trip Conley asked.

"No."

"How are we feeling this morning?"

He shook his head.

"I'm sorry, I can't hear you."

Scott coughed. There is no limit to God's patience, but some discernible limit perhaps to the patience of the creature fashioned in His image, this puny exhaustible lord of creation. For whom time is running out. For whom there's not a prayer or a final goddamn chance. Before she died he visited with Alice Tucker in the room next door, and what she had to tell him—how she got here, who was taking care of her, who screwed around with whom and with which pillar of the town she'd been, as she liked to describe it, *intimate*—was, he tried to inform Trip, a hoot. She had friends in high places, she'd whispered—*tell Johnny, tell everyone, everyone*—in this particular place.

But it mattered to her, not to him; we're the only animal that drinks when less than thirsty or ruts when not in season. Still, he offered comfort, saying *There there, I'll remember, I promise;* with his hand he touched Alice's hand. Of the species' astonishing vitality, its blind persistent habitual aeration, *cell, lung, knuckle, gun, drum, flesh,* the brilliant instinctual or at least the learned advertent locomotion of the walking creature, there was nothing left to say.

The president withdrew. Scott coughed. His guitar, for example, would seem to be air, and the brilliant melody, the sweet mystery of Johnny in the shower, as of this hour half-awake and it goes without saying unshaven, the coffee dripping down as though it were potassium, the caffeine fix of it directly in his vein, cooling, cooling on the stove, no longer lukewarm but tepid, no longer tepid but cool, and often he had asked why bother to heat up the coffee if you prefer it cold? He himself preferred it hot, of course, and with warm milk also, and served in his Italian cup, the one with the chipped rim and black latticework where the glaze had worn thin over time, the one with orange blossoms but his lover had an answer: there's a difference, he said.

Well then if you're so goddamn smart what's the distinction between liquid cooled and that which never has been hot; well, I can tell, said Johnny. And lifted his luminous eyes. Kid gloves, Kid Gavilan, here's looking at *you*, kid, my chickenless egg, and lifting his right arm, suggesting in the very gesture that there's a difference, isn't there, between desire slaked and desire as yet unaroused, between a climax reached and one not yet imagined, and performing his morning *why do we call it* ablution, with the water beading on his face, the soap in the small of his back, the vacant stare that signifies proximity to—do I dare breathe or whisper it?—for God's great sake, help, *help*.

There was someone in the room. Its shape was indistinct. It departed, breathing. There was no one in the room.

April 29

To the Editor:

The city of Bellehaven was a fine and upright place. Used to be how neighbor greeted neighbor in the morning and helped each other out. If your house burned down there was always a roof, if you needed a loan for the mortgage why that was no problem at all. People CARED goddammit and you didn't just go off to pasture if you lost your job. The name of the game was Be Pity-full, Mercy-full, and even at His elbow on Golgotha one of the Thieves was Saved. But nowadays I look around me and there's waste and desolation and a whole lot of foreigners too.

Mr. Editor, you listen up. There's an angel of death in our midst our town is marked in letters of flame for the firstborns are marked unto death. When King David lay with Abishag the Shunammite she was a beautiful creature with terrific legs and tits but he was cold and old and David KNEW HER NOT.

What I want to know is why nobody listens, why don't they pay attention. It's plain as the nose on your face. We're the greatest country in the world and in its history too. Except everywhere I turn there's misery and suffering and none of the medical problems get fixed and everybody wonders when it will be His/Her turn. There are vials of smallpox, don't forget, in storage in two places—near Lenin's tomb in Moscow, Russia, and in Atlanta, USA. There was an evil empire of that particular scourge and it has been successfully vanquished though almost everybody OVER 30 has smallpox vaccination marks let's say inside their arm. But people drive around in cars while other people walk.

What makes you think your Great God Mammon won't be toppled soon? It happened to Karl Marx. So print this, please, and if it doesn't make you rich it will make you HAPPY and what's better in this world, because even the rich man can't pass through the needle's eye without a CAMEL is the way I see it and what else is new.

Allright, fella, cut to the chase. Those who know what they know and would tell it for profit grow heinous in my sight. At Trueman-Andrews Hospital there is murder and rapine abounding and you ought to write about it or you too will lose your firstborn when the trumpet sounds and great leveling wind blows when it's a JUDGMENT call. That's all I have to say and all you have to do. For if thine eye offend thee, saith the Lord.

IX

RICHARD TRUEMAN mourned it; he grieved for what was happening, and how the hospital he'd helped to build was going
down the tubes. It was going to hell in a handcart: going going
gone. Trueman-Andrews was a place he'd thought he could be
proud of, once, and had wanted to establish in the American
way: you put your name on something and you expect it to last.
You want your children's children to be proud.

But he had no children's children, and he wasn't proud. He'd
fathered only one daughter and she in her turn produced nothing, or nothing to write home about and take out of the hospital, home. He'd resigned his chairmanship when Harley
Andrews came on board; once they added on the hospice he,
Trueman, called it quits. So when the Executive Committee
members gave him a testimonial dinner and said how much he'd
accomplished and how the town was grateful, Dick, for everything you've done for us he told them to sit down. They read
the citation anyhow, since it was printed up. They called him a
philanthropist, a real estate developer to whom we're all in-

debted because he understands the value of community and stands for everything that's best about America, and then they all applauded.

He gave his thank-you speech. He said, "I wanted to give just a little bit back to this place that has given so much. I wanted to let you good citizens know how me and my whole family are grateful for your help. And maybe extend a helping hand to those who've been less fortunate . . ."

But it was Job's story all over again, is what he really thought. It's the higher you climb up the harder you fall, it's *Lord, how have I offended Thee, that there be not an honest man or woman in this town?* He himself was seventy years old and living by himself and having trouble pissing and unable to sleep through the night. *For if thine eye offend thee, pluck it out.*

So Richard Trueman, benefactor—no matter what they said or how long they stood and applauded or whether they appointed him vice-president of the Rotary and gave him an honorary lifetime membership to the country club, no matter how they invited him to come on down to West Palm Beach or come on up to Harbor Springs—found himself alone. His wife Elizabeth gave up the ghost; after forty years of marriage—forty years in which, he liked to say, he'd never felt a single moment of anything other than happiness, *bliss*—the Good Lord took her away. Elizabeth had made Him jealous of Richard's own good fortune: well, not exactly jealous, the Lord would have no envy but a kind of disapproval, since it's only up in heaven that a perfect angel waits on you, and in his case he was certain that a perfect angel went ahead, and paradise awaits. Down here it's hell on earth.

"We'll miss you, Dick," the vice-president said.

"But I'm not going anywhere . . ."

Then the recording secretary added to the chorus. "We'd like you to stay on the Executive Committee. We know you've been against this change, but we do need to be flexible."

"Is that what you call it? *Flexible?*"

"You're judging us too harshly, Dick. We're changing with the times, is all, and we want you to watch how it goes."

"As an inmate?" Trueman joked. "As a test case for the hospice? To see if I survive it?"

"As a consultant, maybe."

"Paid?"

"*Ex officio*, is what we were thinking. As a kind of adviser emeritus?"

"All right," he said. "I'll stick around. But I'm an old dog, children, and these are your new tricks."

The land had been his father's way back when. Before that it belonged to Richard's father's father, and his great-grandfather too. Since Northwest Territory days his people worked this particular land, and if it hadn't been for Uncle Sam they might be farming it still. They cleared and homesteaded whole sections of town, and over time the family had prospered.

His great-great-uncle was elected governor. But what doth it profit a man if he gain the whole world and lose his own soul? His grandfather had been a judge, and mostly his uncles were lawyers and bankers, and when the whole family got together they made a raucous crew. On his walls he hung framed photographs of twenty, maybe thirty Truemans at a time—by the riverbank having a picnic, at the fairgrounds playing ball. There were tintypes of the governor surrounded by his nephews, or waving from a Pullman car in his failed Senate campaign. There were women in hoopskirts, holding mallets; there were photographs of parents with their children, with horses and sailboats and dogs.

William, Richard's father, had been the quiet one. He was the youngest son of four, the one who didn't smoke or drink or ever show up at the bowling alley with some peroxide thin-legged thing he introduced as this week's wife. Up every morning of his life and tending to the land and chores and never for a minute sick or never so sick you would notice or that he'd complain— and he preferred it that way. He'd seen what happened to a man when all you worked with was paper, and one day the paper goes bad. It takes a lot longer, his father would say, to ruin a crop or a well.

So William Trueman plowed and planted, and he fertilized and tended fence and one Sunday supper, just when Beth informed her in-laws they'd be grandparents soon, that the family was getting bigger which was why she'd had no appetite and had to pass on seconds, William fell into his soup. He'd milked the cows and watered and fed them and bedded them down for the night; he'd washed his hands and rolled his sleeves down past his wrists and said grace with his customary emphasis, then nodded and started to eat. Richard tapped his water glass and asked for their attention; then Beth said she was pregnant, and while they were congratulating her, while everybody was all smiles his father choked and died.

So then they had the funeral. On the drive back from the cemetery his mother started crying. She said his father was the best of men, the sweetest, and she didn't understand how she could manage without him and didn't want to try. "You have no idea," she said, using her handkerchief. "You just have no idea."

Richard did what he could to console her, and soon enough she dried her tears and asked if he and his new bride might stay in Bellehaven to help. "If Beth has a boy," asked his mother, "you'll name him William, won't you?" The widow stared out of the limousine window at dun-colored fields, the low hills. "The Lord taketh away and He gives."

Therefore they moved to the guest cottage, the one on the property's northeast corner, with its brown shingled roof and the stone fireplace with the clematis blooming. And on May 17, 1953, Christine Addison Trueman was born. Then everything had been exactly what he wanted, and he wanted it to stay that way: the roses and the cradle with the wicker roses climbing it, and Beth and him contented just to watch the cradle rock. So when his mother also died, at sixty-two, of cancer, he sold the herd and clear-cut the hardwood stand his grandfather had planted and retired the farmer and sold the parcel back beyond the river for the high-rise and the mall.

The phone rang. "Daddy?"

"Yes."

"How are you?"

"Tolerable, babycakes. And you?" He cradled the receiver. "I haven't even *heard* from you in . . ."

"Two weeks."

"That's all? Two weeks?" He wiped his hands. He had been standing at the sink.

"I'm sorry to disturb you."

"You're not disturbing me, Christine."

"Good."

"You don't disturb me often enough. You *couldn't*, you know that. Sometimes I think," he told her, "it's like we're living in two different countries. Or maybe you're in California and I'm on the East Coast. Sometimes I forget we're just a mile away . . ."

"Don't start this," said his daughter.

"When I think how you and I—how every night I'd tuck you in, how often your mother and I sat by your bedside watching—when I remember how two *hours* could hardly go by without your calling 'Daddy,' why it's simply an astonishment that it could take two weeks."

"Are you finished?"

"Yes."

"I have to talk to you."

"All ears," said Richard Trueman. "It's what I am where you're concerned. All ears."

"I'm worried, Daddy. Really."

"Where are you? What's that buzzing sound?"

"I'm on the car phone," she said. "I've been driving around, oh, for hours. I'm almost out of gas, I think."

"Where *are* you?"

"In the car."

"That doesn't help me, babycakes."

"Oh but it *does*." Christine's voice rose, shrill. "You asked me where I'm calling from; I told you, *in the car*. So why don't you ask why I'm calling? I was hoping you would ask me that."

"Why are you calling?"

"Good. Now ask me what's the problem."

"Problem?"

She spat out the word. "Rebecca."

"Who?"

"Your son-in-law's mistress," she said. "Your fine son-in-law is a son of a bitch. My husband's new mistress, that's who."

He'd honored it, being a father; it had been his golden rule: do unto others, babycakes, what you would have them do. He'd been so proud he thought he'd bust, and he arranged his schedule so he could take his daughter to horseback-riding lessons or collect her after art class and, for the years she'd studied it, ballet. He attended every single one of Christine's piano recitals and junior high school plays. Often, in the evenings, he and Beth would sit together by the fireside and thank the Good Lord for His bounty and hope they might continue to find favor in His sight. Dear Lord, let this continue, Richard Trueman prayed.

His daughter had been, he was certain, a fine upstanding young woman, and only when she turned sixteen did things go wrong. One night he'd been singing lullabies, sitting in the chair beside her bed, with sometimes his harmonica or hoping she might sing along, and the next night she had a sleep-over date and what he heard was laughter back behind the door. And then she brought home boys not girls, and the boys wore beads and had long hair and then she didn't bring them home but drove around in cars and maybe called at midnight saying, Daddy don't wait up. He said it doesn't matter, I'm not sleepy, babycakes, and she said I've got the key. And then she stayed out all night long and the key she used was to motels and nobody bothered to call . . .

It was like a horse that runs away and takes the bit between its teeth and will not take instruction. Or like a fire you try to control, but what it does is spread. Those were the days when everyone wore flowers and chanted "Flower Power" and slept with people not their wives and shouted "Hell No, We Won't Go" and used what they called Mary Jane or hash and LSD. The less said the better, Elizabeth warned him; it's these times we live in, husband, whatever you tell her she won't want to do. If you tell her turn right she turns left; if you want to make certain she marries Trip Conley just tell her she shouldn't, just try.

Still, he'd felt he ought to *try* and rein her in. Where were you, he asked his wife, when they crucified Our Lord? Where were you when they nailed Him to the cross? What's that got to do with the price of asparagus, asked Beth, why are you asking me that? It's an expression, he told her; it means we take responsibility for what we failed to fix.

I didn't make Trip Conley, she said, I didn't make the birds and bees and I can't control them. I'm not responsible for who our daughter chooses to marry, and I won't take the blame. But when the Lord sacrificed Jesus, Richard had reminded her, He did so for our sake. He offered up His only begotten child, and did so with good cause.

Elizabeth said nothing. There had been no answer to make. Instead she studied him with her old exasperation, with the corners of her mouth turned down so she didn't have to say a thing but what she meant was, husband, don't come on all holy to me . . .

He sat on a stool in the kitchen. "Rebecca? Who's Rebecca?"

"This time it's serious. It's why I'm calling from the car."

He had been boiling water for his Cup-a-Soup. "Trip's seeing someone else?"

"He's *always* seeing someone else. I thought you knew that, Daddy."

"No."

"Well, where have you been all these years?"

"Rebecca who?" he asked.

"The iron maiden, remember? The famous hospice lady that he brought back here from England. The one who wants sick people to manage their own suicides." Her voice rose. "But what she means by assistance, what she wants to get rid of is *me*."

Trueman tore open his packet of soup. He emptied it into his mug.

"I've got to go," she said. "You asked me where I'm calling from, correct? I'm way out here in the middle of nowhere, behind a Burger King. You should see these people, you should see the junk they *eat . . .*"

"I get so lonesome, babycakes."

"Don't start all that," she said.

"Start what?"

"Your *Which one of us fashioned Leviathan?* Your Job-on-a-dunghill routine."

He added water and watched the broth steam.

"So why I called you, Daddy, is you've got to talk to him. You gave him the job, remember?"

Again there was static. He waited.

"And you could take it away."

He stirred the broth. "Okay."

"Well, *couldn't* you?"

"I'll handle it."

Now she was happy. "Promise?"

"Yes. I don't know what I'll tell him, but I promise you I'll handle it."

"I'll visit on Thursday," she said.

So where were you, he asked himself, when they crucified Our Lord? Where were you, he'd ask Trip Conley, while they nailed Him to the cross? On that dark October evening all those years ago when he'd insisted to his wife that we were each responsible, and certainly the life of everyone alive is worth protecting, worth respecting, he had spoken truer than he knew. His daughter was marrying, leaving the house, and Richard had been certain then that nothing good would come of it and Trip Conley should be stopped.

The soup was hot. He let it cool. There'd been a bit of over-reach; he was the first to admit it; he'd needed Harley Andrews and his checkbook to come in and bail them out. So he had looked the other way and noticed nothing, really, not while they built the hospice and restructured the managed-care pay-ment strategy for what they called capitation and refinanced the debt. He himself would take responsibility for what he'd done, or failed to do; he would stand accountable in the presence of the Lord. Because he had been pleased with the offer—making Andrews welcome in Bellehaven, forgetting what his father knew, that if a gift is offered, you'd best look that horse in the mouth.

Warming them, inhaling, he laced his fingers to the mug. Now Trueman-Andrews Hospital proved everything that went wrong in this country, with the government and namby-pamby health officials and the bleeding-heart health-care advocates and city and county commissioners all shoving their hand in the till. It took twenty-six staff persons—that's what they called each other, staff *persons*, but they might as well say staff *infection*—for every single bed. Well, maybe twenty-two.

So an ancient honorable function had been—there was no other word for it—perverted. A doctor was supposed to help the sick and ease their suffering and get them back into the work-place, if that was where they came from, and back into their houses, if that was where they belonged. Now he himself was old and sick and maybe belonged in the hospital but certainly not in the hospice. He was planning to leave on his own two feet, and thank you very much, he told the Executive Commit-tee; once you attach a hospice to a place of healing you're ask-ing Old Man Trouble to walk right in the door.

Elizabeth had known that much; she'd tried to tell him, dying, that the Good Lord keeps a schedule. He marks your name down in His book and nothing to be done. It isn't a ques-tion of whether but when; death comes when it will come. So he was grateful that he'd quit but not entirely; he'd stepped aside as chairman but kept his seat on the Board. What he had forgotten was more than Trip knew; a telephone chitchat, a letter or two, and Trip would toe the line . . .

Their daughter was, he'd admit it, a drunk; when she called him from the car phone he had figured on an accident or maybe she sideswiped a tree. But he couldn't blame her, really; she had no children of her own to protect in case of danger, and when he tried to tell her what it meant to be a parent she poured herself a nightcap or a freshener or pick-me-up and refused to listen.

"It disappears," he tried to say. "It does."

These evenings when he held himself, standing by the vanity, coaxing out the droplets, it felt to Richard Trueman like he was pissing blood.

X

"YOU'RE REBECCA Forsythe?"

"Yes."

"I saw you at grand rounds."

"And I enjoyed your presentation. My pleasure, Dr. Julius."

"Peter."

"Peter."

"When did you get here?" he asked.

"To Bellehaven?" She was standing in the corridor. "Three days ago." She shook her head. "It all blurs together, rather. Five."

"Well, welcome. Do come in."

He held the door. She was polite and self-assured; she promised that she would not keep him long. She was wearing perfume, and a tailored lilac suit: not the grieving widow he had been led to expect.

"I've read your book, *Death's Kingdom*. It's very good."

"Truth, Dr. Julius?"

He colored. "Yes, it is."

She saw, he saw, the photograph of Julie on his desk. "Do show me what you're up to. What you do."

So he walked her through the hospice, its three floors. This was part of his activity each week; he guided visitors often. By now he'd grown familiar with the range of their reactions, the suspicion or uncertainty transforming to relief. Each tour was planned according to the nature of the visit and whether he accompanied a prospective patient, a family member, a donor or local official.

In truth he had grown proud of it: the ramps and swimming pool and common room, the intercom system and closed-circuit relays, the brightly lit and flower-filled reception space. It had been Andrews's stated plan that a person could choose solitude, since every single man and woman deserved a private cubicle— a stateroom, as he put it, in which to make this journey all alone.

"We're on a ship," he liked to say, "a journey downriver together." Then, taking Peter's elbow, J. Harley Andrews repeated, "I want them to travel first-class."

The hospice and the hospital were linked by an underground passage, so machinery and gurneys could pass back and forth. On the surface, however, the building stood alone. There was a parking lot for visitors, a gravel drive, a wide stretch of well-tended lawn; there were flowering fruit trees and yews. The outer walls were faced in brick, and the roof was slate. The effect was of a mansion that happened to be situated next to a modern hospital; the hospice itself appeared old. Not old so much as timeless, as J. Harley Andrews asserted: we're building this baby to last . . .

He made many such pronouncements. He bustled about for the first days and weeks, showing Peter what he wanted and how it should be arranged. Harley brandished a set square and level and wore a yellow hard hat, with the initials T/A. He pointed out the walnut burl on elevator panels and the quality of bathroom fixtures and carpeting design. He took pride in the sauna and pool. He enjoyed himself hugely, it seemed; the philanthropist carried a notebook and Dictaphone and chomped on an unlit cigar. He wanted to keep evidence of illness to a minimum—not in order to delude his clientele, but because they knew it all already and had had enough of hospitals and medical machinery; a bed should just look like a bed.

The architect had been ingenious; he pursued Andrews's motif of disguise. If the building in its exterior looked like a private club or home, its interior resembled a hotel. The personnel wore street clothes; each room had a window and view. The room arrangements were circular, giving onto common space where caregivers had been positioned. Therefore patients fanned out like the spokes on a wheel, and the hub was readily available and no one felt abandoned or, as Harley liked to put it, "lost at the end of the line."

Since many of the elderly had no surviving relatives, some patients died alone. If they wanted company, they were entitled to visitors, and there were rooms with two beds. They had a full complement now and could accommodate thirty. The average period of residence, Dr. Julius told Rebecca, was two weeks. There were exceptions to this rule, of course—those who died while being transferred or who lingered on for months. The outreach program and Hospice on Wheels served those who stayed at home.

"What's your—what would you call it—demography?"
"The patient population?"
"Yes."
They were standing in the upstairs hallway, at the large bay window.
"It's anecdotal, largely, Ms. Forsythe; we're too young an institution to have an adequate statistical database compiled. We're finding all this out, of course, but we've been in business—excuse the expression—less than a year."
"Is there an isolation unit for AIDS patients?"
"No. We don't yet have the population for a separate hospice.

We will, I suppose, sometime soon. This is, as you've noticed, a city—but it's nothing like Chicago or New York. You've been there?"

"No, not really. I did spend a night in Chicago."

In the light his face was lined, and not the carefree innocent's she'd thought it up on stage. She continued with her questions; it was a form of politeness. "The average age of hospice patients is . . . ?"

"A median would be more useful. Eighty-one. The average age won't tell you much; they range from thirty-four to ninety-six years old. They represent our area in terms of race and gender distribution; they are, I think, well above the median in income and education; they come from five to five hundred miles away."

"And how do they find you?"

"Referrals, mostly. Word of mouth. And our president—as you've no doubt noticed—does understand the media; he's good at attracting attention."

"Perhaps too good," Rebecca offered. "There's a limit to the value of publicity . . ."

"Such as, for example, in your case," said Dr. Peter Julius. Surprising her, he smiled. "Correct?"

"Correct." She felt the first faint stirring of that predatory interest she had learned to call desire; she turned from him therefore and moved to a patient and introduced herself and held out her right hand.

The ease with which she greeted orderlies and nurses, the authority with which she moved from bed to bed and through the sunporch and solarium—such professional assurance, Peter knew, could not have come unearned. The clipped succinctness of her speech when they were in his office gave way, upstairs, to chatter, as if she had leisure to spare. Rebecca Forsythe, author, shook each outstretched hand.

Laura Pierce was resting in a wheelchair by the window, holding the *Smithsonian*, with a picture of some brightly colored birds. She held the page out for inspection. Then she remarked upon the photograph, the plumage of the toucan, its bill, its beauty, the variety of species in North America and the pattern of migration, here, for birds of the Great Lakes.

"I always wished," said Laura, "that I could follow one of them. A flock, I mean. To wherever they go when they scoot along south. Imagine: Argentina, isn't that where they mostly fetch up? Yes, I believe it must be: Argentina."

"Have you been there?"

"No." But she continued naming names, ticking them off on her fingers—"Ascension, Barbados, Aruba, Antigua, Barbuda, Brazil. Something like that anyway." Then Laura fell silent. "I never do get past the Bs . . ."

A second patient joined them, advancing by means of a walker. Harriet Anderson wore slippers and a nightgown and pink cardigan; she was pencil-thin, and stooped. Her hair was white, her face a honeycomb of wrinkles, her eyes a faded blue. "You're that English one," she said. "They told us you were coming. You're the lady who killed her own husband."

Rebecca seemed inured to this. "That's not how I'd put it, precisely," she said. "It isn't the way I describe it."

"One thing about this place," Harriet announced. "We call a spade a spade."

"How so?"

"They don't ever pretend you'll get better. They don't coddle you with foolishness."

"No?"

"You know the expression," said Harriet. "Well, perhaps you wouldn't, being English, but there's an expression we have over here. We call it a tissue of lies. Myself I prefer the word 'Kleenex'; they don't offer a *Kleenex* of lies."

"Excuse me?"

"No sob story," Harriet said. She wheezed with what seemed to be laughter, and produced a handkerchief. "Kleenex of lies," she repeated, and then she dabbed at her mouth.

Dr. Julius continued the tour. The third floor, he explained, had been reserved for patients confined to their beds. They did not move; they watched TV or slept. This also was Harley's idea. "Up there," he said, "on top of things they won't concern themselves about what's down below."

In the room called Arizona—the walls were sand-colored, the paintings showed teepees, the carpet and curtains had weaving-motifs—Samuel Eisenhorn lay ashen-faced. He was near death, and knew it; he did not lift his head. One eye was closed, one wandered. His voice was clear, however, and in that space resonant, as though all vitality had lodged within his throat. "Who's the pretty lady? Who's that you got with you, Doc?"

"A visitor from England. Miss Rebecca Forsythe."

"Enchanted," said Samuel Eisenhorn. "A pound is what they spend in England. A shilling, am I right?"

He drifted then, describing Hampstead Heath and the pond at the crest of the hill. He explained to Peter and the pretty lady that he had gone to England when the war was over to see what damage the Luftwaffe did and how they were repairing it and just what was what. He had cigarettes and nylons and some chocolate in his pocket and it had bought him everything you could imagine and some things you couldn't begin to, but a gentleman wouldn't describe them, not in polite mixed company like what we have here now.

He tried to raise his head and failed; he lay back and stared at the ceiling. Liquid gathered at his eye. There were things he could remember, said Samuel Eisenhorn, that he hadn't told anyone, ever, and one of the problems with dying was what you remembered died too.

Her husband in the end had looked like that. He had been younger, of course, but with the same distance about him—the same terrible impatience with their little daily life. In Gytheion she sat beside him in the windswept taverna; they had been eating tsatsiki and lamb; he could not swallow the lamb.

There was sea wrack, the loud cry of gulls. A car ferry departed the dock. They had been speaking of her future and the ways they had been lucky and how he at thirty-eight had had his share and even an abundance of good luck. Arthur toasted her: his overflowing cup. She did not cry.

Their waiter was practicing English and he spoke to them in English and to the customers at the next table in German; the waiter had a cousin in Melbourne and was planning to emigrate by the end of December or at the latest next spring. It's the second largest city full of Greeks, he said, excepting only Athens; everybody and his cousin moves to Australia now.

"What will you do?" asked Arthur, while the waiter fetched her coffee. "Would you consider Melbourne? Or America, even? Where will you go when I'm gone?"

Arthur worked at Lloyds as an insurance adjuster and his future had been bright. Then, as he was fond of saying, the actuarial tables were turned. He called it "appropriate" that someone who deals with catastrophe would have to underwrite his own particular trouble and update the client list; the odds had come a cropper in his case. Against all probability he belied his own statistics; he was the thirty-eight-year-old exception that would prove the rule.

"Stop being ironic," Rebecca had said. "It isn't very funny and it doesn't help."

"It helps me," Arthur said. "There are lines you ought to use. 'The readiness is all.' "

He carried a book of poetry in his briefcase, always, and it surprised his clients that he quoted verse. When she told him that he should have been a poet he said, "Rubbish. It takes talent. I had none."

"Don't, please, use the past tense," she said.

So in the taverna that evening she had told him not to worry, that she would be all right. "You're young," he said. "And lovely. You won't have the heart to refuse."

She told him not to say that and he said it's true; you'll say no to start with, possibly, but then you'll tell them yes. I'll lock the door, she told him, I'll know just the way to behave. The answer will be simple and it will be no.

*   *   *

"Do you have a family?"

Peter Julius shook his head.

"You're married?" asked Rebecca.

"No."

She looked at him, puzzling a moment; on his desk there was that smiling woman by a picket fence. She had been making conversation, asking as another might about his parents or his pets. Now she felt it necessary to continue. "Are you engaged, Dr. Julius?"

"No."

"I'm sorry. In your office there's a photograph . . ."

"My wife is dead," he said. "She died two years ago."

He seemed to need to say no more, and this was so unlike her experience of strangers—her expectant pause inviting then eliciting a breathless or breathy confession—that Rebecca was surprised. "I'm sorry . . ."

"Yes."

"I didn't mean . . ."

"It's not an accident"—Peter Julius smiled—"that I'm involved in hospice work. Harley Andrews knew my wife. We agreed that this would be, oh, a fitting memorial. That's what they call your book also, I think: a fitting memorial tribute, correct?"

"Correct."

"The Bellehaven Book of the Dead," he said.

She had been wrong about him, after all; he was *not* luck's shining child. The air between them was electric, and she drew back, shocked.

XI

"ARE WE finished here?" Trip asked.

"I believe so," said Jim Kelly.

"Any further questions?" Conley scanned the room. His secretary, Martha, had been taking notes.

"No."

"Signed, sealed, delivered?" At his signal, Martha closed the pad.

Peter Julius answered, "Yes."

"I'm late, I have to leave. And we do need a decision."

They looked at him, incurious. They too would be happy to call it a day. "In my opinion," he offered, "this is a nonstory. This is where we call it quits. Case closed."

Martha stood. "I'm out of here. Night-night, you all."

"Did you hear," asked Kelly, wasting time, "about the EKG they took? Just before Raposo died, I mean. Staff did an EKG on him, and they did draw blood. Both are compatible with hyperkalemia."

"What's that?"

"High K+ levels in the blood. Too much potassium."

"What else is new?" Trip found his gloves. He adjusted the brim of his hat. "The guy had renal failure, didn't he? That's what you told us at grand rounds."

"I just thought you'd want to know. The crash cart wasn't fully stocked; when we looked at it next morning, there was potassium missing."

"Next morning?"

"Yes. At least two vials."

"Good night."

Trip's problem was the problem of control. There was too much confusion in the place. He was all for participatory management, of course, had practically *invented* it, but there ought to be a limit, you need to know when to say when. It was like a throttle adjustment on a cold machine; you could go too heavy or too light, could flood the system with your choke or stall it out instead. He could—it was an option, always—call for a full-scale autopsy and examination of procedures in the case. He could launch a security check. Except it wasn't Kelly, it was hot-pants Lampson who was pulling on his chain; she'd taken care of Raposo and the two of them were tight, it seemed, and she didn't like the looks of what she saw.

But for Trip to blow the whistle would be a lot of make-work and a kind of make-believe. Though Kelly and his residents were sticklers for procedure, the procedure had gone wrong; Jim hadn't been too pleased about the EKG they took, you could see him start to sweat. And Julius argued all along for what he liked to call a dignified release. The patient's parents had been notified and hung up without even asking if there was a funeral scheduled; they didn't plan to attend. That idiot Johnny was jumping for joy, just smiling through his tears and sobbing all the way back to the apartment and his bottle of cold vodka and brand-new checking account. The will stipulated cremation; soon enough they'd be sifting through ash.

So there was no one that he knew of who was anxious to pursue the case—not even Nurse-Practitioner Lampson, because it happened on her watch and she could get the kind of fucking-over that she wasn't dreaming of and didn't have in mind. This is one time, Trip announced, when the press is not invited, we'll leave well enough alone. Who counts the potassium containers on the crash cart, for example, and who checks off the stock list and what else was missing if anything *was* missing, and who had access to the cart at what point when? The nurses disposed of the IV bottle, since Raposo's death appeared routine, and by the time they thought to look for it the trash had been recycled.

So there would have been no point. They could have checked the lines for excess potassium levels and maybe a world-class detective could make a case out of probable cause and creatinine readings and personnel logs. But it wasn't worth hiring a world-class detective and the worst that happened, if anything actually happened, was Raposo died a little sooner here than he would have done at home. *If* someone had messed with the lead lines and fed too much potassium, they were speeding matters up and that was all . . .

In the hallway, as he'd guessed she would, Penny Lampson waited. When Trip passed her, walking out, she tried to look surprised. "Oh, hello."

"He's in there."

"Who?"

"Whoever you were waiting for."

She did not blush. He liked that. "Do you mind if I ask you a question?" she asked.

"Of course not, no. Go right ahead." She was wearing make-up: eye shadow, lipstick, perfume.

"Will you order an autopsy?"

"No."

"Why not?"

"We did consider it, as a matter of fact. But the pathologists don't much enjoy an autopsy on AIDS patients, do they? All those cute little bodily fluids of his, they haven't quite dried up."

"In grand rounds," Penny said, "when you were talking about—what did you call it?—collective authority. Participation. Did you mean to include the whole staff?"

He nodded. Jim Kelly appeared in the hall.

"Then would you tell me, maybe, what was going on in there? I know it's not my place to ask, not my business. But I *did* take care of Scott Raposo, and I knew him pretty well. We were neighbors, sort of." Penny smiled. "We came from the same armpit of the state."

"Then check yourself for lesions, Nurse." He waved at the chief resident. "Ask him."

Leaving, Trip tried not to worry; his wife would be waiting, he knew. Christine was on her second drink and staring at the menu, trying to decide if she would forgive him this once. She'd look up while he took his chair and started to apologize and, smiling that good smile of hers, the one that cost three years of orthodontia and a nose job, say "Don't mention it, let's not discuss it, I'm certain you had a good reason." It would keep him guessing, and she liked to do that too.

Or, more likely, she *would* mention it and blame him for standing her up. So then he'd say she could have called him from the car and he'd left a message, hadn't he, or didn't she bother to listen? He'd called to say he would be late, and anyway she wasn't standing up but sitting at a comfortable table at the Hermitage, so sloshed that if she had another she wouldn't bother to order or eat and wouldn't care that he'd been late and wouldn't remember at all.

Then she'd start in on the usual, how if it hadn't been for her there'd *be* no comfortable table, no reservation at a restaurant and nothing to buy dinner with and while he was perfecting his manners and learning the fine art of punctuality why didn't he acquire some gratitude also, you son of a bitch. Her father used to own this town, the land that they were sitting on, and it would be nice to remember every once in a great while to be grateful and polite. He'd remind her at some point that gratitude works both ways, dear, and her money bought them dinner once, but by now she was drinking it—not her money, her beautiful trust fund, but dinner—and this year he himself was earning 300K, remember, Chris, and no thanks to you. She'd warn him what comes around goes around, you could be out on your ass. My my, he'd say, where did you ever learn such language, where did an elegant lady like the one I married learn to look so shitfaced and use an expression like out on your ass? In the gutter, she'd say, where I found you, in the great school of Conley the Con.

So then he'd try to make it up and tell her he was sorry, they both were overtired, and he'd been working too hard. They should take a vacation, he'd say. And halfway through the soup course it would be all right again, they'd be debating Cozumel or Puerto Vallarta for May. Christine would be at ease and talkative and telling him how much of a spectacle some idiot or other had made of themselves at the club. Then she would ask him what went wrong that day, how the publicity aspect of dying had been handled—or maybe *man*handled, *mis*handled. She called it crowd control. But she'd be on an even keel and it wouldn't be a problem, really, so even when he mentioned Isla Mujeres as a possible vacation site she would not get angry; her Spanish wasn't good enough to translate "Isle of Women" or maybe she had also heard that Isla Mujeres was less spoiled than Cozumel.

Trip pulled into the parking lot; he parked near her black Coupe de Ville. He tried to tell himself that it would be all right. She'd be drinking only water and ordering the rack of lamb for two the way they ate it on their honeymoon, remember, darling, rare. She'd be assuring Pierre the waiter that a crown rack was the very thing to order for a honeymoon, though we both know you don't want one, now do you, Pierre, but if you ever change your mind, just ask my husband here.

She'd nod at him across the table, and for the waiter's benefit she'd smile: You choose the vegetables, darling, you order what you prefer. You really should consider it, a honeymoon, I mean, dear Pierre, you must promise to take lessons from our local expert here. And follow the example of the lamb. It's an instruction to us all, the way a crown rack keeps its shape, so pliable and pink and broken-boned and bloody, with its soft little legs in the air.

Then Christine would put down her fork. She'd look up at the waiter to see if he was shocked. And then, so casually it might seem inadvertent and would be over too quickly in any case for Trip to notice or prevent her, she'd reach and drain his wineglass in a single swallow and be cursing him again.

"How are you?"

"Fine."

"I'm sorry I was late." Trip sat. "You got my message?"

"No."

"I did leave a message." He broke a bread stick. "An hour ago, at home. On the machine."

"That's fine," she said.

"We had a bit of trouble at the hospital. A meeting. I'm sorry," he said.

"Would you do me a favor?"

"Of course."

"Stop apologizing," said Christine. "Each time you tell me how sorry you are I believe it a little bit less."

"All right," he said. "I'm sorry. Now I'll stop."

"So what are you eating tonight, the lamb? The paschal lamb?"

"Is that the special?"

"Yes."

"There was an accident," Trip told her. "It's why we had a meeting. We had to decide what to do."

"Bury the body," she said. "There's room."

Then Pierre the waiter returned. "The usual, Mr. Conley?" he asked, smiling, wiggling his hips, and Trip nodded yes. When they were alone again and while he waited for the wine he touched his wife's hand, lightly. She did not move.

"I've been thinking we should take a trip."

"Where?"

"Get out of town a little. Maybe see the Yucatán," he offered. "Or maybe Cozumel."

"It's obvious, isn't it? What do we pay you for, Conley the Con? We pay you to bury the dead."

It happened this way now whenever they went out in public. And at their house it was worse. She'd been crazy all along, he guessed, but he hadn't noticed to start with or, noticing, much cared. He'd figured her for spoiled, at first, with a rich kid's predictable problems and maybe a bit of particular lunacy that dropped off the family tree. Maybe all those uncles in upstate institutions should have tipped him off. But Christine had been rich enough so she could have been cross-eyed and lame and Trip wouldn't have worried or stopped himself from popping the question and tying the knot; he married Daddy's little girl and got a house on a golf course to show for it, and it didn't matter all that much if he found her crying in the bathtub or stuffing her mouth full of blankets or staring at a kitchen knife like maybe her left wrist should be the evening's roast.

For the first years it was worth it, and he'd given as good as he got. When she wanted to ride horses they rented her a stable, when she wanted to go swimming they built an indoor pool. His golf improved. He joined the Hunt Club and bought rifles and handguns and shotguns and went hunting with the men who ran the town. He shot skeet. He took a job in Uncle Alex Trueman's bank and started from the bottom up; he took public-speaking classes and learned how to maximize his potential and acquired a personal trainer and a personal mantra too. He did the rope course to establish trust and got manicured and pedicured and three dozen monogrammed shirts.

But then she got pregnant and William arrived and, after six days, died. Her mother, too, had died that month, though she did so after cancer; she died in "the fullness of time." That was how the minister expressed it at the funeral: "The Lord taketh away but He gives."

And that was when she took the nosedive she'd been diving now for years. That was when she started in to drink and when she learned to be suspicious, saying her life was not worth living, and he was one of the reasons, and some of it was her fault maybe but most of it was his. It isn't a question of fault, Trip had tried to tell her, it isn't a question of blaming yourself, and we could try again. The minister agreed. And so did the various doctors and so did the psychiatrists and so did all her friends.

But none of it made any difference after that. Christine stared longingly at women in the playground and babies in their strollers like she'd snatch the kids and bring them home or strap them to the baby seat she carried in the car. After her mother died and baby William came and went and there was no protection at the bank, he'd lost his job.

She bought herself a rag doll and pulled out its button-eyes and sat in the rocking chair, rocking. It had been all that he could do to keep himself from telling her how she was an investment he could sell short: there's only so patient a person can be and only so long he would wait. It was his time for apron strings and watching while she watched the wall; it was standing on his hind legs, wagging, while she fed him bones.

XII

"YOU KILLED him, Jimbo."

"No."

"You let him die."

"You're way out of line here, Johnny. You don't know what you're saying."

"Yes I do. Of course I do."

"Then stop it," Kelly said.

"It's the truth."

"Truth hurts," said Kelly. "Stop it."

"You're threatening me. Are you threatening me?"

"No."

"Of course you are. It's just exactly what you're doing, you sorry son of a bitch. *Threatening* me. Don't think I don't know what you're up to, and why."

"What I'm up to is my ears in other people's trouble. What I'm saying is the truth can hurt. I've got work to do this afternoon."

Johnny raised his arms above his head, fists clenched. "Your work, it's just wading in shit."

"Have it your own way." He stood.

"I do intend to, Jimbo. Just watch me," Johnny said.

He had seen it happen often; it was a part of his job. He had grown used to abuse. As chief resident, Jim Kelly knew, he had to study bereavement, the varieties of "acting out." You deliver fond farewells and get the house in order; you tell yourself you're reconciled, ready and willing to lose whom you love. Then you go through a mourning period, maybe, and price a coffin and black clothes a season in advance. But the person you're prepared to lose goes off and kills himself or dies while you're not watching, and you end up shocked. You're twice as guilty, twice as much a wreck as you'd have ever guessed.

It was happening with Johnny now; Johnny was falling apart. Day by day and night by night he was coming apart at the seams. He'd tell anyone who listened—and more and more of them *did* listen, according to Trip Conley—how Scott had been improving, was heading home that Saturday when they found him dead. There's this thing about malpractice; you send a person into the hospital healthy and they come out in a box and maybe you've the right to ask and it's appropriate to get an explanation and ask a friendly question, maybe six.

So Kelly pointed out the obvious: the patient had been less than healthy on arrival. Let's not endorse denial here, let's not get carried away. Your friend wasn't exactly the picture of health when we admitted him to Trueman-Andrews—what was it?— two weeks ago. And Johnny said that's true, but it isn't what I'm talking about, it isn't *my* point, Jimbo, not at all. Then he grinned his wacky leering grin and bit his lip and shut his eyes and opened them again. His eyes were brilliant blue. What makes you think I don't intend to find out just what happened here, and who's responsible? What makes you sons of bitches think I'd let my lover die?

We never thought that, Kelly said, what makes *you* think we thought any such thing, and Johnny said I'm not as dumb as you look. Don't take me for a fool.

He was sweating and jumpy and anxious and drunk and it didn't take a genius to see he was in trouble. They'd thought it might be HIV, but he tested negative; then they thought perhaps cirrhosis, or hepatitis C. But it turned out what he had was ulcerative colitis, and Johnny knew enough to know the damage alcohol could do. He knew about restrictive diet and the poor prognosis; he'd spent enough time on the ward with Scott—talking to the nurse-practitioners, entertaining the house staff—so he understood the odds.

"I think we ought to check you in. To work you up," said Kelly.

"All right," said the patient, half-smiling. "Because misery loves company, correct?"

"Correct."

"Well, I just adore your company and I'll let you in on a secret, it's my intention nowadays to make you miserable too."

Kelly signed the paperwork. He pocketed his pen.

"We've got a culture of *cure*," Johnny said, "but why not a culture of *care*. Because there isn't any cure for AIDS, you bastards just don't care."

"Of course we do," he answered.

"On the scale of suffering, from one to ten?"

"I'm sorry. I don't understand."

"How much would you say you suffer, Jimbo? On a scale of one to ten?"

Kelly shrugged. He scrubbed himself off at the sink. "There *is* a limit, finally, to what we can accomplish. If a doctor permitted himself to feel *everything* as acutely as his patients do, then he'd be of no use."

"Where did you learn that? In medical school? In some sort of self-help manual?"

"No."

"Where? In the school of hard knocks? You doctors have

worked up a culture of cure, and if there's none available you wash your goddamn hands and walk away."

So Kelly dried his hands. "Okay. All right. I've got other patients to see."

"God help them."

"You've been drinking, haven't you, and it's time to *quit,* goddammit. I don't need to listen to abuse."

"Oh yes you do, Jimbo. You have to."

"Why?"

"Because I loved him," Johnny said. "And that gives me the right to complain."

And it was funny, really; really, he was right. Kelly had to admit it: the man had a point. He could remember walking in one morning to Raposo's room, 517, where the two of them sat wordless, staring at each other, their faces so suffused with light it was as though he'd stumbled on a movie set, or maybe an old photograph: love, love. One of them was dead already, the other one was dying, but they'd made a kind of peace together after so much shouting. They cared for each other completely since it would be over soon.

And it made him wonder what he himself would stare at in that fashion now. Without what would he be lost? He cared for his own family, of course, but not with that same famished need, and what he wanted mostly was to be left alone. What he wanted were his little friends, a pair of them dissolving: the timed release, sweet sourness, the Percodan blue-plate special for our customers this week. And this was such a change for him, so far from what he'd always thought or allowed himself even to *think* about thinking, that the sight of those two dying men caused Kelly to take stock. It forced him to make a kind of inventory: what was worth the keeping, and what could he call junk?

He'd met Margy on the beach. They'd both been seventeen, and already she had the kind of thick-legged solidity that signified *childbearing, children.* It told him, hey, these hips are built to carry and these arms to squeeze. He could remember the purple bikini, the white line underneath her breasts and sweat above her lip. She was telling him (not right out loud, of course, but just by the way she adjusted her strap, pulling it, providing a quick glimpse of nipple while she shook out the sand from the bright purple shield) how much fun there'd be in making kids and having kids and watching the family grow.

They talked about it, Jim remembered, right away. It would be fun for them both. She asked him where he came from, and he told her: Syracuse. He'd been busing tables at the hotel that his uncle's neighbor managed, and was planning to stay for the summer. Margy had been visiting her cousin; she'd come up from Des Moines. Her cousin Marietta lived in Charlevoix year-round, and worked the Tastee-Freez just one block from the beach.

They walked there together; he bought her a frappé. He could remember, still, the line of foam above her lip, the mustache of pink bubbles she'd licked, and how she offered him a swallow from the paper cup. By the time he left that afternoon they'd made a date for next Monday night at the movies; by next Tuesday he was happier than ever before, and she said she felt the same.

They went to *A Funny Thing Happened on the Way to the Forum*, the only show in town. It was a terrible movie, or at least the parts he could remember had been terrible—full of chorus girls and old fat men in togas, singing—but it made no difference because Margy, lightly, absentmindedly it almost seemed, rested her hand on his leg. It was like there was no armrest and she just needed someplace to spread out her hand, and he sat through the whole movie with an erection so big and stiff he thought he'd pop his pants.

He wondered, could she tell. He put his own hand on her leg, and she didn't move away. Instead she raised the knee a little, pressing back. All this was half his life ago, but Jim Kelly could remember as if it happened yesterday the way she put her arm in his when he prepared to drive her home, because Marietta had a car and let Margy borrow it, and how his erection just wouldn't subside, and how she leaned against his shoulder in the Dodge.

Then it was years of working at the pharmacy and saving to

get married and getting married finally and loving each other at night in the dark, of planning and waiting and making things happen until they turned to ash. It was as if they'd built a fire: first flame, then heat, then ash.

"Don't blame yourself," he tried to say.

"Why not?" said Johnny.

"You two did the best you could, and you don't need to feel guilty."

"I don't, Dr. Kelly. I don't."

"You did everything you could for him."

"Would you say the same thing, Doctor?"

"Yes."

Johnny pursed his lips. He smacked them liquidly. "Have you noticed how most entertainers—Tony Perkins, Liberace— wanted to keep it a secret? AIDS, I mean. And sometimes even when they're dead they don't want it in the papers. Have you noticed that?"

He nodded.

"Well, there's a reason, Jimbo. They worry that they'll lose their jobs. That nobody will hire them."

"But your friend Scott was self-employed. He wasn't worried about *work*."

"Correct. And I'm the entertainer here, and I'm glad it's only colitis, because that means I get to go on stage and strut my stuff and dance my dance and make a million dollars off my talent."

"Which is?"

"Litigation—or, if you prefer to call it that, harassment. Large-claims court. Because before he died he told me what was going down. Because you sons of bitches made my lover die."

And then he dropped his head and rubbed his eyes. His shoulders shook. "Can I get you anything?" asked Kelly, and Johnny told him, "No."

Therefore when Penny Lampson said, let's talk about the death of Scott Raposo, let's have a drink, it was easy to say yes.

It was easy to go to that bar where she knew the bartender and sit in a booth and drink margaritas and eat chili con queso and pretend they were in Costa Rica or Panama City and try to explain to her somehow what he was worried about: not so much malpractice as *practice*, and what they were doing at work. Because through all the fuss and shrieking, through all the lamentation and the bad jokes and hysterics and the threats of lawsuits, what rang out loud and clear was Johnny's actual pain.

She said she understood. She knew, she told him, just what he was saying and felt the same way most days now and every night. She knew what it felt like, she told him, to think you might be helpful to your fellow sufferers and then find out that what you were was not an agent of God's mercy but His terrible swift sword.

Jim had been drinking too much. He was not used to cocktails, or anything stronger than beer, and he thought she'd said "angel of God's mercy," not "agent." So he started to tell Penny that she was indeed a kind of angel, or appeared that way to him, since she let him tell her his troubles and smiled knowingly, forgivingly, across the booth. The way he, Kelly, saw it was they were wasting resources and mobilizing uselessly and that terrible swift sword she mentioned ought to stay where it belonged in—what was it?—"The Battle Hymn of the Republic," not to mention trampled vineyards, not to mention glory, and maybe they should spend more time together the way they were doing this evening. No time like the present, said Penny, just let me freshen up. Then she stared at him unblinkingly and folded her napkin and licked the salt rim of the glass. I wonder if you'd care to take me home?

It was like that night with Margy, their first time upstairs in Charlevoix; it was the old wham-bang exhilaration and a prick so stiff he thought he was a kid again, eighteen. The margaritas helped. The strange room helped, where Penny lived, and that he'd never been there and had to whisper on the stairs and leave the light off in the hall and then she put her hand across his mouth and laid her finger on his lips so he would understand they'd have to keep it quiet.

"I've been wanting . . ." he began to say.

"What? What were you wanting exactly?"

He fought for breath.

She licked her lips. She dropped her hand to his belt. Like a schoolgirl, Penny giggled. "But I have to ask you one question."

"What?"

"Will you respect me in the morning?"

"Oh," he said. "Penny. Of *course* I . . ."

"Don't think about it, lover," Penny whispered. "It's a joke."

So that was the beginning and he had no idea at all of where it was going to end. He would take the car and pick up Penny at the apartment and she'd have packed a picnic lunch and a Styrofoam cooler of soda and beer, and he'd stow the cooler and the duffels in the backseat and point west or maybe south. They'd be out of Bellehaven by breakfast, leaving it behind; they'd head for Indiana or Ohio or Illinois or Kentucky, not caring where they went at first but only where they'd be at night and what motel was open and if it had a swimming pool set far enough back off the road. It would be easy driving, and he would steer left-handed and drop his right hand in her lap, and then she'd raise her skirt and not be wearing panties and put his hand on her and say, "I'm so excited, baby, I'm wet already, see," or sometimes she'd take off her panties and wrap them silkily around his cock and pump until he came. In another of his fantasies he drove her to the airport and they bought two tickets anywhere that you could get to from O'Hare with a passport and visa, one-way.

Trip Conley would page him; he wouldn't be there. Peter Julius would hunt through the office and halls, but he would be long gone. The patients he was saddled with would suffer or improve alone; the kids would order pizza or a Big Mac coming back from practice or not be home to gather at the empty unwiped table, and he and Penny Lampson would be well out of it, together, lying somewhere in the sun. There'd be no trouble with the mortgage and no trouble with the lab reports or hysterical companions of the unquiet dead.

So this was the new dream he dreamed.

XIII

PETER JULIUS was in his office, checking flowcharts, hearing laughter down the hall where they were watching reruns of the *I Love Lucy* show. A shaft of late afternoon sunlight fell across his worksheet, and the blue ink of his fountain pen puddled briefly, drying. And then the telephone rang.

"Hey, kid, it's Uncle Harley."

"Mr. Andrews?"

"Harley. How've you been?"

"I can't complain."

"And what good would it do you, correct?"

"Correct." Peter smiled at the receiver. "I'm just fine."

"Then you're better off than I am."

"Sir?"

"Don't 'sir' me. Don't pull that 'Mr. Andrews' shit. We're in trouble, Pete. I need your help."

"Of course, sir. What's the problem?"

"You're the doctor. You tell me."

"All right." There was a high whine in his ear. "But I'm not much good at answering if I don't know the question."

"So what am I supposed to tell you? It's my ticker, kid, it's giving out. I can feel it all over my chest."

"Where are you calling from?"

"Bellehaven. I'm in town. I was driving up, and something snapped. So I checked myself into my own goddamn Hospitality House, right around the corner, and I need to talk."

"I'll be there in ten minutes," said Peter.

"Room 22. Next to Rebecca Forsythe's. You know the way, I hope."

Death's Kingdom was the sequel to *Undiscovered Country*, and she wrote it in two months. When the first volume appeared, Rebecca was besieged by readers—by those whose tales were similar and drew strength from her account. Then Noel said it's time to publish a companion volume with a series of disclosures of complicity and loving testimonials like yours.

She hadn't liked to put it that way, quite. A "disclosure of complicity" was not the phrase she wanted Noel to use. But they enlarged on Arthur's story to include the suicides of others who had made the same decision, or who wrote her to report a loved one's loss. Noel knew what he was doing, and soon enough they had a second best-seller about suicide and a third book in the works. So what began as mystery had ended up as politics in her experience also; the pure grief of her husband's pancreatic cancer became a source of profit for her publisher. Out of private lamentation they forged a kind of industry, and it had succeeded beyond his wildest dreams.

Noel wouldn't admit it, of course, he reminded her he'd told her so and predicted her best-seller status all along. But he too had been astonished at how many people seemed to need to buy her books; he said, "We've touched a nerve" and, later, "Well, Rebecca, we appear to have opened a vein." She'd become a kind of public image—an icon, nearly—of sorrow. Xanthippe, she was often called, and sometimes the Angel of Death; one magazine called her Medusa and another, for some reason, a Siren and Madonna of the Rocks.

She supposed it was like that for other celebrities also. If you were a politician you would be expected to live, breathe, and eat only politics. If you were a famous athlete you would no doubt play sports all year round; if you worked in the theater at night you were supposed to live a glamorous and theatrical life by day. But since she, Rebecca Forsythe, had grown famous for a book about assisted suicide she was expected to be death-obsessed in public; it was as though all other subjects would seem irrelevant. She had become a *thanatoptician*, as Noel liked to call it; the way that others were beauticians or pediatricians or morticians, she herself was an expert on death.

On Monday evening, after work, Jim Kelly bought her a drink. He arrived at Hospitality House in an ancient, battered Subaru and drove her to the Rooster's Pen and spilled himself over the table, dropping peanuts all the while and shredding his napkin to bits. It devolved upon him, he announced—and used that word, "devolved"—to organize grand rounds.

She flattered his performance at the podium the week before and, visibly, he blushed. He was, she could tell, disconcerted. "The pleasure's *mine*," he said. "I mean it, Ms. Forsythe. The pleasure's all mine."

"Rebecca."

"Rebecca," he said.

Chief Resident Jim Kelly kept ordering Michelob, light. He hadn't read *Undiscovered Country*, but he'd heard of it of course. He wanted her to know his own opinion on the issue, and hear his side of the story. That was the point of their drink. He was like a hundred other doctors with the dying and the vegetal; he thought heroic measures would mean he himself was heroic; he'd grown certain of his savior mission and would destroy to save. And he was so suspicious, so appalled by what he de-scribed as the hospital's "touchy-feely" program of participatory management that he positively jiggled in his chair.

Then he told her that his marriage was going on the rocks. He had a little secret of his very own to share. He was older than the other residents, as she might have noticed, and maybe she'd been wondering what had taken him so long. She hadn't in point of fact wondered, but he seemed to think an explanation was in order. He told her of his history in pharmaceuticals and his faith in life-enhancing drugs and how he'd finally decided that he'd rather be the horse's mouth than horse's ass, pardon his French, and had applied to medical school and had changed his life.

His third beer had taken effect. He told her that his daughter's scoliosis failed to respond to the brace; they might well have to operate; his son was in what they used to call a remedial reading program and now called Studies for the Differently Enabled. His cat was sick; his dog was pissing everywhere; his marriage was what the experts call dysfunctional and used to call a mess.

"I'm sorry," said Rebecca.

"Right," he said. "Of course you are." There were peanut-shell flecks on his lips. "So anyway, why are you here?"

"To visit your hospice, remember? To see if it's working."

"It's working, all right," Kelly said. "It's working like a goddamn clock. It's working so damn well"—he wiped his palm across his mouth—"we got the fastest turnaround of any institution in the country. Except . . ."

"Except?"

"You'll see," he hinted darkly. " 'Bioethical education.' You'll see it if only you look."

She reminded him there were distinctions, and important ones, between assisted suicide and the creed of the hospice itself. Jim Kelly was not listening. He distrusted this new system and its practitioners and president; he would do what he could, he insisted, to oppose a form of health-care delivery that delivered instead—he intended no disrespect—death. He was balding and plump and myopic and his collar was too tight. And this particular chief resident—he wanted to be clear with her;

he leaned across the table and blew foam from the rim of the glass—believed a doctor was supposed to heal the sick and alleviate suffering and *nothing else*. He was conscientious in such matters, and he objected on principle. *"Non Serviam,"* he said.

Laura Pierce had been transferred to Trueman-Andrews Hospital. Dr. Julius had tried to countermand the order, but the admitting physician insisted that a ten-day course of antibiotics was what the patient needed, and the prognosis was good; she'd be as good as new, he said, coming out of the oxygen tent.

"As good as new." Her teeth were out. "What does it mean, Doctor, 'good as new'?"

Peter placed his chair beside the bed.

"It means," mouthed Laura, "good as *old*."

"How are you, Mrs. Pierce?"

She crooked her finger at him, as if to bring him near.

"Is there something I can do for you?"

"Yes."

Lunch had arrived.

"Doctor, please . . ."

He took her hand.

"Take me away from here," she said.

Her hand was brown with liver spots. She had removed her ring. The nurse's aide said, "Back in five," and closed the curtain carefully.

"All right," said Dr. Julius. "When you're ready there'll be help."

"Ready?"

"We'll bring you back across the street . . ."

"Please . . ."

". . . and deal with it."

"What? *What?*" The curtain by her bed was green.

"With whatever's coming next," he said.

She smiled up at him gaspingly.

"Do we understand each other?" Peter asked.

She held his hand. She squeezed it. "Yes."

"It's the reason you're a hospice patient, Mrs. Pierce."

She died on Thursday evening, in her sleep.

Andrews welcomed him expansively—grinning, firm-handed, sucking an unlit cigar. He wore yellow pants, a shirt with bananas emblazoned on the belly, black silk suspenders, a loosened red tie. He was not wearing shoes. His color was good, and what he described as his little discomfort was over; he wasn't worried now. He said you're looking healthy, Doc, but me I'm wealthy and wise.

Peter asked about his symptoms and unpacked his stethoscope. Then he checked Andrews's blood pressure and pulse and suggested that they cross the street and maybe visit the E.R. or run an EKG. But Harley brushed him off. I've had this pain before, he said, and Alka-Seltzer fixes it; I took two and feel fine. Indigestion, mostly that must be what it is. I wanted to talk to you is why I called, and not about my heart condition, my leaky little mitral valve and—he laughed—tacky tachycardia, I wanted to get your advice.

"About?"

"This euthanasia law in Holland. They're letting people choose to die, they're putting in safeguards, correct?"

"Correct. They call it *zelftöding*, I think."

"But *here*"—Harley spread his hands—"in the good old U.S. of A. we're making it a crime. And you know why all that shit goes down, you know why this is happening?" He answered his own question. "Kevorkian. Dr. Jack Alias Death. It's *his* fault that that law got passed."

"Against assisted suicide?"

"The one the Legislature wrote. That outlaws euthanasia."

"But only in this state," said Peter. "And with exceptions, of course. The law itself was overturned."

Again, Harley nodded. He blew his nose, hard. "But then he kills off fifteen people just ahead of deadline. So they paw through his garbage and take away his license so he can't get any chemicals and he has to make do with a hacksaw and carbon monoxide and hoses—teenage stuff, for chrissakes, home remedies, do it yourself." Again, he blew his nose. "So the ones who want his help to die, they hurry up to get to him before it gets illegal; they're practically standing in *line*. The ones who still can stand. And no jury will convict him so they let the doctor out again; *ladies and gentlemen*," Harley intoned, *"the line forms on the left.*

"It's circus-barker stuff, it's talk-show ethics, kid. So that son of a bitch with his Rube Goldberg machine, the one who guides and holds their hand while they pull the little lever, then wipes it clean for fingerprints—*he's* the one who gets the publicity, right?"

"It focuses attention on the problem," Peter said. "That's not necessarily bad."

"But it's the wrong *kind* of attention. This used to happen quietly. All those women with M.S., that guy with emphysema, the one with Lou Gehrig's disease—those poor people afraid they'll get worse. They're not into denial; no, they *need* this place."

Rebecca Forsythe knocked. She kissed Andrews on both cheeks, in the European fashion, and shook Peter's hand.

"Rebecca," said J. Harley Andrews, "glad you could join us. I've been wanting to make certain that you two got together. You've got a lot in common." He made a comic face and clutched at his chest. "Old catastrophes. Like me."

"We've met," said Peter Julius. "At grand rounds and at the hospice."

"Yes?"

"I showed Ms. Forsythe what we were up to . . ."

"And I approved," she said.

"We've been discussing," Harley said, "this guy Kevorkian. And how he's making it harder for everyone—how everything he does brings down this lunatic *posse*, these righteous right-to-lifers. These people who sift through his garbage and call for inquests and what-have-you, the ones who read his mail . . ."

She sat in the chair by the window. Lightly, it started to rain.

"A million people die each year in hospitals," said Harley. "Give or take a hundred thousand, right? And you have to occupy those beds or else you lose your billing, so instead of sending patients home you have to keep them here." He was on his bully pulpit, and would not be stopped. "All this defensive medicine, this legal system, this malpractice; what does it do to our GNP? The answer's 'Nothing good.' "

While Rebecca watched the pattern of the raindrops on the windowpane—dividing, then joining, dividing again—Dr. Julius agreed. We spend too much time in denial, he said, we treat the end of human life like a problem of waste management. What are you saying, asked Harley, we're garbage? Not at all, the doctor said, but it's a part of maturation, an organic stage like adolescence or childhood. And it's wrong to keep our suffering in quarantine or at a stiff arm's remove.

They talked about technology, how Americans have grown convinced machines will solve their problems, and how this also constitutes a form of mass denial. It's like those right-to-lifers, Harley claimed, who think they have the right to kill, and in order to save babies they shoot doctors and receptionists instead. They discussed the AMA and managed health care and how in Holland those who choose to die are doing so for reasons that have nothing to do with the expense of maintenance, since they can afford to continue . . .

Then Harley said it's late enough and if this state had any sun why it would be over the yardarm by now. He brought out a bottle and glasses and said, do the honors, kid.

Rebecca stood. "I'll see you both tomorrow?"

"Not me," said Harley. "I'm traveling on. You'll just have to manage without me. To togetherness." He raised his glass. "To single malt whiskey, Glenfiddich, the best goddamn painkiller made."

"Amen to that," said Peter.

"An old Welsh toast," Harley Andrews proposed: "May you live all the days of your life."

XIV

SHE WAS hearing Muzak of the most insipid sort; they were always playing Muzak nowadays at Kroger's: a ridiculous arrangement of trumpet and guitar. Forty-seven violinists violated "Yesterday." They played it in unison, badly. *Love was such an easy,* such a saccharine arrangement, such a plaintive *game to play,* and could that be a harp she was hearing? The P.A. system blatted out a special on fresh fish. Then the manager called for everyone's attention to our everyday low prices and all this week at Kroger's to our very extra special Combo-Deli deal. But was it possible that she, Christine Addison Trueman Conley, three days before her forty-second birthday, at almost four o'clock on Thursday afternoon, and shopping since she had not shopped all week and in order to replenish what she could not remember having consumed in the first place, in aisle 8 of the supermarket, catercorner to the salad bar and watching a green-clad adolescent make a pyramid of artichokes, mound a berm of escarole, wedged between the jams and jellies, heard a harp?

No, not a harp, she told herself, not possibly, and shook her

head. The child at the vegetable counter had, she saw, a strawberry mark on his chin. She could remember seeing TV footage
of the Beatles when they first arrived in America and sang that
particular song. Now, however, there were no tomorrows for the
Beatles or John Lennon or whoever named that tune or, for that
matter, Ed Sullivan—the pioneer, they called him, did they call
him *pioneer?*—the hatchet-faced impervious M.C., cracking his
knuckles and sucking his cheeks on the seventeen-inch Philco
she had been so proud of once, so elated to have in her room.
Testing testing one two three.

And this reminded her of water she was hunting. She was
looking for the shelf of Schweppes or Evian with lemon or Perrier or Saratoga water or Quibel with a splash of lime, since latterly it did appear to matter which water you drank with what
fruit. *All my troubles seemed to fall away.* Was that the line she
was hunting, or was it *seemed too far away,* and the most irritat-
ing thing about those jingles was how they remained in your
head. How you couldn't dispel them by stopping the song, *tum,
ta-tum tum tum tum tum,* and couldn't get rid of the rhyme . . .

She shook her head to clear it; she was standing in aisle 8.
She was consulting her list. But a woman in a paisley skirt was
reaching for the pretzels, and her shopping cart was in the way,
and she steered past, or tried to, but the obstacle remained.

"Ex*cuse* me," said Christine.

"Excuse *me.*"

They did a little shuffle; she moved right and the stranger
moved left. Face-to-face: lift up thine eyes. And drink to me
only with Perrier or, as it happens, Quibel. As if they were partners in some sort of square dance, doing the do-si-do, once more
they sidestepped and once more they met.

The woman wore sneakers; they squeaked. And at least this
would enable her to banish that *jing-a-ling* inside her *tum, ta-tum
tum* head, thank heaven for small favors, because now instead of
Muzak Christine could focus on the odd coincidence, the
strange way English worked, that she and this fat reeking

stranger should literally lock their wheels and use the same two words and mean such different things. "Try the salt-free pretzels," she wanted to say.

"Excuse me?"

"Not potato chips."

"Ex*cuse* me?"

"Not potato chips!" she said.

For there was mindless repetition everywhere abroad. It was cold in Kroger's now, and a distinct chill threatened her, and therefore she stood looking at the capers in her shopping cart, the avocados and the Boston lettuce and the cereal her husband liked, or at any rate pretended to, to which he added raisins, and suddenly there seemed no point in such a confrontation (the thick ankles of her shopping partner, the shirtwaist, the stain on the paisley) and the insult she intended would have been besides the point.

They were standing one aisle over from the double freezer aisle. It was probably this simple fact, this salient intervention, that kept her from screaming, the wind at her back, *Who goes there, Help, Halt, Help!* Instead Christine attempted to remove her cart and groceries, to back up gracefully and leave it all alone and turn and pay and flee this sordid place.

Except their wheels were locked. The fat woman's handbag was plastic. It had the iridescent sheen of something dead. It was, what was the word, *shocking* red. It nestled on the kiddie tray, that shelf with a green circle and an X-mark through the sitting child, so that you understood you had been warned against depositing your children, and if you lose them cannot sue, as if anyone would balance children up there with the cantaloupe, beside the eggs, as if she had children to balance, or as if the precious darlings wouldn't rather roller-skate.

"Don't you just hate it here?" she heard herself asking. "Don't you absolutely hate it here with this insane abundance? *Choice!* Except for in potato chips, the brand names of potato chips, the illusion, no, *delusion* of variety we have in fact no choice. Think of the people in Russia," she said. "The starving multitudes, the millions out in the Sudan. Left hanging there to dry."

"Are you all right?" the woman asked.

Her green cart squeaked. It squealed.

"Is there something I can do for you?"

Wordless, Christine shook her head. Then at last the sound track altered and a woman with a breathy low loud husky voice sang "Coming 'Round Again," and this was supposed to mean something, no doubt, and be some sort of sign. She smiled, or tried to, or attempted via camaraderie to gloss over the insult and take it all back. "These brand names everywhere," she heard herself saying out loud.

"Here. Let me help you."

"No," she said. "That's why we married, isn't it?"

"Excuse me?"

"I know you, don't I?" asked Christine. "And *not* just from this afternoon. We've met before, I'm certain."

"Here?"

"At some office party or other. Where do you live?"

There was an odd dignity to this pink hulk. It demurred. "I believe you're mistaken."

"Christine Addison Trueman Conley," said Christine. She made herself perform the introduction—because after all they were connected, inextricable, at least for this brief interlude with their cart wheels engaged, front right and front left linked—and there was no alternative, or none she could imagine, and when in Bellehaven do as the natives do. Nonetheless this struck her as ironic, since no one could be more a native than she, more entirely at home on this particular parcel of land if not the steel and brick and glass monstrosity they'd built on it, who had literally been raised above the register and learned to brush her teeth in what became the parking lot . . .

"I'm Marjorie Kelly," the fat woman said. "Pleased to meet you, Chris."

*   *   *

Then carefully they disengaged and went together to the checkout line. They stood together, waiting, and while the groceries were added up and bagged and paid for, first her own few purchases and then the other's, *groaning, bored*, while discount coupons were produced and bottle returns subtracted, and the usual interminable questions asked, *paper or plastic, ma'am, which do you prefer?* (there was a slow and single file of idiots behind them and to the right and left of them and idiots in front), the two women spoke in that desultory fashion such proximity makes possible, of weather and the sales tax and the cost of magazines, of Cindy Crawford on the cover staring out, who was not so much attractive or even seductive as reproachful, an impossible *ideal*.

There were razor blades and gum. There were batteries and film. There was a picture of the illegitimate baby in diapers that Jackie Kennedy Onassis on her deathbed confessed to having had with Gary Cooper on the cover of the newspaper, in 1966, a *grown boy now* her own son would have been, if he had grown, if he had lived, and ever so handsome, so devil-may-care. There was *Good Housekeeping*. There was *TV Guide*. And it developed as she'd known it must that their husbands did indeed report for work at the same establishment, and Christine watched patiently—*too* patiently, it took forever—while it dawned on the lady in paisley that she was standing in the parking lot at Kroger's with the president's wife of Trueman-Andrews Hospital, the daughter of its founder, that Mrs. Trip Conley herself had solicited help, had needed the kind of assistance (*you don't have to, no, don't mention it, I'm very grateful, really, thanks*) a total or near-total stranger might provide . . .

Oh, once her father's father owned this whole section of town. Once they pastured horses here, right on this very spot where shoppers flock to graze. Does a flock graze, she asked her new companion, is that the way to put it, I think it's only a herd that grazes, don't you, a flock that pastures, and wasn't this entire shopping center once her father's farm? Then along came the bankers and the Caterpillar tractors and backhoes and the men who built the cloverleaf where the barn and paddock used to be and the little obedient hirelings who were mounding grapefruit even as she watched, were pawing the produce in cellophane gloves, were setting out boxes of berries to conform with, *consort* with their strawberry marks why even as we speak.

Well anyway, she said again, I remember without any trouble the dust in summer here, the heat-haze where we're talking. Before they built this ridiculous fountain and the shopping mall. My father would sit on the front porch and put his feet up on the rocker and tell me, babycakes, this family's going for broke. It's what a broker does. They made him rich, of course, they made him make me rich. And that's why Trip Conley noticed and married me and the rest, as the expression goes, is history and now I'll have him fired so he'll remain at home. Because on Thursday afternoon I come here to check the investment, to assess the local provender, to acquire the necessities but I don't mind telling you, dear, it's always such a shock.

So what do you think of Bellehaven, she asked, how long have you been in this part of the world? This neck of the woods, so to speak. You have children, I don't doubt, I've met your husband certainly and certainly you've met my own, my splendid perfectly attentive well-tailored son of a bitch of a husband and do you have a family and do you want a coffee or something a *tad* bit stronger while we talk? Remember I'm a farm girl too, or used to be, or anyway my mother was—that teat has been brutally sucked, I can see, but you really should improve your posture, Marge, you ought to take care of yourself and by the way where are *you* parked, where have they stalled you now? The house you live in, is what I mean, the roof over your animal head. And probably it leaks.

"I got to go," said Marjorie Kelly.

"No. Please."

"The kids are waiting."

"No."

"I *got* to."

"Goodbye then," said Christine. "You've been helpful."

"Do you think you'll make it home all right?"

"No."

Because what I have to wait for is only more of the same. Is the gin at five the wine at seven-thirty and the brandy beginning at nine. Is my own heart beating singly where it used to beat for two, in the very town and two miles north-northeast from the very hospital where sixty-seven months ago the bundle that I held to it collapsed on Thursday noon. Is the desolating certainty that nothing will improve.

Therefore Christine Addison Trueman Conley turned her back on her companion who was leaving anyhow, was backing off and, where a woman in a dark green Pontiac was getting out, was closing the door, was lifting up her face expectantly, half-smiling, collecting a cart from the Kart-Corral, she approached her next and new and plausibly a *tad* bit more presentable and enlightened and intelligent acquaintance and said *Hello, fine weather we're having, isn't it? hello, hello, hello.*

XV

SO JOHNNY had them on the run; he had them watching their shadows and looking both ways when they crossed and waiting for the green. He had them by the short hairs, in the palm of his hand while he squeezed; he was offering his hot-wax special and depilatory cream. They were making appointments and offering things and writing prescriptions and begging him not to go public; he had the power brokers in his power finally, and he was making it last.

All right, all right, here's the routine. Why did the chicken cross the road? That was no chicken, that was my life. *And then you do the sidestep and the shuffle, then you take a bow.* Question: Who was that piccolo I saw you with? Answer: that was no piccolo, that was my fife. *And then you doff your top hat, then you twirl your cane. Then you shuffle all about.* Question: How do you get three old ladies to scream *Fuck!* Answer: get the fourth to cry out, *Bingo.*

Oh they loved him at the hospital, they couldn't get enough. He'd begun to bleed again and had been admitted; Jimbo Kelly wanted him around. There was standing room only while he played the patient; the doctors rocked and rolled. O-colitis, where the wind comes rushing round the plain. And the waving wheat, beneath your feet—they adored it, they knew his routine. *Pore Judd is daid.* So he asked them what they wanted and the staff cried out in unison, pleading do it baby, do it, oh play it one more time.

Waiter, waiter, what's this fly doing in my soup? *Answer: the backstroke.* Waiter, waiter, what's this fly doing in my ice cream? *Answer: he prefers winter sports.* Then you perform a drumroll and, at a jaunty angle, cock your hat. Tell me, waiter, darling waiter, what's this splinter doing in my cottage cheese? *Answer: for that price, you expect the whole cottage?* Oh they loved him at the E.R. and the rehab unit and up there, in intensive care, they crowded to the stage and kissed his feet and waved their arms and were very damn thrilled he could make it. They were rolling in the aisles.

Johnny worked the hospice too, the young and old and in between with all of them needing a laugh. He took his skateboard and his microphone and did his Frank Sinatra: *Hush little baby, don't say a word, Daddy's going to buy you a big brown turd.* And then his Harry Connick, Jr.: *Hush, little darlin', can't you see, Doctor's going to give you a D&C.* This was when they ceased to laugh, when they saw that he was serious and knew that he was weeping since they heard it when he sang. *Hush, little blackbird, don't you cry, Mama's going to take your friends, your twenty-three boon companions, and she'll smash them and she'll trash them and she'll mash them in a pie . . .*

Yet everywhere there came the sound of apples falling, of soft wind soughing in the laden boughs, of music music *music.* It was Scott with his beloved and badly cracked Favilla, the Super Bowl at halftime, the moon walk, the "We Are the World." And what it all came down to, really, was how Johnny couldn't cry out loud because, he liked to tell them, the tears are falling continually and what do you think of that, ladies, and how do you like them ripe soft apples, gentlemen. There's a pain in my belly, *dear Jimbo, dear Jimbo,* there's diarrhea often and mucus in my stool.

Question, why did the nun get fucked in the ass by mistake? *Answer: she was wearing her choirboy clothes.*

But it wasn't very funny, and he knew it; it was nothing to write home about, no joke. He was tired; his whole body hurt. This is going to run into money, said the monkey as he peed into the cash register. In the hallways and the waiting rooms, in the power plant and staff garage, daily, his audience grew. The sweet little thing, how it grew. It was swollen and upright and purple and while he was instructing them it absolutely *expressed* this drop of lubricating liquid from the tip. So he held it there in the palm of his hand like the monkey and cash register, like a warm paper cup with its own yellow sample, *drink, drink. To me only with thine eyes,* except the Nardil turned him off, except his balls were soft and small, except his breasts were growing. So they watched him with unflagging interest and paid respectful attention; he was great friends with Jack Daniel's and Jim Beam. He was pals with Johnnie Walker, George Dickel and the gang. He was particularly fond of Ezra Brooks.

Trip Conley came to visit; he smiled his TV smile. "How are we feeling this morning?"

"You're worried, aren't you?"

"No."

"You're worried that I'll blow the horn. Or is it whistle?" Johnny asked.

"You have to remember," his visitor said, "your friend imagined things. In the end he was hallucinating . . ."

"Alice Tucker?" Johnny asked, and so Trip left the room. Which could not be called surprising since, according to his very own and personal physician, these digestive spasms might be due to side effects from the vitamins he took and the antidepressants he needed to swallow and the debilitating aftermath of California wine. Still, he had nothing to complain about and no one to complain to and in any case there was no point complaining, it was how to lose an audience; he had the apartment, didn't he, and his memories, his *memories*, and bank account and most of his muscle and all of his hair.

So there's this ancient couple, married sixty years. And they wheel themselves into divorce court and ask for a divorce. Excuse me, asks the judge, do you mind if I ask you one question? No, no, go right ahead. Well then why did you wait so long: why did you choose to wait until you're eighty-five? *Answer: we wanted to wait till the children were dead.* Next you offer up a version for the regulars, the ones at the bar, the ones who maybe didn't listen first time through. So there's this couple, understand, maybe eighty years old, eighty-five. And they want to get a divorce. But when they approach the bench the judge says, request granted, except do you mind if I ask you one question, why did you wait all these years? And why—now, after all this time—why would you want a divorce? *Your honor*, says the husband, *because enough's enough.*

So he had them by the short hairs, and the reporters were loving it, *yes*, and they were doing a story. Big-time hospice, big-time hospital: what we've got is an *engine of death.* My recently deceased companion, ladies and gentlemen, friends, and I honor his memory daily, Mr. Scott Raposo checked himself into this establishment with a slight cough, a low-grade fever possibly, a little problem with his kidneys that could well have been corrected; then the patient died in Trueman-Andrews, and it's my total certainty, my absolute conviction, and I can prove it, he was killed. By someone in this kitchen who was mopping up the mess; I have the evidence, your honor, since he *told* me what was going down and who put the overalls in Alice Tucker's chowder. And I'll tell you since you ask *who wants to know.*

But I myself have a small problem, a slight procedural difficulty, with U.C. and my MAO inhibitor and fondness for salami and initials and old cheese. And besides I need a drink. For obvious reasons, therefore, I have been admitted to this place and intend to seek an explanation or at least redress, though not *you will agree* impertinently, excessively, and have scanned the morning headlines and exercised my duties as a citizen by voting and have vacuumed the balcony carpet and scrubbed the shower stall.

So today we have good news and bad news. First, the bad. *Help, the paranoiacs are after me!* So we performed this amputation, says the doctor, and now the operation's done and the bad news is we cut off the wrong leg. Well what's the good news, cries the patient, what can you tell me that will possibly be good, Doc, how can you cheer me up? The *good* news, says the sawbones, is your bad leg's doing fine. Oh yes, there are hospital jokes. Did you hear the one about *dis nurse and disorderly*, didja? Or the one about *friend and enema?* Did you hear the one about how when I come in for a consultation, for a simple prescription, an answer or two, what I get instead is lectured on my lifestyle and its risks, my self-destructive and unprotected and promiscuous sexual behavior, as Peter Peter Pumpkin Eater calls it, my *what the fuck business is it of yours, honeychile, did I come on to you did I go all over shivery or what?*

But they have me in their power here at last. And Penny gets her own back after all. Now Jimbo Kelly gets to fix me up and play a game of doctor behind the maternity ward. Not to mention what I don't see fit to mention at this time. Not to mention who. *I was reading a book on schizophrenia the other day. Or, at least, part of me was.* And therefore I give my permission: proceed.

There was someone in the room. Its shape was spotlit, various. It departed, coughing. There was no one in the room.

May 7

To the Editor:

    Yes, it's me again. I've been told you're asking questions and that's good. I've been told you might be curious about who wants to know. Don't think I'm not up to your tricks. What makes you think anyway what you have for postmark is the place I send it from who tells you anyway that this is my machine? What other person would enjoy this kind of access to the files? Who else if you stop to think about it, and you'd better, BUDDY, would be apprised—I use the word advisedly but you could look it up—of every patient's name. Well it's a hard hard rain & why does everybody Dr. Peter Julius takes care of end up dead?

    It says in Corinthians WATCH IT; it announces in Revelation that we walk through the valley of Bones. But it is God's decision only who shall live and who shall die, and that decision must belong to no mortal woman nor man. Which is the reason that I'm writing you and the reason that you're reading, it's the problem with this nation first and foremost don't you see. Back there behind the Hospice is a graveyard for the babies of the poor unmarried mothers of this land. For those who have been murdered in their sleep. And those who fail to take responsibility because of their own actions and think the killer chicken won't come home to roost. You're still reading, aren't you, mister, you're looking for a clue. Look back behind the Hospice like I said. In beautiful Bellehaven which used to be a peaceful place there's riot now and murder in the land, and if the Lord of Hosts sent down His messenger to find an honest man he wouldn't find him in the Hospice that's for sure. Because it be not up to US to weigh or judge the virtue of our fellow citizens, to know for certain that a person lying down will not stand up again. Or that a baby born in direst poverty will not become a millionaire just look at Michael Jordan for example whom the Lord endowed with great leaping ability which permitted him to vault out of tobacco fields and slums. But then look what happened anyhow to Air Jordan's daddy look what transpired with him. Or Miss Aretha Franklin with her God-given gift of vocalese or consider how the baby Albert Einstein could not add. And if even these are saved and rendered precious in His sight then how deny the infant in the mother's womb, the old man in the hospital, the poor and the hungry and tired, the fucking Immigrant Hordes, which is what some people call them, what gives *you* the right to decide?

XVI

"DR. JULIUS?"

"Yes."

"Oh, Dr. Julius . . ."

"What can I do for you, Harriet?"

"Tell me, if you know it, what's the time?"

"Six-fifteen."

"In the afternoon?"

He approached her wheelchair. "It's Thursday afternoon, yes."

"And what's the weather like outside?"

"The usual, I'm afraid."

"Which is? Is it nice weather?"

"You're not missing anything. No."

Her eyes were closed. "I wanted to leave something. You understand me, Doctor, something for the children."

"Yes."

"A little cash money, afterwards. Something to help them with, later. Just so I'm not too poor."

He took her pulse.

"I'm *not* a bankrupt, am I?"

"No. Of course not."

"Bankrupt, without a red cent. Because before there's Medicaid you'll make me be a pauper."

"But we won't let it happen. Nothing will happen here you can't afford."

"Promise?"

"I promise."

"Scout's honor," she said. "A bankrupt. Harriet Anderson who used to be, well, not rich, never rich, but comfortable. And who got sick and wants to die without losing everything, Doctor, and leave her family not a red cent to bury her. What time is it?"

"Six-seventeen."

"On Thursday?"

"Yes."

"What *time* is it?"

"Six-seventeen."

"You'll stay with me? You promise?"

Peter could not bear it. He turned and left the room.

That night his old ghosts came to call; they swept in with the wind. The shutter of his bedroom window banged, and the chimney sang. There was a cat fight in his neighbor's yard; the furnace clicked on, hummed, clicked off.

Marjorie Billings had been in the hospice six weeks. She had congestive heart failure and could no longer walk or stand, but there were arrangements to make. There was, she said to Dr. Julius, the question of the silver in her silver chest, the dispensation of the forks and spoons and in particular the twenty-four knives that had separate initials because—although she never had admitted this to anyone before, and it was heavy on her conscience and he mustn't think the worse of her—she bought them at a flea market, not Schlanderers or Jensen's where her pattern had been registered. He knew, she knew, what Jensen's meant, and Schlanderers also were irreproachable, or in any case had been that way in 1956. But this was the same pattern, except her own set had no fish knives, only cake and butter knives, and so she took the chance.

What chance, he asked, that silver you bought was for sale. But she said, *Think* of the embarrassment, the mortification of having to sell what you own. So it hadn't been an accident that she hid silver all those years but only out of fear that at some supper party the previous owner would sit down to table and shake out her napkin and recognize her beautiful lost polished precious things. Now she wanted to give them away. If the doctor could help she'd die happily, because she had a list of items to take care of, and it was the last one remaining. She confessed all this haltingly, pausing for breath. What she needed as a favor was for him to send the silver fish knives back, to separate them out and give them to her cousin who would otherwise get nothing, who was not included in her will but had the correct initials, and now with this—let's call it by its proper name and admit it finally—act of *restitution* she could die content. Otherwise, said Marjorie, it would have been a shame.

"It's fine," he said. "It's not a shame."

"No, you think not? No?"

"You did the right thing, Mrs. Billings."

"*Really*, Doctor?"

"Yes. I'll send them to your cousin . . ."

"Good," she said. "That's excellent." She jostled her pills in the white paper cup like a child with M&M's.

Rebecca wandered back and forth between the hospital and Hospitality House, restless and ready to leave. Even the photographs of the Grand Canyon and Old Faithful in her hotel corridor suggested some sort of departure; Bellehaven was a mistake.

Its citizens did not amuse her. Trip's hot breath in her ear at lunch or at the hospice staff meeting had come to seem ridiculous; his murmured protestations left her cold. "This evening after work," he asked, "are you free this evening?" and she told him no. When Scott Raposo and then Johnny died, she had the old premonitory certainty: there would be others soon.

On the path between the buildings she encountered Peter Julius; it was six o'clock. The air was mild. They talked about the comforts of stability for home health care and the role of familiar surroundings. "One of the things," Dr. Julius said, "that distinguishes our hospice from those you have in England is how relatively few home visits our staff gets to make. It's not what Dame Cicely intended, of course, but we do get to replicate 'home.' "

"That must be why your Mr. Andrews made this place attractive. Rather more so, in fact, than his Hospitality House."

They gazed at it—the gables, the chimneys, the slate—a replica of someone's clubhouse or resort.

"Partly it's a function of the weather," Peter said. "We lose a lot of time to snowstorms or to ice storms or mud season. The nurses here don't like to travel in the middle of the night."

"I've not been in a private home. Since I came to America, I mean. I'm only just noticing that."

"I'm sorry. Come to mine."

She blushed. "I didn't intend it to sound that way. I didn't mean to be—I wasn't inviting myself."

"Of course not. I'm inviting you. Please pay me a home visit—a 'house call.' When you can."

"You mean that, Dr. Julius?"

"Peter."

"Peter." Of a sudden she decided—surprised at herself, embarrassed at having so obviously given what he thought of as a hint—to accept. "You're not just being polite?"

"No. I do mean it," he said.

"Well, no time like the present . . ." And gaily, feigning pleasure, Rebecca took his arm.

The sun was setting, westerly, and red light illumined the gates of the hospital grounds. He opened the passenger door of his car, then waited while she found the seat belt and then helped her fasten it. She held herself high in the seat. He asked her, would she like some music, and she shook her head. He shut the door and paused a minute, fitting the key into the ignition, letting the engine idle, until everything seemed freighted with meaning: how long he waited, how lightly she breathed.

They drove into Bellehaven, in the increasing dark. They made their way past pharmacies and a dry cleaner with a winking fluorescent sign and a video rental and drive-through liquor shop. The treelined avenues divided, and there were restaurants and bars at intervals: a parking lot, a clothing store, a firehouse and boarded-up hotel. It was called Embassy Suites.

Peter's house was painted white. Inside the door she understood, by the absence of domestic clutter and the faint must of the living room, that her host had had few visitors; he was not a bachelor used to entertaining. The couch had flowered pillows, and there was a faded Oriental on the floor. He opened several cupboards. They seemed bare.

"What will you drink?"

She shook her head. "Not alcohol. I'm sorry. I've got a bit of a headache . . ."

"Some coffee? Tea?"

"I'd like that, yes."

He rummaged and at length produced a red container and one single tea bag. She assured him it was her favorite brand and he put the kettle on. Rebecca found herself explaining that she'd had a migraine ever since she'd reached Bellehaven, that the headaches came and stayed and sometimes were so fierce she'd not remember anything—not what she did or said but only the bright yellow light.

"It's been diagnosed as migraine?"

"Yes."

"By whom, if I might ask?"

"Someone I trusted," she said.

"I didn't mean . . ."

"I understand. But it *is* a migraine, really . . ."

Peter smiled, and so did she. It was the tea, perhaps, the

chipped mug and the empty room and whiskey he was sipping, neat—but she closed her eyes an instant and saw Arthur in his slippers, standing by the fire in the grate. He was stirring a small flame; it flared. He was telling her she would survive him, and that she'd be happy, and she was denying it and telling him "No, no."

"Don't be ridiculous," her husband said. "You will. Of course you will . . ."

Now she forced herself to listen to her host in this dark room. He spoke of Harley Andrews and the risks attaching to angina and the likelihood that they would operate on Harley soon. He said how strange it felt to be at strangers' beck and call, and how the world despises doctors until the moment they need them: a doctor goes, he told her, from villain to priest overnight.

The sugar was clotted, dark brown.

"When you first said you'd come," he asked, "how long were you planning to stay?"

"Two weeks," she said, "a month at most."

"Have you been told," asked Peter, "how many patients have died?"

She shook her head. It did not flare.

"Eleven in the last three weeks. I checked the records this morning."

"And therefore?"

"It's hard not to notice an increase. Hard not to wonder—that's what everyone is asking me—if it could be coincidence. An expert on death, a famous author comes to town, and everyone starts dying . . ."

She stared at him. "And you? Is *that* what you've been wondering?"

"No."

"But it's not a question, is it? You're not really asking me, are you?"

"No."

"Let me make sure I understand. You're saying that because

I'm here, your patients all are dying. The Englishwoman comes to town, and these Americans die."

Dr. Julius spread his hands. "It needn't be cause and effect. It could be mere coincidence—the power of suggestion. I'm wondering out loud."

Rebecca answered carefully. It had been no coincidence; it was in fact cause and effect. Trip Conley wanted her to meet J. Harley Andrews. Then she learned it had been Andrews's money that brought her to Bellehaven and the whole arrangement had been *his* idea. They expected her to soften and counteract the image of that man—what was his name, Kevorkian?—who killed off all those people in that place called Royal Oak. He was rather creepy, wasn't he, a sort of Bluebeard with carbon monoxide and those polyester pants of his and that craving for celebrity. He had quite the reputation for service with a smile; he was a real lady-killer, wasn't he, the famous Dr. Death. She supposed they thought a lady who helped her husband kill himself would provide a counterbalance, a sort of positive force. All that publicity the unfrocked doctor was getting could be turned to their advantage, she supposed.

"You're here for Trip?"

"Not really. No."

"*Because* of him, I meant to say."

"When you put it that way, yes. In a manner of speaking." She made a dismissive gesture. "We met in London."

"Yes?"

"And he wanted me to serve as, oh, I suppose a kind of witness. That seems to be my role these days."

Rebecca was tired; her head hurt, and conversation wearied her. He asked again about Trip Conley and the reason she had come to town and what she hoped to learn. But she did not want to think herself some sort of hostage—a captive, a piece of prized booty—to their warring factions. They were enemies, she knew. She had no notion, really, of what it was they fought about at Trueman-Andrews, in the hospice and the hospital, but it was clear they fought.

"You two belong to Harley, don't you?"

"Excuse me?" Peter said.

"You're both his creatures, aren't you? I mean, he does employ you both . . ."

"If you want to put it that way, yes. But there's no *professional* jealousy . . ."

So she asked him and he spoke about his work. He described the human wreckage that slept by heating vents or wandered into hospitals and sat huddled in the halls. He talked with a sweet melancholy earnestness about the daily round of hospice visits, the model program in Amsterdam, the illusion of assistance and comfort to provide. Yet the best that we can hope to do is help a little, provisionally, and with the foreknowledge of failure, since all of us are born to die, and most particularly those without proper insurance. Meanwhile our patient population, Peter said, is wheeled into the E.R., hemorrhaging, its rib cage crushed, blood pouring out of an eye . . .

"Why did you take this particular job?"

"There was a man I liked," he said. "A janitor in Lakeview where I worked before I came here. And I never knew him well. I'll spare you the gory details, but he asked for help and I"— Peter spread his hands—"I failed to help him. So then he killed himself."

"Violently?"

"Yes. It happened at a time when I—you know about this also—was starting out alone again and trying to make sense of things. Gerontology, you see; that was supposed to be my specialty. And it's very different than, say, pediatrics; it's about coming to terms with the inevitable, with various forms of collapse. But once you start to notice death, it crops up everywhere."

"I didn't mean to insult you," she said. "I'm sorry. I was curious."

Mirthlessly, he laughed. "Curiosity, they tell us, killed the cat."

"You've read about my own," she said. "My experience of loss, I mean. I didn't handle it all that well either . . ."

"It sounds melodramatic, I know," Peter said, "what you called a conversion experience. The need to end things well. What it comes down to, really, is we shouldn't die alone."

She studied him. He did not know, it seemed, what wall he butted up against or maze he wandered through. He was the perfect American boy-man who had been inoculated—or so Rebecca told herself—against grief and disappointment and uncertainty and loss. He was bright-eyed and fair-visaged and aloof.

"Where does it hurt you?" he asked. He came to her and, wordless, she pointed to the ridge of bone above her eyes. Using first his fingertips, then palms, massaging her temples, he pressed. Then he released the pressure, and then he pressed again.

There was a band of pain; it loosened. He cupped his hands at her ears. He worked his way down to her neck. When she opened her eyes to him, weeping, he was radiant, enfolding her, and she embraced him back.

XVII

PENNY WALKED out on the hospice grounds to see what she could see. She bit into her apple: Granny Smith. Lately she'd been working as a "float," dividing her time equally between the hospital and hospice. And it did seem like six of one, half a dozen of another; they died on both sides of the street.

Jim Kelly also worked in both; he was moonlighting nowadays in order to pay off the loans. That was what he told his wife, they needed the overtime check. So he supervised the hospice on Tuesday night, and every other Friday; it was easy work, the patients slept, and she made sure she joined him for the Tuesday night rotation. There was a bathroom they could lock behind the staff lounge on the second floor and, once, an empty bedroom on the third. It was the room called Arizona, with a photograph of the Grand Canyon and buffalo and teepees on the wallpaper and a double bed.

The chief resident was losing it, she knew. Lately he had trouble with his concentration; he'd get soft and drift away and, that night in Arizona, Kelly fell asleep. It hadn't taken long; she moved and he woke up. But she had been so angry at the short fat man above her, sprawled and snoring in her ear, so insulted and ashamed she simply couldn't speak. He'd said, "What's wrong, what did I do?" and she said, "Nothing, nothing" until he got the point.

Lately he popped Percodan for what he said was his rotator cuff, but Penny had grown certain that the trouble was his head. The stress that he was used to was a different kind of stress; it was washing out the diapers, and teaching the dog how to beg and to fetch, not signing off on bodies that might instead be saved. When she offered to massage him he said no thanks, not now. Once or twice she did it anyway and he lay rigid and un-yielding so she had to make a joke of it: oh, lover, you're so stiff . . .

Jim had been a pharmacist and one of his pet peeves was how no one else at Trueman-Andrews knew the first thing about drugs, their power and variety and therapeutic value; it's some-thing we don't talk enough about. Let's talk about it, Penny said, and he said, well why not, only ten percent of medical stu-dents claim they feel competent dispensing pharmaceuticals. Most doctors shy away from drugs until it's way too late. Under-stand me, Kelly said, it's like any other clinical skill, it's learning how to deal with pain, and when she asked him what about pleasure he answered—earnest, blinking, staring at her like he couldn't exactly remember her name—that's your department, lady, mine is pain.

She had dreamed they'd go to Paris and would be welcome there. She imagined strolling up and down along the perfumed boulevards, wearing a white hat and veil, with rings on her fin-gers and rings on her toes, with bracelets and earrings and neck-laces of semiprecious—*precious*—stones, all of them brightly a-jangle. Where she walked along the boulevards she took her suitor's arm.

There was a word for her behavior, not the word her father used: not *murderer* or *slut* but *coquette*. She was being Jim Kelly's coquette. She was trying anyway, and he took out his leather bag, his Dr. Feelgood pharmacy, and that was when the dream went bad and she woke to Bellehaven instead.

So now without her even thinking it but out of childhood habit she offered up contrition: I am sorry, most heartily sorry, *mea culpa, mea maxima,* and what can I do for you, baby, whatever can I do? By the hospice pool she brought him off, and he told her he had never been so happy in his life. You poor bastard, Penny thought, but then she fixed her makeup and said she was happy too.

Her last two patients this morning had both been in denial. "I'm getting better," they told her. "I'm just not ready yet."

"We need to wash you," she told Susan Hollister. Susan was incontinent, and did not seem to notice or, if she noticed, care; her bed smelled like an outhouse back behind the barn.

"No."

"You don't want to lie here this way."

"The other ones will fix me. They take care of cleaning up."

"I'm used to it," Nurse Lampson said. "I've done it all my life."

"But you're not used to *me*," said Susan. "And that's the difference."

"No difference this morning. You've voided."

"Says *you*."

"Well, we can't have a person lying around in wet sheets."

"Okay. Tomorrow, you do it tomorrow."

"Let's get it over with. Alley-oop," Penny said.

It was like gentling a horse. You keep a carrot in your pocket and the horse knows that you've got it, but you don't offer anything until you've had the ride. Then you offer up a carrot, not a stick. Her procedure with this patient was the same; after Penny washed her, only *after* she had changed the catheter and sheets did Susan get a sausage biscuit as reward.

Ernie Potter in the next room wouldn't eat. He weighed half as much as Susan, and probably slipped her his food; it was like that nursery jingle about Jack and Mrs. Sprat. Between the two

of them they licked the platter clean. Ernie used to keep a garden, and he told her every morning how eighty square feet kept
him going all winter, how the brussels sprouts he grew would
make it through the snow. They stayed green right through the
winter, they were just the prettiest things. He raised and lowered his hand cautiously, painfully, sketching brussels sprouts in
air.

Can you help me, Nurse, he'd asked her, can you help me
with the dosage and supplies? It's Dilaudid and morphine and
MS Contin, correct? What had started out as nothing very seri-
ous was serious by now; there had been three deaths this week.
There would be, she was certain, two more. When Penny left,
Ernie Potter was crying; water streamed over his cheeks.

Lately, again, she woke shouting; it happened three nights in
a row. Her nightmare had three versions but it was always the
same. On the first night she lost her baby in a supermarket parking lot, in the second dream she drowned it, in the third version
it burned. There were always people watching with the faces,
yea, of angels, and always they pointed their fingers at her and
threw stones and shook their fists. Always their breath smelled
of cough drops, the ones her father used to chew; in the first
dream they grabbed at her ankles and in the second her wrists.
They accused her of breaking commandments: the one about
Honor Thy Parents and the one about adultery, the one about
bearing false witness, not to mention the Thou Shalt Not Kill.
When she sent her unborn baby to come unto Him in heaven
she was doomed to an eternity of sorrow and remorse, and the
portals opened wide but when Penny approached they slammed
shut.

On the third night of her nightmare, always, she confessed.
She was a nurse, Penny said, and nurses love their patients and
want to help them to stop suffering; if only she could get some
sleep, if they would stop tormenting her, she'd sign the discharge papers even unto the third generation and, yea, the press
release. And that was when, shouting, she woke.

*   *   *

Their president liked to play games. He was a handsome man, if you enjoyed that kind of handsome: no stubble, no hair out of place. Idly Penny wondered how well Night-Tripper Conley would perform in bed, and whether it was worth it to find out. She thought not. There was something finicky about him, too delicate by half, too pleased with himself in the mirror; that skinny English lady he'd been fucking was his type. Or maybe he was closet-gay and what really turned him on were all those orderlies who followed him around, those photographers you couldn't tell (with their slim hips, their ankle boots) were men.

Men were a species Nurse Lampson knew well; she'd studied enough in her time. It was like Chihuahuas and Great Danes. Both of them were dogs, of course, and belonged to the same species, with four legs and some sort of tail. But that was just about where the resemblance ended; you couldn't just say *dog* and mean both dachshund and German shepherd, or Irish setter and mutt. So Penny couldn't really tell if the Night-Tripper and his wife—she'd seen the lady only once, at the Christmas banquet—were happy or unhappy with each other or who picked out and paid for the Jaguar he drove; she couldn't tell, to tell the truth, what made Conley tick.

Which worried her. He wanted, he claimed, to be part of a team; he needed to keep track of things. And when he talked to patients he behaved just like a movie star, or a man bucking for mayor. He wanted to make their acquaintance and get to know each and every hospice resident on a first-name and personal basis; Conley asked her for the list.

So she handed him a printout of this week's patients' names. He said thanks much and she said, can I talk to you, it's important, it's something I saw. What could be so very important, he asked, and she said that's what I'll tell you in private and he said in *that* case, Nurse, come over during lunch. Then he visited with Ernie Potter, and talked about baseball and the best growing weather for gardens, and when Ernie said he'd promised Dr.

Julius he'd make it through to brussels sprouts, Trip Conley told him not to worry, you'll do fine.

The rain did start by lunchtime; just crossing on the walkway she got wet. The garden was a pretty place, with yews and flower beds and shredded bark the gardeners were spreading out for mulch. Fat Martha at reception said, "Go on, go right ahead" and offered her a plastic cup of coffee, the bitter dregs of an old pot, and watched with disapproval while Trip came toward her, smiling.

"Hello," he said. "You made it."

"Yes."

"It's raining?"

"Do you mind if we do this in private?"

Martha sniffed.

"Of course not. Come on in." Trip Conley closed the door. When she brushed past him to the chair she smelled his sweet cologne. And she was conscious, sitting, of the way he watched her sit. She had not been in his office before, and the bank of computers surprised her, and the windows giving out upon the weeping willow trees, and then the hospice grounds.

Trip waited, making a tent of his fingers—the green light at his right hand blinking, the desk a burnished black. Fish swam across the screen.

She took a deep breath and began: "Ever since I saw you there, I've been wanting a chance to discuss it . . ."

"Where?"

"In Johnny's room. Two twenty-five. I saw you there the night he died."

He did not seem surprised. "Johnny. Johnny who? Oh yes, I do remember him. Two twenty-five?"

"He was my friend," said Penny. "And that's what I wanted to talk about, what I came here to explain. I could tell you who was there, and when."

"A hospital's a busy place. There's always someone in the hall—someone running tests or making rounds." Conley turned.

"He was what you'd call a whistle-blower—Johnny," Penny said. "And he was onto something."

"What?"

"Here, at Trueman-Andrews. About his own friend's murder, Scott Raposo, you remember. Or what Johnny kept calling murder." She paused. "Except he's also dead."

Trip swiveled in his seat again. "That's true."

"It was preventable."

He shrugged. "I wouldn't know. I'm not a medical expert. Nor, let me remind you, Nurse, are *you*."

The room was cold. The ventilation system blew at the back of her neck. "I know enough," said Penny, "to know a mistake when I see one."

He studied her. "What are you asking?"

"I'm not asking anything. I'm telling you something, that's all. I thought you'd like to know, I checked the dispensation. The IV record, actually."

His chair springs squeaked.

"I know enough, Mr. Conley, to understand if something's preventable. And when it needn't have happened."

"What *else* are you asking?" He stood.

"Well, since you put it that way, my question is what is it worth?"

"Your knowledge?"

"I could tell you when the Demerol was added. The wrong painkiller. The contraindicated drug for anyone on Nardil."

"I'm afraid I don't follow." He walked to the window and stood staring out.

"Myself," said Penny, "I'm not rich." This was her speech; she'd prepared it. "And I always hoped to go to France. I used to think someone would take me, but I may have to go on my own."

"It's expensive," said Trip Conley. "That's what I was telling Johnny, since you ask. He was talking lawsuits, and I told him what it cost."

"I've got a tape, I listen to it every day. *Merci, monsieur*," she said. "*Pour votre assistance. Votre générosité.*"

"Well anyway," he said, "what information do you have and why is it of value?"

"At eleven-forty-seven," Penny said, "I was coming off the night shift and I know what time it was because I always check the clock. And I write it down, correct?"

"If you say so, Nurse."

"I say so. And I saw something in his room. Someone in his room."

She could have told him *Peter*, it was Peter Julius. He was bending down, checking the shunt; he had his back to her. But Penny would have recognized that back and bent head any-where, that tight ass in black linen pants, and she picked him out at fifty paces and saw him slip noiselessly out to the hall, not looking over his shoulder, not seeing anyone, she was certain, and then when she went to see Johnny later the Demerol was empty, and she knew, she *knew*.

But instead she crossed her legs. She let her ankle swing. The body is a system in a certain kind of balance, Nurse Lampson said, and if you shift that balance things go wrong; you can give a diabetic too much or too little insulin, for example, and either dosage kills. If you order Demerol for someone who's on Nardil you might as well write a prescription for poison; it's like pre-scribing death. Take heparin, for example, which keeps your blood from clotting and is perfect for phlebitis or an embolus— but if you need the blood to clot then it's a lethal additive, just exactly the wrong thing to give.

"You don't say," said Trip Conley, and she stood to leave. She watched him watching her.

"This place is scary, Mr. President. It's getting out of hand."

"You need a vacation," he said.

XVIII

WHEN J. Harley Andrews arrived at the hospice that Monday, he complained about his heart. His skin was pale and blotched; he moved with difficulty, wincing, and his breath was loud. "My ticker, kid, it's giving out. It's giving up on me," he said. "I mentioned it before."

"Are you in pain?"

"I am, indeed I am."

"Where?"

"Here." He pointed to his chest.

"Let's have a look." Peter pulled out a chair and helped Andrews sit.

"I need a bed, Doc, not some chair. I want, what do you call it, an angie balloon."

"Angioplasty, maybe?"

"Right. That's what I need. I heard about it, just the thing. Reams out the tubes. *Brrr, brr.*" His lips were blue-tinged, Peter saw, and he had not shaved. His fringe of hair was lank, his liver spots pronounced. "So what's the odds? Are you religious, kid?"

"Sir?"

"Do you believe in God, I mean."

Dr. Julius unpacked his stethoscope. "In something like Him, yes. Lift up your shirt, please."

"A Jew, correct? You're Jewish."

"Let's just have a listen. Yes."

"Well, do you believe what it says in the Bible? That suicide's a sin?"

"Not really, no. Breathe deeply. Hold."

"But I do," Harley said. "You got to understand that fact. For people like me, it's a sin."

"Exhale," he said. "Now hold."

"And that's what I've been puzzling out. Because the Good Lord makes exceptions—for missionaries, volunteers—for just about any and everyone who ponies up in the line of duty. Who falls on a grenade. Remember 'The Charge of the Light Brigade,' kid?— why, all of *them* were sinners! Into the valley of death, remember, that's where they went galloping. And if you think about the saints, lives of the saints, if you read the *Book of Martyrs* they're a battalion of suicides, aren't they? Holy martyrs to the cause."

"Again. Again."

"If Jesus was the Son of God and *could* have come down off that cross, if He died on purpose and could have prevented it, why then He's a *major* suicide." His fingertips were cold. "A world-class sinner, wouldn't you say? A man who *let* Himself be killed, who *chose* to end His suffering. Who willingly gave up the ghost." He coughed. "Well, couldn't you see it that way?"

"Hold still," said Peter. "Save your breath, please. Breathe."

"I know what you're hearing," said Harley. "And I know it isn't good."

They checked the patient in and worked him up. They scheduled tests and a period of observation; then they would lay out the options and choose the best way to proceed. They prepared a room in the second-floor southeast corner where the patient could have privacy—the one beyond the staff lounge with its own view of the park. It had windows that could open and a separate-access stairway in the hall.

Through all of this J. Harley Andrews stayed tranquil; he sucked on an unlit cigar. He wanted, he told Peter, just to get it over with; he'd thought about New York or Minneapolis or Boston but in the end decided he ought to trust this shop. Imagine, Harley said, if Colonel Sanders hated fried chicken or Henry Ford drove Oldsmobiles; you want to demonstrate some *confidence* in the thing you advertise and prove you enjoy your own product, correct?

He and Peter shared a tray. There were crackers, minestrone, and iced tea. The patient ate the cottage cheese and offered the doctor his portion of peaches; winking, he brought out a flask. What you don't understand, he said, is how this arrangement looks—from the outside, I mean, looking in. You're here to run a hospice, right, you're here to help people die. With dignity, correct? Harley poured what looked like vodka in his plastic cup. Then he added ice. And of course there's the Hemlock Society, that pretty English lady we're so happy to have now in town. It's her agenda, isn't it, to teach people how to kill themselves—he wheezed and slapped his own back, coughing—or with a loved one's help.

Then there's Dr. Death himself, our famous Jack the Dripper, who's getting his rocks off on what he calls *obitriatry* and turning the state into pretzels; each time he hangs his shingle out they write another law. One judge says yes, the other no; there's petitions all over the map. Meanwhile fifty percent of our national costs are entailed in the final months of life, it's crazy, kid, a business that runs this way would go bankrupt in three months at most. You make a profit, don't you, by *not* sending people home. Grow old along with me, he laughed, remember, all that Hallmark crap, that's nothing like the way it works, the way that old age works is misery and silence and if you're very rich like I am it postpones things a little bit maybe so the worst is yet to be . . .

He sighed. He drained his cup. "The trouble here," asked Harley, "is it getting better? Worse?"

"Trouble?"

"Kid, I'm seventy-six years old. And I won't live forever and I don't have time to pretend. And you *do* know what I'm talking about: the death rate in this hospital."

"Yes," said Peter.

"Yes, it's getting better?"

"Yes, there's trouble. No, it's not."

"Well, what are you doing about it?"

"Statistically speaking," said Peter, "it's within the acceptable range. The rate of mortality nationwide in hospitals is high—rather higher, I imagine, than you'd guess. And in some ways the better the hospital, or the better its own record-keeping, the higher the reported proportion of inpatient loss. As for the hospice patients themselves, by definition death is the appropriate result. Within those parameters, therefore, and in that context Trueman-Andrews appears unremarkable . . ."

"Talk English, kid, I'm *dying* here . . ."

Dr. Julius folded the chart. It isn't, he explained, a complicated procedure; angioplasty is intrusive but no longer a real risk. Still, I do have to tell you there are in fact risks, an outside chance of myocardial infarction. What's that, a heart attack? asked Harley, and Peter nodded yes. But if it has to happen it's better on the operating table with technicians at the ready than while you're out, say, fishing or sitting in your plane.

The doctor spoke about stenosis and occlusion, and when Harley asked for a translation he said your blood vessels get blocked. It happens, over time. In layman's terms we'll ream you out, we'll take a little wire and track it with an X ray and there's a balloon we'll inflate and use as a probe till we widen the passage; then it's steak and potatoes again . . .

But the heart is not my specialty, said Dr. Julius, and the patient said, that's fine. What he wanted to discuss was the operation's aftermath; a minor—what did you call it?—myocardial infraction is manageable, right, a major heart attack is something else again. If I go I'm gone, he said, and I want that entirely clear. At my age, Pete, and after all that cheddar cheese and sour cream we'll have none of your Stairmaster crap, I've signed a living will. I've given durable power of attorney, a whole bunch of instructions, to my lawyer except he's in Atlanta and we're up here in godforsaken Michigan and I'm not *sure* of reciprocity between the states or who gets to pull which plug and I'm only willing to take that chance if it's understood between us, Doctor. It's understood between us, Peter said, and Harley said have a cigar.

"Would you mind if I ask you a question?"

"Ask ahead," said Harley.

"You never married, did you? Why?"

The patient laughed. "A wife and kids," he said, "they're in-dispensable, correct?"

The television hanging from the ceiling turned itself suddenly on. There was someone selling record albums. Peter switched it off.

"You wouldn't know about the kids part, yet. You maybe won't ever have kids. But pretty Julie Watson—I do remember her."

In the silence that followed they heard an ambulance siren. It arrived.

When they first met at a party, Julie Watson had complained to him, "It candy-coats reality," about the ending of a movie they both had happened to see. "It's Hollywood's notion of fate," she said, and Peter remembered the phrase. Then reality proved bitter, and the bitterness went deep; with his wife's death all sweetness leached away. Then he had gone to bed at night and gone about his daily rounds feeling hopelessness, not hope. He had behaved, he came to see, like a stunned animal—a sheep before its throat is cut, a chicken on the block . . .

In the next room, doorbells sounded and telephones rang on TV; people laughed. Carts rumbled in the hall. The night shift was starting, the dark closing down; Dr. Julius needed to leave. The patients at the hospice were expecting him, and there was a staff meeting he needed to get to at eight. "I'll look in later on," he said, and when Harley said, "Don't bother, kid, just get some rest," the doctor insisted, "I'm fine."

Still, he lingered at the door. These last weeks things had changed again, and he heard himself whistling at work. He was

feeling light-hearted, high-hearted, and Andrews knew the reason and had engineered it, hadn't he, with his hard hat and his
checkbook and his optimistic conviction that the healer could
be healed . . .

"You're the reason why we moved here," Peter said. "To
Michigan, I mean."

"Yes."

"Were you two very"—he spread his hands—"close?"

"Close?"

"I mean, how well did you know her? I always wanted to ask
you that."

The siren started briefly; then it stopped.

"I was old enough to be her father—hell, I *knew* her father. It
was almost like I *was* her father, really. Me and old Chip Eliot
and others that you never met, we hung around together."

"Julie called you Mr. Wonderful. She admired you a lot. She
never said it, not like that, but she was devoted to her Uncle
Harley."

"Kid stuff," said Andrews, visibly pleased. "But if you're asking why I hired you, why I gave you the job when she wanted a
favor, it's because I was . . ." He shut his eyes an instant, an old
man fighting sleep.

"Are you all right?"

"I'm telling you," said Harley, "pretty Julie kept the faith."

"The *faith?*"

"It's possible," the patient said. "We cared for each other,
okay? Like stepping on my toes at the Lakeview July 4 square
dance, or insisting that I take her out for ice cream or holding
my hand in the movies, letting me beat her at tennis? Well,
that's our little secret."

"Secret?"

Harley put his finger to his lips. "Sssh," he whispered, theatrical. "Took it with her to the grave." He threw himself back at
the pillow, subsiding. "An old man gave her candy, and they ate
it on the porch."

And then he fell asleep.

XIX

IT WAS as though he came alive, as though the years since Julie's death were a long hibernation for Peter, and what he woke to was spring. Things thawed. What had been dark and forbidding and chill now seemed suffused with light. The world had worn a wintry aspect, but it changed. He was embarrassed even to admit this, even to think of the world in such terms or to find himself pretending that nature might mirror his moods. But the embarrassment itself was part of his new wakeful pleasure; he liked feeling foolish, he told himself, and sentimental again. He was a kid with a bright burnished gift, and the gift was called Rebecca, and he couldn't believe his good luck.

She laughed. "It surprises me also," she said.

"Tell me," he asked, "when you arrived in Bellehaven, what were you expecting?"

"Not you."

"Tell me," he urged her.

"Nothing much."

But he was irrepressible. "I can't believe it. I just can't be casual or take it for granted."

Her hand was in his hand. She squeezed it. "Oh, Peter, aren't we lucky."

"Yes. It's like a second chance, a new beginning for me. You just can't imagine."

"I can."

"No, really. I've fallen in . . ."

"Lust," Rebecca said. "You've fallen in lust, darling man."

"That too," he said. "That too."

There was trouble all around him now, yet he found himself whistling at work. There were staff meetings and huddled consultations and press releases and private inquiries and widespread public concern. But it did not concern him at all. It bothered others, not Peter, that reporters and policemen arrived at Trueman-Andrews and took photographs and notes.

There were interviews and visits to the hospice and television news briefs and Channel 7 eyewitness accounts. The deaths were widely noticed and reported on; the *Lakeview Clarion* did a feature on the hospital, and those citizens from Lakeview who played so large a part in it. It upset Trip Conley and Jim Kelly and the rest that hospital procedures were disrupted and lab reports requisitioned and the house staff questioned as to where they had been when. Dr. Julius did not care.

What he cared for was the spring. The birds and blooming dogwood trees and sudden flush of greenery appeared as if they did so for his own particular benefit. The moon rose and traversed the sky, and stars shone expressly for him. He knew, of course, that thirty-four-year-olds are not supposed to be romantic, or to believe as adults what they believed when young. Not everything that matters in the world is mere romance.

Yet it did seem that way. What he thought of was Rebecca, and his chance to be with her at night and see her in the hallways or for a hurried lunch. What counted to Dr. Julius now was how many hours he spent at her side, and how often he could

lie with her and listen to her history and marvel at the great
good luck that brought her to his bed. When they finished making love, or in the lazy intervals, he asked her and she spoke
about herself.

She had had, she told him, the kind of English childhood you
read about in books. There were comedies on television about
her kind of childhood, except it wasn't funny, it was dull. Her
parents were elderly now, but they'd seemed old already when
Rebecca had been young. She was an only child. Her father was
semiretired, and he'd pottered in the garden during the spring-
time and summer and autumn, and in the greenhouse all winter,
making detailed annotations of his plants. He'd paid more attention to them than to her; when he considered his daughter
at all he thought of her, no doubt, as a domestic species of little
interest. At the table if she mentioned something that had happened that afternoon in school he would peer into the soup
tureen or casserole and answer by announcing what transpired
with the roses or the lobelia instead. When they took their Sunday outing it was always to a flower show or horticultural park.

Rebecca had grown used to inattention; it troubled her more
now, remembering, than she'd minded at the time. She spoke
about her solitude, the neighbor's horse she learned to ride, the
coal scuttle where she used to hide and dream of chevaliers ar-
riving in Aston Martins and Bentleys. They would stand before
her window in the moonlight and then pirate her away from
that brick pile she was sequestered in not so much by cruelty as
through someone's inadvertence. She described her sheepdog,
Nana, the room she thought of as a tower cell, the way that she
would braid her hair and pretend she was truly a princess, Ra-
punzel, the long wet afternoons and boarding school and the
aloofness of her family—a judicious disapproval she had mistaken for love.

Her parents had wanted a son. Her father had expected that
he would have a son and heir to help him with the business and
lawn. He used the phrase "son and heir" often, and always with
the implication that the women of his family were inadequate

companions and might have managed things better and it was her, Rebecca's, fault that he'd been disappointed. He complained about the roast, calling it too salty; he said the peas were cold. He called Anthony Eden a namby-pamby ignoramus and Harold Wilson the inevitable offshoot of such ignorance. Edward Heath was a conductor, not prime minister, better suited to waving a baton at nancy boys in evening clothes than dealing with Parliament, surely.

Since Churchill's death there had been anarchy and havoc in the land; that's what her father thought. He'd lived through the dismantling, stage by stage, of the British Empire, the sun that never set now never rising anywhere, and though he had had no role in and therefore could not be blamed for policy, that didn't mean he thought it was correct. Her father wanted no part of it—and neither would have Churchill, he was sure. Then he shifted the topic under discussion to one that more nearly concerned him: his potting shed. The right rear doorpane had cracked. Her mother said she'd noticed it last week.

Rebecca had liked dancing, but at fourteen she gave up. She told Peter how the night of her debut appearance in the school production of *Coppélia* was the night of her first period, and how she'd cried and cried because her tights were bloody and her cramps had hurt so much she fumbled her opening cue. Then she got through the number anyway but fell down in the second act and turned her ankle in the final *pas de deux;* she stopped ballet classes the very next day. When she shot up that summer, with breasts and all the rest of it, she'd felt ashamed. She'd been an ugly duckling, and when Peter said that wasn't possible, how could it be possible, she said I'm not pretending that it's still the case.

Then, smiling, raising her incomparable lips to his, she said, all right, I dare you, I dare you to call me your swan.

My swan, Peter said, and he kissed her and said, there, now watch me become your true prince. What does that mean, asked Rebecca, and he said I was a bullfrog but you've transformed me by your kiss.

Oh please, she said, and he said I wasn't being serious, and she said, reaching for him, please be serious, my prince. You have transformed me—see, see that?—just by your single kiss.

One afternoon she asked him, "You're a purist, aren't you?"

"I believe in what I'm doing, yes."

"A devotee. A zealot."

Peter shook his head.

"When did you have this, this"—she hunted the right word—"conversion? Because of Uncle Harley?"

"No. No more than you did."

"Let me ask you a question," said Rebecca.

"Fine."

"You don't mind my asking?"

"Not at all. Go right ahead."

"And you won't be angry with me?"

Peter smiled. "Why would I be angry?"

"How far are you prepared to go?"

"In which direction?"

"Death."

He frowned. "Explain yourself."

"If an AIDS patient required dialysis, say. If it's clear that without it the patient will die. And if there's no money. Would you counsel six months of dialysis?"

"No."

"And if a baby's brain-dead, would you enjoin its parents from—what do they call it here—pulling the plug?"

He shook his head.

"And if, let's say, a murderer assures you as his doctor he'll go on a rampage again just as soon as he's fully recovered, would you implement recovery?"

"What is this, an interrogation?"

"No. I've only got one question more."

"Then ask it."

"Have you been—what's the polite way to put it?—*facilitating* their departure?"

He turned his face to the wall. Beyond the window lilacs bloomed—purple and lavender and white lilac bushes—profusely.

"I'm trying hard to understand," Rebecca said. "I need to know what's happening and what's in fact at stake."

"At the hospital or hospice?"

"Both. I just can't understand how human life can be so cheap, and also so expensive. You spend hundreds of thousands of dollars in order to rescue a person you've left out on the street. You Americans worry obsessively about what happens at the end and at the start of things. You pass laws about assisted suicide. Abortion. Then everyone ignores the in-between . . ."

Now he rose up on an elbow. He laughed.

"Why are you laughing? What's funny?"

"There's an old song," Peter said. "You probably don't know it. 'Ac*cen*tuate the positive.' " He snapped his fingers to the beat. " 'Eli*mi*nate the negative.' "

She tried to smile.

"And *don't* mess with Mr. In-Between."

Peter's childhood was as foreign to Rebecca as her own must have sounded to him. He talked of touch football and baseball and his classmate from high school who took LSD then killed himself, jumping off a parapet, convinced that he would fly. He talked about growing up after the war, not World War II but Vietnam, with the emotional uncertainty of his whole generation, the guilt of the survivor—not "My country, right or wrong," but "My God, what have we wrought?"

She made herself listen, eyes closed, to his voice and its rough music. He spoke about college and medical school and, later on, his internship. He told her how his parents had believed in education. They thought that if you studied hard enough and worked long hours, hard, you would be judged fairly and squarely and could get ahead. They were fervent in their admiration for the American way.

In Europe their birthright was canceled, because Hitler took his rubber stamp and stamped everyone's passport invalid. Hitler declared Jews valueless; the principal value of the non-Aryan population was what he could melt from their teeth. If they were rich enough, of course, they might be held for ransom, and *Hochbürgerlicher* citizens could be bled for cash and labor, and even the small businessmen might be made to offer tribute until they were bled dry. And then, when there was nothing left to bleed, they could be rendered for soap.

His father used to be a "sunshine man." That was his mother's way of putting it; Frederick Julius had enjoyed a sunny disposition and perpetual high hopes. But during the McCarthy years and then again in Watergate he lost his high good humor and grew anxious and afraid. He saw violence and prejudice and terrorism everywhere, and America no longer seemed the world's best hope. Peter's father wondered if the family should emigrate to Israel; this is the second country we've called home, he said, it's time to consider a third.

He himself had been too small to understand assassination or the loss of hope and growth of rage when President John Kennedy and Martin Luther King and Bobby Kennedy and Malcolm X were killed. He hadn't known what actually was changing but did sense his parents' growing doubt about their newfound land and then their growing anger and then, finally, their fear. They had fled Hitler's Europe only to discover that men who built the atom bomb had also worked for Hitler, and their hero, Roosevelt, was an anti-Semite too. So it had been a narrow thing, that great and shining moment when America entered the war; the FBI might well have been the Gestapo instead . . .

So Peter had been raised, he said, with a sense of what was fleeting and what might perhaps endure. What was fleeting was safety, security; it could be taken from you overnight by those who came to power and sent storm troopers knocking on your door. The trappings of his parents' youth—the ornate furniture and Meissen china and teapots, the ancestral portraits on the walls and Oriental rugs and fine cars waiting at the curb—could vanish overnight. All they had worked for disappeared; the books and musical instruments and albums and chess sets were burned.

But in America you kept what you earned, if you earned it fair and square. That was what his parents thought. They migrated to New York as if it were a refuge for and the last best hope of mankind. In this country, said his parents, there was a premium not so much on privilege as on education; it cannot be overestimated. They urged their only son to work hard and be a doctor, since that profession is always of substantial value to society and properly esteemed.

To be a doctor, said his father, was to have a guaranteed income; to be a doctor, said his mother, was to have people's respect. It was a skill that nobody could take away, the way they could take furniture and teapots and portraits. There were always people dying, always the needy and sick. The powers-that-be cannot tax you on knowledge, nor can they declare invalid the diplomas you have earned. His parents had a touching faith in the title, Doctor; they believed that medicine was a high calling like the rabbinate, and that he had been called.

XX

AT HOME Jim's roof was leaking and it couldn't just be patched. He'd had three bids, each one of them outrageous, each of them worse than the other. The roofers said, we're trimming, Doc, there's no fat in *our* budget and we can't go any lower, we couldn't do it for less. He had hoped to make a difference, to heal the sick and help the poor, but the roof leaked and it rained all month and he ran around with a bucket while his kids were eating bonbons and the puppy chewed his shoe and now that it was house-trained started throwing up. So he lay in bed listening, hearing the rain, or maybe a squirrel skittering across the rooftop or building in the eaves.

What he lived in was a kind of hell: the leaky roof, the screaming kids, the trouble at the hospital, reporters and police. Two detectives made an appointment and arrived at lunch break and asked him questions about the mortality rate at Trueman-Andrews, the deaths of Scott Raposo and Johnny and the rest. They asked about Alice Tucker, and if he remembered her name. They inquired if in his official capacity he noticed anything out of the ordinary or suspicious or if anyone lodged a complaint. There was no evidence, they said, except for anonymous letters and calls, but anyway they had to check it out.

It was paperwork, make-work, a waste of staff time. Captain Harry Lawson and Sergeant William Cutler of the Bellehaven P.D. took notes. They assured him the procedure was routine. When he produced his records they nodded, satisfied; we just need to be sure they're available, it's not a formal investigation, not yet. Sergeant Cutler had his hands full with the drownings in Lake Potawoska; there'd been three drownings off a Chris-Craft, and the driver had been drunk. He told Jim Kelly we wanted to meet you in order to establish acquaintance for the next time, till we meet again; I'm leaving you—he clapped Harry Lawson on the back—in my partner here's capable hands. He's taught me everything I know, there's nothing he don't know.

Then Cutler left and Harry said, you must be asking yourself what's going on and what it's all about. Well, you deserve an answer, and if you've got a coffee I'd be much obliged. He was beefy, heavy-muscled; he tore three packets of sugar across and poured them in his cup, then added a spoonful of powdered milk substitute and stirred the mixture thoughtfully. Some local crazy, he explained, has been sending the newspaper letters, taking credit for killings that aren't necessarily killings or, when he isn't busy taking credit, laying blame.

How many letters have you got, asked Kelly, and Lawson said, three, four. It happens more often than you think, believe me, it's some religious nut. He drank. He smacked his lips and snapped the wooden stir stick in two and said, if you ask me, Doctor, if you want my real opinion there's a Bible up his ass. How do you know it's a *he*, asked the chief resident, and Harry said when you've been in this business as long as I have, Doctor, when you're about to retire you get a feeling in your bones. You can't explain it, maybe, but you know.

Harry rocked back in his chair. He blew on his bifocals and produced a large white handkerchief and polished the lenses meticulously; before I knew you, Harry said, hell, before you was even imagined or *born* I had some room to work in, in this town. And there was real work to do. He sighed. But I've pissed away the last two years just answering the phone, just keeping the customer happy, Bellehaven's finest at your service, you want me to rescue a cat? You want me, maybe, to call the fire department out on this one, lady, asked Lawson in falsetto, and then he imitated the complainant, no, no, I just called to *tell* you, Officer, it's the second time this week. I want you to come over here and arrest the cat's owner, Officer, he's doing it on purpose and I want him put in jail.

Then Lawson drained his coffee cup: You think I need to hear this shit, you think I want to talk about it? The detective sighed, deflating, it's child abuse and bad checks and the perp's missed payments and too many beers at the wheel and crack dealers down on the corner of Madison and Vinewood; it's my bad knee acting up again, and this horseshit every morning where they've got me filing in triplicate. Nowadays there's so much paper it's a wonder we don't drown in it, it keeps me at the desk so much I'm sitting two feet higher from the piles.

He crushed his cup; he tossed it at the wastepaper basket. It missed. Except on Tuesday between coffee and lunch break I get to track down rumors, to read Mr. Anonymous's mash notes to the press and then bring them by the hospital and ask you if it's true.

Penny Lampson showed him a poem. She had been blushing, nearly embarrassed; she said she'd written it for Johnny the night that Johnny died. He said he hadn't known that she wrote poetry, and she said she did it for her own sake only, and in private. But it mattered very much to her and so did he, Jim Kelly, and he should read what she wrote.

The poem went like this:

To my special new friend,
There comes a scene when everything must end.

If only God would give us a reason
Why He makes some of us suffer like an act of treason.
And remember that Jesus did die for our sins
So nobody loses and everyone wins.
The Lord God is preparing for you a wonderful place
Up there above us in celestial space.
Eternally you will be free of pain
With only peace and bliss to gain.
Whatever they told you about getting better
I thought I would tell you again in a letter.
There has been suffering here as we know
So sometimes it really seems safer to go.
And don't be afraid of the place that is warm
Since you're never alone when you walk hand in hand
   through a storm.
Your behavior was always creative and busy,
Now the changes that do happen are hard for your friends to
   see.
Though I've only known you for a few weeks of time,
I feel your fear and despair and pain as though they were
   mine.
You travel before me unto Paradise.
And meeting you there will be nice.

"It's beautiful," he told her.

"No."

"It is," he insisted. "It's beautiful. I wish I could write like that. Say what I feel."

"Do you really like it?" Penny asked him, shyly.

"Oh yes," he said. "Did Johnny see it?"

"No, I never got to share with him. I was planning to. It's one of the reasons I'm sharing with you."

"He would have been flattered," said Kelly. "He would have been honored and grateful."

"I'm writing one for you," she said. "I've been having trouble but I got the first verse ready."

"Will you tell it to me?"

"Soon," she promised. "Not right now. Tonight if we get lucky."

"I don't think I can wait," he said.

"You have to."

"Why?"

"I'll give you a hint," Penny said. "About my first two lines, the ones I've written already, okay?"

"Okay."

"You have to guess. About the first two lines, I mean."

"I'll guess," he promised. "Just give me a clue."

She touched his wrist, then stroked it, and now it was his turn to flush. "What rhymes with pluck and duck?"

He was ass over teakettle crazy about her, head over heels though he knew it was wrong; he felt just like a kid or teenager again. When they met each other in the hallway he went cold, then hot all over; he could have been fifteen. One afternoon at lunch they went to a motel. But Kelly had been worried that the parked car outside their room would be identified as his, and worried that the lunch break wasn't long enough, or that they would page him, using the beeper he'd left on his belt. And he didn't much like, either, how ready she was for a "quickie," since that was what she called it, and how she told him, lying back, oh hurry, lover, hurry. Use it or lose it, she said.

He'd established her on Prozac, since she said she was depressed. One side effect of Prozac in a percentage of users is sexual dysfunction, and he half hoped it worked for Penny; if she needed sex less often he, Kelly, wouldn't mind. But of course he couldn't tell her that and so instead he promised it would stabilize her mood swings and muffle that old biological clock and ease her worried mind. She believed him, she said, absolutely; she batted her eyes and smiled that enthusiastic smile of hers and swallowed two at a time.

In truth Nurse Lampson frightened him, a little, with her matter-of-factness about sex and death. She took off her clothes and spread her legs or sat on the toilet seat wiping herself or talked about Susan Hollister's last wishes (a sausage biscuit, a grave on GreenAcres' hillside two feet higher than her husband's) with an absolute indifference to what he thought of as shame. When he confessed he felt ashamed about what they were doing, she said she never felt that way—well maybe guilty, a little, since if you're born Catholic you're always hooked on sin. You don't divorce the Church, she said, you never can divorce it, you get an annulment maybe or a lifelong separation but you can't get divorced.

"I'm not," he said.

"What?"

"Catholic."

"Then you *could* get divorced," she said. "It wouldn't bother you."

The dinner bell rang: do-re-mi. The hospice had a dining room for those who could sit down.

"Not for that reason," Kelly said. "I don't have to wait for the pope."

"Then what are we waiting for, lover? The last dance?"

"I need some time," he said. "I'm just not ready yet."

She flared at him. Her cheeks went white. "How much?"

"What?"

"Time." The dinner bell repeated its three notes. "How much time were you thinking of?"

He spread his hands.

"A day? A week? A year?"

He shrugged.

"Well, while you're thinking about it, while you're figuring the odds," she said, "why don't you stack these luncheon trays? Why don't you change these sheets?"

So Jim had to make his mind up and figure out which way to go. He could stay at home or move on out and live alone or maybe live with Penny or leave town. The week was long. The work was dull, and what he had to deal with was the bulimic girl next door and the deadbeat motorcyclist who drove into a tree. Lately he brushed up against his mistress in the corridor and went home to his snoring wife and could not fall asleep.

Then Jim Kelly asked himself questions. Why, for example, would a woman with metastatic lung cancer and recurrent laryngeal nerve paralysis develop a tolerance for opiates; why would a 27-gauge butterfly needle placed subcutaneously not have done the trick? He had tried, in sequence, hydromorphone, levorphanol and methodone; he had used placebos with equivalent success. What, for example, was the likelihood that seven hospice patients would die within a week?

So something was up, something wrong. But it wasn't up to *him* to explain to a bored detective on a coffee break that the statistics in Bellehaven were perhaps significant and did indeed bear watching; it wasn't part of his own job description to explain to Harry Lawson that maybe he was right. If he blew the whistle he'd be fired as whistle-blower; Trip Conley would be on his ass so fast it would be grass.

The truth is, Kelly told himself, that he disliked his patients—or at least distrusted them by now. It hadn't been that way to start with; he'd been full of good intentions and the milk of human kindness, so much a cow he'd leaked it out each morning on the ward. Even though it was slave labor, the loans taking half of his paycheck and the IRS a quarter, leaving him with not enough for Margy and the kids and mortgage and a second car, he'd jumped at it: the chance to make a difference in this world.

But do the work he'd done for years and see how far it takes you; see how long you stay in love with medical advance. You tell yourself you *want* to play with this week's toy, the latest technological triumph, and that you'll keep abreast of those who do their medicine in labs or at the bench. In the great forward march of science you're a foot soldier, happily, and happy to join the parade . . .

But what you get are charts and balance sheets and cost analyses and double overtime; what you hear are jokes about why the nurse-practitioners get called physician extenders and how Penny feels about that. What you worry about is bankruptcy and empty beds; what you miss is the news of recovery, and your reward each evening is a fistful of calls to return. In private practice, maybe, there's a chance to know your patients, but here at Trueman-Andrews what they're calling capitation is a way to cut the system off below the knees. What he handled now for workload were a list of faceless faces and an insurer's covered procedures and his interns' fumbling imprecision and Trip Conley's flowchart: *consumers, clientele*. It gets hard to love your neighbor when your neighbor has no name.

And the ones he *could* remember were no bargain either; they were his cross to bear. They came into his office full of questions and complaints. They'd read some self-help manual that recommended snake oil for cancer or garlic for arthritis or preventive surgery for inflammation of the tonsils or maybe just athlete's foot. They wanted every possible procedure and then they questioned the bill. They said, "Doctor, I just hate to bother you," and then they bothered him; they said, "I don't like to call you at home," and then they called him at home.

Trip Conley told a joke. He said, hey, Jim, you'll like this, listen up. It's about an old man and a magic lamp and a genie who arrives to do his bidding. Master, rub my lamp. So the old man says, I've had a happy life, I've got nothing to ask for a favor from a genie except maybe a bit more variety in sex. So what I'd like is a week with the three most exciting women in America, and I don't mean only those centerfold types, I mean the ones with *power* because that's what I find exciting. Master, who do you mean? Why, Tanya Harding, Lorena Bobbit and Hillary Clinton, of course. All right, Master, says the genie, bowing, your wish is my command. And so he returns a week later and the old guy's satisfied, blissed out. He says it was terrific, it was everything I dreamed of, it was just like a dream. Of course, I've got no knees, no cock, and no health insurance . . .

Then Trip laughed. Go figure, he said, and moved on.

*   *   *

Once Penny made him meet her in the Hospitality House. She'd found a key, she told him, from someone who was checking out—the forgetful mother of a salesman with diverticulitis, some old lady with a suitcase and a plane to catch and no time to return the room key to room 36. Nurse Lampson promised the visitor that she herself would take it back, and then she waved the key at him and said I get off at five. How would you like to, Jim, she said, and when he asked her, like to what? she said, get off at five? Then Penny kissed the air; I'll be waiting for you, she announced, just knock three times, Hernando, it'll be our hideaway . . .

So at five o'clock he crossed the street, still wearing scrubs. Peter Julius was in the parking lot, nosing his car through the gate. He waved and did not stop. When Kelly found room 36 and knocked three times he was still puzzling over Julius, what he'd been doing in this place, and when Penny turned to him, her skirt unzipped, her sweater off, he asked her who's Hernando, what was that supposed to mean? It's an old song, she told him, *Knock three times and whisper low*. It comes from *Pajama Game*, a musical, and I'll teach you how to play it, Penny said. Then she led him past the kitchenette and into the bedroom and bed.

The Percodan was kicking in and he felt lazy, distant, but the Prozac didn't have the same effect. It made her even wilder, though he wasn't sure she really came; it made her batter at him, hissing "God, my God," with a glinting urgency that had him—he'd admit it—running scared. And then after they were finished, Nurse Lampson kept the key. She said we might as well make use of it, there's just that English bitch downstairs and those who're passing through. You shouldn't call her that, said Jim, and Penny said why not, does that mean you're fucking her too? Don't *talk* that way, he told her, and she said, oh, right, I'm sorry, Mr. See-No-Evil, Speak-No-Evil, I should wash my mouth with soap . . .

Hell hath no music, he remembered Johnny saying, like that of a woman playing second fiddle. Or maybe it was some TV comedian who said it, but in any case Jim sometimes felt that Penny thought him second best, some sort of consolation prize for the game she played. "Two more today," she told him, "two more old people dead today. There's no point waiting, baby, till we get too sick and old."

XXI

"WELL, HERE we are," said Harley. "Here we all are finally. All present and accounted for."

"Aye aye, sir," Richard Trueman said. He was not amused.

"It's good to see you, Dick."

He nodded. He did not agree. "How are you feeling?"

"Fine. It's only what they call a workup . . ." Andrews lay back in the pillows. He had, it seemed, lost weight.

"Heart trouble?" Trueman asked. "Is that the problem for you now? With me, they say it's prostate . . ."

"We're getting old, Dick, ancient . . ."

There was someone else, he noticed, in the corner of the room. Peter Julius was holding what appeared to be an X ray up against the light; he lowered it, then turned. The doctor wore his uniform: a white jacket and polka-dot bow tie, a stethoscope around his neck, a beeper at his belt.

"He's leaving," Harley Andrews said. "I kept him here till you arrived. He says he has to go."

"I'm late," the doctor said. "A consultation down the hall . . ." and shut the door behind him carefully and left.

Now Trueman sat. The chair seat squeaked. "They treating you okay?"

"Like royalty. Like"—Harley smiled, expansive—"somebody who *owns* the place."

"He's a worker," Richard Trueman said. "That much I'll give him, anyhow."

"Who?"

"Julius."

"The place looks swell." Lifting the arm with the IV attached, the patient waved at the window and, beyond, the slate-roofed hospice. "Looks just the way I hoped it would—a combination, mostly, something old and something new." He dropped his arm. "What's that wedding jingle: 'something borrowed, something blue'?"

"I wouldn't know," said Trueman. "I never heard it said, myself."

"Me either. But of course I wasn't married, not happily the way you were. For how long was it . . . ?"

"Forty years."

"Amazing," Harley said. "And what about your daughter?"

"What about her?"

"Her own happy marriage, I mean. Would you call it happy?"

"Are we here for a meeting, or did I get it wrong? Did you ask me up to admire the view—do you want my opinion on marriage or was there something else?"

Andrews reached across the food tray and into his briefcase and pulled out a leather cigar case and extracted a cigar. "Depends."

"What are you saying, Harley?"

Andrews clamped his lips around the cigar—unlit, in the cellophane—and began to puff.

"On what. Depends on *what*?"

"Trip Conley," Andrews said.

*   *   *

Richard Trueman had believed that Michigan could use another hospital. He'd thought you shouldn't have to travel for medical assistance, but you could be proud of Bellehaven and everything it stood for, and one of the things that it stood for was the right to attend to your health. What's the pursuit of happiness if it excludes the healthy life; which inalienable rights has the Creator endowed us with if not among them the right to the best goddamn care available, and at reasonable cost? We hold these truths, he liked to say, to be self-evident: no taxation without representation, no town without a doctor or church or post office or jail.

So he built Trueman Hospital. He donated the site and arranged the tax abatement and floated the bond issue and ponied up a million five to get the whole thing going. It had been a good deed and a business proposition, an act of two-way charity. And everything worked fine for years and then costs started rising and there were questions about siting and the landfill was declared unsafe and then the regulators came and the unions organized and picketed and struck expensive bargains and the hospital administrator had to resign because he was caught with his pants down and his assistant up on the desk, administering to her a little too particularly, and then he hired his own son-in-law since Trip might as well work for a living.

If it ain't broke, don't fix it; that's what he always said. But lately it was just the other way around, lately it seemed the reverse. The thing he'd planned and built to last was Harley Andrews's plaything now, a place where people entered not to get better but die. They used to walk out on their own two feet and just as soon as their condition stabilized. Now they enroll in a funeral home and what they expect is a coffin.

But a doctor is *supposed* to fix things, isn't he? not stand around and watch them break and have a patent on replacement parts or maybe do some dealing on the side. When you prescribe the drug you're working on, the FDA gets interested; when you say, "This patient needs a heart valve and right here in my pocket I just happen to have the new valve he requires," the patent office damn well better *ought* to get concerned.

For it flies in the face of Our Lord. It's not the American way. It has nothing to do with His precepts; it violates the very con-stitution of America that we should be so busy writing every-thing in triplicate and not just taking a grown man's word and taking his handshake as contract and looking him straight in the eye. Because the billing agencies do everything in triplicate; they itemize and argue and prepare the fatted calf and charge each other premiums until the whole system goes bankrupt. They have overhead so high these days you can't see the roof. And then they raise the roof and haul each other into court and pay each other off.

So all the time behind His back the devil quoted scripture. If he'd known way back then what would happen today he'd never have permitted it; he'd have said to hell with them and built himself a nice profitable racetrack or a casino instead. When Christine was young he would sit by her side; he'd read her the Three Little Pigs and Aesop's fables and Mother Goose rhymes, and just when she'd flutter her blue eyes and start drift-ing off to sleep disaster would arrive. It was like London Bridge in that kids' song, or Joshua razing Jericho: you huff and puff till the windows fall in, till the walls come tumbling down.

And she'd raise her head from the pillow and ask him, Daddy, can you fix it, and he'd say of course I can, don't worry, baby-cakes.

"He's wrecking things," said Harley.
"Who?"
"Your son-in-law. We need to set him free."
So Trueman stood. "It's not my business anymore."
"These hospitals," said Harley. "This top-heavy administra-tion. Why do they have to bother us; why's everyone in every-body else's pocket, why can't they just leave us alone?"
"All right. So what's Trip's problem?"
"You tell me."

"What are you talking about—*set him free?*" There was pressure in his lower back and, trying to relieve it, he pushed at the base of his spine.

"Autonomy, beneficence and justice, that's the legal triple standard, right? Make sure the patient knows what's up and then make sure he or she *desires* it to happen; make sure that what you're doing has been done with good intentions and serves for the general good . . ."

"Are you saying he'll be fired?"

"Except he comes to visit, your president does, and now that I'm a patient here I get to watch him work." Andrews paused to gather air. "Chatting up the patients and the nurses and the house staff, oh, every goddamn person on the floor. And he's got this agenda, this personal program . . ."

"Unlike the rest of us . . ."

Now Harley rose. He pressed a button and came forward in the bed like a fish surfacing. "What's *that* supposed to mean?"

"Just what I said," said Trueman.

"The *program*, pal, is that we leave the staff alone, not meddle with them all the time, not obstruct our Dr. Julius in . . ."

"In?"

"His mission of mercy, remember. His errand in this wilderness. His willingness to help me."

"How? What way does he help you?"

Andrews shut his eyes. "To die."

Richard Trueman shook his head. He shifted his weight on his heels. It was ironic, he wanted to say, how they each had their different reasons but finally they could agree. He'd been planning to remind his son-in-law of their agreement way back when: *forsaking all others, in sickness and health.* Christine was a grown woman, sure, but still and all his little girl, and nothing she could do or say would change how he felt about marriage; in matters of fidelity Trip Conley had been lax. So stand on line, O Faithless One, down at the unemployment office and study the want-ads and wait . . .

He himself was getting up each night and standing at the toilet bowl, dribbling, his stream split in two. It wasn't that he'd put on weight, just that it got moved around, as though what used to belong to his shoulders and arms had gotten tired of the strain and accepted gravity and slumped down past his belt. We all have our own problems, he wanted to tell Harley, and you're getting a new neighbor soon; there's no monopoly on sickness and old age.

Three doctors laid it out for him: the verdict on his prostate had been handed down. The diagnosis was recent, and the biopsy showed well-differentiated cancer—which was, or so they assured him, no particular cause for alarm. In the consulting room they said it was a better prognosis than if he'd had a poorly differentiated, more aggressive cancer. Thank heaven for small favors, Trueman said.

The doctors did not smile. They were careful with him, and they wanted to make sure he understood. Fifty percent of men in their sixties, eighty percent of those in their eighties have prostate cancer when tested, and the natural history of his tumor had yet to be assessed. They could in fact choose to do nothing and then see if things got worse. Radiation was one treatment course, they said. It would cause discomfort; it would have some side effects, but in two out of three such cases, potency can be preserved. On the other hand the tumor would not be completely removed, and some patients—here the urologist paused, checking his file folder—prefer aggressive measures. It should be stressed that the proper treatment course for a condition like this one is at this stage controversial, and would be his call.

Outside, it was raining. An ambulance wailed. On the other hand, the surgeon said, we won't pretend you're a stranger and that we aren't concerned to give you the best possible advice. You're like any other patient, Mr. Trueman, only more so, and we've laid out our options in advance. A radical prostatectomy should be considered. Here the operation, if done properly, will result in impotence, and the psychological effect of impotence is something you must take into account. The doctor with the mustache spread his hands: an inflatable penile implant could be inserted during surgery. But your prostate, on examination, proves only moderately enlarged, and with contained tumors, so a transurethral prostatectomy might be the preferred procedure . . .

"What's that?" asked Richard Trueman, and the surgeon said it's not as serious as it maybe sounds. "Sounds serious enough to me," he said, and now for the first time the doctors smiled. "So it's just the roto-rooter?" Trueman asked. The doctors nodded yes.

XXII

Trip locked himself into his office. He planned to spend the night. At college and in business school all-nighters pulled him through. Certain puzzles had no answers; certain riddles made no sense. But if he focused, he was sure, he could make some sense of this: this was a problem he knew he could solve. So Trip laid it out on yellow paper; he compiled a list.

(A) Mortality is natural.
(B) The deaths are a coincidence. What seems like a pattern is not.
(C) In fact there is a killer.
(D) More than one?
(E) If D, then one or more killer works in the hospital.
(F) Or hospice.
(G) If C, (s)he has access to both.
(H) In which case the deaths are neither natural nor a coincidence. Assisted?
(J) Preventable?

(K) If a murderer is found and charged, what happens to hospital billings?

(I) Lawsuits?

(M) The police? The press?

(N) My job.

All this was clear enough. What he needed to establish next
was access: who had it when and where. The administrative staff,
the doctors and nurses and orderlies and support personnel each
had access to one or the other: of those employed by the hospital
there was a population who worked in the hospice too. If cate-
gory G were true, then this was the crucial subset; on a whim he
added transferred patients, and then Rebecca Forsythe's name,
since she also had access to both.

He fired up his computer. A kind of excitement washed over
him now, a clarity of attention. It was the old displacement and
the mantra's discipline: you close your eyes to see. As though he
had a second self, a shadow presence in the room that would
emerge once summoned, Trip focused on the problem posed:
within this labyrinth lay a way, within this maze a thread . . .

That afternoon he'd visited with Peter Julius. They discussed
the issue of support groups for the families of patients, sensitiv-
ity training, and the billing for transferred accounts from hospital to hospice. At four o'clock the doctor stood. "Can I ask you
one last thing?"

"Yes."

"Is there something I'm doing that you don't approve of?
Some procedure you object to, Trip?"

"What makes you ask that?"

Dr. Julius waited. He studied his hands.

"Well, maybe there's a reason, yes. Just imagine there's a cat
you've, oh, elbowed from the table—then guess how he's going
to feel. About the thing he used to have and what he thinks he's
losing here: control . . ."

*　　*　　*

Control: Trip liked the way he kept and how his partners lost it—the weepers, the screamers, the polite ones swearing shamelessly and then the proud ones begging, stripped of pride. He liked what he learned about women from the way they behaved in the dark. There was nothing else—well, drowning or torture maybe, but he wasn't into drowning—that could teach you so much and so fast. They say a person's life can pass before his eyes and everything you've done comes back in the last minute, so you watch it like a movie while you drown. They say your heart stops beating, briefly, when you sneeze, and also when you come.

Therefore he schooled himself, coming, to think of it as death-in-life, as if every lay-me-down-to-sleep might be the final time. From the first time he had watched himself in mirrors to the last mouth he had photographed he liked display—not so much for what it shows you as for what it strips away. From the moment he first understood how people change without their clothes, how what they're hiding *matters* and you can get their secrets when you get them into bed, Trip understood the game. And everybody played. He *knew* her, says the Bible, and Eve swallowed knowledge when she ate the apple and offered a piece to Adam and then got dressed and left . . .

It wasn't as simple as fucking for money or payment for services rendered, which is how whores behave. It wasn't as simple as toting up scores or doing the arithmetic, a boy-in-the-locker-room boastfulness he'd stopped long ago. No, the satisfaction was *discovery*—how you never knew beforehand what a person would reveal to you when you had your cock or hand inside them and were bearing down. You never knew till you were trying them how they would respond. And *that* was the pleasure a player could take and *that* was the reason he needed to play; sex is a game you can lose, tie or win, and what it takes to win is absolute control.

Which is why Rebecca Forsythe was a problem. No matter how he worked on her she simply turned away. When they first met in London and then again in Chicago and she took him up on Harley's offer it seemed more out of indifference than interest, as though coming to Bellehaven were a thing she would try later on to remember but would most likely forget. There'd been no mastery or rush of risk; nothing he could do or say made any impression at all . . .

So Trip felt like a kid again, outside the kitchen door, saying "Mommy, my throat hurts" and finding Harry Stringfellow naked—or, later, in the Roxy, waiting for his mother to collect him and finding his father instead. Upstairs the professor lay bleeding; upstairs they were taking photographs, but down here where he lived it was empty space and popcorn smells and people taking tickets and waiting in the lobby for the second show.

The computer's Screen-Saver clicked in: purple fish. They chased each other right to left, then back again pinkly, then red right to left. If he had been the sort of man who let himself feel pity, he'd feel self-pity now. He'd spent the best years of his life on other people's business, other people's problems, and now when he could use some help they were telling him go take a walk. He worked his fingers to the bone to keep the boat from rocking, but anyhow it rocked.

The Joint Commission on Accreditation of Healthcare Organizations was slated to visit come fall. By then his operation had to be in apple-pie order again, with all of this forgotten, and everybody taking care of everybody else. He rubbed his eyes. There was a man on a wheel, Trip saw: arms and legs akimbo. And Christine Addison Trueman was part of the picture somehow also: lying in the hospital, surrounded by flowers, wearing perfume and ribbons and brushing her hair but paying no attention to the comfort that he offered, refusing it, turning away. She was cradling the pillow she called their child, keening, crooning soundlessly. "Hush, little baby," she sang.

"Are you happy here?" he'd asked Rebecca that morning.

"Yes."

"I don't get to see you much."

"You're very busy, Trip."

"I told you it would have to be catch-as-catch-can in Belle-haven. But I'm going to Boston on Friday—would you like to come along?"

"And?"

"And," he repeated. He smiled.

"You're kind to ask," Rebecca said. "But it's not a good idea."

"A *good idea*," he echoed her. "What's wrong with it?"

"I have a prior engagement."

"Then break it."

"It's not that simple, Trip. It's with your hospice patients. I promised I'd be there on Friday."

"Reschedule the damn visit. We'll be back on Monday morning."

"No."

He'd grown tired of it anyway: excuses and arrangements and the complicated business of bringing a stranger to town. He was tired of *her* anyway, her snooty English attitudes, her holier-than-thou insistence on what she said were the rules of the game: no cheating during the party and not in your hostess's garden. This has become, he told the fish, more trouble than pleasure, more worry than fun: it was time to let bygones be bygones and then to call it quits.

"You're in trouble, Trip," said Richard Trueman.

"Sir?"

"I made you, I can break you; it's back to the drawing board, friend. There's a thing you promised when you got married, remember—a thing about sickness and health?"

"Excuse me. What?"

"As soon as I get out of here. When we're done with this little procedure . . ."

"Sir?"

"I'm talking to you." The receiver squawked. "Am I *talking* to you?"

"It must be the connection."

"Christ. The phone's not working . . ."

"Yes it is. I hear you," said Trip Conley.

Then there was a shuffling, a shift in his ear and "Daddy's angry," said Christine.

"Yes."

"You've noticed?"

Trip watched the receiver. "I noticed."

"Why is he angry, I wonder?"

"You tell me."

"He doesn't like being fooled with, I think. And now they plan to operate and he's scared, maybe, a little . . ."

"Do you blame him?" Conley asked.

"He thinks you two are fooling him."

"Who?"

"You two."

"And who's the other person?"

"You tell me."

They had it wrong, they misunderstood; he sat in his office alone. For all the talk about consensus and participatory management, it was only in the mirror that he found himself reflected, and one was a sufficiency. He yawned: two more would be too much. And therefore what he witnessed might as well be mirrored images, his own face fading in the dark, his single self enlarging, doubling, *leaking* over into Dr. Julius, one to the other, each from each . . .

"Lawson here."

"Detective Lawson?"

"Speaking."

"It's Trip Conley. From the hospital."

"Right, Mr. Conley. What can I do you for?"

"I've got a problem," said the president. "Well, maybe it isn't a problem. I need you to tell me about it."

"Shoot."

"As it happens, Officer, that's precisely the reason I'm calling. What you said, I mean: shoot. I keep a gun. Or kept it," Trip told the screen of moving fish. "For personal security, you understand, a handgun. Here."

"Where?"

"In the office. Where I'm calling from."

"Okay. It's registered?"

"It is."

"With us?"

"I suppose so," Conley said. "I mean, I bought it in Bellehaven at, what's it called, the Tack and Tackle Shop. A Smith & Wesson .38. It's loaded, I bought it last year."

"Except," said the detective, "you've not told me what the problem is."

"I lost it," Conley said.

"*Lost* it?"

"Well, misplaced it. Can't find the sucker anywhere." Trip bit, on his right hand's index finger, the cuticle. Then he examined the nail. "I keep it in the right front desk drawer, safely. Locked. There was that man in Ann Arbor, remember, the one who wasn't satisfied with his doctor's treatment program. And who walked into the hospital and blew the guy away."

"I remember," Lawson said.

"So I thought I might—well, not *need* it—be glad to have it, understand. Except it isn't here."

"You've looked around? You've asked your staff?"

"I have. I can assure you, Officer. I've put out, what would you call it, an all-points bulletin."

"All right," Detective Lawson said. "Come on down to the station and file us a report."

Trip yawned again; he pulled a second sheet. He positioned it next to the first, under the assumption that there was in fact malfeasance in the hospital and therefore at least one suspect. For the Accreditation Commission, not to mention the police, he needed it all written down. Motive was the question now: who had what motive when? Who stood to profit from what? He kept the motives general, and therefore this list was brief.

(A) Power.
(B) Money.
(C) Revenge.
(D) Self-protection, the fear of discovery.
(E) Faith.

Next Conley made a cup of tea and settled back to look. The screen was bright. He brought up the records of the hospice patients and studied them for patterns: age, gender, attending physician, presenting symptoms, cause of death, and time in the hospice till death. Then he scanned for similarities outside of their medical history—creating categories such as place of birth, profession, insurance agent and religious affiliation. The tea was hot and, when he added Equal, sweet.

He drank. He scrolled through the medical workups and entrance interviews. He cross-referenced them, watching for overlap, hunting for what would come next. Then he turned to Trueman-Andrews and brought up the files of Alice Tucker, Scott Raposo, Harley Andrews, and Scott's lover, Johnny. The hard thing was to concentrate, keeping his mind on the problem at hand, and come up with a plan.

He did; he had a plan.

XXIII

OUTSIDE, THE world was changing; there were calls about
Richard Trueman and Harley Andrews and how both men
would be treated in the hospital at once. There were rumors
that the patients did not get along; would the doctor care to
comment and if not why not? Peter joined discussions as to
whether Andrews could withstand a bypass operation and how
long the surgeon could wait. Richard Trueman had been scheduled for a transurethral prostatectomy that week.

But what mattered was Rebecca, and he saw her every day.
All he wanted was to see her face, to hold her in his arms. It was
how he'd felt with Julie, in the brief bliss of their marriage, but
had kept himself from feeling since her death. If the doctor had
an hour or a cancellation, he called and ran across the avenue
and through the lime-green hallways of what she hated, Hospitality House, and would knock on her door twice, lightly, and
once hard. She would be naked already and watching through
the keyhole to let him in and bolt the door and her hands
would be everywhere instantly—unbuttoning his shirt, unzip-

ping him, pulling at his shoes, his socks, his loosened tie—as needy and eager as he. Then they'd tumble to the floor or chair or sprawl across the turned-back bed and he'd spill himself inside her like a boy.

At night they had more leisure, and she visited his house instead. Sometimes she brought food along and sometimes he would cook for her, but they were rarely hungry, or hungry only for each other with an appetite that fed on satisfaction. They made love in the shower stall and kitchen and his single bed. He was, she said, insatiable, and you make me that way also and isn't it wonderful, darling, and what did we do to deserve it and how did this happen to us?

He pillowed her head on his arm. Rebecca lay beside him, talking, with her clipped English accent and her throaty fluency, her fingers tracing patterns on the sheets. You have to tell me everything, Dr. Julius insisted, you can't leave anything out.

So she told him of her first employment, at an import-export firm in Leadenhall Street. Her supervisor—the nephew of her mother's cousin's neighbor, as it happened, and the son of the firm's managing director—would expose himself routinely to the secretarial staff. At the Christmas party, he took off all his clothes. Then he sent the bowl of eggnog crashing to the floor, and then he lay down on the floor and put his head in the bowl. She would have liked, she said, to invite her parents to the office Christmas party and introduce them formally to that scion of the company they so much hoped she'd marry or, as her father put it, "snare."

She worked in London for two years, and then she spent a year in Brussels, at the firm's European headquarters. The job kept her busy and lonely and she flew home for the holidays to spend a week with her parents. Her father's new bee in his bonnet was the European Community, and he ranted about Maggie Thatcher and how Winston Churchill would be having none of it; old Winnie would know what to do. Those Frogs and Wops and Bolshies, said her father, should all be set to building their famous Chunnel together, and when the project was finished and all the heads of all the governments arrived to cut the ribbon, why Winnie'd just trip the sluice gate and they'd all be swept away. Then he showed her his night-blooming cereus and her mother asked if she was warm enough in Brussels or would like another knitted cap.

She changed her travel plans. She declared an emergency in the office and told her parents that she'd have to leave on the day after Christmas because they expected her, absolutely unexpectedly, at work. Her father nodded, doddering on about Maggie Thatcher and the Frogs and Wops and saying he wasn't surprised. It was a shame, her father said, that Churchill wasn't still around to fix the Sambos and Bolshies and Huns. Rebecca kissed her mother and shook hands with her father and fled, but on Boxing Day there was an enormous snowstorm and she found herself stranded at Heathrow, attempting to depart. The man waiting beside her was Arthur, so that was how they met.

"How old were you?" asked Peter. "When you got engaged, I mean."

"Twenty-two."

"How long was the engagement?"

"The usual," she said. "Six months, to make it seem decent. That way everyone in Dorset could come and admire the plantings and deposit presents and congratulate my parents . . ."

Then she described her marriage—the early and tedious years. She had married, she told Peter, in order to escape, but at least in the beginning marriage meant more of the same: boredom and good manners and a helpless anchored drifting that was called respectability. They acquired a circle of friends. Arthur had associates, and the associates had wives. The truth is, said Rebecca, that before the final, fatal months she'd not much liked her husband. The things he found uproarious seemed silly to her, faintly, and the things he found exciting she thought dull.

It was then her migraine started—or, more exactly, returned. It was the way she'd felt in childhood, as though the room had been suspended just above her head, a band of pain pinching, descending. She felt caught in a tightening vise. He had no idea, she told Peter, how *stultifying* provincial England could be. Its pleasures and its pastimes and its sport were all constrained. She had thought perhaps that Arthur would provide excitement, not constraint; he was eight years her senior and well-off and experienced, and the world she'd begun to explore was one with which he'd been conversant.

That, too, was an expression from her married past. Arthur was always telling her that he had been "conversant" with the opera or Rachmaninoff's virtuoso piano recordings or solid geometry or actuarial tables or Greece. He bought her chocolates and perfume. He furnished her handbags and hats. He treated her as though she were an ornamental acquisition, one which he was pleased to have and display beside the mantel, but which he could replace. Once he brought home an orchid, and the expression with which he set it down on the counter and examined it, lifting the leaves, to see if it had yellow spots or required water or had been properly situated within the pot was so familiar that she felt her headache coming on; it was as if she'd married her father's pale and dreary shadow and not managed to escape.

Yet Arthur had surprised her, over time. He liked to play rummy, for instance, but would cheat at cards. When she caught him at it, the first time, she'd been too surprised to mention it, and then when she mentioned it later, he said, but naturally, Becky, that's the point. Of course one has to cheat. He dressed each morning for the office as though he were only playacting, as though he were an actor and the part he'd been assigned to play was that of a middle-class upwardly mobile official. He was "conversant" with poetry, too, and there had been a sly obliqueness to him that kept her on her guard. When he talked about the family they someday planned to have, the cottage in the Cotswolds they would buy and then improve, when he visited her parents and discussed the Common Market with her father or, with her mother, the lamentable condition of the House of Windsor and the prospect of Prince Charles and Princess Diana ever reconciling, she had had the sense that nothing mattered to him actually, and he was only going through the motions of respectability—as if he'd known that none of it would ever come to pass. He'd known it all along.

Rebecca did not mean by this that Arthur lied about his health; she believed him when he said the doctors surprised him with news. Cancer of the pancreas is not the sort of information that you carry with you unannounced; it must have been a shock. Yet he *had* had a sort of foreknowledge. When he confessed that he had pancreatic cancer that dark afternoon in March, and very much wanted to see the Peloponnese again, and intended to show her the region of the Mani and the Hermes by Praxiteles, when he told her that he fully planned to kill himself with her assistance, and that she should write it down, there'd been a sort of ease to him—almost, a sense of relief. " 'The readiness is all,' " he liked to say. " 'Let be.' "

"He quoted *Hamlet* to you?" Peter asked.

"Yes. That's what I mean by playacting. It's as if he had his lines prepared, and he had rehearsed them."

"I read about that," Peter said. " 'Absent thee from felicity awhile.' I remember you discussed it in *Undiscovered Country*."

"Yes. Let's change the subject. Let's talk about anything else."

"All right." He propped himself up on an elbow. He looked at the window, the three-quarter moon. "I'm glad you had that migraine."

"Yes."

"I'm very glad you chose to stay."

"It was the migraine," Rebecca said, smiling. "Don't flatter yourself."

"I don't," he told her. "Not at all. I just feel so damn lucky."

"Oh, Peter. My beautiful Peter. We're two lost creatures, aren't we?"

"Yes."

"And now," she said, "we're found."

*   *   *

He doubted it. He watched the blue vein beating in her neck. When she lay beneath him, eyes shut, hands clenched, in the very height of pleasure there was pain. While she clung to him, shuddering, moaning, he felt her slip away. He feared she was playacting also, as full of irony as her dead husband, with that self-deprecating and wordy detachment he thought of as British reserve. Each morning when he left for work, he wondered if by afternoon she would have packed and taken the train to Chicago and departed from O'Hare.

While Arthur was dying in London, she said, and for the first weeks afterwards, she made of their bedroom a study. She sat beside him, writing, at her old dressing table, and when he died she continued what felt like dictation. Rebecca had not left the flat except for shopping outings, and then only briefly, furtively, wearing dark glasses and a scarf and Arthur's shapeless macintosh. She would slip around the corner for whatever she needed by way of provisions—food or drink or a new box of typewriter ribbons or a ream of paper. She did not answer the phone. It had not rung often but it frightened her each time.

And then her neighbor Noel coaxed her out of her burrow and into the light. And then the book appeared and she was a celebrity. Her ballet instructor and schoolmates and friends of her husband and parents and the women she'd worked with in Leadenhall Street all remembered or invented an ancient spurious intimacy. They invited her everywhere and wanted her autograph and photograph; the barrage had been incessant, and she needed to get out of town.

But when Rebecca did escape to Wessex or Sussex or East Anglia it was with a driver, on a book tour, and exhausting and no fun. So she had to get out of the country but didn't dare return to Greece, and then she met Trip Conley in London, at a publishing affair, and he had convinced her that the hospice network in America could profit from her presence. Then he underwrote her visit from what seemed his personal checkbook, and—she shrugged her shoulders—what could she do but accept?

For she was tired of publicity and tired to death of repeating herself and tired of attention that was servile or rapacious or, more likely, both. What she wanted was Peter's attention, and she hadn't had enough of it, not by a long chalk, darling, not enough of you this afternoon, and I just can't let you withdraw . . .

He feared it; he felt her withdraw. She apologized, not meaning it, for his lack of sleep. They were responsible adults, said Rebecca, teasing him, and they couldn't just drop everything and lie in bed all week. She mentioned friends in New Orleans and her desire to see the Grand Canyon; she was a tourist, after all, and there must be something better in America than downtown Bellehaven to see. She would visit Old Faithful in Yellowstone Park and watch it spout instead.

Rebecca bought new boots. The boots were beige. It had been their first shopping trip, to Wilkinson's Leather & Shoe Shoppe in the Bellehaven Mall, and she selected this pair. They laced above the ankle: high-heeled, Italian suede. While the salesman went behind the counter to ring up the purchase Rebecca said, "A little thing like this"—she touched Peter's cheek—"how lovely to do it together. How nice to think you chose them. This color, I mean. This particular pair."

Afterwards they went to dinner, appearing in a public place, ordering Vouvray and salmon and swordfish from the grill, holding hands across the table.

"Are we declaring ourselves?" she asked. "Are we coming out of hiding?"

Peter said, "We're going public, yes," and later she came to his house.

Yet even as she whispered that she would not let him leave, not even to work at the hospice, most especially not at the hospice, not for the morning or the endless interval until he might return at lunch, or till nighttime an impossible eternity away— even when she promised this it seemed to Dr. Julius that she was preparing to go.

May 16

To the Editor:

Okay Smartass you didn't believe me. So what happened to those faggots is the question now. With an IV up their nostrils with a needle in their ass, with a nice pine box for Johnny and a urn for the one who wanted cremation—what was his name again?—Scott. And no matter what the President says no matter how many hundreds of thousands of them gather to do their unspeakable buttfuck in Washington it is written that they may not fight this cuntry's wars and AIDS is a scourge on the nation just ask the men who died. The one of them of renal failure HAH. The one of them with what they call Ulcerative Colitis BullSHIT. And too much gin and water since I know whereof I write thus spake the Lord of Hosts, mercy Lawsamercy me. There will be fire and brimstone there will be unspeakable torment forever and ever amen, a creature who is married must stay married, sayeth our Creator and the Father-in-law of us all. Or is it better to burn? I have a lawyer, understand, and he's negotiating at this very minute with some very influential people in New York. And also on the coast, where I have got the ear of influential friends. And an appearance scheduled on Donahue and Oprah and maybe A Current Affair. This is my last letter to you until I read the story. This is your last chance to get the Schoop. If you don't do it and I'm warning you I'll go to the police. And then how will you look.

XXIV

HE WAS perfect, he was wonderful, the best there'd ever been. Rebecca smiled. There was real irony, she knew, in even thinking such a thing or permitting herself to believe it. She could have laughed out loud. Absurdity resides, she knew, not only in private or public behavior but the interaction of the two; the distance between them may well prove ironic. And of the ironies with which an adult grows familiar, the spectacle of passionate infatuation is one of the most comic: how *could* a grown woman behave, she asked herself, as she behaved in his arms? She could remember thinking, not four weeks ago and at grand rounds that morning, how all of these men were absurd.

Trip Conley had been that way, surely, with his athletic expertise and his preening self-awareness, his devotion to the mirror. He was the sort of Narcissus who made the world his pool. Chief Resident Jim Kelly had been that way also, though she had no need to sleep with him in order to find him absurd. With his prickly bantam combativeness and his overweening anxiousness for everyone's approval, Kelly shattered in frustration what he failed to fix. He would have been the sort of child who hammered at his toys. His speech about what doctors should and shouldn't do, what is and isn't possible, which procedures were discretionary and which ones the law enjoined— well, Rebecca had been weary in advance.

So this visit to Bellehaven had come as a surprise. She had had no intention of starting again, and certainly not in Bellehaven, and certainly not now. In the back of her brain a puppet was having hysterics: *eat your heart out, eat your words*. Since Arthur's death she'd had a habit of dismissiveness, and she nearly dismissed Peter too. These great American boy-men; she'd thought him a part of the crew. But she'd been wrong, she told herself, admitting now, burying her head within the circle of his strong left arm, how very wrong she'd been . . .

"One month," he said. "I'm keeping count. A month since you arrived . . ."

"But you were slow about it, darling."

"Yes."

"We wasted whole entire days. You ought to be ashamed."

"I'm sorry. I apologize."

"But aren't you glad you waited? Wasn't it worth waiting for?"

"I waited *years*," he said. "Not days."

"That's sweet," Rebecca said, "you're being sweet," and cradled his head on her breast.

Of such inanity did their conversation consist. There'd been a film she went to with Arthur, in the art theater in Hampstead: a creaky American comedy with a title that must once have been risqué. *Pillow Talk* starred Doris Day and that actor who would die of AIDS; it described a love affair and the titillating nonsense men and women whisper. And it was, Rebecca knew, absurd that she—a more or less successful adult briefly in a foreign town—should whisper titillating nonsense to the pillow now. But that was how she found herself behaving, and she could not help it, no matter how she tried to bring old ironies to bear.

"I'm not," said Peter.

"Not what?"

"Not being, as you put it, sweet."

"That's true enough, then. You're not being sweet."

"I mean it," he said.

"Mean what?"

"It feels like I've waited for years."

Then he rose above her on his knees and kissed her lips and—splendidly, tenderly, brilliantly—took her in his arms.

It was, again, like those last days with Arthur. All night, it seemed, they talked. They were strangers who shared an estrangement, and they clung to each other, explaining. Now nothing was too trivial to learn about, and everything mattered and proved consequential—part of the perfect symmetry, the great skein of coincidence that brought them to this place. She'd learned on March 18 that she would lose a husband, he a wife.

The doctor draped his leg on hers; he stroked her collarbone. There was a Yiddish word, *qvell*. It meant bubble over, overflow, and his mother *qvelled* with pride. For every semester of medical school she would make him come home Friday nights, and spend the night if possible, and always he'd return with a package of cookies and slices of cake and cheese and special jams and his shirts freshly laundered and ironed; always she told him she feared for his health, since a doctor in particular can't afford to neglect his physical appearance or his health or sleep. He was losing too much weight. He was getting too little sleep. Imagine, said his father, what you'd feel like learning tennis from a man who couldn't hit the ball; imagine what you'd do if at the Arthur Murray school the instructor had no sense of rhythm and couldn't dance the tango and had a wooden leg. Well, that's why a doctor has a *particular* obligation to stay healthy, his mother insisted; eat, eat.

Talking, he gestured; he ruffled her hair. There was such a thing as too little attention, he said, but there could also be too much. Since her own parents had been distant and aloof, she would have to take his word for it: the reverse could be equally true. His father was a constant looming presence, with his enthusiasms and his twenty questions at dinner and his business around the corner so he could return home for lunch. And Peter's mother smothered him; she breathed in all the air. His childhood had been filled with expectation and, if he did not meet their expectations, with reproof.

So when he took his internship he took it far away. He had wanted to spend Friday nights some somewhere that wasn't the Bronx. And for a while—he cupped her breast; lightly, he pressed it—he'd planned to be the sort of doctor who made so much money that he could please his parents with a condo, say, in Sarasota or Palm Beach. He could give them a Mercedes with the profits of his surgery or buy them a new Porsche with his consulting fees. But of course they wouldn't want a Mercedes or a Porsche or BMW or any sort of car produced in Germany; of course they wouldn't want to go where old Jews go in quantity, because they would be fearful, once again, of a pogrom. And what they really wanted was for him to heal the poor.

They hadn't liked it, Peter said, that he married a Protestant girl. The word for that was *shiksa*, and it reeked of trouble. They hadn't minded when he went away with blondes or, on occasion, if he introduced his ladyfriends while driving by to Boston or to Montreal. But they did object to marriage; it was asking for trouble to marry a *shiksa* and to mingle passionately with the *goyim*, as he was doing now.

Is that what they call it, asked Rebecca, is this what your parents called passionate mingling? She reached for him—"You think they'd mind?"—and he told her yes, certainly, yes.

"What do you think of Trip Conley?"

"Why?"

"His ability, I mean. His job as Trueman-Andrews's boss."

"I haven't thought about it," Peter said. "You trust him, don't you?"

"No."

He looked down at her, incurious. "I thought you two were friends."

"Not precisely, darling. No."

But she could not bring herself to tell him what their relation was, precisely, and how he brought her here. It felt like infidelity, though she had known Trip first.

"I think he's a fool," Peter said. "If you don't mind me saying so, I believe our boy's a fool."

She touched his ankle. "Why?"

"Because he should have kept you. Shouldn't ever let you go."

So Peter had known all along. Or perhaps Trip had been boastful, or it was obvious in any case; Rebecca did not care. She was not ashamed, exactly, of having found her love among the ruins. It was like that Robert Browning poem Arthur had recited: "Pippa's Song." *God's in his heaven, all's right with the world:* that was the poem's last line.

But if God were in His heaven, then heaven was Bellehaven: a guest suite with green wallpaper and a Gideon Bible in the bedside bureau, or a split-level underfurnished clapboard house that a widower rented windswept streets away. Then Pippa passing by would be a widow, and needy, and on a business trip. Except that she, Rebecca Forsythe, was neither young nor hopeful, nor a heroine of Browning's verse, and all was not right with the world.

She watched television these days in a way she had not done before, wasting the time until Peter returned. There was a CD player also, and sometimes she listened to music: the Mendelssohn he loved. But mostly she watched dance shows and talk shows and comedy hours and sporting events on TV. She knew, by now, more than she ever imagined she'd know about the way Americans behaved when people menaced them with whistles or ran around with basketballs or played a game named Jeopardy! She listened to earnest discussions of abuse and sexual addiction and various forms of dependency and incompatibility and child molestation and the rights of adoptive parents and identical twins who met only in their twenties, having been reunited by accident in a shopping mall. She saw interviews with those who won the lottery or were aided by heroic real-life policemen when they dialed 911. She watched evangelists and exercise shows and something called MTV.

In her room in Hospitality House, awaiting his arrival, Rebecca watched the news. It was rarely good. There was catastrophe everywhere: starvation and genocide and factories being dismantled and threats and counterthreats and deportations and rapes. There was a family of seven dead in Grand Rapids of smoke inhalation; the father smoked in bed. He had been unemployed since the previous November; he was drinking, neighbors said. There was a teenager arrested for selling crack cocaine in Benton Harbor, then robbing a convenience store, then shooting the night clerk and three customers, one fatally.

She read the local trash in newspapers and, in magazines, the national trash. She could not concentrate. Peter would be watched, she feared, and weighed and sacrificed to that voracious demon of publicity that had swallowed her in England and spat her out again. He would be a scapegoat soon. The demon of publicity is insatiable, Rebecca knew; it hungers daily, weekly, for some new victim to describe and, having described, to destroy.

The hospice and the hospital were a "technological killing field"—so claimed the *Lakeview Clarion*. "Kevorkian Disciple Pretending to Be Mercy Killer!" read the Thursday article, though on Friday they described this as a rumor and not established fact. On Saturday there was no article; Trip Conley saw to that. And on television the reporters were more scrupulous or, perhaps, more fearful of a lawsuit; the *Channel 7 Eyewitness News* anchorman raised the question, merely, arching his expressive eyebrows until they approached his toupee.

"What's going on at Trueman-Andrews: coincidence or plot?" he asked. "Should you think twice before you send your loved one there?"

Dr. Julius was mentioned, twice, on Channel 7. He had arrived in Bellehaven, said a reporter, from the Andrews Clinic in Lakeview where Samuel Green had killed himself in that fiery explosion many of our viewers will recall. It was an eyewitness exclusive; we broke the story first.

So she knew with a kind of instinctive conviction that Peter was at risk. She was terrified he would not come or might be detained. And she was eager to the point of panic for the sound of his quick footsteps in the hall, his rat-a-tat-tat at the door. And when her lover did arrive she threw herself upon him. He had survived that morning or that afternoon or night but might not be so lucky *now*, *today*.

The poetry is in the data, as Arthur told her, dying, the art in the flat fact. We live by little detail and not by large abstractions; we believe that our personal story might stand for a general truth.

Rebecca wrote it down. It was *this* the critics praised and *this*, as Noel liked to say, that caused the jolly bells of all those jolly registers to ring. *Death's Kingdom* had been hailed for "its resolute lack of avoidance," its "refusal to seek comfort in the merely representative."

Now Peter Julius became her personal and particular and abstract representative truth. He played the piano for her in the hospice solarium. He had not practiced for some time, and his hands were rusty and fingers thick. The music in his head— Schumann's *Kinderscenen* or Mendelssohn's *Songs Without Words*—was difficult music to make, and Peter started slowly; she listened and approved.

He was Galahad and Lancelot, her knight on a white charger, her frog-prince. He complained that she was joking but she'd never been more serious, she told him, in her life. He had delivered her from bondage like the chevalier she'd dreamed of in her childhood, in her high cold room, staring out the mullioned window at the driveway and the road below, waiting for a Bentley or an Aston Martin to arrive. He would take her in his arms, her *preux chevalier*, and carry her away from this forsaken place. He was everything she wanted, and she told him so.

"I owe you an apology," Rebecca said.

"No."

"Yes," she insisted. "I do. I thought, when we first met, I thought . . ."

But she could not tell him, truly, what she thought. Instead she kissed his palm. She fluttered her lips at his wrist. She raked her fingernails along his chest—gently, so gently he stiffened. Then she dropped her hand, caressing him, and then he entered her. As always, she was ready, wet, and as always she was shocked, unready also, and heard herself as though from a great distance crying out.

He adjusted to her rhythm, she to his. She scissored her legs to his waist. Rebecca closed her eyes. It was happening, again; it was the temple at Kranae and the shabby lighthouse and her doomed implacable husband in the hotel room in Gytheion, and then in London, in their bed; it was what she felt for Arthur when he died. As though from a great distance, she heard herself whispering, "Love."

Book III

I

THE PATIENT rested easily and was not in pain. The prostatectomy had been a success. A Foley catheter was put in place, and
the drainage from the bladder flowed correctly. The patient's
vital signs were good, his condition stable, and Penny Lampson
would remember and tell Jim Kelly later that when she passed
him on his way out of the operating theater his eyes were open,
blinking, and he smiled.

Richard Trueman spent three hours after surgery in the recovery
room. Postoperative bleeding had been well controlled. There
were other bodies in the room, and the low hum and clatter of machinery to listen to, and for some time he watched the flickering
illumination and shadow-play along the walls. The walls were, he
decided, white. Shapes drifted past him, hovering, then disappeared. The respirator to his left sounded like Ezio Pinza in *South
Pacific*; its voice was deep and sonorous. Except the record had a
scratch and kept repeating, burbling "Some Enchanted Evening"
in his ear: "You may *see* a . . . you may *see* a . . . you may *see* a . . ."

"Stranger," he wanted to say.

Where they wheeled him on the gurney the hall clock read 7:15. A rear wheel of the transport squeaked; it needed oil.

"Have yourself a *fine* night," someone said. "Take care of yourself, darlin', hear?"

The elevator door was yellow and the room door green. His room had *R. Trout* on the door. This precaution was unnecessary, Trueman had protested when they told him how to register the night before. No one knew him any longer or, if they knew him, cared. But the hospital administrator had been adamant; he wanted no more publicity. "You're a big fish," he insisted. "And this is a small pond."

The floor supervisor agreed: this was a private not a public matter, and best left that way. Trout's daughter and her husband came to call.

They signed in at 9:22. Permissible visitors included the patient's surgeon, his anesthesiologist, the urologist and his assistant, the chief resident, Dr. Peter Julius, the referring physician, the nursing staff, Christine Addision Trueman, three cousins, a sister-in-law. The list did not include Trip Conley, but that was a mistake. That was what Trip Conley said when the hall monitor showed him the sheet.

Then the president smiled and held out his hand and without looking at the monitor's laminated ID called him Tim by name.

"Well, I suppose so," the hall monitor said. "If you want to, Mr. Conley. You two just go on in."

"We thank you," Conley said.

And in any case, as Tim repeated next morning, it wasn't up to *him* to tell the head honcho of the whole fucking place which doors were off limits when. You obey *that* kind of order and you're standing in the street.

Room 238 was single, opposite the supply station and the stairwell at hall's end. They let themselves in and sat down. There was only one visitor's chair. The patient appeared unresponsive; when his daughter said how well he looked he did not bother to answer. His left eye was closed.

Richard Trueman's mouth was dry. He lay in what he saw as a spotlit darkness, and the mattress raised him weightlessly when he began to sink. The air itself was heavy with the weight of expectation, and he wanted water, and he moved his mouth. There were ice chips in a pitcher, by the bed. He ran his tongue around the inside of his lip, but his visitors paid no attention; they had the sheen of health about them, the abrupt excitability of people in their prime.

"You need to rest," his daughter said.

Trueman made no answer.

"You'll feel much better in the morning."

"Right," he managed.

"Get some sleep." She kissed him where he lay. "I'll see you first thing in the morning."

"Me too," announced Trip Conley. "I'll be by."

They signed out at 9:46.

Discomfort was the word for it, not pain. From time to time a nurse appeared and something was added or taken away, and once he saw a plastic bag of his own urine: red. That deep-pitched baritone, that growling bass subsided, the monitor blinking and Demerol dripping: *on, on.*

He was, he knew, supposed to settle something, *handle* it, but he could not quite remember what he had promised to do. So instead he remembered a stranger, a you may *see* a, you may *see* a *stranger* across a crowded room. The first time that he noticed her, Elizabeth was wearing slacks; she had been holding peaches and studying a can of soup and reading the label intently, as if she could already taste the food. There was a grumpy thin man who owned the store and a cheerful fat woman he'd married: Setwell, Stewell, *Sewell's,* that was it . . .

Trueman's mind was wandering, and he knew it even as he wandered: the soup had been split pea and ham. The shadows on the wall were intricate: a mirror and the bathroom light and jacket that hung from the door. There were his father, his mother, his twelve-year-old basset hound Red. On a pillow stuffed with cedar shavings, his dog slept by the bed; Red barked and twitched and snuffled in his sleep. There were the days he drove Christine to school and later on to piano lessons, the years he watched her step so gallantly, so bravely through the stable gate, and drove away, not wanting to, but because it made her nervous and then angry if he stayed. There was the morning he decided not to become a farmer and the night his father—not complaining, saying nothing, saying maybe "Pass the butter," or "Could I have some more of them pickles, Mother?"—fell into the stew.

Mine enemy grows older. Trueman slept. There were no complications; the prostatic bed would heal. When the door to 238 slid open it did not figure in his dream: a woman and a pink-and-purple-striped umbrella like Elizabeth's and, for some reason that he could not but would understand in a moment, *be right there*, a pair of hunting springer spaniels and then Trip Conley smiling at him, wiping his face with a leaf. They were drinking from a flask. It was an act of charity, a gesture of concern—so why should it seem fearsome, a swift avenging angel in the case of harm, *Yea, though I walk*, and wherefore in this darkened place the sudden shocked impulse to scream?

The shadow Trueman lay beneath was no shadow he could see. The noise was nothing he could hear nor steady ticking of the clock a form of interruption. In the updraft from the ventilation unit, a white curtain billowed. The patient did not wake. The clock read 11:14.

It was a simple matter to remove the IV bottle and add heparin in quantity, then connect the tubing once again and wipe the IV bottle and the tubing clean. What had oozed around the catheter became a crimson stream. When they found him in the morning—the blanket carefully arranged, the room with no sign of a struggle, the *No Visitors* sign intact at the door—it was important that the sheets be wet. Since Richard Trueman had complained so loudly and so often that the hospital was bleeding cash, that the money he invested had been hemorrhaging, drained away, it was important that the patient bleed to death.

II

I WILL look upon him who shall have taught me this Art even as one of my parents. I will share my substance with him, and I will supply his necessities, if he be in need. I will regard his offspring even as my own brethren, and I will teach them this Art, if they would learn it, without fee or covenant. I will impart this Art by precept, by lecture, and by every mode of teaching, not only to my own sons but to the sons of him who has taught me, and to disciples bound by covenant and oath, according to the Law of Medicine.

The regimen I adopt shall be for the benefit of my patients according to my ability and judgment, and not for their hurt or for any wrong. I will give no deadly drug to any, though it be asked of me, nor will I counsel such, and especially I will not aid a woman to procure abortion. Whatsoever house I enter, there will I go for the benefit of the sick, refraining from all wrongdoing or corruption, and especially of any act of seduction, of male or female, of bond or free. Whatsoever things I see or hear concerning the life of men, in my attendance on the sick or even apart therefrom, which ought not to be *noised abroad, I will keep silence thereon, counting such things to be as sacred secrets.*

Annabelle-Mae Simmons could not speak. She blinked her answers instead. One blink meant "Yes," two "No." She could signify agreement also by nodding or shaking her head.

"How are we feeling this morning?" asked Penny.

The patient made no answer.

"Fine?"

Annabelle-Mae shook her head.

"Do you want some breakfast?"

Twice, she blinked.

"A nice bath, maybe? Cereal?"

She blinked.

"I'll fix it for you. Won't be a sec."

Annabelle-Mae nodded.

"Let's get you to the window. It's a nice morning," Penny said. "They say it might rain later, but it's nice out there right now."

She shut her eyes.

"What else is new?" said Penny. "About the rain, I mean. The fact that it's going to rain."

Four times, she blinked.

"That 'Great gettin' up morning,' am I right?" Nurse Lampson said. "Rise and *shine*."

The clock read 8:15.

"Except I'll need some help from you. Some cooperation, right? At the count of three."

Penny positioned her left arm beneath the patient's back, then prepared to lift and roll. "Who's counting with me here, who's ready to *assist*?" she asked. "And *one*-and *two*-and *three*."

Annabelle-Mae was blinking rapidly. She tried to raise her arms. She battered at the air.

"*Up* we go," said Penny. "Thatagirl."

She bundled the old woman into the chair. She wheeled it to the window. "You're looking fine. Tip-top."

The patient stared.

"What we have is oatmeal." Penny bent to change the sheets. "And when you take your pills this morning do you want water or juice?"

Trip was playing solitaire. He laid out the cards in ranked rows. It wasn't serious cheating, mostly a matter of slipping the six or doubling on a king or working the deck for a fourth time, though the game should have been over with a third. Since losing is a waste of time, he did not let himself lose.

This morning he had done his Stairmaster and Exercycle and Nautilus and then, as on every other morning, showered and drove off to work but by the time he reached the office all hell had broken loose. Martha was standing by the fax, holding tear sheets and a coffee cup and looking like the sky had fallen in. He asked her, "What's wrong, Chicken Little?" and she said it wasn't a joke. She gave him the news about Trueman and he hurried to the second floor and supervised the cleaning up, then turned around and headed home and delivered the verdict and the personal effects—the watch, the wallet, the framed photo of Elizabeth—in person.

Christine reached for her Valium. There was a corked bottle of Cabernet Sauvignon by the sink and, even at that hour, she took the pills with wine. When he asked her to go easy, please, she looked at him with that glazed dismissive absolute indifference of hers and said, "Oh, really? Why?"

So he kept himself busy with details, greeting the neighbors and family and the members of the Rotary who had heard about the death at lunch, right after the local announcements and before they sang "God Bless America"; Trip stayed home all afternoon. He prepared the news release and the obituary notice and only when he'd been assured that his wife would be well taken care of and was properly sedated did he return to the office. There would be explanations to make.

Richard Trueman's treatment plan would have to be assessed. There would be an investigation, and he'd do what the Board instructed; he would offer to resign. Then he would accept their refusal, their statement of absolute confidence; he'd say that he was grateful for their trust in him, moved by their confidence, and that he wasn't a quitter and would see this project through. The death of each individual was a great personal tragedy, of course, but Trueman-Andrews Hospital would continue nevertheless. We must not confuse a cause with its proponent or the doer with the deed; we must not allow ourselves to be discouraged in our mission of general mercy or distracted from the task. The matter of the hospice must also be addressed.

Trip slapped the nine of clubs beneath the ten of diamonds, and lifted those two cards and dropped them on the jack of spades and hunted up the queen.

"*Clarion.*"

"Is this the *Lakeview Clarion?*"

"Mm-mn. Which department did you want? Subscriptions? Community calendar?"

"Editorial. I need to talk to a reporter, please."

"Hold on."

Then there was a ringing sound and then the voice changed. "Editorial."

"Hello. Have I got a story for *you*, friend."

"Excuse me? Who's this calling?"

"A feature story. Scoop. Isn't that what you characters call it? A *scoop*."

"Who is this? What's your name?"

"No one who wants to be quoted. But let me ask you something."

"Right."

"Am I bothering you, maybe? Wasting your valuable time?"

"I'll give you one more minute, I don't take anonymous callers. If you've got something to tell me, then tell it for ascription."

"Well, take a look at Trueman-Andrews. That hospital up in Bellehaven."

"Trueman-Andrews?"

"You need me to spell it? T-R-U—"

"No. I need you to tell me why bother."

"Remember Dr. Julius?"

"Can't say as I do. Sorry. No."

"Dr. *Peter* Julius? Kevorkian's kid brother."

"What?"

"Okay. Pretend you're Dr. Julius."

"Why should I?"

"Because I'll hang up otherwise. Pretend I'm calling in for help."

"Two minutes. That's what I'll give you, two minutes."

"Dr. Julius?" The voice was high. "Oh, Dr. *Julius?*"

"If you say so. Shoot."

"I need assistance, Doctor."

"Why?"

"*I want to die.*"

"Now hold on. Just a minute . . ."

But there was only a dial tone; the phone had been hung up.

Rebecca wrote a letter.

Darling Noel,

I find myself in Bellehaven, Michigan, and it's the strangest place. Don't ask me why I'm here. It's an hour from anywhere, the middle of nowhere, and it looks rather as though they dropped Liverpool on the Salisbury Plain. Or perhaps Newcastle directly in the center of the Sussex Downs. And then all around the outskirts planted corn. There's a hospital I'm visiting, with an inpatient hospice attached, and many warring factions and alarums and excursions; they pretend that you're in Disneyland—or is it Disney World?—where Death is just the ticket, a Magic Kingdom Carpet Ride. It makes no sense at all.

I'm having an extraordinary time of it out here in the Wild West. Well it's not precisely the Wild West, at least not in terms of America, but it must have seemed so to Buffalo Bill or Kit Carson or whoever settled the region—the French, perhaps, canoeing down from the

Great Lakes. I'm a little bit embarrassed to admit this to you, actually, but I seem to be seeing a doctor. And it's serious. Not in terms of my physical health, don't worry, I'm healthy as a horse. And rather disgustingly happy. Because Peter Julius—you'll meet him soon, I hope—has brought me back again from thinking it's all over and that there's no point.

That's the point of this letter, of course. You warned me eighteen months ago that I would take a year or two to sort my way through— the whole business of Arthur and the books and the celebrity—and you were prophetic, as usual; I'm halfway through the second year and have, I think, sorted it out. I've doffed my widow's weeds. It's over now, it's Goodbye to All That. Or 'Good riddance to bad rubbish,' as we used to say in school.

Wise one, you'll have to bear with me; I'm giddy and hopeful and not in the slightest inclined to sit upon the ground and tell sad stories, or to produce Volume Three. He's good for me, my doctor is, he makes me want to live. Not write. Which as you should know better than anyone is a departure for your friend. Who's happy, happy happy and hopes the same for you—how's Mopsy, by the way, still chewing her way through the curtain?—and sends you her very best wishes and pleads for contractual forgiveness. Or, if not forgiveness, delay . . .

More soon. These lines seem the most I can manage; I've gotten stupid and tongue-tied and can't seem to concentrate and may not send this letter; it may be a Letter Not Sent. I'll introduce you two, I promise, and then you'll understand. Hugs.

R.

So now, Trip Conley told the staff at their 5:30 meeting, there'd be some explaining to do. It has been—Trip rubbed his eyes, he ran his hand across his cheeks—as most of you are well aware a very damn difficult day. At some point late last night, or early this morning, he couldn't be sure, his father-in-law Richard Trueman expired. The founder of their hospital and ex-chairman of the Board had succumbed to postoperative complications from elective surgery, and it was a great shock as well as shame.

There would have to be some cleaning up, some form of damage control. He wasn't speaking, understand, about personal damage or personal grief, he was talking about public trust. It's the one indispensable thing. It's hard to pinpoint maybe, unreliable as hell—but with it you've got everything and without it you're nowhere at all. What happened to Dick Trueman was inevitable, maybe; at this point in the procedure, Trip was assigning no blame. With Harley Andrews down the hall (and that midnight pileup on Route 94 where the tractor-trailer jackknifed and the E.R. working overtime on seven new arrivals) they'd been shorthanded anyhow, and nobody could have predicted where the patient would hemorrhage when. As the deceased himself liked to observe, Let Him Who Is Without Sin Amongst You—that was a favorite saying of Dick's, and if we've heard him say it once we've heard it all a hundred times—Cast the First Stone.

It's the old joke and old story: If I owe you twenty dollars, that's no problem. If I owe you twenty thousand dollars, that's my problem, and I need to pay it off. But if I owe you twenty million, why it's *your* problem, sucker, and you'd best help me out. Because we're talking about family in the extended sense, and therefore we share in the loss. More to the point, perhaps, we learn from old mistakes and consequently can avoid them in the future; we capitalize on what we've learned and have the opportunity to invest anew.

He paused. He shot his cuffs. He gazed at the conference table as if there were an answer hidden in the waxed wood's patina, the polished mahogany under his palm; he sighed. But I don't have to tell you, do I, we have a problem, folks. There will be action to take and announce; the president of Trueman-Andrews is responsible for what happens in both hospital and hospice and must be personally accountable to the Executive Committee and in the court of public opinion: the buck stops here, Trip said. *Horseshit*, he told himself. *Crap*. So he was terminating forthwith the practice of open access; he wanted it to stop. He would encourage those members of the staff who wished to use their sick leave, or vacation days; he would guarantee there'd be no loss of job security or penalty attached. He would suggest to their distinguished visitor from England that her visit should hereafter cease.

To signal the meeting's completion, Trip stood; he himself would spearhead the investigation into hospital staff procedure, and he expected each and every one of them to help.

"Dr. Kelly?"

"Speaking."

"Dr. Kelly, this is Detective Lawson calling. Harry. Would you mind if we ask you some questions?"

"We?"

"You remember, Doctor, I'm the guy with the notepad— Bellehaven P.D. And we just got another letter and I need something explained to me. For clarification, okay?"

Jim had been expecting this. "Okay. What can I tell you?"

"You could inform us, for starters, what drugs they use there in the hospice. The kind you call depressants; does that mean you get depressed? Is that the same as *downers? tranquilizers?*"

"More or less. In layman's terms."

"So could you tell me their names?"

"Depends."

"On what?"

"How much you want to know," he said. "There are different brands in different countries; in Italy, for instance, what we call Seconal is Immenox, in Switzerland Dormona or Vesperax; Darvon is known as Abalgin in Denmark and Antalvic in France. Demerol in Germany's Dolantin and Dilaudid in Canada's called Pentagone; you have to know what to get where . . ."

"Well, what are the generic kinds?" Captain Lawson asked. "Of downers, if you know their names . . ."

So he ran through the litany: *amobarbital, butabarbital, secbutobarbitone, codeine, diazepam, flurazepam, chloral hydrate, hydro-*

morphone, meprobamate, methyprylon, meperidine, methadone, morphine, orphenadrine, phenobarbital, secobarbital, quinalbarbitone, propoxyphene, pentobarbital . . .

"You're an expert," Lawson said.

"Not really, no. It's part of my job. And I used to be a pharmacist."

"Your favorite part?" Lawson asked.

Jim Kelly halved the distance from the telephone to the receiver, and then he halved it again.

From this north corner of his office Dr. Julius could see the hospital and its obstetrics ward. When babies were delivered and the rooms were lit at night he liked to watch the mothers, the green sheets and the delivery table and the delivery room. After each successful birth the nurses and the attending physicians, always, paused at the window and, facing the hospice, held up the new arrival so that those who were dying might see. It continues, they seemed to be saying, it does continue: life.

Trip checked his watch and called Christine and when she did not answer told his own voice on the tape he would be running late. She should start dinner without him; he'd join her when he could. Join *them* was more like it, *everyone*; the whole house was crawling with guests. Every Trueman in the county was offering condolences and sitting in his living room and staring out over the golf course and drinking his juice and his Scotch. In the middle of his message a relative picked up the phone—Lavinia, Aunt Laverne?—and when Trip asked "How is she?" the woman answered "Asleep."

"Okay," he said. "That's fine, that's good, I'll finish things up at the office and then I'll hurry home."

"Don't worry," Lavinia said.

Or maybe she told him don't *hurry*; he needn't hurry home. There was a whistling in his ear, and it was hard to hear. So Trip forced himself to focus, taking calls and making calls and gathering his energy for the assault to come. His action had the

logic, the pure sequential continuity of solitaire: one move engendered the next. He wrote a letter, folded it, and put it in his
pocket. It was eight o'clock.

The person who came to his office was pushing a vacuum
cleaner, with its high hysterical drone. Outside, the cleaning
lady trailed a mop. There was a tattooed janitor with a wagon
full of trash.

When the Emperor puts on his clothes, what exactly does he
wear and who does the dressing and what precisely happens to
the boy who blows the whistle?—it's an interesting problem.
Conley yawned. When the Emperor puts on his clothes, the citizens stop watching; it's business as usual and everyone is satisfied and soon enough the crowd disperses and goes home. A
grateful populace applauds and falls asleep.

III

IF YOU come right down to it, Harley was prepared; he'd been around the track a time or ten and had nothing to complain about and had made his peace. *Now I lay my burden down. Now I ease my worried mind.* For this was what he wanted: *soft focus, a slow fade.* He had memories to keep him happy where he lay, and they were playing his own private movie on the wide white screen. It was a silent movie, like the early ones he went to, and there were instruments—a player piano, an accordion. So it was just the way it used to be, a ticket booth and all that tinkly music in the hall, with upholstered seats for viewing comfort, and there would be popcorn and soda for sale. His friends sat all around him as if they were at school again, out double-, *triple*-dating, and a couple in the back row whose names he couldn't quite remember—Jim and Betty? Billy?—were, what was the word for it? spooning: *J. Harley Andrews, this is your life!*

Some of it was black-and-white, so he watched the trailer first. Not that he himself was all that old or born to silent movies—but it did feel that way these evenings in the hospital;

he couldn't always understand what the announcer was saying, and the video quality was second-rate. Flickering, faded, the numbers ran backwards: *nine, seven, six, five, three*. Now suddenly he saw the picture of his mother's ankle, then her thigh, the varicose veins protruding, the sieve and sand shovel and plastic bucket he used to use at the beach. There was a beach ball too. He was building a castle and digging a moat, working till dinnertime, till the loud gong, and the water filled and swirled brownly through but did not flood his moat, and the drawbridge was a challenge and the tide would be high at 5:30 so he had to concentrate.

Except it was an album, not a movie, and some of it was torn across: the part about going to bed by himself, the part about being upstairs. *Do I have to?* he asked them, *yes yes*. Harley climbed the steps reluctantly, haltingly, taking his time, or as much time as he dared to, taking comfort from the chatter of his parents in the kitchen or, if his uncle was in town, the laughter in the living room, the clink and scrape of dishes while he drifted off to sleep. Next he remembered seventh grade—the blackboard, the coatroom, the knife they used for mumblety-peg and how you have to twist your wrist to go around the world. Then there was archery also, a dietitian called Miss Brock who insisted on broccoli spears and then broccoli soup every week, and wore a wig, and tuna fish salad on Friday for the Catholics at school.

"What's going on?"

At morning recess he could hear them in the hall. "What's *happening?*"

"Room 238. Trout."

"Trueman?"

There had been bells and whistles. Miss Brock was serving broccoli. She was gutting trout.

"A reflux . . ."

"From the catheter?"

"Blood from the Foley all over the floor . . ."

J. Harley Andrews, Jr., heard it all: Sweet dreams, my darling boy. And while he laid him down to sleep he could remember fuss and perturbation in the corridor, the racket of employment, framed dollar bills above the drugstore counter, the motto in needlepoint *Waste Not, Want Not*, and then for some reason a baseball game also where he missed a ground ball and looked up to see his father, to try to explain that the ball hit a rock. That was why the bounce went crazy and it wasn't his fault, really, *really*, the projector malfunctioning, stuttering, and he hated baseball anyway and wanted to go home . . .

But his father had his hand on their neighbor Betty Eldredge's knee and paid him no attention and was turned the other way, *so that was that*. And then Betty Eldredge came to their kitchen and pretended nothing happened and they were all great friends, weren't they, but there was nothing for Harley to answer and nothing left to say. Instead his father's mistress sat with her great friend his mother—whom even then she was betraying, had been planning to betray—as if she wasn't planning to and wouldn't disappear next week forever with his father, heading west, sending letters, money orders, postcards from Niagara Falls or the Garden of the Gods or Bryce Canyon all the way out to the Golden Gate Bridge. And then she bent her bobbed head down to swallow the hot sweet tea, slurping, showing her teeth, her long pink tongue, explaining things to Harley as if he could be fooled or maybe bribed. She was saying who do you like in the World Series, and what do you want for your birthday, big boy, and don't you just adore a lump of sugar in your hot tea, hon, *cat got your tongue?* But he had refused to answer and he hated Betty Eldredge till that hatred modulated to distrust and then disdain and then became a form of general contagion.

Therefore he turned the page. He leafed past childish things. *Christopher Robin went down there with Alice*, and something in the hospital was, or so the sign announced, *Temporarily Out of Order*. They were changing to the night shift, Harley knew, and what was the rhyme again? *Buckingham Palace*. Like that bridge across the peculiar river and into the troubled roiled water it came falling, *tumbling* down.

But he himself was rising, gazing down upon the planet from the cockpit of the Lear. His captain invited him forward and— past the little blinking lights, the dials and gauges and intricate embellishments of all such bright modernity—out the window of the airplane he saw clouds like peaks of cotton that were in- corporeal, the very *stuff* of paradise above which their engine roared, soared. And there were no distractions, nothing petty or importunate, just the wings beneath him glinting and the pres- ence of the past. Oh it's wonderful, said Harley, I have never been so happy, look, the Great Wall of China, look there . . .

Therefore he rolled his eyes. He could accomplish this. If the patient cannot blink he may require a lubricating agent, an at- tendant with Murine; without a blinking reflex the patient will go blind. *Would you like to make a call? If you'd like to make a call . . .*

Yet in Technicolor nonetheless J. Harley Andrews, Jr. (*So what's it stand for, Jimmy? Jack? No, it's only an initial, J., that's the thing it stands for, simply the thing itself . . .*) could *see* the maroon Buick Roadmaster, the black leather seats, the oil pan he cracked on that dirt track near Auburn while driving to some football game because it was autumn—or why else would he have been there, on what fool's errand wearing his father's rac- coon coat and brandishing his silver flask and singing "Boola- Boola," why otherwise would sugar maples and the oak trees and the copper beech be part of the memory, the whiff of wood- smoke somewhere also, and crab apples at his feet? He could in- hale the vinegar, their sweet spoiled acrid wine.

So it must have been a football game with his friends beside him, cheering—but who they were or why they were with him had gone out of focus, forgotten. And then he closed his eyes again and watched a mechanic in coveralls shaking his head, wiping his palms on his pants, the car gliding noiselessly into extinction, the man's red curls beneath his cap and the ancient, hand-cranked lift. In the edges of his vision, there was snow. But that wasn't likely, was it?—no, he told himself, that couldn't be possible, not in October, not in Auburn. Nonetheless, the snow. For it *had* been a hill where his old Buick died, the engine just seizing up, useless, and a farm full of Christmas trees, Scotch pine, white pine, Austrian pine. He could remember getting out and heading for a farmhouse and what he hoped might be a telephone, with a girl in a tire-swing strung to an elm, rocking, saying nothing, a strawberry mark on her cheek. Dogs barked. Up past the barn, in the pasture, cows were watching them, incurious. A guernsey took a piss. His friends were laughing, slapping the fenders, writing *WASH ME* in the road dust on the hood.

So that was the end of the Roadmaster and the beginning of his Oldsmobiles—a midnight-blue 76, a Rocket 88, a white Super 88 convertible, a two-tone 98, a dark green Toronado—and then for no particular reason, or none that he could follow, he was old and sick of driving and other people took the wheel and clicked their heels and tipped their caps and inquired of him, "Where to, sir?" while they shut the limousine door. How many hundreds and thousands of miles, how many millions finally, can a person run around in Oldsmobiles and not end up weary, how often in the private plane before the mighty mountain Himavant and its glorious ascension now, today . . .

"Sleepy, are we?" Harley heard.

"Is he sleeping?"

"A transient ischemic attack . . ."

"Eighty-one over sixty-three."

"*Hike* . . ."

"An embolus dislodged in the procedure . . ."

"How do you . . . ?"

"Fine, it's fine. Fine, fine."

"Your blue-eyed boy . . ."

First it was spring then summer and he watched the kids in Lakeview, swimming, playing volleyball or tennis, and then there were the years when everything he touched was gold, so that they called him Midas and asked his opinion and sought his advice. And next they started naming him to—seventeen by last count, or was it nineteen? he'd stopped counting—Boards, since one such position leads to another, one such appointment the next, and brought him his coffee in white china cups, and placed Perrier on long corporate tables, the polished mahogany surface of things. They were deferential, circumspect, they were saying here's the balance sheet for your inspection, the prospectus, the information you requested, sir, the hostile bid, the takeover investment plan, its dividend, the illustrated chart of transferred capital, and from their numbered accounts in Geneva, Zurich, Lichtenstein, the Bahamas, from their gleaming briefcases these gentlemen extracted private offerings on the float, their leveraged buyouts, the stock split, the travel arrangements, the hedge fund, his heart, his beating heart . . .

Whatever they would say of him they'd say he tried his best. He had done what he knew how to do. With lire, with dollars and pounds and promissory notes and French francs and Swiss francs and German marks and dinar and drachmae and yen. With calls on the margin he would alleviate the sorrow of the poor benighted multitude; he would stay here till the morning came and establish things. J. Harley Andrews, Jr., who was nobody's father and no living somebody's son could yet repose at journey's end within this loud imitation of silence, for who was in the room beside him was not perhaps as clear as he could have wished.

Well, what did he regret? The bankruptcy at ITL, the Christmas he stayed in Australia when he should have flown home instead to see his mother, dying, the Montecristos that he used to smoke and, on doctor's orders, gave up. There were games he missed also, of course: tennis, Ping-Pong, the pool he liked to shoot on Friday nights, in college, on the Union's second floor. He was sorry, Lord, heartily sorry, for what had happened in 1962 in Leadville, the sale of the mine, the way he insulted a secretary, once, for being deaf then learned she was, the way his partners and associates took or disregarded his advice. The motion of the blood.

And he regretted the Snake River certainly, the salmon-fishing trip to Iceland he never did manage to schedule, the fly rod he loved that was stolen, the Kodiak bear that he missed. For he had made mistakes and would willingly acknowledge them: breathe, *breathe*, exhale, hold, breathe. Again. And he regretted angina pectoris, myocardial infarction, and how we live much longer now who should depart the igloo with wandering steps and slow and lie down on the ice to save the tribe's allotted food or pitch ourselves over the gunwale to lighten the swamped lifeboat's load . . .

"Cat got your tongue?"

But still there's the feel of a river at sunset, the kingfisher feeding, fresh trout in the creel, the way the water eddies at your feet like rocks, the grass, the long grass, long green grass. He coughed. He tried to rise. For everywhere he heard the sound of someone singing, someone committing himself to the flame—that fluttering and fibrillation in the chest, that glad relinquishing and lights on at show's end—the sound of seats released and then the reel reeled backwards, ending happy, happily, his classmates applauding, standing, whistling, people buttoning their coats to leave, to brave the winter weather; dear sweet Julie Watson, don't die.

So he fought his way up through the tangle of sheets, the lifelines and trout lines and netting and dials. He had provided well. And lifted his head from the bed. He had lived every day of his life. But the question of a waterfall persisted, that old chestnut whose answer is *yes, of course, of course, yes, yes,* but does it make sufficient sound if there is no one near to hear, is a toppling tree noiseless with no one to listen, and what was he crying if mute? So he lifted his bed from the head. There was no one in the room.

IV

"MAY I come in?" Trip Conley asked.

"Not really, no."

"Is that polite, Rebecca?"

"No."

But Trip had his foot in the door. "I'm the president, remember? Of the hospital you're visiting. You're supposed to be flattered the boss comes to call. Your host and your, what shall we call it? admirer."

"If you insist." She stepped aside. "I have five minutes, I suppose."

"Thank you, don't mind if I do." He did not seem to bridle at her conscious rudeness. As if his shoes were muddy, as if there were a floor mat, Trip Conley shuffled his feet. It was 8:15. "There are things we have to talk about."

"Such as?"

"Don't rush me, please." He closed the door behind him carefully. He was carrying a briefcase and still in his business suit. "I

waited as long as I could. I just didn't want to disturb you. You're alone?"

"The truth is, Trip, I'm busy. I was expecting someone else."

"I know that, darling, I know who you mean. Except this is important. You could offer me a drink."

"All I have is brandy."

"Fine. And I did bring you something."

"What?"

"You've read this, probably—the *Handbook for Dying*." He laughed. "Hell, you practically *wrote* the thing. But I wanted your opinion on the parts I've highlighted, I wanted you to look at it. What's that you're playing?"

"Mendelssohn."

"That's fine," Trip said. "Just perfect."

She did not ask him why. She produced a bottle and a pair of brandy snifters and he washed and dried them carefully and poured them each a drink. Then he set them on the counter, side by side. "Rémy Martin," he said. "My favorite. You found the liquor store downtown?"

Rebecca shook her head.

"No, of course not," Trip said smilingly. "It must have been a gift."

She excused herself and went into the bedroom and pulled up the coverlet and, in the mirror, checked her face. She had been expecting Peter and had showered and prepared herself; she wore no underclothes. By the dressing table there were panties, and she drew them on. But it would take too long to find a bra, and instead—half-irritated at the impulse, half-smiling at the precaution—she buttoned her blouse to the neck.

When she returned Trip had his back to her. He was standing at the window, looking down; there was, she knew, nothing to see.

"Your health," he offered. "Happy days." He pointed to her glass.

"Cheers."

The brandy tasted wrong. She glanced at Trip to see if he too noticed, but he smacked his lips, appreciative, and said he had some things to say and hoped she didn't mind. There was trouble, as she no doubt knew, with the press and Trueman-Andrews, and maybe she had heard and maybe she hadn't that Richard Trueman passed away and, quite aside from his sorrow, of course, they could ill afford the publicity. But Trip prided himself always on how he dealt with journalists, and he wasn't worried, really, about how to handle them; what worried him instead was what he'd call *internal* politics, the lack of trust *inside* the shop, and then he spoke about a rope test and beginner's rock climb; he had devised a procedure for their administrative meetings in order to establish trust; what did she think?

"Think?"

Rebecca licked her lips. The brandy had an edge to it, an acid aftertaste. Still, Trip was talking rapidly, saying that paralysis or at least a sense of lassitude and incapacity was common, or hadn't she noticed, and the thing with the human condition is that all of us are tied in knots, but some of us know it and some of us don't. He asked her to sit in the armchair; she did. He turned the second armchair so that it was nearly touching hers, not four feet off. His motions were unhurried and precise.

Then he placed his briefcase on the table and rummaged inside it and said, just a second, I brought a book along in case you haven't read it lately, the poems of John Donne, the one about "Death be not proud," that's what you wanted, isn't it, that's why you let me in the door though you were making a mistake, I think, confusing me with Peter. Oh you mustn't look so shocked, my dear, it's not a secret anymore, it's the reason that I need to sneak up here all by my lonesome now you don't invite me in—and just a minute, just a minute, he said, chuckling, producing a pair of white surgical gloves and donning them elaborately, adjusting them finger by finger. Next, feigning astonishment, he extracted something that gleamed dully in his fist. It had a silencer fitted. For a moment she thought it had to be plastic, a water pistol, be unloaded; for a moment she assured herself that surely he was joking, and she tried to laugh.

"Well, looky here." He seemed surprised. "Imagine that."

"What?"

"This funny little instrument. This Smith & Wesson in my hand. Why it's the very model that I reported missing . . ."

"What are you *talking* about?"

"My hospital safety insurance. My little office number, if you follow what I'm saying."

"I don't follow," said Rebecca. "No."

"Permit me, it's important. I need to get it right." Trip was elaborate, polite; he moved with practiced ease. He knelt at her feet and, from his briefcase, extracted a set of dark blue ten-pound straps. "These are aerobic weights," he said. "I'm conducting an experiment. Put your ankles back, Rebecca. Please."

She complied. Holding the pistol loosely, negligently, and using his right hand he looped a rope around the chair leg, then fastened her right ankle and then did the same with her left. The weights were self-fastening, cool to the touch; they were made out of nylon and Velcro. Next he played a line between her ankles in what he called a half hitch. He secured her at the waist. This was done without apology and in so amiable a fashion that she made no protest and did not attempt to resist. She felt, instead, a kind of yielding weariness, as if she soon would sleep. He strapped a cord around her wrists and said, remember, anytime you wish, whenever you ask me I'll take the weights away. I'm a little tired also, yes, but it's *important* to establish trust, important that we have this talk, I've missed them very much you know, our bedside chats . . .

Rebecca attempted to stand.

"Don't bother," said Trip Conley. "Are there any questions?"

"No. Untie me, please," she said.

He smiled at her. "Of course, of course. Because I have to let it look as if you did this to yourself." Trip was cheerful—garrulous, even. "So anyway, about this gun, I called the police de-

partment and told them—wrote the report last night, in fact—
that someone in the hospital, someone with access to my office
since I always keep it in the desk drawer, must have stolen or
maybe only borrowed it. And now just looky here. Little Lulu,
here she is."

"I don't understand," said Rebecca.

"That way the murder weapon will be traced to me. But I
don't possess it anymore, I did report it missing. And once they
find it in your palm they'll know what to make of it, won't they?
That's why I brought this pamphlet along, this little instruction
on dying. Which is why I'm using gloves. But I'm getting ahead
of myself," Trip said. "You're a lefty, aren't you?"

Despite herself, she nodded.

"I thought so, I've been watching. So we'll need to release
your left hand."

Dreams are like that, often; you shout yourself awake. She did
not think he meant it; she could not believe it quite yet. But
this was not a dream.

"Ain't Velcro wonderful?" He took a swallow of brandy. "It
makes a neater job."

The straps were tight. Her two ears hurt; her tongue was
thick, her pupils were dilated and refused to focus.

"It's my favorite invention," said Trip Conley. "Next to the silencer, of course; that one's terrific too. A *fabulous* invention. So
when you're dead they'll say you killed yourself. It's obvious, it
seems to me—wouldn't you say so, Rebecca?" He appealed to
her happily, winking. "You're a quick study, you'll figure it out.
Best-selling author practices what she used to preach."

There is, at times, in silence, a second self that thinks for
us—a voice that declares an intention. Call it self-consciousness
or conscience; call it an inner instinctual prompting or the
adrenal gland. When we feel *fear* or *hunger,* when we recognize
hate or *desire* we mean instead the body's signal: go or stay. The
dream or fragment of a song or trembling hand or hair that
prickles at neck's nape or shift in blood sugar that triggers re-

sponse—all these are versions of that voice, the animal instruction: *run, duck, turn.*

"All right," Rebecca tried to say. "You've made your point.
Let's stop this now."

"Stop what?"

Her hands and feet were tied. She could not move. "I'm not
enjoying this," she said. "It's not amusing, Trip."

"Trust me. R&B," he said. "Don't you get off on this?"

"No."

"Sure you do. Of course you do." He was wearing latex gloves.
He had a handkerchief.

"Stop being silly," said Rebecca, and he slapped her—
"*Silly!*"—open-handed, twice.

Now Trip grew voluble. "Do you know what my wife calls me?
You haven't met her, I imagine, you haven't had the pleasure. It
would have been a pleasure, though one we'll have to forgo."
He shook his head. "Well, she calls me Conley the Con. And
like all such accusations there's a grain of truth in it, like any
truth it hurts. Speaking of which I trust your wrists are free of
pain, your ankles also, darling? I wouldn't want them chafed."

She could not see. His head had blurred.

"So talk to me. Open your mouth."

She opened her mouth then, obedient. The barrel of the pistol was neither warm nor cold.

"That's better, that's much better."

It tasted neither of metal nor smoke.

"You shouldn't have come here," he said. "Not to Trueman-
Andrews. Not to Bellehaven, ever. You shouldn't have fucked
with him, ever. Or *me*, come to think of it. Big mistake." Now
he withdrew the pistol till it cracked against her teeth—then
pushed it forward, probing. "But anyway you're here. *We're* here.
And you understand my problem."

She was crying. She tried not to cry.

"Don't do that, I'm warning you. Take it *all* in."

She had allowed herself, it seemed, to let him tease and cajole her, to pretend it was a parlor game they played. What was happening was actual: a nightmare of flat fact.

"We'll miss you. Yes. We'll have a funeral service. I'll say you were a martyr to the cause."

Though she shook her head to clear it, she could not clear her head; there was a kaleidoscope across her eyes, a ringing in her ears. And now she did taste metal; he was scraping the roof of her mouth.

"On second thought I think I won't. I'll just be quiet, watching. I'll be overcome with grief. And since it's a suicide, we've finished off the story. Closed the book."

He was jabbing at her teeth.

"Would you like to put your hand on it? We need your prints here anyhow." His breathing changed. "Caress the trigger, baby?"

She was gagging; her tongue tasted bile.

"It's yours, you know, this .38. I'll leave it here, I'll curl your little hand around it, *yes*. I click the safety *off*."

His left hand was waving, weaving. He had taken off his glove. "I'll do it later, probably. When I've finished packing up the rope. It makes a neater job."

She tasted blood.

"There's a song they taught us, baby. Would you like to hear it? Tum ta tum, ta tum," he sang. His voice was high. "Well, here's the way it goes: *This is my pistol, this is my gun. This one's for shooting, and this one for fun.*"

When she opened her eyes she could see him, erect, his prick sticking out of his pants. The tip of his cock was engorged. He was masturbating with his right hand and steadying the pistol with his left. "Bitch," he grunted. "Slut." But that such a thing would seek its pleasure from her now, that this madman's fantasy could come to pass and leave her drugged and terrorized and gagging on a silencer—that such a horror happened in the world she still inhabited made what she knew must happen next a kind of heart-ease, a sliding release. Rebecca shook her head.

She kicked at him, or tried to. She threw herself back in the chair.

"Don't do that, bitch. Just help me here."

"No!" She did in fact pull free. Her mouth was, of a sudden, empty while his pistol wavered and she filled it with her rage, her scorn and unempowered misery, and spat. The globule was too small. It dribbled down her chin. She tried to spit again. This time he shouted, coming, but Rebecca did not hear his shouting and did not see what happened to her final small defiance or taste or smell or touch her death because he pulled the trigger and blew out the back of her head.

V

SO NOW he had completed what he came here to accomplish; that was the end of that. Trip found himself repeating: *that was the end of that*. Or maybe he should say, instead, *this was the end of this*. He tried them both out loud. In any case one aspect of his evening's work was finished, over, done. This was Part One of the plan. He laid down the pistol: *complete*.

He did not want to look at her or the mess at the back of the chair. His cock was sore. He folded it inside his pants and zipped up his zipper and straightened his belt; there was a not unpleasant tingling, a ringing in his ears. His hand, too, tingled from the Smith & Wesson's recoil; his palm hurt. There would be a bruise on the heel of his hand. He pressed his hands over his ears.

In this position, hands at his head, he remained by her side for some time. When the ringing had subsided and he felt calm enough to do so he removed the Velcro strapping from the body's arms and legs. He did not look at her head. He focused instead on her ankles and wrists; when they were unfastened she slumped. The nylon filament, he noticed, was the same blue color as her skirt; he left these knots intact.

He wiped off the brandy bottle and started to wipe down the book, then said "The hell with it" out loud because the book was his. Rebecca did not move. "The hell with it," he said again, "the absolute hell with it," testing his voice. For no particular reason, or none that he cared to consider, an image came to him of naked women on a wheel—a drawing, no, a *photograph* of bodies at their perfect rest, a symmetrical arrangement in the shape of a mandala.

Trip turned off the overhead light. He let his eyes adjust. He did not think he had been heard or that they had made noise enough to attract attention. Therefore negligently, casually, putting himself in the place of the doctor he fastened his own right ankle to the rear leg of the chair. He did the same with the left.

The man who patented Velcro made a fortune, Trip was sure. It was brilliant, it was foolproof, it was nature's little joke. You walk through a pasture, you brush past a bush or maybe only a weed or pod or thistle, maybe only step outside and stand there upright in the breeze while burrs and hooked seeds stick to you; they need to get across the road and you're the carrier pigeon. They decide to get a transfer and you're the crosstown bus. That's how nature works. He flexed his thighs, then calves. There was comfort in inertia and pleasure in anticipation, and he sat back and, arching his back, stretching, let both legs extend.

He poured a second drink. From the unadulterated glass he drank; he smacked his lips. Then, although he had no wish to *tamper* with the evidence, your honor, he knocked Rebecca's cognac to the floor. Spilled, it spread. When they tested for the sedative they'd find it on the carpet, according to Hemlock procedure. Now Trip could smell the cordite and the acrid mash of bone and brains, and he lifted himself in the armchair to make sure he still could do it, and—satisfied with his preparations and to pass the time till Peter came—turned toward the window, looking out. In this position, moreover, he could not see Rebecca. He focused instead on the willow tree, the crescent moon, the north wall of the Trueman-Andrews Hospice, with its illuminated parking lot and its security lamps.

Dr. Julius was out there and coming over soon. The doctor would announce himself; this was Part Two of the plan. He would knuckle at the peephole the way he had been doing every night for weeks. Or maybe he would have a key, since Rebecca had a copy made, and Peter would let himself in. Then, before his eyes adjusted to the surrounding darkness, while he was calling out "Honey, I'm home," or whatever little joke he made by way of saying he'd arrived, Trip would display the gun. It would be a small surprise but after all a doctor must grow used to small surprises, little shocks, and anyhow this would explain the purpose of his visit and the things they had to talk about and settle up and decide.

He would take his own sweet time. Peter would glance at the closet, the bathroom, and perhaps call out "Rebecca?" but for obvious reasons hear nothing and—again with the invaluable assistance and by virtue of the gun—be persuaded to occupy the second chair, the one that faced the window, and the ropes and straps would be—what was the word?—*applicable*.

The procedure would take only a minute, chaff sticking in the Velcro breeze, with Conley smiling, chatting, saying it had come to his attention that a patient in the hospital—all those postoperative old folks in the corridor, shuffling along in their slippers, attached to the IV and pole—must learn to walk a different way than was the case before. You talk the talk and walk the walk and everything feels different once you're tied. Now this half hitch for example, he said, provides the kind of restraint that everybody in Trueman-Andrews has grown accustomed to, and each physician should acquaint himself with it because only by means of such empathy might he and other members of the staff find themselves empowered. *The rod and the staff*, Trip would joke. Dr. Julius would smile. And only at that moment would he notice what had been Rebecca, sitting silently behind him, and it would be too late.

But he deserved an explanation, did he not. Trip would explain it all. He would describe how Peter's work had replicated his, Trip's, own, and this was inefficient and wasteful from the point of view of management; there's an ancient Chinese proverb, Peteyboy. Man cannot step in the same stream twice; you should have left this English cunt alone, just look what you made, *make* me do.

It had started long ago, with pretty Alice Tucker. She had been the perfect candidate for a bone-narrow transplant, well maybe not the perfect one but in an imperfect world you make do with what you've got. Trip made her a test case. And you yourself, he said, would have enjoyed her way back when; two years ago she was like our Rebecca here, a pleasure, and only when he'd learned how Peter's own wife went—that's the polite term for it, isn't it, *went?*—had Conley made the connection. Because Ms. Tucker grew confessional and wanted to go public and that had been a problem so when she lay down in her hospital bed and got horizontal and *went* it did seem natural to indicate that the person who might be involved—here he smiled—was one of the men in this room.

The phone rang. Trip ignored it; after six rings ringing ceased. He made himself remember all those westerns and the murder mysteries and spy stories he had watched when young. A train comes speeding down the track where our hero lies half-conscious, or a shark is approaching him widemouthed, or a bomb with a timing device has thirty seconds left. He is hanging by his fingernails to a rooftop or a cliff, and the bad guy stomps his hands. He is tied up in an elevator or a tunnel or a steam vent, and the building is burning or the tunnel crumbling or the steam vent fills with steam. There is no hope, no chance.

Then always the killer comes clean. Always when he thinks he has the good guy in his power he is tempted to explain himself—while holding the rope or the gun. The villain files his fingernails; he drinks champagne; he strokes the cat or blonde. He tells the condemned man the truth. He says something like, *You guessed it, you're a clever fellow—but it doesn't matter anymore. It's too late, Mr. Bond.* And always, in those movies, at the very last possible instant, the hero escapes and the bad guy is caught and justice is finally done. Then virtue is rewarded and the vicious man is punished and his plot is foiled . . .

Trip laid out his red deck of cards. There were three aces— spades, diamonds, hearts—in the first five cards he turned, and he took this as a sign: his good luck was going to hold.

Because, as Peter ought to know, once we begin a game like this we learn to play by rules. We come to understand that there are those who fail to have our own best interests at heart, who desire us out on the street; some people or persons unknown, your honor, are no doubt after our job. And because we've learned a little something in the hospital, with our extensive vocational training, we assist our dear father-in-law to make a graceful exit so he cannot help with ours. We do so in the very manner that has become, in fact, characteristic of our shop; we rearrange the feeder tubes and provide what he doesn't quite need. Potassium or Demerol or heparin the STP for tired blood—you name it, Dr. Julius, it was brilliant Part Three of the plan. We lose our patience—get it, Pete?—we lose our talkative *patients*, our Alice and Johnny and Scott . . .

But now the moving finger points, it *points* accusingly to the medical director of the Harley Andrews Hospice, your honor, for what further evidence could anyone require than his guilt this very night made manifest by an act of such contrition, in the company and with the no-doubt-willing assistance of Rebecca Forsythe, author, and Exhibit A. The lady to my right. Therefore as preparation we compose a letter to the newspaper, or three, and decide to call the editor and pay off Penny Lampson, who has maybe watched too carefully and will decipher my initials on the sign-off sheet for Johnny or remember about heparin and publicize those patients that Dr. Julius sees. Saw. Trip corrected himself; it's all past tense by now.

So that's the long and short of it, the start and end of everything, it's my shop, Pete, my own responsibility, and everything that happens here happens on my watch. I don't know what you did to all those old folks at the hospice, and I don't really care. We're talking assisted suicide, maybe, but give or take a week or two it isn't a federal case. Bellehaven, Michigan, is its own little world, of course, its small remarkable planet, and we are the north and south poles. We two are peas, your honor, in the same individual pod. In case you weren't aware of this, Trip Conley would say, smiling, the thing we talked about tonight is your squeeze here, your particular cunt believed I was jealous and we set her straight. She's not my squeeze, Dr. Julius would answer, she's not my particular cunt. Truer words was never spoke, said Trip, she belongs to no one now.

This was regrettable. He had his own regrets. He hoped the doctor would believe him when he said he killed reluctantly and would of course provide a full accounting to the newspapers; it would be, he promised, a kind of workers' comp. So you should try not to hold it against me—here Trip laughed—at least not the way he was holding the Smith & Wesson, the good old S&W, the splendid Smith & Wesson, the pride of the Old West up against this particular practitioner's head. And with his dextrous right hand and intricate fingers, opposable thumbs, he took the final Velcro weight and strapped and secured the left.

Then he would place the pistol carefully against Peter Julius's temple, or perhaps the rib cage just above the heart, saying he needed to confirm the angle, it had to be an angle that a left-handed person would use, because he wanted it to be quite clear that what was happening to the doctor, my colleague and admired friend, was that Rebecca Forsythe shot him and then she shot herself. It might have been the other way around, of course, or maybe he could shoot himself and she would do the same, he hadn't decided, there was time to decide which one of them was chicken and which egg. It would certainly help with the autopsy, the pathologist's report. They were equally guilty, your honor, they both had transgressed and paid the supreme penalty and it didn't really matter who had been the murderer and who the suicide, or perhaps they both were suicides and Peter had gone first . . .

This was Part Four—he couldn't remember, six, jack, queen?—of the plan. This was what they call the coup de grâce. Trip would jab the barrel slightly forward and release the trigger so the shot was muffled, strangely unimportant, and the doctor's head would alter only slightly, drooping, and the powder burn, it seemed to him, would be at least as visible as blood.

Except he was alone. He had rehearsed the scene sufficiently and now he needed to rest. There were no steps in the hall. There was only Rebecca here with him, and she was not much fun. She was dead, and dripping, and Peter had not yet arrived.

It was late, it was too late. He thought he might go home. He could get in the car and drive through Bellehaven and have a shower and sleep. But he would have to see his wife and console her for her father's death, his father on the kitchen floor, his mother escaping in only a towel, and then pretend to her and everyone and then again tomorrow at Trueman-Andrews Hospital while the shocking revelation of this double suicide went public that nothing very much had changed nor irretrievable had happened, and in the morning assure them all that this too would pass . . .

Trip had been hunting quail. He was new to shooting and his reactions were slow. He scratched himself on a thorn-apple thorn and his boots pinched and his legs were soaked. He picked his way across the hill. Where he walked, birds flew. To his right and left were hunters; they reached their limit by noon. The others had him cornered; he was their target now.

But his right hand was free, unfettered, and he used it to beat back the brush. Things clung to him beseechingly: blood, gristle, a spur of brain bone, weeds and seeds and burrs. He removed them from his pants. He wiped his sweating neck. He was climbing with his safety on, seeing nothing, bagging nothing, hearing the swift scurrying escape of what he planned to kill.

Then the thicket exploded noisily; quail fled. He alone was empty-

handed, and when they called to him he shouldered his rifle and, not aiming, shot the sky.

Trip thought he should practice; he raised his right hand. He let the barrel find its purchase up above his heart and, balancing, practicing, watching the silencer, squeezed.

VI

"HE'S DEAD."

"Who?" asked Peter Julius.

"Your patient. Harley Andrews."

"When?"

"I can't be sure. A half an hour, maybe."

"Did you try to revive him?"

"No. He was DNR."

"What *happened* here?"

She shrugged. She spread her hands.

"What do you *think* was the cause of his death?"

"Heart failure," Penny said.

He studied her. She seemed composed. "Were there witnesses?" he asked. "Was anyone else present during the . . . episode?"

"No. Not that I'm aware of."

"Who had the floor? Who saw him last?"

"Jim Kelly," Penny said.

"Where is he? Let me talk to him."

"That's the funny part." She shook her head. "He left without reporting it. He went off duty, I think, around seven."

"Then how do you know he saw Harley?"

"He told me," Penny said.

The room had its lights off; the monitors glowed. The machinery, too, was turned off. What struck Peter first was the silence; he stood at Andrews's side. He touched his patron's face. The nose was cold and white, the nostrils pinched, the mouth already stiffening. He cupped his hand over the chin. His palm was on the dead man's Adam's apple, his fingers on the lips.

Dr. Julius remained this way a moment, watching; there was a bruise above the collarbone and, where they had drawn blood, discoloration of the wrist. Later, he would mourn.

It took some time to complete the procedures, to pronounce the patient dead and sign the death certificate. He sealed the room. It should be examined in the morning, he told the floor supervisor; he needed to order an autopsy first, and there would be an internal review and nothing should be touched. Why are you doing this, the supervisor asked, and Peter said because I'm tired of not knowing, because we all deserve to know and the patient would have wanted it and now it's nine o'clock and I've been working here since six o'clock this morning and am going home. "Aye aye, sir," said an orderly, saluting. Dr. Julius was not amused.

Nor was he going home. He called Rebecca's number, but there was no answer; she was in the shower, possibly, or taking a quick nap. He hung up his white jacket and, in shirtsleeves, crossed the lawn; a rabbit froze in front of him, then bolted and zigzagged away.

A woman in a wheelchair said, "Evening, Dr. Julius," and he called out "Good night."

The moon was full. Driving out through the mechanical gate, in an ancient Volvo, backfiring, a minister waved. Then the yellow and orange gate arm descended, blocking unpaid access.

Dr. Julius hurried through the parking lot and tried to put the spectacle of Harley Andrews behind him, at least until he told Rebecca, at least until she asked him what was going on. He had the sense, once more, of something he was missing—some clue to a puzzle he'd missed.

There was no one in the lobby, and that was a relief. He did not take the elevator but used the stairwell instead. He let himself in with his key. He let his eyes adjust. The first thing that he noticed—in the foyer, pocketing his key once more, calling out "Rebecca?"—was the smell.

She had no lower face to speak of left beneath her eyes. He shut the staring eyes. The hand on the armrest that once was his darling's was not something that he wished to hold, but Peter took it anyhow and closed its fingers carefully and out of years of training tried to find a pulse. There was no pulse to take.

Behind him, not four feet away, Trip Conley sprawled undead. He was, the doctor saw, still breathing. Veins fluttered in his neck.

For some seconds Dr. Julius stood above the wreckage, staring down. He studied the pistol near Conley's right hand, the Velcro restraints fastened loosely, and upright in the heavy chair the body of Rebecca Forsythe with its brains blown out. Brain matter had festooned the neck rest of the chair; it spattered on the armrest also, and blood was on the wall. The woman had been killed, he saw, and then the man had shot himself but had done so through the lung not heart. There was blood at the edge of his mouth. He could perhaps be saved.

Once more out of habit he reached for a pulse: fitful, faint. In the pocket of Trip's brown suit was a letter; Dr. Julius extracted it. The patient's eyelids fluttered, and he licked his lips. Trip had brought his props along: a deck of cards, a handbook, and a copy of John Donne. He seemed to be trying to speak.

Dr. Julius walked to the window. He steadied himself on the sill. He fought back his vomit; he breathed through his mouth. A CD was playing. It stopped.

June 5

To the Editor:

Well what do you think about that? Well what do you know about what happened over on Division Street with Miss Rebecca Forsythe and Dr. PJ. **???** I told you I warned you I wrote you of course but you just didn't listen or is it you couldn't be bothered and is it you just wouldn't care? Thus ever is a profit without honor in his native land, a voice crying in the wilderness repeatedly repeatedly: have Mercy on us all. **666** is a serious number, and the beast of the Apocalypse was hungry here last night, it swallowed two more victims, did DREAd DEATh. But I gave you fair warning, correct?

We must accept, I tell my sisters and brothers on Donahue and Oprah just so you check it out, the *responsibility* for action and so while it is important to feel sorry for the souls of our dearly departed it is important to acknowledge that they did this of their own free will, as consenting adults, and anyone who tries to stop it will be committing a CRImE.

So look what you made me do now. His name was Peter Julius who will bend before your awful wrath and, on your *knees* now, counsel, approach the judge. Like that crooked one in New York City who got jilted and then changed his voice and tried to get his mistress back again or anyway to pay. Hah hah don't make me laugh. Hah hah he went to jail. Except too late too late.

Because in the case of yours truly I'm done explaining things. I've finished, believe it or not. Physician, heal thyself. This is my last letter, fans, this is my final announcement.

And a great silence fell upon the land.

For an interval he could not gauge, leaning, standing at the window, the doctor willed Rebecca Forsythe back to life. He repeated "Darling, darling, darling," in the rhythm of what would have been her breath. He inhaled for the count of eight then held his breath for eight and then again exhaled. But even as he listened he heard only the loud gargle of the killer in the chair, only his own blood beating and his own assaulted heart.

"Why did you kill her?" Peter asked. "Why didn't you kill me?"

Trip Conley moved his tongue.

In the dining alcove there were chairs. Dr. Julius chose a ladder chair and, moving stiffly, slowly, carried it across the carpet to the coffee table and placed it between the two bodies. There was a mirror on the wall. He positioned the seat on the angle, so he could not see Rebecca.

Then he sat.

But he could not keep from seeing her: her arms, legs, ankles, shoulders, shattered face. In the slant light from the hallway fixture Peter saw himself reflected. A brightness played about his eyes, a wild flaring rage in his stare. What he embraced he lost.

"How do you feel?"

"Fine." The right side of the patient's chest moved rapidly; he leaned toward the left.

"Tell me the truth," Peter said.

"I didn't mean to . . ."

"Kill her? Pull the trigger? You didn't mean to shoot yourself?" Trip Conley shook his head.

"What? *What?*"

There was red froth on his shirt.

"You're thirsty. Are you thirsty?"

"I'm tired," said Trip Conley. He said this clearly, audibly. And then he shut his eyes.

Dr. Julius, too, shut his eyes. The covenant that governed his profession had been broken; it could not be repaired. There is a difference between the secret uttered in strict confidence and an exchange between practitioner and patient which in the eyes of the law can be construed profane. This injury was not yet hopeless; he would have to wait.

Now, trying not to open them, he pressed his fingers to his eyes and within his eyelids' screen viewed colored sunbursts, starbursts, little implosions of light. The phone was on the bed-side dressing table; he could use the phone. He knew the number to call. He could alert the hospital, and they would arrive in ten minutes while he waited at the door. They would ask him what had happened and, to the best of his ability, he would explain what happened while they covered up Rebecca and laid Trip on the stretcher and, using the gurney, departed; they were efficient, not easily shocked, and each of them had dealt before with homicide and a self-inflicted but possibly not fatal gunshot wound. In their hurry to transport him, they would complicate the evidence; they would remove Rebecca also. Time would be important; they could not afford to waste time.

So the ambulance crew would take their president across the street at speed, and the surgical procedures would be accorded top priority and the emergency team would assemble and the life might well be saved. Trip Conley would be lying on the operating table in half an hour at the most, since his vital signs were weak and internal bleeding at a certain stage would prove irreversible. With every minute lost, the chances of survival would diminish, the patient's breathing fail . . .

He had had a teacher in medical school, a doctor who'd had polio. Dr. Rangely walked with a slow rolling limp, a cane that he used as a pointer. He washed his hands often and spoke softly, in a southern accent, of the need to pay attention to the large arc of an illness, not the daily fluctuation of a chart. Dr. Rangely's hands were pink and clean; he was a cardiologist and, according to hospital gossip, in line for chief of medicine. His hair was cropped and worn in a brush cut; his neck, too, seemed a soldier's. He had, it was rumored, five daughters; his wife wanted a divorce.

Peter saw him in the cafeteria once, paring an apple with surgical precision, removing the peel in an intricate spiral. When he said, "Good morning, sir," the doctor blinked at him. There were tears in Rangely's eyes. When Peter asked, "Are you all right?" his teacher said, "Oh, Julius. Sit down, my boy. Who was it, can you remember? Which poet said that famous thing: 'This long disease, my life' . . . ? Who was it called his life *disease?*"

"There was a time," said Dr. Julius, "when you and I, the two of us I mean"—he gestured at Conley, who breathed—"could maybe have been friends. We could have worked this out. The first time that we met I had this feeling, I think maybe you did too, now *here's* a worthy adversary, *here's* a complicated person, someone to discuss things with. To take into account . . ."

Trip was breathing rapidly. His index finger twitched. His lips had been blue; they turned pale.

"But what I didn't guess," the doctor said, "was how much it would bother you, how crazy you would get because Rebecca left—or you were crazy anyhow, an accident waiting to happen . . ."

"I want," Trip said, "I want . . ."

Dr. Julius stood.

"Help," the patient said, or tried to.

His knee brushed Conley's knee.

"Help."

And, imitating a gunman, Dr. Julius raised his right hand. He aimed his index finger and sighted with his thumb. "I can't forgive you, brother, I can't be asked to help."

Blood puddled at Trip Conley's mouth.

The dead, the dead, the legion of the dead; the ones who collapse in the fullness of time or early or aborted, the ones who claim they do not care or give no seeming thought to it—to each of these death comes. To the shocked unready fisherman beneath the tidal wave, the warrior on battlefield or villager on hillside where the lightning strikes, the passenger in trains and planes, the children in a school bus colliding with a truck, to the elderly in traffic or standing in line for a movie or bus or switching television channels or waiting for an ambulance or lying in a hospital or hospice death arrives. It is not a question of *whether* but *when;* it comes without exception. Mortal, we partake of shared mortality.

Dr. Julius knew this; it was no surprise. It surprised him nonetheless how few of his patients were ready, how little they prepared. He himself was unprepared. The dead are numberless, he knew, and those who make ready to join them may be delayed, a little, but cannot be denied. He pocketed Trip's letter and took his chair back to the dining alcove and wiped it clean of fingerprints, not carefully, since traces of his presence would in any case be everywhere in the apartment.

He turned toward the remnant of Rebecca Forsythe's face, the nothing there to salvage. He put his hand on her shoulder; he stroked her reeking hair. Long ago and far away, he had been sitting with Julie. His wife had wanted him to help, but his lover acquiesced in nothing and did not seek release. There was no mercy in this killing, none at all. It was as brutal and as lunatic as Billy Morris years before when all this horror started in the dark lethal furnace room of Huron Acres, Building C . . .

What Peter needed to explain was how a man might start out planning to be helpful, a force for good, a man could hope to heal the sick and cancel or at least control their pain, then plan to help the living live and dying die but get *confused*, since after all the living die and all the dead have lived. This was a distinction of some consequence, and Dr. Julius, attempting to control himself, pressed his fingers to his cheek, since in this dark room on the second floor of Trueman-Andrews Hospitality House it mattered a great deal to him to fashion a distinction between the dead and quick.

He tried now to see what Rebecca had seen. He tried to imagine what she had endured: the violence enacted. Outside, a siren wailed. It was, he wanted to tell Trip, grotesque; it was a madman's parody of how he himself had behaved.

A doctor is supposed to do as little harm as possible; great harm had been nonetheless done. He did not use the phone. He closed and locked the door.

Epilogue

～

PENNY LAMPSON did travel to France; her passport took two weeks to come, but the wait was worth it. It arrived in the mail from Chicago. The dark blue cover with its letters and numbers incised, the seal, the list of countries U.S. citizens should be advised are dangerous, the personal statistics, her name and date and place of birth, the date of expiration—all this felt official in just the right way. Even the photograph pleased her: bright-lipped, the blank white screen behind her making her eyes look more blue. She told Jim Kelly it was what the doctor ordered, exactly what she wanted in her purse. She was psyched, she felt excited, and hoped that he did too.

There was a travel agency in Bellehaven, one door down from the Republic Bank and catercorner from Willis Insurance. Jerry Heineman, the manager, handed her brochures and pricing indices for package tours. She wasn't sure, she told him, how long she could afford to stay, and he said in that case he would recommend Plan C, the plan for travelers on a budget. He suggested a "family hotel" on the Left Bank of Paris and a ticket on open return; it makes good sense, said Jerry, to save your shekels when starting a trip.

"Shekels," Penny asked. "What's that?"

He smiled at her, not answering, and said, "Wait a minute, wait a minute," to someone on the phone.

The flight was long but peaceful; she read magazines. She had flown two times before—once to Denver with her family and once, on a school trip, to Washington, D.C. Jim was planning to meet her as soon as he could; he had some mopping up to do and some replacement arrangements to finalize and thought it would be advisable in two or three days at the latest if he took a separate plane. Penny flew from Chicago direct. She drank two beers and, as soon as they darkened the cabin, fell asleep. There was no one in the row beside her, and in the morning when she woke she followed the example of the televised in-flight instructor and did aerobic exercises in her seat. The clouds outside her window were just like cotton candy, and every time the captain spoke she followed his directions—looking at the left horizon if he urged her to, then crossing over to look out the right.

When the plane landed in Paris, Penny told herself she'd died and gone to heaven. "I've died and gone to heaven," she announced to the next couple in the passport line.

Her hotel had dark green shutters and geraniums in window boxes and a lot of people that she thought were probably Egyptians smoking in the lobby, with a fat woman reading at a desk. The elevator no longer worked, the woman explained to her, pointing, so she would have to climb. Her room was on the fifth floor. One of the Egyptians carried up her bags. She said "Sphinx" and "Pyramid," trying to pronounce them correctly in French, but after she said, "River Nile," he shook his head and said, "Moi, je suis Algérien." Then he waited in the room until she found some money and dropped it in his hand.

Penny sponged herself clean in the sink. The hallway bathroom stank. Her window had no screens. She put on her flared pink cotton slacks and Top-Siders and wandered the wide avenues and the narrow streets. There was a great deal of traffic, and the drivers all leaned on their horns. The streets smelled of urine and fruit. She walked along the River Seine, seeing barges and old motorboats and something they called the Bateau Mouche and the huddled bums.

She began to be afraid. Her language tapes had not prepared her properly for what she saw in Paris; her clothes proclaimed her an absolute hick from Hicksville, U.S.A. The natives failed to answer if she explained that she was lost and asked them for directions—or, worse, they answered in English. The fashionable shops and storefronts with their mannequins made Penny feel self-conscious, just off the boat from Bellehaven; so did the narrow-hipped elegant salesmen, the women fingering handbags or earrings or scarves at prices that—when she did the arithmetic, dividing by five—seemed insane.

At lunchtime she stopped at an outdoor café, with ropes to keep the cars away, and sat down at a table underneath the awning. The waiters ignored her; men smoked. When finally she stood to leave a waiter sauntered over; his shirt had sweatstains, and his bald head was shiny, and he licked a pencil and asked what she desired. She pointed to an omelette on the menu, and he brought an omelette and bread. She could not explain to him that the eggs were runny and the bread too dry. Then she ordered what at home she had learned to call *café au lait*. The milk was sour, the coffee too strong, the sugar in the blue bowl brown and thick and wet. "I've made it," Penny said, attempting to cheer herself up. *"Je suis là."*

The first night she could hardly sleep; a cat in the alley screeched, yowling; the hall light flickered on and off, and the night concierge knocked at her door. He stood in the dark in his undershirt, shifting his weight on his feet. His breath smelled of onions and wine. Then in English he inquired leeringly if she had everything she wanted, if there was any additional service she might like him to provide. She knew *that* answer, anyhow, and told him *"Non, merci."*

Over and over again, the next day and the day after that, which she knew was called *le lendemain*, Penny heard herself repeating: No thank you, *"Non, merci."* Men shoved bunches of flowers at her, or tried to sell her watches and postcards and a model of the Eiffel Tower and gaudy rhinestone combs. One man brushed her right breast, passing; another one grabbed for her purse. The French did not resemble those gallants she'd imagined, and she prayed that when Jim Kelly came things would be different, be better. Meanwhile, the women were haughty; the children were derisive and jostled her out of the way. If this is heaven, she admitted to herself at last, it's expensive and too crowded and too hot. The paradise she'd landed in was noisy and commercial; when she shook her head, refusing, the vendors passed her by as if she had no further reason to exist.

She was standing by the church she'd seen on posters and in photographs, la Cathédrale de Notre-Dame, and there were tour buses and tour guides, hawkers everywhere. She had a sinus headache, and her period was late. She swallowed a licorice twist. While she watched the pigeons wheeling past the gargoyles that were downspouts, according to her guidebook, and the flying buttresses and the bell that Quasimodo rang, from the corner of her vision she saw something advancing. It was bright and various; it came at her like flame. What she saw above the entrance portal—hovering, corporeal—was her old despair.

It was not a shape so much as outline; it had no substance of its own but everything could fit inside it nevertheless. It surrounded her, and squeezed. She could not breathe. It engorged the available air. Familiar from her time in Lakeview and Bellehaven, it had crossed the wide Atlantic to pursue her even here. It was a desolation so absolute, so total that Penny fell to her knees.

Tourists hurtled through the square, making for the catacombs. Dear Jesus Christ have mercy, please, she whispered, *mea culpa, mea maxima,* dear Jesus, please, please, please. No kind citizen bent to help her, however, or paid the least attention. Someone said *"Tiens,"* someone *"Bien."* She could remember Peter Julius, that first night she had cooked for him, so long ago and far away, and she thought how terrible it was that everything she'd hoped for had come true.

*　　*　　*

Jim Kelly drove to O'Hare. He pulled into the parking lot, dreaming, and carried his suitcase and waited in line; he used his passport and ticket and took the magic carpet ride to where his mistress waited. She was wearing a garter belt, lying in silk, and she welcomed him extravagantly and curled her legs around his head and, whimpering, moaning, repeated, "At last, baby, baby you're *here*."

But it was too much trouble, so he went to the bathroom instead. Avoiding the mirror he reached for his pills and let the water run; when it was cool, not tepid, he filled the yellow plastic cup and brushed his teeth with Crest Tartar Control and took his morning Percodan and, hoping he could sleep again and that he would not wake his wife, got back into the bed.

Christine Addison Trueman Conley believed in creature comforts, or so she told her doctor, and her doctor—what else was he paid for, why else would she see him?—agreed. At three o'clock each Thursday she departed her house and drove to the mall and foraged for what she might need. First she liberated a green Kroger's shopping cart from the Kart-Corral, then waited for the automatic doors to slide sideways, yielding, and pushed herself into the store.

She bought tonic and rolled anchovies and artichoke hearts and mushrooms; from the gourmet shelf she gathered sorrel soup in cans. She picked lemons and onions and limes. For forty minutes in the frigid and recirculating air, Christine selected things, collecting them, the wagon supporting her weight as she walked. By the butcher's counter or standing at the service desk she heard herself conversing, for there was a story to tell. "Once upon a time," she said, "come, listen to my tale . . ." It began with seduction and ended with death; it had villains and a tangled web of cause and consequence. At the Deli-Corner salad bar or leaning on the freezer case she offered up her history of innocence betrayed . . .

Richard Trueman had been born beneath her feet. Her father

had died in his hospital bed; so too had her one son. But then her husband killed himself, and although a suicide is supposed to be unkind to the survivor—although a person who destroys himself is supposed to punish those who stay on afterwards—she did not feel that way. She felt, in fact, released. For she could not now remember what her husband said and wore and smelled like, in the mornings, after shaving. Though he came home full of self-pity and pride, and in the living room or bedroom had wanted something, clearly, it was no longer clear to her what he appeared to want. Always, Trip had been ambitious; always, he had yearned for ten minutes' worth of fame. Well, now he had acquired it; he'd been a headline for ten minutes and would no doubt be gratified—but those were not the articles his widow chose to read.

Having his mistress die also had helped; she could despise them both. The double suicide had been such a public gesture it canceled private grief. Since the policemen and the journalists and the insurance adjusters were so busy with the spectacle, Christine could afford to ignore it. What interested everyone— the newspapers, the neighbors—was, of course, a bore. It was, of course, yesterday's news.

Her friends and relatives wrote letters to condole. They gathered to offer advice. They said, "We're here for you" or "Darling, I never *dreamed* . . ." or "Did you ever notice?" or "If there's anything that we can do, don't hesitate to ask . . ." But there was never anything, and she did not ask.

They painted the walls and cleaned the carpets of Hospitality House. There was a funeral service and there would be a plaque. Of what happened to the Forsythe woman she did not bother to inquire—whether the body had been returned to England or cremated on the spot.

Death's Kingdom sold out in Bellehaven; people pointed to the chapter where the woman claimed that "dying" was interchangeable in certain poetry with "coming." The orgasmic instant and the "little death" have been equated since the troubadours; ecstasy, the author wrote, is not unknown to lovers in the final heartstopping instant and the lingering last breath. In the conventional formula, *die* means the same as *come*. *Undiscovered Country*, too, explored the connection between sex and death; *eros* and *thanatos*, according to its author, may prove inextricably linked.

Christine bought fat-free pretzels and potato chips and Gorgonzola cheese. She accumulated beer and dry white wine. The lame and halt were of her company, and she did like to take them aside. With overweight and acne-covered adolescent baggers in the checkout lines she discussed the weather; with some regularity, on Thursdays, standing in front of the baked goods display she met the chief resident's wife.

When this happened, and when she remembered, she asked about the kids. She followed their adventures with feigned interest and the account of their progress with the satisfactory illusion of concern. One of them had scoliosis and one of them had ADHS. But things were improving, said Marjorie Kelly, and then she made a joke. One of my children is straightening out and the other is straightening up.

How nice for you, Christine declared, how very very nice. She lingered by the frozen foods as if in her own doctor's waiting room, with its *Thank You for Not Smoking* sign and its *Quiet, Please*, and its *Vanity Fair* and *House Beautiful* and *Newsweek*, as though there were an answer to the riddle she had posed and predictably—clearing his throat, drumming his fingers on the coffee table—he would fail to answer: *where did I come from and where will I go to and why am I here?*

Peter drove to Lakeview. It took him three hours; he started in fog. By ten in the morning, however, the day was clear and bright. At the outskirts of the village, a circus had encamped; he drove past trailers and a Ferris wheel and tents and industrial cranes. There were horses in a pasture and, surprisingly, an elephant. At the shore road, he turned south.

The drive-up window at the Stop 'n' Shop had a blue banner taped across it, saying *Closed for Renovation; Bear with Us While We Build!* The FISHAUS now offered ANTIQUES. What used to be the hardware store announced it was *For Rent*. At Dunkin'

Donuts he bought himself coffee; he was the single customer so he ordered a glazed cruller also. The man behind the counter studied him. "To go?"

He nodded.

"Nice morning, ain't it?"

"Yes." He returned to the Dodge, drank and ate.

Two men walked past, vociferous. The first one said, "It isn't just the spotted owl. It's a marker for a whole entire ecosystem, understand." The other asked, "Well, what about our indigenous peoples? Would a traditional Spanish community according to your definition be a marker too?"

Dr. Julius drove to the boathouse; the mailbox had not changed. His old home had new tenants: a woman planting impatiens, two boys playing catch in the yard. They threw grounders and high flies. "Two men on base," the fielder called. "One out. Line drive to third."

Now an image came to him and would not be dislodged. His father, Frederick Julius, sat at the kitchen table in the house on Edgemont Road. He was reading the newspaper, folding pages noisily, his shirtsleeves rolled above his wrists and the black hair on his forearms curling. It was Saturday morning, or Sunday perhaps. The doctor *heard* the kitchen fan, the radio on WQXR, his mother saying something that he could not hear or was not meant to understand, in German, urgently, repeatedly. And all of this felt palpable: his yawning arrival in the kitchen where still the adults lingered, his problem in his parents' hands and therefore not his problem. He *saw* the toasted challah and the marmalade, the currant jelly and strawberry compote and herring in brine, the orange juice hand-squeezed while he had been asleep, with sometimes a half grapefruit too, with a maraschino cherry leaking redly from the fruit's eviscerated center, and a plate of Jarlsberg and Gouda and what his family called *stänkekäse*, stinky-cheese. There a boiled egg awaited him in its pink crocheted cap, the teapot in its cozy, and cornflakes with a sliced banana or for cold winter breakfasts hot oatmeal with a pad of butter melting, or dry Rice Krispies in a bowl, so that, stirring, he could hear them *snap* and *crackle* and, when he added milk, *pop*.

A small dog yipped at him until he backed out of the driveway, pretending to be lost. Day sailors made their energetic circles in the cove; a Boston Whaler planed past. A man without his shirt on and tattoos across his shoulders was hosing down a car. The wind smelled of pickles in brine.

Next a young girl on a bicycle, waiting for the traffic light, long-legged, in beauty's early bloom, a tennis racket strapped behind her, a yellow baseball cap high-riding on her hair, stared down at Peter where he sat. For an instant he thought he saw Julie. The light changed, and he started off, but it had all come flooding back; he thought his heart would crack.

At the J. Harley Andrews Clinic, the doctor failed to stop; there was no one he needed to see. There was no peace to make. That week, he had resigned. When he informed the Medical Center Board of Directors that he would leave Bellehaven and his job at Trueman-Andrews, they did not try to change his mind or urge him to return. J. Harley Andrews and Richard Trueman and Rebecca Forsythe and their president, Trip Conley, were chapters of a book they wished to close. The staff, too, seemed relieved.

Over Alice Tucker, Scott Raposo, Johnny and the rest the dust of oblivion settled. A joint hospital and hospice spokesperson said it was a great shame that their mission—which was to alleviate suffering—should seem in this way to go wrong. Eight patients canceled their elective admissions; eleven applications to the hospice program were withdrawn.

Harley Andrews, it turned out, had died of natural causes and in the manner he might well have chosen; his heart had simply failed. The right coronary artery proved upon examination to be more than ninety percent occluded; the front wall of the left ventricle, too, had been involved. Of Richard Trueman's hemorrhage no formal notice was taken; at another time and place an inquiry would have been ordered, but the chain of command was broken and the Internal Review Committee had more pressing matters at hand.

The hospital president's death, and that of his companion, were ruled a double suicide. Given the nature of Rebecca Forsythe's work, and what the papers called "her professional obsession," it came—so the reporters concluded—as no real surprise. The medical examiner identified the sedative Ms. Forsythe had ingested, and the ejaculation on her clothing was shown to be Trip Conley's. This information was not made public, but it seemed compatible with the original finding: a fatal lovers' pact.

The Smith & Wesson was Trip's. That he reported it missing had been duly noted, but Detective Lawson offered two explanations, both of them sufficient: either his lover had borrowed the pistol without his prior knowledge, or he forgot to inform the police when it turned up again.

President Conley, his secretary insisted, had given her no hint of what he was planning to do. She would have tried to talk him out of it, and anyway she blamed herself, Martha never would forgive herself, it was her *job* to have known. The Channel 7 anchorman questioned workers at the hospital coming off the day shift; one woman called it "Fate." He asked her what she meant by that, and she said, "Myself, I thought the English lady was, you know what I mean, *weird.*"

Dr. Julius was cleared of all suspicion; the newspaper stories and TV accounts no longer used his name. He was no longer news. He would take his mother on a cruise, then settle in Ohio or Missouri or possibly the Finger Lakes in upstate New York. He would volunteer his services for food kitchens or community shelters; he would answer telephones or do the paperwork for supervisors at the local hospital and perhaps work with the E.R. staff and, for the Mobile Clinic, drive the van.

The quality of mercy, Dr. Julius assured himself, is like the rain, the rain. He would begin again.